George W. Curtis, John Lothrop Motley

The Correspondence of John Lothrop Motley

Volume 1, Second Edition

George W. Curtis, John Lothrop Motley

The Correspondence of John Lothrop Motley
Volume 1, Second Edition

ISBN/EAN: 9783337399252

Printed in Europe, USA, Canada, Australia, Japan

Cover: Foto ©Andreas Hilbeck / pixelio.de

More available books at **www.hansebooks.com**

THE

CORRESPONDENCE

OF

JOHN LOTHROP MOTLEY,

D.C.L.,

AUTHOR OF "THE HISTORY OF THE RISE OF THE DUTCH REPUBLIC,"
"THE HISTORY OF THE UNITED NETHERLANDS," ETC.

EDITED BY

GEORGE WILLIAM CURTIS.

IN TWO VOLUMES.—VOL. I.

SECOND EDITION.

WITH PORTRAIT.

LONDON:

JOHN MURRAY, ALBEMARLE STREET.

1889.

LONDON:
PRINTED BY WILLIAM CLOWES AND SONS, Limited,
STAMFORD STREET AND CHARING CROSS.

PREFACE.

THE admirable Memoir of Mr. Motley by his friend Oliver Wendell Holmes, renders the addition of any biographical notice to these volumes unnecessary.

The letters now published were written mainly to members of his family, and have been collected by his daughters. In preparing them for publication, the editor has withheld whatever he believed that the writer's good judgment and thoughtful consideration for others would have omitted. This rule excludes comments upon persons and affairs which, however innocent or playful, might cause needless pain or misapprehension. It excludes, also, much of the repetition which naturally occurs in such letters, and a large part of the domestic and friendly messages and allusions, which although illustrating the writer's generous sympathy and affectionate disposition, are essentially private. If much of such matter is still left, it is because, with all his interest in literary pursuits and in public affairs, Mr. Motley was essentially a domestic man, and a more rigid exclusion could not have been made without injustice to his character. Otherwise the letters are printed as they were written.

Occasional breaks in the series of letters—especially after the death of Mr. Motley's mother, with whom he maintained a full and affectionate correspondence for forty years—are due chiefly to the fact that, when surrounded by his family and engrossed by many cares, he had but little inclination or leisure for friendly letter-writing. This was the case in 1870;

and the editor has been able to give but two letters written during that year—one addressed to the Duchess of Argyll, and the other to Dr. Holmes.

The circumstances of Mr. Motley's resignation of the mission to Austria, and of his retirement from the English mission, are told accurately and adequately in Dr. Holmes's Memoir. The publication of private correspondence upon the subject would add nothing to the facts as related by the biographer, and would needlessly re-open controversy. Mr. Motley's deep feeling upon the subject, however, which was well known to his friends, is expressed in a few brief allusions which have been retained in the letters now published, and for the facts the reader is referred to the Memoir.

CONTENTS TO VOL. I.

CHAPTER I.

EARLY YEARS.

CHAPTER II.

GERMANY; UNIVERSITY LIFE.

CHAPTER III.

AUSTRIA—FRANCE—ITALY.

CHAPTER VI.

PUBLICATION OF 'THE RISE OF THE DUTCH REPUBLIC.'

PAGE

CHAPTER VII.

BRUSSELS—AT WORK ON 'THE UNITED NETHERLANDS.'

CHAPTER VIII.

LONDON SOCIETY.

CHAPTER XI.

ROME—PARIS.

CHAPTER XII.

RESIDENCE IN ENGLAND—PUBLICATION OF 'THE UNITED NETHERLANDS.'

CHAPTER XIII.

THE CRISIS IN AMERICA.

LETTERS

OF

JOHN LOTHROP MOTLEY.

CHAPTER I.

EARLY YEARS.

Letters from school — Studies and pastimes — Death of Governor Brooks —
'Lionel Lincoln' — Goes to Round Hill School — Cooper's novels — 'Hope
Leslie.'

[At this time Motley was ten years old, and a pupil at the
school of Charles W. Greene, near Boston.]

To his Father.

Jamaica Plain,
May 13th, 1824.

MY DEAR FATHER,—I want to see you very much. I suppose you remember that it is my turn to come home on
Saturday next? This is Thursday, the day on which we speak.
I was third best. The pieces which I spoke were Mr. Sprague's
Prize Prologue and a most delectable comedy entitled and
called 'The Cruel Tragedy of the Death of Pyramus and
Thisbe,' in which I took the part of Thisbe. My nose has
bled very often lately, but I believe it will not bleed much
more. I have had a pain in my side once or twice. I hope
you, mother, and all the family are well. Mr. Greene is very
well. Mrs. Greene has a headache.

I am, dear father,
Your affectionate son,
LOTHROP.

To his Brother.

Boston,
February 21st, 1825.

MON CHER FRÈRE,—J'espère que vous êtes bien ; je suis très bien. Éduard a été indisposé, mais il est mieux. Nous reçûmes votre lettre aujourd'hui, et nous fûmes bien aises d'apprendre que vous êtes bien. Vous avez été mépris, car Monsieur Adams est le Président. Nous cappons maintenant, l'examen doit avoir lieu le prochain Mercredi. Nous tous sommes très bien et nous envoyons bien de l'amour.

Votre affectueux frère,

J. L. M.

(N. B.—This letter was lost, or it would have been sent before.)

L'inauguration du Président était aujourd'hui : l'école d'Éduard n'était pas ouvert ; il n'allait pas. Éduard a reçu les lettres. Écriez-vous à me s'il vous plaît le prochain fois que vous écriez à eux.

J. L. M.

Edward is now writing you a letter, which he makes quite a business of. Our shop is an excellent one. We have made a drawer, a thing to wind twine on, exactly like those in grocers' shops. We have to write exercises now, and I have got used to them, so that I can write them without many mistakes. There is a report that a flood was to have been to-day, but I suppose that it was put off in deference to the President. Mr. Thos. K. Jones sent round a card saying that he would be at his house on the 4th of March (to-day), at any time after twelve o'clock, to congratulate each other on the election of John Quincy Adams to the Presidency of the United States, on which occasion he expects the favour of Mr. ——'s company. Father and Uncle Edward received one of them, and went (his house is in Roxbury) and dined at Faneuil Hall. Messrs. Sprague, Percival, and Wells wrote an ode on the occasion, of which that of Mr. Percival was considered the best.

I believe Mr. Labasse is going from Boston to New York,

to teach there during the summer. I have not told you that the flood is postponed till Monday next. A great many guns were fired this morning, and continued through the day. Mr. Leverett's father is very sick, for which reason he was not at school on Wednesday afternoon and Thursday.

Governor Brooks died Monday morning, and was buried Thursday privately, as he made that request. I have read ' Lionel Lincoln,' which I think very interesting. There is a great deal about the Revolutionary War in it, and it contains a full account of the Battle of Bunker's Hill. Lionel Lincoln is an English lord, and is the principal character in the book. When he comes to Boston, which he does in the beginning of the book, he goes to a near relation, called Madame Lechmere, who is very rich, and is another very principal character in the story. Mrs. Lechmere's house is in Tremont Street, which Governor Phillips now lives in.

Good-night!

Yours affectionately,

J. L. M.

To his Mother.

Northampton,[1]
May 29th, 1825.

DEAR MOTHER,—I intend to have now the pleasure of writing you a few lines. I do not know when I have enjoyed myself so much as I did yesterday (Saturday). In the morning the gardens were distributed, and I worked in it an hour before school, and in the afternoon we worked a good while in them. After that we went to ride in a nutshell, otherwise a monster of a carryall, with five seats in it; each seat holds five, so we had twenty-five in it; and another carryall behind us as full as it could hold. After we came back we went into water, and it refreshed us very much. I wish you would send me up some nankeen pantaloons, as my woolenet ones are so tight that they are uncomfortable, and besides that woolenet is too

[1] The Round Hill School at Northampton, Massachusetts, under the direction of Mr. George Bancroft and Mr. Joseph S. Cogswell, was at that time well known throughout the United States.

thick. I should like to have you send me up my French dictionary. I am reading Hume's 'History of England,' which Mr. Cogswell lent me, and think it very interesting. I wish you would write as soon as you possibly can. I have commenced Spanish, which I like very much. I think this is a beautiful place. From my bed I can see a branch of the Green Mountains; Mount Tom and Holyoke too—I should like very much to go up them.

Give my love to all at home,

And believe me,

Your affectionate son,

J. L. MOTLEY.

To his Mother.

Round Hill, Northampton,
May 31st, 1825.

MY DEAR MOTHER,—I am going to keep a journal this week, and have begun to-day, Tuesday, as you will see by the date. Our gardens are excellent ones, being twenty feet broad and eighty long. Three other boys and myself own one together. We have made several beds and planted a good many things, such as corn, radishes, water and musk melons, etc. It is now about a quarter to one o'clock, so that, as we eat dinner at one, I shall not have time to write much, but I will continue it in the evening. A boy of the name of Barrett came to Round Hill just now and into the school, where I am sitting now; he is an old scholar and has cheeks as big as pumpkins. We have several new scholars, amongst whom is a boy by the name of Wilkinson, who owns a garden with me, and two Jews, by name Moses and Aaron David, and two Baltimore boys by the name of Treeze. I have been working in my garden this morning, and very hot work it is. We went into water yesterday, and last Saturday, so that we have been in three times this season. Mr. Bancroft said that the boys who pleased might go and work in their gardens, and that the rest might go in a swimming; and I assure you that there was not one that did the former.

I study 'Charles XII.' in French, which I think very interesting, and it is much more by its being in French; I can read French books very easily, which I do very often.

Half-past one o'clock, I have just finished my dinner, and I have a half-hour to write you before school. You must certainly send me up some thinner clothes than woolenet.

In the morning, from half-past five to seven, I study French; after breakfast I study Spanish, from nine to half-past ten, when we go out and stay about ten or fifteen minutes; and when we come in, I study Greek until twelve, when we are dismissed; and in the afternoon I study Cicero and recite to Dr. Beck, a German.

I think there is near sixty scholars in the school. We go down town to "meeting"; we go, Thomas and I, to Mr. Hall's. We had a blind man preach for us last Sunday; he had got the hymns and his sermon by heart.

Good-bye for this afternoon!

I have got acquainted with all the boys now. I translate a Spanish book, 'Collections Espagnol,' with T. Bond. I wish you would send me up, if you can find it, my old French exercise book that I finished.

I like Northampton every day more and more. I sleep in the same room with Tom, W. Brewster, and a boy by the name of Forbes, a boy from South Carolina.

Good-night; it's about nine o'clock.

J. L. MOTLEY.

To his Father.

Round Hill,
April 29th, 1826.

DEAR FATHER,—I hope soon to receive a letter from you or mother. Almost all the boys are here now, a few from Baltimore and Philadelphia are wanting. Some of the Philadelphia fellows came yesterday afternoon, and with these came a new boy, the smallest boy by far in school, I don't believe he is a bit bigger than Preble; I suppose he is older though.

I wish I had some marbles up here. It is what the boys

principally have up here, but there are not many up here in all.

I received my paint-box by Tom Appleton. I am in the upper school this term. There are not half so many this term as there were last. It is not very long before I shall come home in August, about four months.

Mr. Cogswell says he should think I might enter Sophomore, but I do not think I could, or at least if I should manage to shuffle in, I should always be the worst in my class, and should not be able to take any part at the end of my stay there, nor I don't believe that I shall be able to get a part in the Freshman class, but I will do my best.

There have been very few new fellows this term, about ten, no more. All the Salem and Boston boys have come now. I never knew the Boston boys come so late—some did not come till Thursday night; some of the Salem boys did not come till Friday evening (day before yesterday).

I study Virgil and Tacitus in Latin, 'Græca Majora' in Greek, and Lacroix's 'Arithmetic,' and Euler's 'Algebra' in Mathematics, besides which, out of school time, I review the 'Greek Reader,' with Dr. Bode, and am going to study the Greek Testament.

Good-bye!   Yours affectionately,
                                         JOHN L. MOTLEY.

To his Father.

Round Hill,
May 13th, 1827.

MY DEAR FATHER,—I received mother's and Thomas's letter. I received mother's a week ago, and Thomas's two or three days ago, more than a week after it was written. The reason was that the boy to whom Mr. Cogswell gave the letters to give to the boys, lost it, and it was found about a week after.

The apple and pear trees have all been in blossom for a good while; the trees in the woods are beginning to have their leaves.

There are six or seven boys going down in August besides myself. We had our gardens given us a week ago. I have got some radishes growing. We do not ride yet, but I heard we were going to ride to-morrow. I wish I had some books up here to read. I wish, when you send me up my paint brushes, you would send some. I do not want you to send me up anything to eat or drink, but I wish you would send me some books by the stage with the paint brushes. I guess you have some in the house that I have not read ; you may have some possibly.

The drawing master has not come yet ; he comes to-morrow, I believe. I believe Charley Appleton is going to write to Edward to-day, he told me he was. Everything goes on the same as ever, and I close my letter with entreating you to send me up some books and paint brushes.

Your affectionate son,
J. L. MOTLEY.

To his Father.

Round Hill,
May 16th, 1827.

MY DEAR FATHER,—As I wrote you so lately, I of course can have nothing to say. I asked you for books. If Cooper's new novel is out, I wish you would send it to me—but stop, I have thought of something. Mr. Cogswell has fixed a reading-room for us. That is a very good thing, and what the boys have long wanted. Mr. Cogswell told the boys that if they chose, he wished that they would put in their newspapers after they read them, and he said that he would' put his own in too, so I wish you would send me up the paper regularly that you used to send me, that I may put it in after I have read it. There are also going to be books there too.

Your affectionate son,
JOHN LOTHROP MOTLEY.

P.S.—Cooper's novel was to be published on the 12th of May, I saw in a paper, so I suppose it is out, the name is 'The Prairie.' Don't forget to send some books by the stage.

To his Brother.

Round Hill,
July 26th, 1829.

MY DEAR BROTHER,—I have received yours of 24th this
morning. We had not had another for nearly three weeks,
except Edward's note in 'Hope Leslie,' which I received a
week ago. Tell Edward my next shall be to him. I do not
think I am bound at all to write you long letters, for I
always write as long ones as you, and about three times as
often. I wish your next would be as long as this, and do
write at least once a week. I have had but two letters in six
weeks, for your last was three weeks ago, and the last before
that was three weeks before.

I think 'Hope Leslie'[1] is a great deal better than 'The
Prairie.' It is the best new novel that I have read for two or
three years, excepting Scott's.

We ought to have gone to draw from nature the day before
yesterday, but we did not because there was no time, and I
am afraid we shall not go Saturday; and it is so rainy to-day
that I am afraid it will continue so for a week, and we have
nothing at all to do in rainy weather. Perhaps you will ask
me why we do not go to the reading-room ; there is never any
papers in there but what are a hundred years old : the boys
will not put them in now, and with reason, for they are all
torn up before they have been in there an hour. *Drawing*
is about the only thing to do now in rainy weather. Reading
is not to be thought of, as there are no books in school.

George Gardner came here last night, and some of the
boys saw him. Bill Edgar, Bill Sturgis, and Sam May, and
Wadsworth are coming up, too, I believe.

I have finished Euler's 'Algebra,' and our class was partly
examined in it yesterday, and is going to be examined more
in a day or two, Mr. Walker says.

Tell father and mother they must write to me. I will write
them more to-day or to-morrow. Do send in your next a
recipe for making good large T's ; I never can make a good

---

[1] A tale by Miss C. M. Sedgwick.

1829.]   LEAVING SCHOOL.   9

one. Tell father to do the same; when I am in a hurry I always make very bad T's.

I have just finished reciting geography, and in a few minutes shall go to breakfast.

I believe there is to be an examination or exhibition in speaking before we go to college. I am going to speak 'Antony's Funeral Oration,' the whole of it. There are several dialogues, both comic and serious, to be spoken at this exhibition. I hope it will be a good one. I have not decided, and I leave it to father, whether I shall study in Boston or go to college the first year. I do not want to come up here though any more. I have been here now two years and a half.

Bill Edgar has been up here, and stayed two or three days, and has gone now. I shall be glad when the time comes to go. Tell father that I want him, if he pleases, to come up and bring me down about the middle of August. W. Gorham is going down in a little more than a week, but the boys will not go till the last of August, and then we shall not have a bit of vacation. I don't want to be examined the very day I get to Boston. If I do not have a vacation before commencement, I shall not have one till the middle of winter. I have to study a good deal now. Tell father to write to me directly, to tell me about this; and tell him also that I had rather study in Boston the first year than go into college, if he is willing. I think that I have fulfilled my promise to write a long letter.

Give my love to father and mother and all the family, and believe me   ·

Your affectionate brother,
J. L. MOTLEY.

CHAPTER II.

GERMANY; UNIVERSITY LIFE.

First voyage to Europe—Cuxhaven—The weather during the voyage—Incidents of the voyage—Göttingen — Arrangements for his first *Semester* at the University—Plans for the vacation—The German language—Account of journey from Hamburg to Göttingen — German postillions — The Hartz Mountains—German University life—Costume of the students—Duelling customs—"Brüderschaft"—Plesse castle—George Washington's letter on the Humane Society—Berlin—Studying law—Public galleries and public money — Daily routine at Berlin — Amusements — Taglioni — Devrient— Goetz van Berlichingen—The "Vons and the not-Vons"—Visit to Potsdam —Plans for the future.

[Mr. Motley graduated at Harvard College in 1831, at the age of seventeen, and after a few months went to study in Germany.]

To his Mother.

Brig *Cyclops*, at anchor off Cuxhaven, mouth of Elbe,
Thursday evening, May 24th, 1832.

MY DEAR MOTHER,—I hope by the time this letter reaches you, you will not have become anxious on my account, for although we have had a long, and in part rather a stormy passage, we have at last arrived at this place in safety.

I hoped to have had a chance of writing to you in the English Channel, but although I had a thousand opportunities of sending a letter ashore, either to France or England, yet as I knew nobody in either country to direct it to, there was no possibility of its reaching you.

It is now 12 o'clock at night, and ye brokers and ye doctors and " ye like" have just left us, and all hands have turned in, and I take the first moment of leisure to write you an account of my voyage. Of course, as we have not yet got to Hamburg nor left the ship, I can tell you nothing else. We are at anchor for the night off a small town called Cuxhaven, just at the mouth of the river, where the vessels are "cleared" before going to Hamburg, which is between fifty and sixty miles farther up. To-morrow morning, between two and three o'clock, we shall probably be under way again, and if we have a fair wind, shall be at the city early in the afternoon.

It is just seven weeks to-day since we sailed—making fifty days' passage, which is an exceedingly long one in any season of the year. We came out in half a gale of wind, and before we were out of the bay, it blew a whole one, and the wind very soon shifted to the east, where it continued to blow for about a month. We were about a week beating about the Grand Bank, in a north-easter, and were regaled with a series of rain storms and wind storms and all kinds of storms from the time we left Boston till we made the English coast. I have not been at all sea-sick (with the exception of the first few hours), but the weather for a long time was so excessively cold that I was below for the principal part of the time, and had plenty of time for reading and rumination—although one is not able to study or reflect to much advantage in the cabin of a small brig in a gale of wind.

The last day of April and the first of May we had a severe gale from the north-east, and were obliged to "lay to" under bare poles for forty-eight hours, and I had then an opportunity of seeing and feeling what the ocean is. I was on deck the greater part of the time, although it was impossible to stand or sit without being secured by a rope or two, and in the cabin I was able to realise what "King Corny," in one of Miss Edgeworth's stories, means by "not being able to lie on the ground *without holding on.*" I should have been very sorry to have crossed the Atlantic (or the pond, as the sailors call it) without a single storm, but one every day in the week is rather too much. However, I enjoyed them well enough, and I considered myself very fortunate in being neither sick nor nervous, as Mr. Grund and his wife were generally. She was very anxious when the vessel leaned over on its side, and as the brig is built very narrow in proportion to its length, it did that all the time; and she was not out of her berth eight-and-forty hours the whole passage from sea-sickness. I contrived, however, in the course of the voyage to learn a good deal of German, by talking and reading and writing, and I have been talking all day with the German pilot (who speaks very little English), and have acted in some sort as an interpreter between him and the captain, as Mr. Grund a few days ago went ashore in the Straits of Dover, to proceed to Hamburg by land, on account of his wife's sickness, but of that I will write you presently, so that I think I shall not have much difficulty in speaking the language pretty soon.

We made the English coast (Start Point) May 4th, and since that time the passage has been very pleasant, although until within these last three days we have not had a single fair wind. But the weather was very fine, and we were sailing between *France and England*, in sight of both sometimes, and always between one and the other, and fishing boats were coming alongside twenty times a day, from which we had fresh news and fresh fish in plenty, and there were always fifty or seventy vessels in sight of all nations and all descriptions, and the shore was constantly offering something or other of interest (although the seaboard of England and France on the Channel has not much of the picturesque), and the idea of being really in sight of those two countries was exciting and pleasing in itself. We were at anchor a whole day (to prevent drifting to leeward with the tide), in a dead calm, off Dover, and I amused myself with reconnoitring the old turrets of the castle with the glass; but the town is built so low that I could not see much of it.

Of course I can tell you in this letter nothing about my arrangements, as I am still at sea to all intents and purposes, although I expect to dine in Hamburg to-morrow; but I shall write in a day or two to father, telling him about the whole, and both letters will probably reach you at the same time.

I had nearly forgotten to tell you that I have become quite a sailor since I have been on board. I have been several times up to the top-gallant masthead, and my usual seat in fine weather is the "maintop," where I sit smoking, reading, and "chewing the cud of sweet and bitter fancies" for hours together. By the way, it was lucky that I did not forget my cigars, for they have been of great service to me *pour tuer le temps* in disagreeable weather. "You know my old ward," as Falstaff says, and tell Edward that I am very much obliged to him for getting them for me the morning we sailed, and that I have thanked him in every puff. I hope by the time this letter reaches you that Tom will have safely arrived; and do not be anxious if he overstays his time a little, for it seems to me now that one is as safe at sea as on land. In a gale of wind I can half join in the sailors' song—

> "Lord help me, how I pities all
> Unhappy folks on shore now."

And, by the way, that puts me in mind that my old friend, the ship *Corso*, has kept us company for the last two or three days, and is now anchored close by. Good-night, my dear mother. Give my love to Edward and Preble and Emma, and give little Annie as many kisses as she will accept for me. I shall write to father to-morrow or next day, and tell him of all my own arrangements and expectations, and send him all the news in Europe, which, by the way, is somewhat surprising. There is no need of my asking you to write, for I am sure that you will do so by every opportunity. Remember me to all who may recollect me; and when you next write to Cousin Anne, tell her that I shall open the correspondence that we agreed upon very soon, although not exactly from the same place, and tell her she might send a letter to me enclosed in the very next she writes to you.

Affectionately your son,
LOTHROP MOTLEY.

P.S.—I do not know that you will be able to read half, or understand a tittle of what I have been writing.

My ideas are in such a whirl that I cannot string them together intelligibly, and I shall write more at length and more coherently from Hamburg. The hurry and confusion that we have been in for the last six to seven hours with doctors and pilots and merchants and brokers, etc., etc., has confused me, and this has been the only hour in which I have

been able to be alone. But good-night, I am going to turn
in now, and hear for the last time the "gurgling noise of
waters in mine ear," which has been my lullaby for the last
forty-nine nights.

To his Father.

Göttingen,
June 23rd, 1832.

MY DEAR FATHER,—I have delayed writing to you during
the fortnight I have been here, because I wished to wait till
I could inform you of what I was about, and how I was settled.
I have now got rooms, etc., etc., arranged what lectures and
lessons I shall take this term, and provided in some degree
for the next *Semester.*

I got here about a fortnight since, just when the Pentecost
holidays began, and consequently had to wait till they were
ended before I could do anything except engage rooms.

I found here, much to my satisfaction, two Americans, one
Englishman, and one Scotchman. The Americans are both
from Charleston—one is Mitchell King, of exactly my own
age; and the other, Amory Coffin, about a year older, with
both of whom I am very intimate, as also the Englishman and
Scotchman, who, however, are going away very soon. I have
got rooms in the Buchstrasse (Book Street), the next door to
King's, and a few minutes' walk to the Library and to my
lectures. I breakfast either at my own room or my neighbour's, and we all dine at the "Crown," the best hotel here.

My room for the rest of this *Semester,* that is to say, from
about the 1st of June to the 1st of September, costs me three
louis d'or and a half, about fourteen dollars. Dinner at the
"Crown," eight rix-dollars a month; and then there is the
house bill, for coffee, etc., etc. Each course of lectures costs
from one to three louis d'or; and I have a private lesson in
German from Professor Benecke three times a week for the
rest of this *Semester,* which will probably cost eight more.
This term (about ten weeks are left) I intend to devote to
German, for I have not enough of the language to understand

the lectures well, and so it is, of course, useless to take them.
I, however, attend one lecture (five times a week), of Professor
Hugo, as the introduction to a course of Civil Law—of which
I am able to understand the general drift, by taking the text-
book with me to the lecture-room. Next term, however, I
shall have a lecture in the Pandects, a lecture on the Institutes,
a lecture on Natural Law, a lecture on the history of Roman
law, which, with the introductory lecture of Hugo—which I
now attend, and which I shall hear again next *Semester*—form
a complete course of Civil Law. Besides which I shall probably attend Heeren's lectures on History, Saalfeld's Political
Lectures (he is a tremendous Liberal, and lately a member of
the Diet), which altogether will be quite a sufficiency.

The rooms which I have taken, I have engaged only for
this *Semester*. Next *Semester* (which begins six weeks after
Michaelmas), King and myself intend taking rooms in the
same house, as we shall be the only Englishmen—I mean
Americans or Englishmen—left in Göttingen. I cannot, of
course, tell you what my expenses are likely to be, and of
course they have been at first more than they will be. But I
think that my necessary expenses will amount to between five
or six hundred dollars at the most, probably to about five
hundred and fifty dollars; and if I travel about in the vacation,
which everybody does, and principally on foot, which everybody does, my whole expenses will amount to between six or
seven hundred dollars, probably not so much as seven hundred;
but I state the maximum rather than the minimum, that I
may not in reality exceed what I say, and this is about the
amount of credit you have given me with Mr. Gossler.

I have not exactly determined what to do or where to go in
September, when there are six weeks' holiday. But I think
of going on foot to the Lake of Constance, and returning down
the Rhine, and so home to Göttingen. This would take about
six weeks, I should suppose, and I do not know how many louis
d'or, but I suppose not more than thirty or forty, which, as I
told you, I have left with the banker.

Neither can I exactly tell how long I had best remain at
Göttingen. It is seldom the custom with German students to

study more than one year at one university—since, by staying
on one or two *Semesters* at Göttingen, another at Berlin,
another at Munich, another at Jena, and so on, they combine
the advantages of all, because in each *Semester* a student may
hear a course of lectures from each of the most eminent
professors in each university, and a year studied in one
university counts in another, and so on.

But I shall certainly stay here this *Semester* and the next,
and after that I do not know whether I shall go to Berlin or
Munich, or remain in Göttingen, but I shall have time to
decide and to advise.

My first object at present, as I said, is to possess myself of
the language, and I study it five or six hours a day, and, as I
said, have a lesson from Professor Benecke from seven to
eight every other morning. As soon as I have acquired
enough of the language to write it and speak it and understand it, I shall feel at my ease and ready to begin my
lectures, and that will undoubtedly be by the end of this
Semester. This has been a long, stupid letter, about louis d'or
and rix dollars, and in fact I hope you will not consider it a
letter, but merely a necessary statement of statistics. To-
morrow is Sunday, which is *Feiertag* (holiday) all over
Germany, and I shall then write a voluminous letter to
mother, telling her all about the miraculous things seen,
heard, and acted in Germany by

Your affectionate son,
J. LOTHROP MOTLEY.

If you ever see Fred Brune, Tom Appleton, Hillard, or
John Sullivan, or Mr. Snow, I wish you would tell them that
they have all got to write to me too.

I know that you will not excuse this writing, so I say
nothing about it.

To his Mother.

Göttingen,
July 1st, 1832.

MY DEAR MOTHER,—I wrote you just before I left Hamburg, and my journey to this place was as uninteresting as can well be imagined ; in fact, it surpassed my *beau ideal* of a bore. The first day was through the Lünenburger Haide (or heath), and the greatest rate of travelling a German mile an hour (4½ English). The two next days (for it took me three days to come about 130 miles) were little better, except that I was a little amused by the coolness of the German postillions. I came from Hanover by extra post (as there was to be no diligence to Göttingen the day I arrived there), and being alone, was almost at the mercy of the postillions. These creatures are certainly the most phlegmatic specimens of mankind that exist. I recollect in particular one fellow who drove me out of Celle, who incontinently determined on first setting out to walk the whole way. He did go for about a mile, and at last I asked him if he could go no faster. "*Oh, ja*," he said, and continued the same pace for another ten minutes. I began to get incensed, and to remonstrate in broken German, but he turned a deaf ear to my invectives, and instead of mending his pace, laid his whip on the top of the chaise, took out his bugle, and solaced himself with practising the overture to 'Tancredi.' At last I recollected a very convincing argument in all languages, and took out a rix-dollar, and said to him, "*Schwager*" (*Schwager* means brother-in-law, and is a very pleasing title to a postillion), "if you go no faster you get no *Trinkgeld*" (drink-money, a regular item in every reckoning in Germany). The appeal was decisive, and he whipped his horses into a trot. Göttingen itself is an unpleasant town enough, and the country about it uninteresting. But the Hartz country (that El-dorado of superstition) is in sight, and there are some lesser hills nearer. You know how celebrated the Hartz Mountains are for goblins, etc. On May-day night they have from time immemorial kept carnival on the Brocken, although I have

not seen a ghost yet, but mean some fine dark night to go
there on a ghost hunt. There is nothing here to mark out
the University, except the Library and the students that you
meet in the streets, for there are no University buildings for
the students, as with us, but the Professors lecture in their
own houses, and the students lodge with the *Philisters* (tradesmen) of the town.

The Library is an immense collection of books, and all have
been purchased in one hundred years ; the precise number is
not known, but it is thought about 400,000. It contains,
however, few rare books and manuscripts, and but few splendid
editions of books. Everything is for use, and the students
may have almost as many books out at a time as they wish by
obtaining a number of cards from a Professor.

I got here, as I told you in my last letter, in the Pentecost
holidays, and had to wait a few days before I could be
matriculated, which matriculation is simply this : I was
summoned before the Senate of the University, and then
wrote my name and my whences and whats, etc., etc., in
a great book. I then gave the member of the Senate who
officiated three rix-dollars for his trouble, and put another into
the poor-box. I have signed an immense list of promises
(which are, I believe, never in the slightest degree kept by
any of the students, and, consequently, a very improper exac-
tion), the principal of which were, to obey the laws *in toto*, to
join no *Landsmannschaft*, drink no beer, fight no duels, etc.,
etc., etc. The next day I went to the Pro-Rector of the
University (Herr Hofrath Goeschen), who gave me my matricle
and legitimation *cartes*, observed that the laws were binding,
and, shaking my hand, informed me that I was a member of
the University. The next day I was introduced to Professor
Hugo, who has been a very celebrated lawyer and professor,
but is now "a noble wreck in ruinous perfection." His
lectures now are dull and stupid, and his titles of Aulic Coun-
sellor, Guelphic Knight, Hofrath, Professor, etc., etc., cannot
bring more than three or four students into his class-room.
He still lectures, however, on the Law, but his great peculiarity
is an unbounded passion for thermometers. He has four or

five hanging in every room of his house, and two on each side
of his head in the lecture-room ; the window opposite him is
raised and lowered by a cord which crosses the room, and is
hitched just over his head, by means of which he very carefully
regulates the temperature of the room at the conclusion of
each paragraph of his lecture. He presented me with a book
which had been lately published in England and dedicated to
him, and I presented him with a louis d'or for a course of
lectures on Roman Law.

But I have said nothing yet of the students because I am
afraid of attacking such a boundless and inexhaustible subject.
The German students are certainly an original and peculiar
race of beings, and can be compared to nothing.

The University towns are the homes of "*outré-ness*," or
rather, they are places where it is impossible to be *outré*, except
by dressing or behaving like "a Christian or an ordinary
man." You can hardly meet a student in the streets whose
dress would not collect a mob anywhere else, and, at the same
time, you hardly meet two in a day who are dressed alike,
every man consulting his own taste, and fashioning himself
according to his *beau ideal*.

The most common outer garment is a red plaid or a blue
velvet frock-coat, twenty of which you find to one of cloth.
The head is covered with a very small cap with the colours of
Landsmannschaft to which the individual may belong. The
boots are garnished with spurs universally, albeit innocent of
horse-flesh ; the fore-finger of the left hand always with an
immense seal ring (often of iron or brass) ; and the upper lip
and chin fortified with an immense moustachio and beard (in
fact, I have seen several students with a depending beard
more than four inches long, and there is hardly one who does
not wear moustachios). A long pipe in the mouth, a portfolio
under the arm, a stick in the hand, and one or two bull-dogs
at the heels, complete a picture not in the slightest degree
exaggerated of a Göttingen student! The most promising
article in the formation of a German student's room is the
pipe. There are generally about twenty or thirty of different
kinds hanging in his room—of porcelain. meerschaum, and

stone, all ornamented with tassels, combining the colours of
his *Landsmannschaft;* and you have no idea how beautifully
some of the pipes are painted with landscapes, portraits (there
are often beautiful miniatures painted on them), or coats of
arms.   Pipes are a favourite present among the students (and
you have anything you wish painted on one when you wish to
give it away).   Every one smokes, and smokes at all times,
and in all occupations (except that they are not allowed to
smoke in the streets), reading, writing, talking, or riding.   I
prefer a pipe now to a cigar, and I am hardly ever without
one in my mouth (for instance, I have been smoking a great
meerschaum all the time I have been writing this), and I
always breakfast at half-past five o'clock (!) on a cup of coffee
and a pipe, and continue the "cloud compelling" occupation
through the day.   I find I grow fat on it, for I never was in
such health in my life.   I find that I have said nothing as
yet about the German duels.   These things are such a common
and every-day occurrence that I have ceased to think at all
about them.   I must, in the first place, tell you that the
accounts you have read in Dwight, etc., of the frequency of
these things is not in the slightest degree exaggerated, in fact
it is entirely impossible to exaggerate them.   I have been here
now about three weeks, and during that time as many as forty
have been fought *to my knowledge*, and I know of as many as
one hundred and fifty more that are to take place directly.

I have seen a few of them, and though you have read
accounts of them in Dwight's ' Travels in Germany,' I suppose
you will be willing to hear a short description of them.   The
duels are not allowed to be fought in the town, and accordingly an inn, called the " Kaiser," just outside one of the gates,
is a very celebrated rendezvous.   As they generally take
place between members of different *Landsmannschafts* (*Landsmannschaft* means countrymen-club, or society; there are as
many of these as there are sets of students from the different
States of Germany.   The most prominent are the " Hanoverian," the " Lünenburger," the " Bremensen," and " Westphalian " Landsmannschaften.   Besides which there is a club
called the " Börsenschafte," which is composed in reality of

the refuse of the whole University), the arms offensive and defensive required in the duel are provided for the duellists by their respective *Landsmannschafts*. These arms are a *Schläger* (or sabre) about four feet in length, blunt at the point, but very sharp-edged, and a suit of stuffed leather to protect all the vital parts, leaving only the face and breast exposed. The last time I was at the "Kaiser," about sixteen duels were fought in the course of the day, ten of which I saw; and they are on the whole stupid affairs, and I think could exist nowhere but in Germany. It is not, however, a perfect trifle to fight one of these duels, although it is very seldom that any lives are lost, or even important wounds received. But the face is often most barbarously mangled, and indeed it is almost an impossibility to meet a student who has not at least one or two large scars in his visage.

In the two that I saw the other day, one man was cut, not very severely, in the breast, and the other received a wound that laid his face open from the left eye to the mouth, and will probably enhance the beauty of his countenance for the rest of his life.

Both these affairs were *Landsmannschaft* duels; the Hanoverians and the Bremensers and the Lünenburgers and the Westphalians being " los "—that is to say, at variance; in which case each Lünenburger has to fight with a Westphalian, each Hanoverian with a Bremenser, till every member of each *Landsmannschaft* has fought. In these four *Landsmannschaften*, I suppose there are from eighty to one hundred students. So here, you see, are a pretty number of duels to be fought directly. Besides this, a single Westphalian has challenged every one of the Lünenburgers to fight him (which challenge has been accepted), and a single Lünenburger has challenged every one of the Westphalians. Here, you see, are two men, each of whom has about twenty-five duels to fight this term. This Lünenburger who has challenged all the Westphalians is somewhat noted for the number of his duels. He has already fought seventy-five, and has been second in about two hundred, and he has here twenty more to fight. Besides which he has yesterday challenged another student, who had insulted his *Landsmannschaft*, to pistols at ten paces, to be reloaded till one is hit. This same fellow who is thus challenged is also challenged by each member of the insulted *Landsmannschaft* to one "gang" of sabres. The meaning of this term is, a duel to be continued till one of the parties falls, or confesses himself unable to fight longer. These duels arise in every sort of way ; a very common one is the one which you have read in 'Dwight,' of pushing or being pushed into the gutter.

There is also a regular code by which the different offences are meted, and the degree of sabre satisfaction determined. The most common and slightest insult is the "Dummer Junge" (stupid boy), which demands a duel of twelve Gangs. (A "Gang" I cannot exactly describe. It is the closing of the two combatants and a certain number of blows and parries.) The parties have each a second at his side to strike up the swords the moment a wound is received. The doctor then steps in, examines the wound, and if it proves to be "*An-schiess*" (a wound of a certain length and depth), the duel is discontinued.

A more gross insult demands twenty-four Gangs, and a still more important one, forty-eight. But the most severe duel is that of one "Gang," in which, as I have said, the duel continues until one drops.

You need be under no apprehension about my returning with a disfigured visage, for as a foreigner is seldom or never insulted, and if he be, has the right of choosing his own weapons (which in my case would be pistols or rifles, and the Germans have an aversion to gunpowder), in which event the offender generally makes an apology and backs out of the business. I assure you I have not at all exaggerated this duelling business. If you cannot have faith in it, you have only to say—

> " Travellers ne'er did lie,
> Though folks at home condemn them."

And though it is beyond all contradiction . a brutal state of things, yet I cannot help thinking it is not without its uses. For instance, some of the students are perfect knights-errant, and if they hear of a lady being insulted (for it is not un-common for a German student, who wishes to manifest his independence, to push a lady off the side-walk), are sure to seek out the offender and salute him with " Dummer Junge," in which case twelve Gangs of the *Schläger* must necessarily ensue.

You will probably not have imbibed a very exalted opinion of the character of German students from the picture I have sketched, but I have found a few friends here whom I admire very much, and with whom I have already drunk " *Brüder-schaft*"; and here, I suppose, an explanatory note is needed. The usual way of addressing a person in German, as perhaps you know, is in the third person plural; the second, as with us is seldom or never used. But between brothers and sisters, parents and children, and very old and intimate friends, the second person singular, " *Du*," thou, is used. The students have a way of cementing a friendship by dropping the third person plural in conversation and substituting for ever the " *Du*" in which case they drink a glass of wine together, ringing the glass, crossing their arms and kissing, after which ceremony the parties can never fight a duel together, or speak to each other otherwise than with " *Du*," in which case they are said to be " *Du*" together.

The Germans are certainly the most musical nation on earth. It is almost impossible to meet a student who cannot sing a thousand songs and play at least one instrument. We have at dinner a full band of music playing, and there are concerts in the public gardens here as often as once a week. The Germans appear to me the most affectionate and (but you will not think it) the most enthusiastic people on earth. Certainly they are infinitely the most industrious and studious. Almost all the students study somewhat, and the greatest part of them immensely, besides writing off at the lectures nearly every word the professor says. But the character of these students is a labyrinth out of which I cannot find my way, and must snap the thread at once if this letter is ever to cross the Atlantic, and it is now of unconscionable length and weight.

Your affectionate son,

J. L. M.

To his Parents.

Göttingen,
August 12th, 1832.

My DEAR PARENTS,—I believe that it is a longer time than it ought to be since I have written home, and I am now so much pressed for time that I shall almost be ashamed to send the letter. The vacation begins in two or three weeks, and my lessons and the one lecture that I had is ended, and to-day at one o'clock I am going off with a party of three students on a foot journey to the Tyrol, a part of Switzerland, and through the Rhine Valley. I have no doubt you will be very glad that I have had the opportunity of travelling through this part of the country in the manner in which I shall now do it—that is to say, as a German student and with German students, and on foot the principal part of the way. The expense of the journey will be very small, considering the time we are to be absent and the length we are to go; and by the arrangement that Mr. Gossler has made about my money, I shall not throughout the year spend a groschen more than you have allowed me, including the expenses of the journey. You must not think that I am neglecting my business to amuse myself; the vacation begins in two or three weeks, and we return before the beginning of the next *Semester.* But of course I shall be back in time to arrange my lectures and lessons (the rooms which I have now I shall retain). This term I cannot pretend to have done much in the way of studying law, because it was impossible for me to attend lectures with any profit before I knew enough of the language to understand them perfectly. But I have studied German a great deal this term, and by mixing a good deal with the students on all occasions, I have made some progress in speaking and understanding the language. By reading a great deal of German every day, too, I have become able to read it almost as easily as English.

Next term I shall remain here, and attend a course of lectures on the 'Institutes' and the 'History of the Civil Law,' which I think I shall be able entirely to understand;

and after next term I shall go either to Munich or Berlin to continue. I shall advise with some of the Professors to know which is the best University for the summer term and which for the winter term, and arrange my plans accordingly. It is at all events not worth one's while to remain long at Göttingen, because most of the Professors who were ornaments of the University are dead or decayed, and the town itself is excessively dull. I am, however, myself very pleasantly situated here. I have formed very agreeable acquaintances among the German students, and I have mixed with them on all occasions and in all places, like one of them. I believe I told you in my last letter about the ceremony of drinking "Schmollets" or Brotherhood. It is a very pleasant way of sealing a friendship, and I have drunk it with several of the best students here.

There are five or six ruined castles near Göttingen, the finest of which are the Hardenburg and the Plesse Castles, both complete and deserted ruins, but very well preserved. The Plesse is much the finest of the two. Large parts of the walls are standing, and two turrets ; but the moat is choked up with shrubs and bushes of a century's growth, and there are great oaks growing in the midst of the hall. It is probably near a thousand years old, and has been a ruin for centuries. It was, as all these German robber knights' castles were, built upon a very high and steep hill, and surrounded by a deep moat with a drawbridge. The hill still remains in its primeval steepness, as my muscles could vouch for many days after my visit ; but the moat is now a thicket, and only the ruins of the portal, to which the drawbridge conducted, remains. The deep cellar vaults are also still perfect, where plenty of Rhenish wine has ripened, and the part of the donjon and the watch-towers, with their deep shot holes and broken staircases, still remain.

The great hall, too, is marked out by its broken and weed-covered walls, and a huge stone fireplace is hanging on the wall, half covered by the branches of the trees that have taken quiet possession of the banqueting room of the Grafs von Plesse. I could not help thinking that the last party who sat

round that fireplace would be somewhat surprised if they could
come into their old premises again, and see what a fresh supply
of firewood was close at hand.

I have been giving a very tame description of a ruin, and I
shall undoubtedly see many a thousand times more interesting
on the Rhine, but the effect which this first antiquity had
upon my brain was so turbulent that it effervesced for some
time, and at last evaporated in a disagreeably long ode in the
German taste, which, however, I will not increase the postage
of this letter with. There are two or three things which I
have yet to describe, and which illustrate well the character
of the students, such as the "Landsmannschaft Kneipen,"
or drinking parties, and the ceremony of the "Landsvater."
I will, however, on the whole postpone them till I can
give a fuller account of them, which will not be till after
I return.

With best love to all my brothers and sisters,

I am

Your affectionate son,

J. LOTHROP MOTLEY.

P.S.—Do write, write, write. I have had no letters for an
age.

To his Parents.

Göttingen,
November 25th, 1832.

MY DEAR FATHER AND MOTHER,— . . . . With respect
to my local habitation after this term, my intentions are
somewhat altered. I think after Easter of removing to
Munich, which has now become one of the most eminent
Universities in Germany, and where are several very useful
and wise expounders of the laws, and which, moreover, is a
much more agreeable tarrying-place in the summer (besides, my friend King and another American friend of mine,
Amory Coffin, who was here last summer, are both going to
Munich next summer), and then of passing the winter in

Berlin, because it is only in winter Savigny, the most celebrated jurist of Germany, reads, and him I have been advised
by everybody by all means to hear. By the time I have done
with Berlin, I think I shall have the 'Civil Law' tolerably
perfectly, that is in a year from April next, and then—but
we won't cast so many "retrospections on the future," as
Mrs. Malaprop says; but some day, when I am in a very
philosophical mood, I will write you as practical and wise
a letter as I can about the way and means I must find to
open what ancient Pistol calls "this oyster world," being a
setting forth of the praiseworthy ideas which every young
gentleman is oppressed with at the time of life when he leaves
off writing bad verses, and discovers that immortality is not
seated in every goose quill. Thank Heaven!—and I am
sure you will join in the thanksgiving—I have quite done
with Pegasus, and begin to affect the "beauty of utility."
But till such time as my philosophical humour cometh, we will
leave all reflections on future destinations.

Will you indulge me in one request? Don't wait always to
send your letters direct to Hamburg; they seldom come one
bit sooner, if the vessel sails the moment the letter is sealed,
than if they came by England or France; and if you write to
me once in two or three weeks, and drop the letters into the
post-office, _via_ Havre or Liverpool, they will be always in my
hands in seven or eight weeks. Here am I now with my direct
letters (I ought to have thanked you before for all those
pleasant letters) in the end of November knowing nothing
at all about you since the end of July. And King has plenty
of September letters, because they come by the packets, and
through France.

I am very much obliged to you for Washington's letter,[1] and

---

[1] _From George Washington to Motley's grandfather, the Rev. John Lothrop._

Mount Vernon,
June 22nd, 1788.

REVERED AND RESPECTED SIR,—Your acceptable favour of the 16th of May, covering a recent publication of the Proceedings of the Humane Society, has within a few days past been put into my hands.

I observe with singular satisfaction the cases in which your benevolent institution has been instrumental in recalling some of our fellow-creatures as it were from beyond the gates of eternity, and has given occasion for the hearts of parents and friends to leap you may be quite sure I shall keep it very religiously, and should like very much to have Franklin's letters, which mother speaks of, and can certainly very easily send. I have also received your 'Morris,' which was a very agreeable present.

I am,

Your most affectionate son,

J. LOTHROP MOTLEY.

To his Mother.

Berlin, Friedrich's Strasse, No. 161, up one pair of stairs,
September, 1833.

MY DEAR MOTHER,—I am settled in this most right-angled of cities, in very comfortable lodgings. I dine in a neighbouring hotel. Every morning my expounder of the divine science of LAW comes to my room for a hour and a half. I have an *abonnement* at a circulating library in the neighbourhood, and

---

for joy. The provision made for shipwrecked mariners is also highly estimable in the view of every philanthropic mind, and greatly consolatory to that suffering part of the community. These things will draw upon you the blessings of those who were nigh to perish. These works of charity and goodwill towards men reflect, in my estimation, great lustre upon the authors, and presage an era of still further improvement.

How pitiful in the eye of reason and religion is that false ambition which desolates the world with fire and sword for the purposes of conquest and fame, while compared to the minor virtues of making our neighbours and our fellow-men as happy as their frail conditions and perishable natures will permit them to be!

I am happy to find that the proposed General Government meets with your approbation—as, indeed, it does with that of most disinterested and discerning men. The Convention of this State is now in session, and I cannot but hope that the Constitution will be adopted by it—though not without considerable opposition. I trust, however, that the commendable example exhibited by the minority in your State will not be without its salutary influence on this. In truth it appears to me that should the proposed Government be generally harmoniously adopted, it will be a new phenomenon in the political and moral world, and an astonishing victory gained by enlightened reason over brutal force. I have the honour to be,

With very great consideration,
Revered and respected sir,
Your most obedient and humble servant,

G. WASHINGTON.

as soon as the term begins (I forgot to tell you in what good season I got here, for the holidays are not finished till after two or three weeks), I shall have myself matriculated at the University.

In the winter, there is generally a good deal of society here. I have a letter to Mr. von Savigny, a celebrated professor, who sees a good deal of company, I believe, which I intend to deliver in the course of a week or two; and with the help of one or two old acquaintances whom I have met here, I shall see as much of society as I wish.

I suppose I ought to describe the wonders and sights of Berlin, and I shall take the first opportunity to drive to Potsdam, and see the Palace Sans Souci, of which you have heard.

When I see here in Europe such sums of money spent by the Government upon every branch of the fine arts, I cannot help asking why we at home have no picture galleries or statue galleries or libraries. I cannot see at all that such things are only fit for monarchies, and I cannot give myself any reason why our Government should not spend some of its surplus money upon them. They have certainly money enough, and in many respects the United States may be called the richest country in the world; at least, if we may reason, as Lovelace in the play does, who calculated his wife's fortune, not by the definite number of pounds, shillings, and pence which she has—for she had nothing—but by the many possible species of extravagance which she has not—thus, £500 a year because she does not *play*; £500 more because she has no passion for dress, etc., etc. So we may say of America, $50,000 a year because we have no army; $50,000 more because we have no debts, and so on to the end of the chapter.

Now, why cannot the "good and senseless" men (as Dogberry tells them) in Congress vote a sum for a library or a gallery or anything of the kind, instead of going to loggerheads about surplus dollars which are lying so comfortably in the treasury?

In every possible improvement that is strictly utilitarian,

America is taking the lead of Europe. One finds nowhere better railroads and steamboats, warehouses or ships than at home; but there is not a library worthy of the name in the whole territory of the United States, from Passamaquoddy Bay to Okafonoke Swamp; and in Germany alone there are dozens of public libraries, any single one of which would weigh up all that we have put together; and so there are in England, France, Italy, Spain, etc., etc.

I shall fold up this letter now, that it may be ready for the post to-night. I shall write again in the course of the next week or two, and I hope you will be as liberal to me. I have heard nothing yet from home since I left. Why can't you write regularly by the New York packets, which sail to Havre or Liverpool half-a-dozen times a month?

With love to all at home,

Your affectionate son,

J. LOTHROP MOTLEY.

To his Parents.

Berlin,
November 4th, 1833.

MY DEAR FATHER AND MOTHER,—I told you in my last that Berlin had no great menagerie of lions, and I have since seen very little to alter my opinion. My "way of life" is very regular. After tea and the newspaper every morning, comes my *Rezensent,* that is, a Doctor of Laws, who reads and expounds to me for a couple of hours the Institutes and Pandects of the *corpus juris;* and I then spend another couple of hours in "stuffing noting" books with the wisdom I have gained. Savigny, whose lectures on the Pandects I intend to hear, does not begin to read for a few days. His lecture will probably be the only judicial one I shall hear, and I have not determined on the other. My principal study is, of course, the Roman law and its history, and this I hope to have learned tolerably, with the assistance of the above-mentioned "learned Theban," by the end of the *Semester,* that is to say, somewhere in March,

and then I shall have done with Berlin and with Germany as
a residence.   There are three theatres—the Royal Opera, the
Royal Playhouse, and the City Theatre—all equally good.   The
first is, however, the finest house, in which all the fashionable
operas and theatres are given.   In the Playhouse is an excellent French drama; and in the City Theatre an Italian opera
and a very good comic company.   The ballets are particularly good in the Opera House.   The Terpsichore of Berlin is
Taglioni, not the Taglioni of London and Paris celebrity,
but her sister-in-law.

The great tragedy star of Berlin and of Germany, Devrient,
is dead.   He was particularly celebrated in Shakesperean
characters, Shylock, Lear, Richard, and others, and, singularly enough, the study of Lear's character was the cause of
his death.   In order to perfect himself in the character of
the crazy king, he spent daily many hours in different mad-
houses, observing and imitating all possible kinds of madness;
the consequence of which was, that after a short time he
became raving mad himself, and died a victim to Melpomene.
At present they have no one to supply his place.   Shakespeare's tragedies are seldom given, and notwithstanding the
richness of the modern German literature, they have very
few fine-acting tragedies.   The *chefs-d'œuvre* of Goethe and
Schiller are not adapted to the stage.   Some of them are
occasionally given, but seldom with success.   The other evening the drama of 'Goetz von Berlichingen with the Iron
Hand,' a magnificent picture of the old time in Germany, and
one of Goethe's masterpieces, was given, but with so many
stage alterations, that from a serious martial tragedy it was
metamorphosed into a farce or a sort of Tom Thumb melo-
drama, full of scenes excellently fitted "to amuse the ears of
the groundlings," and to disgust everybody who had read a
line of the original.   The character of Goetz von Berlichingen, the best possible portrait of a knight of the middle
ages, part robber, part soldier, and part *preux chevalier*, was
given by a thickset, periwig-pated fellow, whose sole effort
was to represent Goetz as a lusty knight "most potent at
potting," who could never keep his fingers from the flask of

Rhenish, except when he was slaughtering legions and com-
mitting unheard-of exploits with his iron fist. And this same
Mr. Rott, as I believe they call him, had the other day the
impertinence to play Shylock, which I was so lucky not to
see.

A favourite author of mine, Lichtenberg, in his lifetime a
celebrated wit and professor at Göttingen, said that he never
knew his own language until he had learned another. The
opinions in Germany concerning America are singularly contradictory. The Germans generally may be divided very
conveniently into two great classes—the Vons and the not-
Vons. Those who are lucky enough to have the three magical
letters V O N before their names belong to the nobility, and
are of course aristocratic to the last degree. Those who have
not these three may have all the other letters of the alphabet
in all possible combinations, and are still nothing but ple-
beians. This proud class are all *ne plus ultra* radicals. It is
as impossible to persuade one of the first class that in the
United States anything exists but democracy and demagogues
as it is to convince the others, particularly those of the lowest
and emigrating class, that they will not find the streets paved
with dollars and their pockets stuffed with bank-notes as
soon as they arrive in New York—that El Dorado of their
expectations.

Your affectionate son,

J. L. M.

To his Father.

Berlin,
January 17th, 1834.

MY DEAR FATHER,—Day before yesterday I took a drive to
Potsdam—which I had not before seen. You know it was the
favourite residence of Frederick the Great, and it is only on
his account that it is interesting. It is about twenty English
miles from here, and looks like a continuation of Berlin,
having the same right-angled streets and yellow-stuccoed
houses. We drove there in the diligence, after having first

" legitimated " ourselves, as the German phrase is—that is to
say, informed the post-office what our names, characters,
religion, etc., etc., were. (How amusing it would be if one should
be obliged always to take a passport with him when he went
in the stage coach, for example, from Boston to Salem! and
yet the Prussian police is as strict as that would be.) The
first thing we looked at was the Palace Sans Souci, which was
built by the famous Fritz. Here everything has been left in
the same state as at his death. You are shown into his study,
where his table stands covered with ink-blots, into his bedroom, etc. The whole house is very simple, and the gardens
around it in the French style. You know he was a passionate
admirer of everything French, which he spoke and wrote
much better than anything German (in fact, he knew very
little of his own language, and all his works are written in
French). Near the house are the tombs of his favourite dogs,
and not far from them the white horse which he rode so often
in the Seven Years' War lies buried.

There are two other palaces here—one of which is a fine
building, and the only splendid residence which the King of
Prussia has, the palaces in Berlin being all very simple,
private-looking houses. Here is also a very elegant and
tasteful villa in the Italian style, belonging to the present
Crown Prince.

In the evening we were invited to a kind of military ball,
where, as is proper and fitting in Prussia, all the ladies were
of ice-gray nobility, and all the gentlemen were officers, with
a profusion of gold lace and orders, or civilians with most
portentous stars on their breasts. It was rather dull, but it
must be confessed that the Germans are very polite to
strangers, and I have experienced nothing but kindness and
civility in every town that I have been in. The most important part of my letter is to come, although I have already
nearly finished my paper.

You remember I was to stay in Berlin for the winter, that
is to say, about six months. I now write to tell you my plans
for leaving, and I beg of you to answer me as soon as possible,
and by the way of London or Havre, because your letter

cannot reach at soonest before I am ready to leave Berlin.   I
shall not give you a long *compte rendu* of what I have done
since I have been here; you must examine for yourself when I
return.   I think I could bear a tolerable examination in the
Civil Law in a few weeks, at which time I shall have finished
the study of it.   I hope in the course of two months to have
some knowledge of the German Common Law and of the Law
of Nations, which I have also been studying.   Of my other
studies, which have been merely for myself, I shall say
nothing.

As soon as your answer to this reaches me, which I hope
will be early in April, I should wish to leave this for Weimar
—from thence to Leipzig, Dresden, and Vienna, and so to
Paris, where I should not wish to stay long, but rather spend
the summer in the South of France.   I wish to stay long
enough to perfect myself in speaking and writing the language
and to see the country, which I could do I think in the course
of four or five months—no longer. (With the Italian language
I hope to do the same afterwards.)   My plans for the winter
are not fully arranged, as I said, but before that I have time
enough to send them for your approval.   Those for the
next summer are so, and I hope that you will consent to
them.

Your affectionate son,
J. L. M.

CHAPTER III.

AUSTRIA—FRANCE—ITALY.

Vienna—Madame de Goethe—Tieck and his works—Journey from Vienna to Styria, Tyrol, etc.—German postillions—Styrian Alps—Molk—Amstetten—Neubach—St. Florian—Salzburg—An ancient hermitage—Burial customs —Hallein — Salt mines — Salzach Valley—Bad-Gastein—Nassfeld—" Old Testament scenery"—A remote village—Rome—The Apollo Belvedere— Naples—Hadrian's villa—Reviving old scenes—Guido's Aurora—Reflections on the art treasures of Rome—Tour in Sicily—Catania—Taormina—Classical associations—Etna—An ascent under difficulties—An arduous climb—And a disappointment—Girgenti—A perilous voyage to Malta—Return to Paris —Salisbury Cathedral—Comparison of English and Foreign cathedrals— Stonehenge.

To his Mother.

Vienna,
June 2nd, 1834.

MY DEAR MOTHER.—

* * * * *

Madame de Goethe, of whom I spoke in my last letter, gave me a letter to a Countess Finkenstein of Dresden, an old lady who lives in Tieck's family, and by whom I was introduced to this author. I had been very much disappointed, as you know, in not having been in Germany before Goethe's death, that I might have seen that Nestor of literature, and this has been in some sort a compensation. I do not know if many of Tieck's works have been translated into English. If they have, you will get them at the Athenæum. Inquire for 'Fantasas' or 'Puss in Boots' or the 'World upside down,' or Tieck's novels (which last are a set of exquisite little tales, novels in the original meaning of the word), full of old German legends and superstitions, and the authorship of which will entitle him to the title of German 'Boccaccio.' The other works are the old nursery tales of 'Fortunatus,' 'Puss in Boots,' 'Blue Beard,' etc., etc., done into plays (not for the stage), and as full of playful and sharp satire, poetry

D 2

and plain sense as they can hold. If they have not been translated we shall have a chance of reading them together one of these days. I was invited by Tieck to tea on Sunday evening, when there was a small party. He is at present just about finishing his translation of Shakespeare (in company with Schlegel), and is in the habit of reading a play aloud to a party of select auditors. I did not hear him, and rather regret it, because he seems to be rather vain of his elocution. His head and bust are fine, and it was not till he got up from his chair that I observed he was slightly deformed (hump-backed). His conversation was like his books, playful, full of *bonhomie*, good-natured sort of satire, and perhaps a little childish vanity. He spoke of Cooper, Irving (whom he knew in Dresden, and whom he admired very much), steamboats, homœopathism, himself, elocution, with Shakespeare and the musical glasses. His conversation was pleasing and quiet, but without any great show or brilliancy; "and so much for Buckingham."

Extract from Diary sent to his Parents.

Paris,
July 8th, 1834.

June 11th.—Leave Vienna for Styria, Salzburg, and the Tyrol, meaning to go afterwards by the way of Munich to Strasbourg, and so to Paris. An old *calèche* (a Vienna acquisition), drawn by two post horses tied by ropes to the carriage and driven by a postillion with gold lace, cocked hat, feathers and spurs enough to set out a whole dozen militia generals, is our conveyance for the present, because in Austria two together can post cheaper than they can go in the diligence. The postillions all over the Continent are certainly the most perfect race of caricatures in existence, and the Austrian was the most absurd of all. Road up the Danube—misty, moisty morning, and hills covered with clouds. Clears up towards noon, and shows us the chain of Styrian Alps on the left, but not quite near enough, except one fine broad-shouldered old mountain (the Eschenberg), with ribands of snow hanging about his head. Pity we took the upper instead of the lower road, and so missed seeing the best part of Styria. Dine at Molk, where we revisit the glimpses of the Danube. Molk monastery, a pretty old abbey on the edge of the river and in the very midst of the fattest and sleekest part of Austria. Road continues through an ocean of wheat and rye, with snug cottages, white villages, distant Alps, and occasionally the Danube, the mother of German rivers. Sleep at a little town called Amstetten.

June 12*th*.—Drive out at four. Mountains more gaunt and grim. Styrian and in part Salzburg Alps. Pass another sleek abbey with two hunting lodges appertaining and wide fields and farms. These are your true monks—none of your bare-footed, rosaried and roped friars, but jovial old gentlemen, living complacently on the fat of the land and the peasants' expense—to whom—

> "They show the steep and thorny way to heaven,
> While they the primrose path of dalliance tread,
> And reck not their own rede."

Weather all day perfect. Fields all waving with wheat and corn and clover, and in this carnival season of the year the old earth looked as if dressed for a planet's ball and determined to eclipse all other stars. Alps all day on the left, with Traunstein, black, shag-eared, beetle-browed old mountain, tallest of the clan. This mountain is near Ischl, is the highest in Upper Austria, and was our companion all day.

Dine at Neubach, wide, dry, unfruitful-looking plain for two or three German miles, cross the railroad, which, wonderful to relate for Germany, is actually begun, and is to go from Gmunden to Linz on the Danube, and thence to Prague, opening the communication, in conjunction with the Danube, between the salt mines in Salzburg in the south and the interior of Bohemia in the north with Vienna, owned by a company of which Rothschild and houses in Hamburg and Vienna are the principal, but is to revert to the Government in fifty years.

Houses becoming more Swiss-like, wooden, with porticoes

and large stones on the roof, which last is universal in
Switzerland and Tyrol. Among other Catholic images which
are strewed all along the roadside, one in particular puzzled
me for a long time—the figure of a saint in armour with a
sword in the right hand and a bucket of water in the left,
which he is emptying on a burning house. I have found that it
is St. Florian, the patron saint of burning houses and firemen,
and also, according to the popular legends, of innkeepers and
brewers, to whom he always sends a sufficient quantity of
water to temper their wine and other potations, and who in
gratitude, as I have observed, have always his figure over their
doorways.

Night at Frankenmarkt, twenty German miles from Amstetten, where we stopped last night. All day weather as perfect
as if sent express from Eden.

June 13th.—Two posts through—better and better mountains
—to Salzburg on the Salzach, a town too beautiful for reality.
A rapid river and the greenest valley. On one side an old
cloister, on the other a magnificent impregnable-looking old
castle. Streets and houses all white and Italian looking, and
the whole in the richest little valley (just large enough to hold
it), where summer is eternally smiling, while around and above
are immense ice mountains, where everlasting winter sits
shivering on his throne. In this town, where we stayed but
six hours, and would have been content to have stayed as many
weeks, besides its natural beauties, which are beyond those of
any town I ever saw, there are a great many curious things
worthy of note; as, for instance, a very handsome gateway to
the town, cut 400 feet through the solid rock of one of the
enclosing mountains, projected and accomplished in ten years
by an ambitious archbishop, Sigismund.

There also still exists a curious and very ancient hermitage,
consisting of a cell and little chapel, cut in the very heart of
the mountains, originally belonging, according to tradition, to
the holy Maximus, a Roman monk of the 5th century, who with
his brother were pitched over a precipice by Odoacer the Goth
as a reward for their labours. This little chapel hangs over
the church of St. Peter, an ancient but of a later date than

itself. I amused myself for some time in the churchyard here
in looking at a few queer old family tombs, which are adorned
with some rude and fantastic paintings representing Death's
doings, with queer explanatory inscriptions, for instance, the
figure of Death playing at skittles with nine cross bones and a
skull for a ball. Another, Death shuffling off the body of a
courtier into the grave in a very unceremonious manner. On
most of the tombs I observed the singular custom of preserving
the skulls of the deceased in a little open case. I took up one
which the inscription informed me belonged to a " beautiful
and accomplished young lady, who spoke four languages,"
I suppose, as Sir Toby says, " word for word without book," and
I daresay too " played the viol de Gamba and had all the good
gifts of nature." Just above it was one of old Death's doings,
pictures of a much earlier date, in which the old gentleman is
making very merry with a scholar, whom he is tumbling with
all his library into the grave, with an inscription which is
rather too long for quotation.

Pass through the mountains one post to Hallein, where are
the celebrated salt mines, which we visited, formerly belonging to the sovereign archbishops of Salzburg, and furnishing
for them a very comfortable revenue of some millions of
florins. They are now a monopoly of the Austrian Emperor,
and, like all the Austrian monopolies, are so dear that they
do not produce half as much as they should. After enduing
ourselves at the entrance in the graceful and picturesque
costume of a miner, viz., a yellow canvas jacket and brown
leather breeches and a red woollen night-cap to keep out
the damp air, we entered the principal shaft (which is for a
considerable distance cut through the solid marble) in order
to descend to the principal receiver, " Behalter," or basin,
which is 1500 feet below the surface of the earth. The descent
is principally made in a peculiar kind of slide, on which you
lay yourself almost horizontally, feet foremost, and taking hold
of a rope made fast above and below in one hand and holding
a torch in the other hand (which answers no earthly purpose
that I could discover except to make darkness visible), you
slip down as mechanically and almost as fast as a weaver's

shuttle, in which operation you may believe that the above-
mentioned brown breeches were of no small advantage. Here
we go, swift as lightning: the picture is enough to make
one's blood run cold, is it not? We soon arrived at the basin,
which, as I said, is about 1500 feet below the earth, and had
leisure to look about us. Such a basin or receiver (of which
there are thirty-two in the mines) is a part of a shaft or gang-
way enlarged on all sides into an artificial cavern of perhaps
a hundred yards in diameter, and some ten or twelve feet in
height.

Fresh water is conducted by wooden pipes into the cavern
till it is nearly half full. The salt of which the inside of the
mountain is almost entirely composed is then dissolved and
mixed with water, which, after becoming sufficiently impregnated, is conducted out of the mines into the valley, where it
is boiled, etc. While the water remains standing, which of
course it is suffered to do for a considerable time, the whole
cavern appears or is in fact a gloomy subterraneous lake. The
miners employed there row about it in little canoes; the whole
appearance is most surprising, and when the cavern is lighted
up, as it was when we were there, and the little lighted boats
flitting across in all directions like fire spectres, you might
believe that you were assisting at the carnival of the cobolds
and gnomes and all sorts of sprites, such a strange, bewildering,
unholy aspect as the whole scene was. We emerged through
another shaft, and after resuming our earthly habiliments, we
returned to our caleche and our journey.

7 to 10 P.M.—Drive through the narrow pass of the mountain towards Werfen, got out to look at the opening of the
River Salzach, where the stream makes its way apparently
through the rock, and where the hills are jammed so closely
together that nothing but a river could get through. Drive
continues through the dark, deep valley of the Salzach, faint
moonlight, black gloomy mountains with glittering snow-
tops, fire-flies, cascades, pine forests, an attempt at a thunder
shower, a precipitous road, and a postilion fast asleep the
whole way, altogether romantic enough to have enchanted the
whole Fudge family. At 11 P.M. reach Werfen, where we stop

for the night, tired enough, having been on the road since four in the morning.

June 14*th*, 4 A.M.—Two posts to little town of Lend. Morning, as usual, cold and foggy. Summits of the mountains covered with snow, and clouds in so singular a mixture that it was impossible to separate the one from the other, and it looked as if the scene were all sky or all *mountain*. Lend, a cascade and a fine rainbow. Detained two hours by a broken bridge. Drive through the Klemme, a narrow pass, much resembling, though I think not quite so magnificent as, the Scotch and White Mountains. Road built along the side of the mountain, for there is no valley, and the immense masses of rock reach from the region of clouds and ice down into the bed of the River Acha, far beneath us in the smooth, unbroken perfect precipice. The bridge over the river, with St. Melchior story on the roadside.

Continue a few miles to Bad-Gastein, a wild and primitive-looking village with a mineral spring on a plain nearly 4000 feet above the sea. Mountains all round, cascades in great number, and the fine fall of the Acha in three separate leaps, all foam and thunder.

Walk in the afternoon to Nassfeld, a little valley about a thousand feet higher than Gastein, three waterfalls, two tolerable but rather commonplace cascades, but the third, the Schleierfall, very beautiful and singular. A thin narrow unbroken snow brook, falling from the tiptop of an iced mountain, with the bed of a river below, and so blue and clear and transparent that it looks, as it is called, like a veil for a giantess, for Queen Cunegunde or for the Spirit of Solitude who is at home in this valley. A strange, silent-looking valley, with snow lying unmelted in large patches in the middle of June, no signs of life excepting a few goats, all shut in by immense mountains, and looking like a very fortress of solitude. Walk back by another path through the same patriarchal, *Old Testament kind of scenery*, to Gastein.

15*th June*.—I suppose that no transatlantic travellers ever happened upon this little place before, for as soon as we had written our names down in the Travellers' Book as Americans,

a most prodigious sensation took place among the bath company. I never was such a lion in my life. Everybody, the
ladies and all, were determined to make our acquaintance, and
a jovial old Austrian Field-Marshal (whom I afterwards found
out was no less a personage than the Governor-General of
Bohemia) patronised us particularly, and we were pressed to
stay on all hands. But fearing that some Sandwich Island
ladies or New Zealanders might arrive if we stayed too long,
and strip us entirely of our *lionship*, we determined to vanish
while we were in our zenith, and such exchanging of cards
and such tender farewells among acquaintances of twenty-
four hours standing I never saw before. I expected that on
our departure the children would come out in procession and
strew flowers in our path, but it was very early in the morning
there was nobody stirring, so we went off quietly.

To his Parents.

Rome,
November 24th, 1834.

MY DEAR PARENTS,—

*   *   *   *   *

The common casts, prints, etc., had given me no better
idea of the Apollo Belvedere than they had of the Venus de
Medici. I have heard of persons being disappointed in both.
This term " disappointment " is a cant and favourite phrase
which I don't profess to understand. If a person expected an
elephant and found an Apollo, I can conceive of his being
disappointed, but if he was looking for a divinity when he
saw the Apollo, and was then " disappointed," I can only say
that the fault was in him. The whole figure of the Apollo is
slight almost to spareness, but at a little distance the nose is
a thousand times more scornful than I expected, and the whole
face has almost a chilling repulsiveness. But on approaching
nearer, this expression melts away, all the anger concentrates
in the nostril, and the eternal beauty of the face and figure
dissolves itself and floats almost like a drapery around the

whole statue.   The god, the divinity speaks, breathes, moves
in every line, limb, muscle.   Every deity of the ancient temple
has lent this face his brightest attributes.   The forehead of
Jupiter, when it was pregnant with the Goddess of Wisdom,
the eye of Juno, the lips of Venus, and the hair floating on
the shoulders and bound on the forehead as if by the very
fingers of the Graces.   The very first sight of the statue
transports you to Delos.   The Muses in their hallowed vales rise
around you, and in the midst of them, and presiding over
them, and over everything which makes life lovely, stands
the god of eternal youth, and light, and beauty and poetry
in his full divinity before you.   It is no longer a piece of
chiselled marble which enchains your eyes, the figure expands
into life, into immortality while you are gazing—the ground
seems to sink away before his lofty godlike steps—you see
the glittering chariot of fire, and hear the snorting steeds, and
you start lest the god of the sun shall have already sprung
into his car, and be already rolling in light and glory and
divinity above the earth.

There is on the whole more divinity, more of the godhead,
in the Apollo than in any ancient statue, at least that I have
seen.   One may have more loveliness (as for instance in
Meleager) and another more nature, but the Apollo is not
flesh, is not marble—there is nothing earthly about him.   It
is a being to whom none but Ganymede or Hebe have administered.   He has never been fed but with nectar and
ambrosia; there are no protruding veins, no swelling muscles
—all is perfect, godlike, beautiful repose.   He is the embodi-
ment of the ethereal essence which is the being of gods, and
there is not a particle of materiality about his whole system.
It seems impossible that labour and time should have created
such a statue.   It seems to have waked into existence like a
single thought, a single impulse.   It seems the sudden and
startling realization of the brightest dream which the genius
of its artist had ever conceived.   It is impossible to imagine
that it could have been produced by degrees, that the sculptor
could have seen the future divinity concealed in the heart of
the shapeless marble, that he could have watched his own

bright original thought gradually unfolding itself from the bosom of the stone, breathing upon him slowly and mysteriously like the birth of day and night, and bursting at last from its marble chaos in full, perfect, immortal loveliness of his first burning conception. It seems impossible; it seems to be the thought itself waked into immortal existence by the stroke of a wand, so ethereal, so immaterial, so godlike is the statue.

There, I have prosed so long about this same Apollo, this Dandy of the Vatican, that I have left myself no room to speak of the other treasures of this Museum. As I may as well have a little method in my madness, and a little system in my letters, I will discourse in my next of St. Peter's, the Capitol, and some of the endless villas, palaces, and churches stuffed full of pictures and statues which occupy our mornings and will occupy them for some time to come.

Very affectionately your son,
LOTHROP MOTLEY.

To his Parents.

Naples,
December 28th, 1834.

MY DEAR PARENTS,—

*   *   *   *   *

Two miles beyond are the vast remains of the Emperor Hadrian's famous villa. This is an immense heap of ruins, and as in most buildings of this kind (see the baths of Caracalla, Titus, Diocletian, etc., in Rome) little remains to testify of their former magnificence but their extent.

This villa is supposed to have been seven miles in circumference, and contained besides the Imperial palace, baths, temples, theatres, libraries, barracks of the Prætorian Guard, and, in short, everything necessary to constitute that counterpart to a cockney's paradise, the *urbs in rure*, always supposing the latter to be the much-coveted *rus in urbe*.

It was built under the direction of Hadrian on his return from his seven years' tour in the East, and seems to have been a sort of embodied epitome of his voyage. The "Canope" was in imitation of that near Alexandria; the Lyceum, Poecile, etc., were copied from those at Athens, and the vale of Tempe was made in imitation of the famous happy valley of Thessaly.

The cicerone conducts you round to several different portions of ruins, to which names, but in general most arbitrary ones, have been given, and the giro commenced with the " Grecian Theatre."

Here the forms of the Proscenium and the seats of the spectators are still distinctly to be traced, and in the neighbourhood are the ruins of the porticoes, etc.

The next is the Poecile, in imitation of that of Athens; and next the library.   Afterwards an immense heap of rubbish with one entire wall, dignified with the name of the Imperial Palace; next the barracks of the Prætorian Guard; next the Canope, near it the remains of another theatre, other baths at the entrance to the vale of Tempe.   The ruins are generally of brick—sometimes a vault, sometimes a portico, sometimes a wall remains entire, but it is generally a confused mass of rubbish, from which the most interesting remains, such as statues, vases, etc., have been extracted and carried to Rome.   And thus is repeated for the thousandth time the often-told and dull catalogue *raisonné* of the ruins of Hadrian's villa.

If you will allow me to mount my hobby, as Tristram Shandy would say, and call fancy to the side of history, the scene will be different, and at least more lively.   The shattered columns rise, the mouldering walls, the fallen arches, the broken statues, the faded pictures, and all the pomp, pride, and circumstance of the luxurious abode of the most glorious Roman Emperor start again to life and grace and beauty.   The palaces, the temples, the theatres, the baths, the halls of sports, the fields of military exercise, the haunts of the poets and philosophers revive and appear as they were thousands of years ago.

The scene becomes alive and animate, and is repeopled with the dust which has long since floated and vanished on the wind.   The forms and voices of the long-forgotten dead

rise again to being, and the halls and courts of the stately
villa swarm with their shades, and in the gay phantasmagoria
of a dream, and ring again as they were wont to the mirth
and laughter of the crowd. Here rises the proud, commanding form of the imperial Hadrian, there lounges the graceful
Antinous, from the neighbouring courtyard is heard the
steady, martial tramp of the Prætorians.

In yonder theatre rises a buzz of admiration or a shout of
laughter at a gay comedy of Terence or Plautus.

In the neighbouring and stately library are seen the
dignified forms of the old philosophers and poets, they
saunter leisurely through the lofty alcoves or descend through
the luxurious mazes of the gardens, and the voices of wit and
wisdom fall again upon your ear as they join in sweet com-
munion together. From yonder Palaestro the roar of merri-
ment rises on the wind and proclaims the assembly engaged
in the light-hearted games of the baths.

A serious crowd in the distance are bending their steps to
the temples, the priests in the splendid array of their office
are administering the rites of the altar.

Farther off a careless crowd are thronging to the luxurious
baths. All around the voices of command, of mirth, of admiration, of discussion, of devotion, float through the air and
mingle in strange variety together.

Everywhere is *life*, cheerful, busy, bustling, noisy, impatient
life. Baths, halls, temples, theatres are all swarming with
human figures, and resounding with human voices. The
stately fabrics of Imperial grandeur are around you, the
masterpieces of Roman and foreign genius decorate the apartments; the porticoes, the gardens, all look as if for eternity,
strong, stately, durable, magnificent.

The day before we determined to leave Rome for Naples I
had taken my last look at the Apollo and Meleager and the
rooms of Raphael, and at midnight I had walked to the ruins
of the Palace of the Cæsars, and taken from thence my last
look at the Forum, and the Curia, and the temples, and the
Coliseum; and the next day, having a call to make in the
vicinity of the Capuchin church, I paid a farewell visit to

Guido's wonderful archangel (which is the Apollo of canvas in spite of all gainsayers), and then, as it was not far off, I thought I might look once more at the wonderful Aurora.

This is painted in fresco on the ceiling of a garden house in the Palace Rospigliosi. The ceiling of a private nobleman's garden pavilion adorned with one of the most immortal pictures of the immortal Guido may be a fair offset to a niche in the basement story of an emperor's palace filled with a group of the Laocoon; but search through the world out of Italy and you will scarcely find in all the palaces and pavilions of all the emperors and noblemen of all the world such a refinement of luxury.

The design of this painting is one of matchless poetry, and executed by the hand of a magician. The chariot of the sun is just rolling over the first grey cloud of morning, preceded by Aurora, who drops flowers and dew over the still-sleeping land and sea, and by Light, in the figure of a boy, whose torch is just beginning to touch the cloud with the brightness of daylight; and surrounded by the train of Hours, every one of whom is a being of eternal youth and grace and beauty. The whole is wonderful—there is not a stroke of the pencil that does not breathe of morning and daylight; all is fresh, brisk, and startling, in the step of Aurora, and the individual and different beauty of each figure is almost incredible. If I should find a fault it would be with the figure of Apollo, who is in fact no Apollo, and furnishes the only exception to the vivid and godlike beauty of all the other figures. He has, in fact, no business in the clouds, being a most earthly figure—a red-haired, clownish-looking bumpkin, who looks as if taken from an ox cart, and is totally unfit to drive the four-in-hand of Phœbus, whose place he is clumsily usurping.

Generation after generation shall throng these places, and still the pile shall endure—the delight and wonder of Rome and of the world. Alas! throw down the wand of imagination and look around you. What meets your eye? Heaps of confused and shapeless ruins—a dreary and desolate mass of decay and corruption, overgrown with weeds and ivy, and choked with rubbish. The theatres, temples, porticoes, palaces,

lie alike in one mighty and indistinguishable mass of ruin and
desolation; and not a voice is heard through the vast and
dreary silence to testify the existence of humanity.

After indulging in all these heroics, which you will perhaps
think excusable when one is " putting his foot on such a
reverend history" as this villa of Hadrian, we continued our
route up the hills, and through a forest of olives to Tivoli.

*   *   *   *   *   *

To his Parents.

Naples,
April 30th, 1835.

MY DEAR PARENTS,—I sent off a very short letter yesterday
to let you know where I was and whither I was going, and
intended writing you a very long one to-day. I have, however, already taken my passage in the steamboat from this to
Genoa, whence I shall go directly to Paris, and I shall accordingly hardly have time to give you the whole of my tour in
Sicily; for I find, on looking at my notes about it, that it is
the most voluminous one I have made. Besides, as I shall see
you all in a few months, I may as well leave something to be
told _vivâ voce._ We came down, as I believe I have told you
in a former letter, through Calabria to Reggio, and so crossed
over to Messina. From Messina we went down along the
eastern coast of Sicily to Catania; from Catania we ascended
Etna; afterwards came to Syracuse; from Syracuse to
Girgenti, the site of the ancient Agrigentum; and from
Girgenti we crossed in a small vessel to Malta. From Malta,
as I have already told you, I returned in a brig to Naples.

24th March.—Left Messina for Catania in a carriage, for this
distance, about 120 miles, is the only part of Sicily where one
can travel in any way but on mules. The two days we were
coming, the weather squally, rainy, wretched, and the road,
which should have presented different and constant views of
Mount Etna, presented nothing. But the island is so beyond
all description lovely—such a wild, fabulous, overflowing

vegetation; such millions of flowers and fruits; lemon trees and oranges springing again into blossom, while the boughs are still golden with fruit; grain bursting ripe and ready bearded from the ground, for all the fields are at this moment in full ear, the banks all gaudy with anemones, marigolds, daisies, violets, and a thousand garden flowers, springing wildly and spontaneously into existence at the first breath of spring.

And then, as one draws near Catania and the base of Etna, such wild, wonderful contrasts—a boundless ocean of lava, black, dismal, awful; and yet, such is the eternal and ever-vivid quality of the atmosphere, that the gaudiest flowers and the most luxuriant vegetation, springing in the very bosom of the lava before it is hardly cold—all this together makes a drive in Sicily, although not under the most favourable sky, a thing to be remembered.

Half-way between Messina and Catania is Taormina, the ancient Taurominium, and here are the beautiful ruins of an ancient theatre; and the second day we passed the pretty and finical town of Aci, which is immortally associated with one or two exquisite fables of the Greeks. The river which runs by the town is the Acis, the liquid lover of Galatea, for it was here that the jealous Titan crushed the unfortunate shepherd as he sat by his beloved sea-nymph, and the river into which he was changed by his mistress still rushes impetuously to the ocean, as if to seek and console the sorrowing sea-nymph. Two or three miles from the town brought us to the beach, to look for seven small islands or rocks close to the shore, and which are said to be the rocks of the Cyclops—the rocks which the same ill-tempered Polyphemus threw down upon Ulysses and his companions. According to accurate people, they were thrown into the sea by Etna and not by the Titans; but the long point of Cape Mollini on the left, the seven mysterious rocks on the right, the sea black and angry in front, and Etna, which ought to have been smoking, behind, made up together a very epical picture, and so I resisted the volcanic theory, and in the midst of the scene I recollected the adventures which occurred on the spot to Æneas. I saw the ancient

Anchises grasp the hand of the unfortunate and defeated
Achæmenides. I listened with him to his tale of distress, and
was startled in the midst by the appearance of the truculent
Titan. I saw the grim, ungainly form of Polyphemus striding
from his cave, and beheld Æneas and his companions scamper-
ing into the boats to escape him, and I heard the disappointed
roar of the infuriated giant, which shook the sea and the earth,
and even Etna itself, to the centre—but I will spare you the
rest of the description.

   I see that although I have carefully left out the description
of the two days' journey to Catania, I am already loitering on
the way, but I have no time to spare, for we have got Etna to
ascend, countless ruins to explore, and a shipwreck to outlive,
before we get to Malta. And so let us hasten at once to
Catania. Catania is just at the base of Etna, and is the most
volcanic town possible, literally built on its own ruins, whole
foundation in land made from water by fire. The sea formerly
reached beyond the Porte di Ulysse, now considerably beyond
the city on the outside, for the ocean has been filled with lava,
and on that stands the town. The harbour is the most singular spectacle in the world, high rocks and cliffs, in as wild
and fantastic shapes as those of Nahant, but all lava, which in
1669 swept from the top of Etna, over and nearly destroying
the town, and ran far into the sea, thus forming a breakwater,
and thus a safe harbour which subsequent eruptions destroyed.
Catania's history is all earthquake—leaving ancient history
out of the question—and beginning with comparatively modern
times. In 1160 every house and every inhabitant was destroyed; in 1348 it was devastated by the plague; in 1669
the lava overwhelmed and destroyed it; in 1693 it was again
destroyed by an earthquake, and still, at this moment, it is a
gay, flourishing and, for Sicily or Italy, a neat and thriving
town; and even now its light-hearted inhabitants live and
laugh and dance and sing with an abyss of fire yawning
beneath them, Etna thundering over their heads, and in
danger every moment to see striding back upon them the
ancient awful chaos. There are no human battle-fields here—
no places celebrated by the wars of the Greeks or the Romans

—the Romans or the Hohenstaufen, as are to be seen in most parts of Sicily and Italy, but other and far more imposing battle-fields. Two great elements have been on this spot continually at war—fire and ocean. The plains and places of this terrible encounter are distinctly, awfully visible, and of the wrecks and ruins which have attended them, the least are man's; and even now, when one sits on the rocks of fire and hears the sea foaming and howling around them, old Ocean seems to be sounding his defiance to the god of fire and daring him to another conflict.

March 28*th.*—Start from Catania at 11 A.M. to Mount Etna. My most exquisite reason for joining in the party I should be puzzled to say, probably because Abbate's and my own opinion were decidedly against it. Mules from Niccolosi, twelve miles, through the first region, or Reggio Coltivato, of the mountain. The greatest peculiarity in the appearance of Etna, and one which renders him the most striking mountain I have ever seen, not excepting even Mont Blanc, is his single and solitary situation. Other high mountains are usually the highest of a chain of mountains, and generally the vicinity of a multitude of hills detracts from the effect of the highest peak. But Etna rises all alone from a dead plain; suddenly and singly with one stride he is in heaven, and there he stands and stood to-day, with the sunshine wasting itself on his icy forehead—all alone—the whole sky and the whole earth to himself, and looking like the god and ruling spirit of the island. The three regions into which naturalists divide the mountain are the Reggio Primo or Fecondo, Reggio Secundo or Selvoso, Reggio Terzo or Nevoso—the fruitful, the woody, the snowy, and desolate. · They are in fact paradise, purgatory, and hell. Nothing can surpass the overflowing wonderful fertility of the first, the mystic gloom of the second, nor the wholly infernal, hideous, sulphureous sights and smells of the last. Gradual ascent towards Niccolosi. Soil of the side of the mountain all ancient lava, which in the course of centuries becomes the richest mould, and is covered with a prurient and fabulous vegetation. Thus here nature is cradled in fire and nursed by earthquakes, and a new Sicily seems constantly springing from the ashes of the old one, for the hackneyed phœnix is no trope here, but reality. Wide base of Etna, which is nearly one hundred miles round.

Life and laughing with plenty—cornfields, vineyards, flower-gardens, fields of flax in flower, Indian figs, mulberries, lemons, oranges, golden with fruit and fragrant with flower; in fact, wherever one looks one sees Ceres, who was anciently, with justice, the presiding deity of the island, sitting in beneficent majesty with the boy Bacchus laughing in her lap. At Niccolosi finishes the first region; here are the Monti Rossi, two tolerable hills thrown up in the tremendous eruption of 1669, and the course of the lava down the side of the mountain to the sea is still darkly and awfully distinct. This side is girt round with a line of *bocce* or craters, and the whole scene is black with lava and ashes. The previous sight of Vesuvius had not enabled me to conceive of such a scene of horrible and unearthly desolation as I saw here. The black broad line of lava looks like the wake of a ship of fire. It seems as if the ancient Chaos had strode from Etna to the sea and left the trace of his footsteps and desolation behind him.

At Niccolosi, which is a little village about a sixth of the way up Etna, we dismounted and ate a dinner brought with us from Catania. A certain Dr. Gemmalaro, a fat old professor and a kind of second Empedocles, lives up in the clouds here, apparently to study the mountain and make notes thereof. This seeming to be his only occupation, Abbate, our landlord at Catania, had advised us to hold converse with the learned Theban, and we did, but to no purpose except that he sent us our guides. At 8 P.M. mount mules again, for, as if the difficulty of ascending the mountain at this season of the year were not great enough, we must needs increase them by going up in the night, in order to enjoy the cool breezes of March at midnight among the snows of Etna. From Niccolosi to the Casa della Neve is about ten miles, the second stage of the journey, and comprehends the second or woody region. Night pitch dark but starry—guides with lanterns. In an hour commence patches of snow, increasing, and night cold. Arrive

at Casa della Neve at half-past eleven, expecting to find a
tolerably comfortable hut with a dry floor and perhaps the
Sybaritish luxury of a chair and table; have the inexpressible
satisfaction to find the house of snow well deserving its name—
a stone hut, minus its roof, and filled with snow about two feet
deep. Make a fire of branches before it, and cower shivering
over it in a most melancholy state, listening to the wind
soughing through the trees and howling hideously on the still
distant and icy top of the mountain.

After indulging for half-an-hour in pleasing anticipations
of our night's walk, leave the paradisaical house of snow at
about midnight to perform the third and principal stage of
the journey. At midsummer the ascent from the Casa della
Neve to the Casa degli Inglesi at the foot of the cone
is practicable to mules, the distance nine miles, and then
there remains only the ascent of the cone, which is, however, for a mile nearly perpendicular, to be made on foot,
consequently in warm weather and by daylight it is an easy—
comparatively easy—affair. At present from the Casa della
Neve to the top is all deep, hard-frozen snow. The guides
had told us we must leave the mules here and make the
whole ten miles' ascent on foot. Attempt riding a little
farther through the thrilling regions of thick-ribbed ice.
Mule and I flounder about a few hundred yards through the
snow, until at last he tumbles fairly over, and we roll together
most amicably head over heels some dozen yards down the
snow bank, till we are stopped by a thicket of ilexes. Get up
and shake myself, and finding myself unharmed, saving a few
bruises, proceed, with the help of the guides, to assist the
amiable companion of my misfortunes to his legs again.
Finding that the girths and bridle are broken all to pieces,
and experience showing that the slippery side of an iced
volcano is not the best place to show off one's horse- or
rather mule-manship, determined to accede to the prayers of
the guide, and all leave the mules and commence the ascent
on foot.

The ascent to the Casa Inglese lasted from a little after
midnight to 5 A.M. Cold gradually increased, the ascent

excessively steep, the ice intolerably slippery, the wind piercing. The remainder of the journey and the ascent of the cone, which must be always performed on foot, is difficult. Difficult on a warm summer's day, and after dismounting, fresh, comfortably warm and untired from our mule's back, and taking repose and refreshment in the Casa Inglese before commencing the ascent,—*ecco la differenza!* On a cold piercing night in March, in the coldest part of the twenty-four hours, viz., an hour before dawn, arriving at the base of the cone, fagged, half-frozen, and worn out from a nine miles' and five hours' walk up the steep, slippery ice of the mountain, through the whole night, too, instead of dismounting from an agreeable ride, finding the Casa Inglese buried deep in snow, and with nothing for it but to commence the last and closing scene of the momentous history without resting, with the addition to our misfortunes that the guides had neglected to take up water or even an orange, so that there was nothing to slake our constant thirst but the ice which we had been so much warned against that it seemed like swallowing poison to attempt it. On my arriving at the Casa degli Inglesi, one of the party was a little ahead, and the other was half-an-hour behind. My guide was an old man, quite unequal to his office, and being very much fatigued himself, advised me to stay and see the sun rise from thence instead of from the summit, adding coolly that any farther ascent was quite impossible. Spur him on, and, both nearly exhausted, commence crawling up through the ice and knee-deep ashes which form the almost perpendicular and almost mile-long ascent of the cone. Both drop with fatigue every dozen yards, till at last the guide fairly tumbles over in the ashes and refuses to budge another step. Leave him to his fate and scramble and creep through clouds of hideously smelling sulphur to the top; see the sun rise just as I reach the top of the ridge, and such a lame and impotent conclusion to the night's labour was intolerable.

The night had been clear and bright, but towards morning mists had begun to collect in the south, and at last the sun rose red and lurid above the sea, and after glaring a few

seconds like a culprit from a barred prison window through
the long dun vapoury mists which stretched all across the
horizon, hid himself from the day in a dark heavy mass of
clouds, which almost filled the whole heaven. I was in no
favour with Apollo certainly, and looking down towards the
islands, which was the only part of the vaunted prospect
not quite obscured by the vapours, I found that the king of
the winds was not in a bit better humour ; he seemed to have
unchained every one of his tempests, and they came sweeping
coldly and dismally across the top of the mountain, and had
nearly blown me into the sea. Struggle against them a little
while, and look about me. The objects to be gained by our
ascent were—first, to see the sun rise ; second, to see the celebrated pyramidal shadow of the cone formed on the southern
side of the island ; third, the extensive view of the island ;
fourth, a sight of the crater. Of these only the last were
attained. The sunrise was anything but brilliant, the clouds
prevented the phenomenon of the shadow, and the darkness
and mistiness of the atmosphere towards the south obscured a
great part of the view. In fact, the Lipari Islands, the ex-
tremity of Calabria, and the coast of Messina were almost all
that could be seen. All that I got was a look at the crater ;
but that was, after all, worth all the trouble. Such a hideous,
horrible, infernal sight I had never conceived of. The yawning and almost fathomless gulf, its sides formed of precipitous
cliffs of ancient ice and brimstone and lava and ashes, the
dull heavy sulphurous vapours rising along the sides and suf-
focating all who attempt to inhale the atmosphere, and seeming
like the breath of the rebel giant who lies chained and howling and writhing in agony beneath the mountain, altogether
gave me an idea of the Inferno which I could never have
conceived of : the fumes of Vulcan's workshop, the breath of
the demons who infest the mountain, the cradle of Chaos,
nothing is too vile, hideous, and ghastly to be associated
with the place.

Forgot to mention what was one of the most striking
circumstances of the whole expedition. At about two hours
after midnight, when we had gotten about a third of the way

up, and were toiling through the snow half tired and half
frozen, we descried what seemed a black ridge of lava above
the snow, and promised a deal of satisfaction in resting there.
It seemed about five minutes' walk. We hastened towards it.
Five minutes passed, and it seemed still five minutes; another
five minutes, still the same. Another half-hour, another hour,
still it receded before us, and I got nervous. It was as if
some of the demons with which the caves of Mount Etna are
peopled were mopping and mowing at us from that black
and ghastly mass of lava, as it still fled in silent mockery
before us. At last morning broke, and lo! the ledge of rocks
where we were to have reposed ourselves when about a third
of the way up the mountain now hung still high above us,
and was—the summit, the black, awful summit itself of
Mount Etna. After five minutes spent in gaping and
gasping at the crater and endeavouring to make something of
the view, return to the base of the cone, seat ourselves and
warm ourselves by the sulphurous and stinking fumes of a
bocca, and thaw some of our hard-frozen food in the steam, and
in that moment I think I never saw six more unearthly and
devilish-looking individuals than we three, with the three
guides, as haggard with the want of sleep and the night's
fatigue, half famished and half frozen, we hung over the
deep, sulphurous fumes of that infernal *bocca*, gnawing our
frozen victuals. Descend from the Casa Inglese to Casa della
Neve in about two hours, which in ascending occupied five,
fold cloak under me like a sledge, and slide down comfortably
and quickly. Reach Casa della Neve at eight, devour a cold
chicken and a bottle of wine, and resume the mules. Jog
down to Niccolosi, falling asleep on the mule two or three
times, and reach Niccolosi at half-past eleven. Rest until
3.30, and then proceed through the paradisaical region to
Catania again. As we approach the base, weather fine again.
Sunday, and the peasants in holiday suits, air full of perfume
and earth full of flowers, butterflies swarming, bees humming,
lizards creeping, etc., etc. Reach at last Catania and the
most excellent Albergo della Corona, and rejoice in a good
dinner and a good bed. The latter, you may be sure, was

acceptable after having ridden on mules fifty miles and walked twenty without sleeping.

On the 9th of April, having been the day before rolled and half drowned, mules and all, in a river, we arrived at Girgenti. After having admired the beautiful temples here for two or three days, we joined a party of English, who had hired a small vessel to take them across to Malta. The distance is about one hundred miles, and we hoped to get there in about twenty-four hours. The vessel was not quite thirty tons burthen, and besides ten passengers and seven sailors, had been loaded with brimstone, contrary to our express contract. We got on well enough the first night. We set sail at nine in the evening, but as there was nothing like a cabin, and the hold would only contain two or three at a time, the night, which was an excessively cold one, was anything but pleasant. Towards morning, however, the wind, which had been pretty strong all night, increased to a hurricane. One of our sails, not taken in in time, was blown to pieces, and the others being furled, we drifted under bare poles quite at the mercy of the wind. The sea rose to a height which I think I never saw in the Atlantic, and our vessel, which in calm weather was hardly a foot above water, was now washed over by every wave. She was heavily laden, and laboured excessively, and strained to every wave almost to cracking. We were drenched through by every wave and expecting every moment to be swamped The captain lay in a corner, crying like a child, and calling on St. Joseph; the crew were praying to the Madonna; and at last all the passengers, at the request of the captain, by a sudden impulse commenced discharging the cargo in a very summary manner.

After having thus presented Mr. Graset's brimstone to the fishes, the vessel rode lighter, and the wind lulling a little, we became encouraged. The captain and crew resumed command of the vessel. And we all lay drenched, shivering, and miserable on the deck. At last we made land, and then commenced a violent dispute among the sailors whether it was Sicily or Malta. Conceive of these sages, men who have spent their whole lives in navigating between these two

islands, and not able to distinguish one coast from the other !
At last the wind, which luckily was in our favour, blew us
about twenty past twelve of the second night into Malta ;
and there we had the inexpressible satisfaction of waiting close
to shore in our wet boat till morning, no vessel being allowed
to discharge its passengers after sundown. When the sun at
last rose I think it never shone on a dozen more forlorn and
wretched-looking individuals. Sick, pale, haggard faces, be-
grimed with brimstone, clothes torn and drenched and water-
logged, we looked altogether more like a deputation of the
devils of ' Der Freischütz ' than like human creatures. At last
we were let out, and the first thing I did on reaching the hotel
at eight in the morning was to jump into bed and sleep until
nine the next morning.

My letter of the 15th of April has informed you of my disappointment at Malta, and you may believe that the eight or
nine days which I was allowed to spend there waiting for a
vessel to the Continent, instead of going with my companions
with the steamer to Greece, where I should have been the
third day after leaving Malta, were anything but pleasant.
The English fleet was there, and as I had acquaintances in
some of the officers, I went on board most of the vessels. My
voyage from Malta to Naples hardly contained much of interest.
The first five days were my usual luck, constant head winds ;
so that on the close of the fifth day we were not fifty miles
from Malta. At last, however, we got a fair wind, and came
through the Straits of Messina and past the Lipari Islands and
made the coast of Naples the sixth morning, thus having seen
Etna, Stromboli, and Vesuvius, the three celebrated volcanoes
of the world, in one and the same day. On arriving I find to
my great disappointment that I have lost a great eruption of
Vesuvius which has taken place since I have been gone, and
this is almost as mortifying as my other disappointment. I
have taken my passage to Genoa in the steamer which sails
day after to-morrow. I should have taken it as far as Marseilles,
but the cholera at that place and the consequent quarantine
at Naples prevent the boats from running thither. I shall
probably consequently go by land from Genoa to Marseilles,

and from thence to Paris. At Paris I shall wait until I hear
from you in reply to my last letter; you will think me to
blame, but I cannot feel that I have anything to reproach
myself with the miscalculating the expense of my journey, and
having been almost in sight of Athens without going there is
a disappointment which cannot be forgotten.

I remain your most affectionate son,

J. L. MOTLEY.

To his Mother.

Dublin,
July 27th, 1835.

MY DEAR MOTHER,—The last time I wrote I was, I think,
on the point of leaving London for a tour in England, Scotland, and Ireland. This is the first time we have been
stationary in any place for as much as twelve hours, and, consequently, the first time I have had any chance of writing.
As it is, I am afraid I shall send you but a short letter; we
stay here only till to-morrow (having arrived yesterday), and
during this time we wish of course to see as much of the town
as possible. We cannot of course help returning to Dublin
on our way back to England, and shall stop here another day
or two to see what we leave unseen now. The day I left
London I reached Salisbury, after a drive in a stage-coach of
five or six hours. Here, as I daresay you know, is one of the
finest cathedrals in England, and decidedly the finest specimen I have yet seen, not only of what is called in architectural
technology the Early English, but generally of English architecture. The evening I arrived I strolled out with my
pocket stuffed full of cigars to see the lions of Salisbury (or
rather the lion, for the cathedral is the only thing of interest).
This was the first specimen of English Gothic I was to see,
and as I walked thither my head was full of the Continental
Gothic, which was as yet all I knew. I thought of the Cathedrals of Cologne, of Vienna, of Rouen, of strange, unfinished,
unfinishable buildings, built according to no plan, or rather
according to a dozen different ones, and rising helter-skelter

from the midst of a multitude of old, sharp-gabled, red-tiled, ten-storey houses, all looking as if built in the time of the Crusades. The idea of a Gothic cathedral was associated, in my mind with hundreds of tumble-down hovels, booths, and shops, mixed grotesquely here and there with a magnificent palace of half a dozen centuries, and with groups of amiable ragamuffins and lazzaroni, which on the Continent form such a constant and indispensable ingredient of every picture. Although I knew I was in England, I could not help thinking of the filth and misery, squalor and magnificence, neglect and decay which usually makes up in equal portions every scene of the Continent, so that on the whole, when I came to look on Salisbury Cathedral, I was most ridiculously half disappointed.

It was my own fault or my own stupidity. The church is of beautiful proportions, of the most beautiful (at any rate the most regular) of the Gothic styles (namely, the Early English), is built of a fair coloured stone, which looks as fresh as if of yesterday, and with its light and graceful and very high spire, its long lancet-headed windows, its massive walls and stately buttresses, is certainly one of the finest cathedrals I know. Influenced by the associations I have mentioned, I thought the whole scene at first too tidy, too notable, too housewifish, but, as I said before, this was only my own dulness; on second thoughts I acknowledged to myself that filth and poverty and ugliness were not necessary concomitants of a cathedral, and I confessed that I had rarely seen a more lovely picture than this same church presents. The scene is so softly and sweetly English. The stately and graceful cathedral with its green and smooth-shaven lawn in front, the surrounding elm trees in their magnificently massive foliage, the tidy cottages half covered with honeysuckles and rose-bushes, the hawthorn hedges, and the green meadows with their sleek cattle (to say nothing of the macadamised turnpike and the new hotel), altogether made up a scene purely and exclusively English, and perhaps, after all, as pleasing a one as you can find any-where. From Salisbury I made a short *détour* to see the celebrated Stonehenge, of which I daresay Preble will give

you a more vivid description out of Worcester's Geography
than I can do, although I have seen it so lately. In fact, a
very barbarous monument (in the matter of the fine arts at
least) has no particular interest when one has seen the much
older monuments of much older nations, which preceding
ages have only been able to gape at and admire without
even being able to imitate, much less to equal. Stonehenge
is merely a rude and rather awkward grouping together of
about a score of huge and shapeless stones. It may have
been a Druid's temple or Queen Boadicea's drawing-room for
aught that I (or I believe any one else) know to the contrary,
and I can't find enough interest in the grotesque monuments
of a parcel of barbarians to detain me from the continuation
of my tour. I shall turn it over to the antiquaries.

                                    Your affectionate son,
                                              J. L. M.

CHAPTER IV.

RUSSIA.

[In 1837 Mr. Motley was married. In 1839 appeared his
first novel, 'Morton's Hope.' In the autumn of 1841 he was
appointed Secretary of Legation to the Russian Mission.]

To his Wife.

Halifax,
Friday morning, October 8th, 1841.

MY DEAREST MARY,—I write again this morning in order
that there may be a double chance of your hearing from me.
I wrote yesterday by the brig *Arcadian*, which sailed this
morning for Boston, and you will probably have got that
letter before this reaches you.   I told you in that that we had
experienced very rough weather and heavy gales from the
north-east which delayed our arrival here three days beyond

the usual time. I flatter myself that nobody can beat me in
long passages, go whither or how I will.   However, we have
every reason to be thankful that we arrived at last in safety,
and I make no complaint at the length of the passage.   Of the
accommodations of the boat I do make complaint, and I may
as well tell you now, if you come out in the spring, by all
means come in one of the best and largest New York packet
ships.   The average gain by taking a steamer is only a week,
and the loss in comfort—no, not comfort, for there is no such
thing at sea, but the loss in those appliances which make
existence endurable at sea—is immense.

Everything is dirty, disorderly and disgusting.   There is no
room in the state rooms to put so much as a tooth-pick, not a
drawer nor a shelf, but everything is left to knock about on the
floor at its own sweet will.   There is no cabin to sit in, the
narrow piggery in which we are fed being entirely filled up
with the troughs and benches.   There is no deck to walk on,
as the whole or nearly the whole of the space is occupied by
the upper cabin, the state rooms being below.   As for the
ladies' cabin, I have not been in it, but I am told that they are
much worse off than the gentlemen.   Recollect, my dearest
Mary, that I am not painting this disagreeable picture because
I have been myself so uncomfortable, but only to prevent you
from being exposed to the same evils.   It has been my
greatest consolation thus far, that you and my little darlings
were not on board the *Caledonia* with me.   I believe you
would have been driven to despair, and I am very sure that
if you had been with me, we should have all stopped in
Halifax and gone home as soon as possible.   Neither do I
know that a great many of the discomforts of these ships can
be avoided.   They are mail boats, intended for speed, and so
carry the greatest number of passengers in the least possible
space.   We are accordingly packed down like salt fish, com-
pressed into nothing, and are of course uncomfortable.   Now
this is worth bearing in going to America, where the saving
averages two or three weeks, but in going to England it is
most " tolerable and not to be endured."

The captain seems to be a thorough seaman, and always at

his post, and inspires us with perfect confidence. The boat has proved herself a staunch and admirable sea-boat. These are the great essentials before which everything else is as nothing ; but you can unite all in a first-rate packet ship from New York, and if ever I should go to Europe again—but no, upon that point my resolution is taken most decidedly. If I get home in safety I shall never leave it again. I knew I should be home-sick enough, but did not anticipate the reality ; I can hardly bear to think of you and all at home for an instant without being sick at heart, and as I cannot say a word upon the subject without becoming very foolish, I shall say nothing.

I shall say nothing now upon the point of your coming. I intend to keep an exact account of the expense and of every-thing else bearing upon the subject, so that in the course of the winter you will have the whole matter before you, all the pros and cons, and then I shall trust you to decide for your-self; you know I have often told you, my dearest, that you always decide right and that I always repent not taking your advice ; I tell you so still, that in order that you should decide upon this point you must have everything before you, and look fairly at both sides. Above all things, do not be governed by your feelings, but by your judgment.

If we are to be separated till my return, of course my return will be so much the sooner. If you join me, the pleasure of being together will be embittered by the length of the journey and the great fatigues which you and the little ones will have to endure, to say nothing of the expense, which will of course be great. However, it is premature to attempt to form an opinion now.

Good-bye. We sail from here at three o'clock this afternoon.

Ever your own

J. L. M.

To his Wife.

Manchester, of all places in the world,
October 20th, 1841.

MY DEAREST,—I have just opened this letter to add a word or two. I came round this way, having nothing to do in Liverpool, and because Tom was coming to this place. I dine here, and go up to London to-night. I saw the Mackintoshes in Liverpool, whom you will see very soon, as they go in the *Britannia.*

The Macleod case causes an inconceivable fuss and anxiety throughout Her Majesty's dominions. The first question asked at Halifax was about it, and in Liverpool we had hardly got into the hotel coffee-room, reeking from the *Caledonia,* when several stout elderly gentlemen rushed frantically across the room, leaving their beer untasted, to inquire concerning the Macleod case. In short, everybody in the house scented us and came upon a point at once. I thought that the ferocity on the subject was confined to the provinces — provincial patriotism is always ferocious, but the excitement was very great in London. God bless you.

To his Wife.

London,
October 21st, 1841.

MY DEAREST MARY,—I arrived here this morning by the railroad between five and six o'clock, having left Manchester at seven the evening before. The whole tour being in the dark, you will hardly expect a description of the journey. I left Tom at Manchester, who, after stopping there some days, intended to go to Scotland.

Contrary to my expectations I found Colonel Todd[1] still in London. He had a passage of twenty-five days, so that

---

[1] United States Minister to St. Petersburg.

after all I did better than he. Our steamer, however, was
beaten by several of the packets; that of the 1st October
from New York arrived before us; and the *Great Western*
(unquestionably, from all I hear, the best steamer between
England and America), which sailed some few days before us,
made her passage in thirteen days. Mr. Frank Gray goes out
in her the day after to-morrow. He is here at the same hotel
with me (Long's in Bond Street). He will see you probably
on his arrival; and if it gives you half as much pleasure to see
him as it would me to see any one who had lately seen you,
it will certainly be a satisfaction to you. I cannot tell you
how much I long for letters, and yet I must leave England
without any.

Augustus Thorndike is also at this house; his family are
in Paris. Mr. Stevenson leaves in the *Great Western;* Mr.
Everett has not arrived, so that ridiculously enough, at the
present critical period of our English relations, there is nobody
in London accredited to the Court, the Secretary of Legation
having left some time ago.

I am not yet decided upon my route. Colonel Todd had
made up his mind to go by the Hamburg and Lubeck line,
but is somewhat inclined to adopt my plan of going by way of
Stockholm. There is some difficulty in getting information
about several points. It is plain sailing enough as far as
Stockholm, but some question whether there be a steamer running at present between that place and Abo in Finland.
London is such an immense place that nobody knows anything about anything. I am going with Colonel Todd to-
morrow morning to see Baron Brunnow, the Russian Ambassador here, who will give more information probably than any
one else can do, and I shall be guided a good deal by what
he says.

It is unfortunate, my dear Mary, that I am obliged to write
thus a second time without having anything to say to you,
except . . . how heart-sick I am at being separated from you.
It is indeed " to drag at each remove a lengthening chain "
to be thus pushing onwards towards the Finns and Calmucks,
while my heart and my eyes are ever turning backwards over

the thousands of miles which separate me from all I love in
the world :—

> " But where my rude hut by the Danube lay,
> There are my young barbarians all at play,
> There is their Dacian mother."

Tell me all about the rude hut on the river when you write.
I suppose it is nearly finished by this time. Be sure and
attend to it in all its details, for I hope it will be our home
for many years, and I shall never be happy till I see it again.
Tell me all about little Lily and Lottie, and mother and
father and all of them. Tell mother I shall certainly write to
her from St. Petersburg. I am so hurried now, and shall be
till I get there, that I have hardly time to scrawl these
jejune and most unmeaning lines to you.

Ever yours,

J. L. M.

To his Wife.

Hamburg,
November 1st, 1841.

MY DEAREST MARY,—I have again a roosting-place for a
few hours, and hasten to employ it by writing to you. I
reached this place an hour or two ago in the steamer from
London. We sailed last Wednesday morning, and ought to
have made the passage by Friday noon, from fifty-five to sixty
hours being the average passage, instead of which we were
six days about it. We had a head wind and very heavy
weather the whole voyage, so that it seems that I have only
to form a resolution, however secretly, to go by sea to any
given place for the wind instantly to make a point of blowing
a gale exactly from that direction. I found here a couple of
notes from Colonel Todd, who has been expecting me at
Lübeck every day according to our agreement, but this most
unconscionable passage has kept me beyond the day of sailing
of the Lübeck packet, in which we were to have gone together,
and as it is the last boat which goes all the way to Petersburg
this season, he was obliged to go without me, and I have

to make the journey by land. This is nobody's fault but the steamer *John Bull's;* and on the whole I do not much regret it, as a November voyage up the Baltic is not a very desirable amusement, and, from my experience of steamboating lately, I daresay it would prove quite as tedious and fatiguing as the journey by land.

Let me see, I wrote you last, I think, by the *Great Western*, a day or two after my arrival in London. After that I left my letter and card at Lord Lyndhurst's, and also at Mr. Clarke's, his cousin, to whom Copley Greene, or rather Mrs. Greene, was kind enough to send me letters. Mr. Clarke called upon me immediately, and was particularly attentive to me. I dined with him once, and received another invitation from a friend of his during my short stay there. Lord Lyndhurst was in the country when I arrived, and came to town only the day upon which I left. He however wrote me a very polite note, hoping to see me when his family returned from the country the next week, and, upon my informing him that I was leaving that day, he sent me a letter of introduction to Lord Stuart de Rothesay, the British Ambassador at Petersburg, and hoped to see me when I returned to London.

Mr. Clarke is a very agreeable gentlemanlike person, and I feel much obliged to the Greenes for their introduction, for which I wish you would make a point of calling upon Mrs. Greene and expressing thanks. Tell Sumner that I left his letter and my card at Sir Charles Vaughan's door; the servant, however, told me he was leaving town the next day, so that I expected to hear nothing from him. However, he came round to my hotel within an hour, and sat some time in my room with me, expressed great regard for Sumner and great regret that his departure from town and mine for St. Petersburg, etc., etc. In fact, everybody is out of town as a matter of course; the end of October and the beginning of November is the hanging season in London and the commencement (I believe) of the hunting season in the country, so that of course everybody is supposed to be hanging themselves or hunting, and I was very lucky to find as much as I did in London. Sir Charles is a plain, unaffected, agreeable man, and I hope to have the pleasure of seeing him again in London some time or other.

I leave this to-morrow (at noon) I believe, for Berlin, and shall stop one day there and then push on for Königsberg. I expect to meet a fellow-passenger on board the *John Bull,* a young man [1] (son of Lord Minto) who is attached to the British Legation at Petersburg, and who left in the diligence for Berlin to-night. Being both upon the same expedition, we have agreed to rough it together in the diligence, and I hope we shall reach Petersburg by this day fortnight.

Colonel Hamilton of New York stopped at the same hotel with me in London. He came out in the *Kamschatka,* which arrived two or three days after us, having made a very long passage, delayed originally by the same severe gale which attacked us between Boston and Halifax. Schuyler did not come up to London, but stayed at Southampton with the frigate. I shall find them there undoubtedly, as they were to sail again on Tuesday for Cronstadt, the day before the one I left London for this place.

To his Wife.

St. Petersburg,
November 18th, 1841.

I wrote to you last from Hamburg; the next day I went in an abominable diligence to Berlin. Stayed there two days. Saw Mrs. Kirkland and George Cabot constantly, they were both perfectly well and perfectly tired of Berlin, but uncertain whether they should leave this winter or remain. Staying in the same house was young Welch, who has joined the university, I believe. I went with Cabot to the Fay's one evening (the Secretary of Legation); he and his wife are very agreeable people. Mr. Wheaton [2] I called upon, and he upon me, but I did not see him, both being out. The next night left

---

[1] Now Sir Henry Elliot.
[2] The distinguished writer on 'International Law,' then United States Minister to Prussia.

with my travelling companion, Mr. Elliot, for Königsberg, a long pull of fifty-eight hours in a diligence. We had the cabriolet or front part, where one is very comfortable. The roads are excellent in Prussia, but the country most uninteresting, our whole route in fact, from Berlin to Petersburg, traversing a portion of that immense plain which reaches from the Netherlands to the Ural Mountains. It is a good country to travel at night in, because there is nothing to see, and the roads having all the smoothness and directness of a railroad without its rapidity, you are able to sleep in the well-cushioned diligences very comfortably.

Prussia has no history—the reigning family is an ancient one; but the State is new, and an artificial patchwork, without natural coherence, mosaiced out of bought, stolen and plundered provinces, and only kept together by compression. A Prince of Hohenzollern-something-or-other-ingen bought the Mark of Brandenburg with the dignity of Elector of the Empire, and his successors, after having in the course of two or three centuries subjugated the barbarous Prussia Proper (already well hammered by the Teutonic Knights and the Polish kings), helped themselves to a slice of Poland, and stolen Silesia, had the pleasure at the beginning of the present century of seeing their ingeniously-contrived kingdom completely sponged out of existence by Napoleon, and then repaired and put together again by the Cabinet-making of Vienna. Since then, Prussia is a camp, and its whole population drilled to the bayonet. It is the fashion to praise its good administration; but I have no sympathy with your good administrations.

Prussia is a mild despotism to be sure. 'Tis the homœopathic tyranny—small doses, constantly administered, and strict diet and regimen. But what annoys you most is this constant dosing, this succession of infinitesimal Government pills which the patient subject bolts every instant. Everything, in fact, is regulated by the Government; the royal colours are black and white, and Government is written in black and white all over the kingdom. The turnpike-gates are black and white; the railings of the bridges are black and white, and so

are the signs of the taverns, post-houses, etc., etc. In every inn
a royal *ordonnance* stuck up against the wall informs you how
much you have to pay for everything—for your dinner, your
bed, your schnaps, or your glass of sugar-and-water. This is
well enough for the traveller; but a sort of arrangement
neither complimentary nor gratifying to the inhabitants. But
what nonsense it is for me to be wasting all this time in such
a tirade. I believe it is because I was annoyed at having to
go back (after having walked down to the Berlin Post-office to
take my place in the diligence) for the sake of having my
passport put in order; for unless the American Minister, the
Prussian Minister for Foreign Affairs, the police inspector, the
Russian Minister, and the Lord knows who beside, all signify
in writing their perfect approval of your taking a seat in the
Schnell Post, the said seat in the Schnell Post is refused to
you by the prigs of the Post-office.

At Königsberg we waited a day—

> " A town, whose greatest vaunt
> Besides some mines of zinc and lead and copper
> Has lately been the great Professor Kant;
> But we, who cared not a tobacco-stopper
> For metaphysics, still pursued our jaunt
> Through Germany, whose somewhat tardy millions
> Have princes who spur more than their postilions "—

like the respectable Don Juan, who went to Petersburg by the
same route that we did. We, however, killed one lion there,
and the only one worth killing—the old cathedral, a building
five hundred years old, as the sexton said: built by the
Grand Master of the Teutonic Knights, and containing
several tombs, monuments, and rude portraits of the old Grand
Masters by whom Königsberg and "Prussia Proper" (I like
that expression, because all Prussia is so extremely proper)
was governed in old times. One of the monuments, rudely
representing a knight in a reclining position and dying, with
some singular devices scattered about, attracted my attention,
and the old sexton insisted upon giving me a long legend
about it, which had a strong resemblance to the story of the
maid and the magpie. This story, in three words, was that

the knight lost a favourite ring from his finger—circumstances convinced him that his favourite servant had stolen it, and so he incontinently cut off his head ; afterwards, a raven's nest was found with the ring in it, and the dead servant's innocence being thus demonstrated, the knight had nothing for it but to die himself. So, upon Tristram Shandy's principle, "that man bears pain best in a horizontal position," he threw himself at length upon his elbow with his toes to heaven and so died. "So Johnny Pringle he laid down and died." A device of a raven with a ring in his mouth, and a servant with his head cut off, and other quaint devices, decorate the monument. The church itself is venerable from its age, but very plain. The windows are the narrow lancet-shaped ones, without tracery, which in England are called the Early English ; but there is very little of ornament in any part of the building— none of that elaborate carving, that needlework in stone, that sculptured Brussels lace, which is the charm and the wonder of the more splendid Gothic cathedrals.

The same night we went to Tilsit, twelve hours from Kö-nigsberg (if you take any post map of Europe or even any common map, you may easily trace our route), a place where Napoleon dictated peace upon a raft in the river Memel to the Emperors of Russia and Austria and remarkable for no-thing else, where we stopped a day and night—these stoppages by the way were owing to our having neglected to inform ourselves at Berlin about the diligence hours of starting from the different places. If we had used due diligence in using the diligence we might have shortened the time four or five days. However as that would not have shortened the road, and as our fatigue was the less, it was of no great consequence.

From Tilsit, we went to Tauroggen on the Russian frontier, passing through the custom-house so much dreaded by travellers unscathed and untouched, thanks to our diplomatic capacity (which, by the way, has carried us through every custom-house with flying colours). At Tauroggen we stopped a day and night, the inn or post-house most comfortable, giving one an agreeable impression of Russian arrangements. The next morning at ten, we took our seats in the Russian

mail for Petersburg; these carriages are without exception
the best public conveyances in Europe; they carry four persons only, and the vehicle consists of two *coupés* or chariots,
one placed behind the other, and each containing two persons;
they were filled with spring cushions, leather padded pillows,
lamps to read by in the night, and in fact as comfortable as a
private carriage.

The road from Tauroggen to Petersburg is 1400 wersts, and
half of it is what is called in Europe very bad, and what
we should call pretty good in America. We got stuck in
the mud regularly every night, but as we were only passengers
we did not mind, and slept comfortably until they lifted us
out; this lasted only two or three nights. At Riga, the
capital of Livonia, we got our first snow storm, after which
the weather became very cold (13 of Reaumur one night
(the 12th of November), equal to about zero of Fahrenheit, but " it was fine times for those who were well wrapped
up, as the ice bear said when he met the gentleman a
skating," and I was uncommonly well wrapped up. I was
immersed to the hips in a pair of fur boots (furred on both
sides), without which an attempt to make such a journey
would have been a bootless undertaking, and had a pelisse
lined with fur reaching from my eyelashes to my heels: thus
attired I was independent of the weather. It was, however,
not very cold long. The weather in fact, since the 12th of
November, has been like our average weather in January
and February. How it will be later you shall know as soon
as I do.

I have nothing more to say of the journey. The country is
dull and uninteresting beyond all description, and as we had
sixteen hours of dark to eight of daylight, " the whole of its
tediousness was not inflicted on us." I had provided myself
at Berlin with some new novels of Balzac and Paul de Kock,
and passed most of the time in reading, slept very well every
night, and breakfasted, dined and supped very comfortably at
the stations or post-houses along the road, which are in general
very well regulated establishments. The villages through
which we pass are all of wood, generally log huts thatched;

the houses in the towns are mostly of wood, painted of a dark colour and sometimes stuccoed, and the people dirty, long-haired, long-bearded, sheepskin-shirted savages. We reached St. Petersburg, the 17th of November, at half-past two in the morning.

This letter I consider both entertaining and instructive, unfortunately it is illegible. It will puzzle the spies at the post office, if they undertake to read it.

J. L. M.

To his Wife.

St. Petersburg,
November 19th, 1841.

I am about moving to-morrow, from the hotel where I am just now, to apartments in the house which Colonel Todd has taken. Lodgings are very high in St. Petersburg, and I am assured by Mr. Gibson, the Consul here, that these are very cheap compared with other lodgings, and that though more elegant than I should care for, they cost actually less than many much more ordinary ones elsewhere. They are well situated in the Admiralty quarter, large and handsomely furnished, and when you come, if you conclude it best that you should, there are additional rooms sufficient to accommodate us comfortably, for a very small additional rent.

You ask about Colonel Todd. I cannot say anything farther at present, but that he seems to me a very amiable, kind-hearted man, and disposed to make things agreeable to me. We shall probably make a common table together this winter. He is undecided yet whether his family will join him or not. Colonel Todd has not yet had his audience of the Emperor, who is in the country. He is expected, I believe, to-morrow. I daresay I may be presented next week, but know nothing yet. As soon as I am settled in my quarters, I shall make my calls of ceremony which the etiquette prescribes.

I hope before long I may be able to send you something amusing in my letters. Thus far I have hardly looked about

me at all. The weather has been cold, though not disagreeable, since the 12th November; good sleighing since
that time, with the thermometer in the daytime a degree or
two below the freezing point. The Neva has been some time
filled with ice and the bridges taken up, although the ice still
floats slowly, so that there is no crossing at all at present, and
everybody is waiting for the ice to fix, which is expected
every day. Tell me about the weather you have, when you
write. I should like to compare it with this, and besides it
gives an additional touch to the picture of home. I was
delighted with your description of Riverdale at that delicious
season (the middle of October). There is nothing in the
whole world besides like an American autumn. How absurd
it is in you to call your letters dull. You know they are not.
I only hope you will write me thousands just such dull letters
as your last. They had the effect of enchantment upon me,
and while I was reading I heard the voice of my darling little
Lotty, and saw my little Lily's bright eyes, and for a moment
was transported quite across the dreary waste of land and sea
which separate us, and was at home again. You are very
right in agreeing with me that I have the worst of the separation. New scenes and new faces, what are they to home
scenes and home faces? Besides, new scenes and new faces
are to me no novelties. I do not know how much to ascribe
to the lonely feelings I experience, how much to my having
already travelled a good deal, and how much to the character
of the place I am in, but I actually feel at present a perfect
want of curiosity, and the lions of St. Petersburg are likely
to remain a long time unkilled in their cages for all me. I
shall, however, make a business of it soon, and I hope to be
able to entertain you a little, if not myself, with the process.

　God bless you!

Your own
J. L. M.

To his Mother.

St. Petersburg,
November 28th, 1841.

I have not yet been presented. I am writing this in my
chancery or office, from which Colonel T. has this moment
gone in full rig to have his first audience of the Emperor.
On account of the Colonel's not having had his audience,
I have been unable to make any calls on the *corps dramatique*, I mean *diplomatique* which is much the same thing.
He had sown his preliminary quantity of cards broadcast over
the town and had reaped his return crop before my arrival.
Etiquette prescribes to a Minister to renew his calls after
his presentation, and accordingly to-morrow I shall accompany
him in his coach-and-four to honour the whole of them with
my pasteboard. After that I have a right to expect return
calls and occasional invitations ; if I get none, it will be no
fault of mine, for, like the General in 'Tom Thumb,' " I shall
have done my duty and have done no more." I have as yet
made no calls, except that day before yesterday I left my
letter from Lord Lyndhurst and my card upon Lord Stuart de
Rothesay—he was out, but called upon me the next day and
sat half an hour with me—a veteran diplomatist, having been
Minister here in the year one—that is to say 1801. He says
that Petersburg has degenerated since that time. That generation, the grandparents of those he is now associated with, spent
all the money, and left them only the great empty houses.

The weather has been most extraordinary. The river
closed a day or two after my arrival (about the 20th, I think)
and up to that time it had been a steady cold (not very cold)
weather, say 28° of Fahrenheit at noon. But for the last week
it has thawed every day, not a warm, sunshiny thaw, such as we
have in January, "not by no means," but a cold drizzling,
something between a fog and a rain, with the glass a degree
above the freezing point, under the influence of which the
snow and ice which covered the ground have nearly disappeared, and the droskies, the most awkward and inconvenient
of all jarvies, have succeeded to the sledges, which were

cutting about when I arrived. The worst of it is that if we get no snow soon, I don't know what I shall do for a vehicle. To keep something is as necessary here, where it is as far across a street as it is from one end of some towns to the other, as to keep a pair of india-rubbers in Boston. It is not decent for a Secretary of Legation to go about in hackney vehicles, which are all very dirty, but luckily it is perfectly correct to go about in a one-horse sleigh, which you can take by the month and which does not cost much more than half a coach-and-two, which would be the only alternative. But without snow there is no sleighing; fortunately it is snowing now, and perhaps we may have a change of weather.

This brings me to speak of the expense of this place. Tell Mary that if my opinions and experience do not soon change very much, the expense alone will make me beat a retreat immediately. Everything is dearer here than in Boston, which you know is a high standard, but besides that, very great expenses are incurred for things which I should dispense with there. I should be afraid to tell you how much I have been obliged to spend for furs, and that not to please myself, for I hate the very sight of them, but because they are indispensable in themselves, and although I tried to keep as near the bottom of the ladder of prices (up which you may go for a single wrapper to $10 or $12,000) as was consistent with decency, yet the price was tremendous and would have clothed me for a year in Boston and three in Dedham. . . .

I remain,

Your most affectionate son,

J. L. M.

I forgot to say that owing to the death of the Queen Dowager of Bavaria the Court are in mourning for twenty-four days, so that I shall not be presented until the 18th of December. Colonel Hamilton of New York (son of the great Hamilton and whilom Secretary of State under Jackson) and Schuyler, his son-in-law, who both came in the *Kamschatka* are to be presented on the same day. They are my only American acquaintances except the Consul, Mr. Gibson.

To his Wife.

St. Petersburg,
December 14th, 1841.

MY DEAREST MARY,— . . . I pass my time almost entirely
alone. There lie upon my table, to be sure, cards by the
dozen of princes and potentates, diplomatists, cup-bearers and
functionaries of all possible names, some of which, being
printed in French, I can read but can't pronounce, and some,
being in Russian, I can neither read nor pronounce, but not
one of the owners of which do I even know by sight. With
the exception of a slight acquaintance with the members of
the English Embassy and with the Dutch *Chargé d'Affaires*,
I do not know a soul. I know that it is in part my fault, and
that many men in my situation would have rushed round the
town, established intimacies with people whose names I have
not yet learned, and been quite at home by this time. But
this is what I can't, and never could do. I cannot take root
so easily anywhere, and in such an inhospitable and ice-bound
soil as this it requires more than I am capable of.

I am going to a party at the Grand Master of Ceremonies
(Count some long name or other) to-morrow, and I believe
I am to be presented at Court on Saturday next. As it is the
"name's day" of the Emperor, he will probably give a great
blow-out of some kind or another—ball or "swarry," or something to make us comfortable, I suppose, of which see further
particulars in my next. Whether there have been any parties
or not hitherto in the town I know not, there have been none
at Court; and, with the exception of the English Ambassador's
levee a few days ago, where we all went in our gold-laced
coats, made bows and walked off again, I have darkened
nobody's doors but my own since I moved into my quarters
in the same house with Colonel Todd.

In the absence, then, of anything agreeable to tell you, I
propose giving you some statistical and topographical facts,
which may enable you to come to a decision after reading
this letter, as well as at any other time, concerning our future
plans. First, with regard to the climate, I cannot speak with

very great certainty from my own experience, because this, they tell me, has been the most extraordinary winter hitherto that has been known for forty years. When I arrived here first, a month ago (17th November), the ground was covered with snow and ice, the sleighing was excellent, the Neva was filled with floating masses of ice (which stopped about three days after the 20th, making the river passable), and the thermometer ranged every day a few degrees below the freezing point. The winter appeared to be settled at about the ordinary time of its setting in. About the end of the month, however, there came a thaw, not a warm sunshiny thaw such as we have in January, but a cold, drizzly, foggy thaw, which gradually broke up the ice, melted the snow, and *opened the river again,* a thing which does not occur twice in a century, before the end of April or beginning of May. This weather has continued without intermission up to this moment, that is to say, the glass varies from two or three degrees below the freezing point, with a sky constantly overcast, and occasional slight showers of rain and snow. This is unnatural, and therefore probably unhealthy. I am, however, very well myself, but it is a great consolation to me to think that the children are not here, shut up in these close, stove-heated, double-windowed, unventilated rooms. As to going out, it would have been out of the question, with the exception of two or three days; and it is a positive fact that since I have been here there has not been one clear, bright, sunshiny day; and as to their length, you may judge of it by the fact that I shave by candlelight very often at half-past nine, and just now, when I sat down close by the window to write this letter, I was obliged to order candles, although it wanted a quarter to three.

I know that it is not fair for me to judge conclusively of the climate—neither do I. I am only giving you facts. But it is certain that the only chance of a change is that of extreme cold weather, which everybody is looking forward to with great anxiety—the more so as at this season of the year all the supplies consist of frozen meat brought hundreds of miles from the interior to this market, which of course at

present is impossible. I cannot quit the subject of the climate
without quoting to you a passage or two from the erratic John
Randolph's first and only despatch from St. Petersburg during
his five weeks' residence here :—

"I shall avail myself of the indulgence which the President
has been pleased to accord me, and leave this worse than
Stygian atmosphere in time to escape the rigours of its arctic
winter. This country may well be likened to a comet; we
are now in the perihelion—I shall not wait the aphelion.
Never have I seen so many severe cases of summer disease.
St. Petersburg, built upon a morass, resembles Holland in
everything but cleanliness and wealth. An inundation of the
Neva, the only outlet of the vast Lake Ladoga and its tribu-
tary swamps, lays the city under water. The mark of the last
inundation is four feet above the surface of the streets, which
are all on a dead level. The water for drinking is detestable,
worse even than that of Norfolk or New York, and never fails
to engender the most fatal diseases. Dysentery in its worst
form, bilious fever of the most malignant type, are now raging.
The *Concord*" (the ship which brought him) "is a perfect hospital. I have written thus far interrupted every quarter of
a minute by innumerable flies, gigantic as the empire they
inhabit, which attack the face in all its vulnerable points—
nose, mouth, ears, and eyes under the cover of the spectacles.
This is the land of Pharaoh and its plagues. It is Egypt in
all but fertility. The extremes of human misery and human
splendour here meet. Although I succeed an Anglo-Russian
(in his house) who considers himself very neat, yet an exact
description of the house prepared to receive me, the public
rooms excepted, would not be very pleasing to him or the
reader," etc., etc.

Is it not a hearty ebullition of spleen?

I like the office part of it very well. In fact, the only part
of the whole business that I do like is the office business—that
is to say, I should like it, but there is none of it. The relations between the United States and Russia are at present so
completely settled, that there is nothing at all to do. But, as
a stepping-stone, it is nothing. The fact is, the profession of

diplomacy, which I should prefer to any other (and which I conceive myself better fitted for than any other), does not exist with us.   There is no promotion, and if there were it would not be desirable ; for I assure you that if I were offered the post of Envoy Extraordinary to St. Petersburg at this moment, I would not take it unless I could spend at least from $15,000 to $20,000 per annum.   To me it would be a constant mortification and annoyance to fill such a post, unless with proper respectability and dignity.

Your own
J. L. M.

To his Wife.

St. Petersburg,
December 25th, 1841.

This is Christmas Day, my dearest Mary, according to our style of reckoning, which is twelve days ahead of the Russian calendar, and I hope to-morrow will prove a merrier Christmas to you than to me.   I feel that I have no right to communicate any portion of the depression under which I am constantly labouring to you, and so I will say no more about it.

Since I last wrote, I have been a little into society, and could go a great deal more if I chose.   I go to two or three balls a week, and might go to one every night if I chose to make the least effort to do so, but to say the truth I am totally unfit for society.   Staying at home here by myself is bad enough, but it depresses me still more to go into society and see other people dancing about and enjoying themselves. " They have dancing shoes with nimble souls, I have a soul of lead," and if it were not for the fear of being snubbed too much by you, when I see you, for neglecting what you will call my advantages, I would go nowhere.   As it is, I go quite enough to see the general structure of society, which is very showy and gay, but entirely hollow and anything but intellectual.

Now as you will wish to hear about the ceremony of presentation at this paradise of ceremonies, the Russian Court, I may as well describe it to you at once.

The " Winter Palace " is one of the largest domestic buildings in Europe, being about 750 feet upon the Neva by 550
feet towards the Admiralty, but as I intend to go one of these
days and kill all the lions like a man, and as this, with its
adjoining Hermitage and its Spanish pictures, is one of the
principal, I shall reserve a description of the palace, of which I
have only seen a few rooms, and content myself with describing
my own exploits.

We drove round to the Neva side of the palace, where we
alighted, walked in through a moderately sized door, up a few
marble steps into a long vaulted corridor, with a tessellated
marble floor.   Coming to the end of this gallery, we ascended
a broad and splendid staircase upon the top of which were
several pages-in-waiting, dressed in a fantastic uniform combining the Highlander's bonnet with the chequered clothes
of Harlequin.   One of these skipped out and led us through
several fine large rooms to the " Hall of the Throne," where the
diplomatic body were assembled.   There we were left with our
companion in arms to await the arrival of the Emperor and
Empress.   The room is spacious, with crimson hangings, the
walls are starred all over with little double-headed eagles in
gold, and a richly decorated throne occupies a large recess
upon the side opposite the windows.   Here we talked and
walked about mingling in a mob of gold lace dignitaries,
amongst whom the ubiquitous Nesselrode was bobbing about
as usual, until a flood of courtiers, pouring into the hall from
an inner one, and passing out followed by a stately procession
of dames of honour and ladies of the Court, with golden tiaras
and sweeping robes of velvet and brocade, indicated that their
Majesties were approaching, having despatched the victims
which had been offered up to them in the hall immediately
preceding.   We were now drawn up in " solemn column " by
Count Bosch, the master of the ceremonies, and formed a very
respectable semi-circle, beginning with the " dowager of St.
Petersburg " (as he calls himself), Lord Stuart de Rothesay, at
one end, and tapering off with those who had not yet been
presented.   By this arrangement I was of course very near
the foot of the class, and stood between a Danish *attaché* and

Sir Robert Porter, British *Chargé d'Affaires* at Venezuela. Presently a file of ladies marched in and stationed themselves along by the windows of the hall opposite the diplomatic circle. Among these were the Grand Duchess Helena, the Grand Duchess Olga, and various others whose faces I was too blind to distinguish, and who were too great to be aimed at with an eye-glass, and immediately afterwards came their Majesties male and female.

They attacked the Ministers first, beginning with the English Ambassador, and so on along the line of diplomats stationed according to their official rank and seniority of commission. His Majesty, on reaching our end, despatched each victim with a bow or a single question, passing to the next man as soon as each name was fairly announced. My introduction consisted in the announcement of my name and office, and an exchange of bows, for just as he was about to address me with probably the usual question of " How long have you been here ? " his eye caught sight of Sir Robert Porter, who had lived formerly a great many years in St. Petersburg, and whom the Czar welcomed with great cordiality—very flattering to me, wasn't it ? The Empress stopped a moment after I had kissed her hand in my turn, and the following amusing and instructive conversation took place, which, as you like details, I give you *verbatim.* " Did you arrive with the Minister ? " " Non, votre Majesté." " How did you come ? " " By the Berlin route." " Ah, did you stop some time in Berlin ? " and with this she tottered off to the next man. After she had reached the bottom of the class and heard us all say our lessons, she passed with the Emperor into the next hall, and the school broke up, or rather we had a recess. The old stagers were dismissed, but the youngsters who had not yet gone the rounds were requested to stop to be presented to the Grand Duke Héritier and his spouse.

We waited accordingly, and after a little while, Count Bosch again took charge of us, assisted by a quizzical old chamberlain as whipper-in, and marshalled us through other rooms (a description of which is of course out of the question, because we passed so rapidly through them, and because there are more than a hundred splendid apartments upon this floor) till we reached a long, high, vaulted hall in white and gold. The walls and pillars of this room are of white stucco (they ought to have been marble), the floor, like all the floors, of beautifully polished and inlaid woods of different colours arranged in graceful figures, the ceiling was massively gilt, and in the centre of one side looking out towards the great quadrangle of the Admiralty Square, with the column of Alexander in the centre, and the triumphal arch with its car and horses of victory. Beyond is a deep spacious oriel window. This is the size of a small boudoir, the three sides are formed of vast plates of glass, comfortable *fauteuils* are in each recess by the window, and in the centre is a fine statue of a ball player. We lounged about this hall for some time, dancing attendance upon their Imperial Highnesses, who were probably taking a comfortable lunch in the meantime, while every now and then a covey of maids of honour and that sort of people would flock into the hall, and stately *dames de la cour* would sail into the room and sail out again with their long trains sweeping after them. The morning court costume of the Russian ladies by the way is very beautiful, and was introduced, or rather restored, by the present Emperor. The diadem-like head-dress and short tunic, which constitute the historical costume of Russia, and which, made of ruder materials, you see constantly worn by the better sort of the lower orders, has a very picturesque effect when united to the long velvet trains, and is very becoming to pretty women.

Moreover the halls of the palace are so vast, that they have plenty of room to sweep about and display their finery, without danger of being jostled or incommoded. For these reasons a *fête* at the Czar's Court is a very picturesque show. As Sir Philip Sidney's life was " poetry put into action," so a Court circle at St. Petersburg is a *ballet* in real life. All this pomp and procession, the gorgeous *locale*, the glittering costumes, the fantastic ceremonies, the farcical solemnity of the whole, remind me constantly of some prodigiously fine ballet. The *tableaux* were constantly varying, the grouping was good, the colours were gaudy, yet harmonious, and excepting that the materials were brocade and bullion, instead of fustian and tinsel, and that the scene was a real instead of a mimic palace, you had every element of a successful spectacle.

At last we were ushered into a room (adjoining the one in which we had been waiting), which was crimson and gold, the drapery and furniture being crimson satin and the walls actually plated or sheathed in gold. This is but natural in a city where they gild the domes and spires of nearly all their churches and public buildings. Here we were again drawn up in a phalanx, " still as the breeze but dreadful as the storm," and presently the Grand Duchess Marie Alexandrine, wife of the hereditary Grand Duke, made her appearance, and commenced operations by flooring Gevers, the Dutch *Chargé*, who was at the head of the row. She is a sweet, pretty, blonde and bright-eyed creature, a daughter of Hesse Darmstadt, whom the young duke married for love, and she went through the present task very gracefully. Her conversation with me was pretty much the stereotyped form, consisting of two questions, *videlicet*, " Have you been long here ? " " Only for a week." " Is it the first time you have been in Russia ? " "The first time I have had that honour." With that a bow and a smile, for she has rosy lips which can smile, and she passed on to the next man, my friend Sir Robert. The Socratic method, by the way, is the one universally adopted by sovereigns. Their observations always come to you in a questionable shape, and I should think a little catechism might be composed for them with which they might make themselves familiar beforehand, and which would make the bore of presentation much less fatiguing and embarrassing to all parties. A few staple questions such as " How long have you been here ? " " Did you ever see a white bear ? " Such questions as these, varied a little according to circumstances, and framed to combine amusement with instruction, should form the *vade mecum* of sovereigns, and would, if diligently committed to memory in early youth, answer the double purpose of imparting pleasure, and eliciting information.

As the Grand Duchess retired, her page, immersed to the hips in military boots, tried very hard to tread upon her train or to lift it up, I could not exactly make out which, but I could not sufficiently admire the incongruity of his boots with his office, and comment upon the necessity of our shivering in our silk stockings and small clothes to the ball the next night, while the Grand Duchess has a squire in jack boots to carry her petticoats.

After we were bowed out of this room, we marched back through the hall with the oriel into a suite of two or three rooms filled with pictures, where we were to wait the Hereditary's leisure. I amused myself so well with the pictures, among which were several fine Velasquez, a fine "Descent from the Cross" by Rubens, one or two Paul Potters, and a good many fine Spanish pictures, that I came near being left behind. I came up with the rest, however, before they left the room where we were served up to the Grand Duke, a fresh-looking young man, who, like his august father, swallowed half a dozen of us at a mouthful, myself included, only bowing as we were successively introduced, and asking questions of but one or two. However, as the ladies talked to me, I have no reason to complain. After this ceremony we marched off and went home.

The Czar is deserving of all the praise I have heard of him. He is one of the handsomest men I ever saw, six feet three inches at least in height, and "every inch a king." His figure is robust, erect and stately, and his features are of great symmetry, and his forehead and eye are singularly fine.

> "The front of Jove himself,
> An eye like Mars to threaten and command."

In short he is a regular-built Jupiter; and so much for the Court circle, or what would be called in England the Drawing-room. Now for the ball, of which, however, I am afraid I shall not be able to say anything new or anything very interesting. The small clothes being "de rigueur," I was obliged to exhibit my unlucky legs

> "In brilliant breeches spotless as new milk,"

without, unfortunately, being able to add

> "On limbs whose symmetry set off the silk."

However, as there was no help for it, I endued myself with
fortitude and the dreaded breeches at half-past eight, and we
drove off early in order to see the grand "star and waltz
entrée" of the Royal family into the ball room. We arrived
"au perron indiqué," as the etiquette book directs, alighted,
gave our fur and boots to our faithful Jäger, and then marched
along across the tessellated marble of the corridor, up the
same grand staircase, upon the top of which a cluster of the
same pages were lounging as upon the day before, and, after
being led by one of them through a few "halls of dazzling
light," we were at last met by the quizzical old Chamberlain
who had been our yesterday's Palinurus, and who now piloted
us safely into the "Salle Blanche." The Imperial family had
not entered, so we had leisure to look about a little.

This ball room, as its name indicates, is white, richly and
massively decorated with gold. It is of vast dimensions,
spacious enough for a whole nation to dance in without jolting,
and absolutely overflowing with light. The great charm of
scene was the extraordinary brilliancy of the hall. White and
gold light up well of course, particularly when a few millions
of candles are stuck into the myriad sockets of the many
massive, glittering chandeliers. There were three rows of
these immense chandeliers hanging from the ceiling, thousands
of candles placed along and in front of the massive, gilded
gallery which runs completely round the hall. This gallery
was completely filled with spectators, all female, well dressed
and some of them pretty, realising in part the suggestion of
the imitation of Tom Moore in 'Rejected Addresses'—

> " If, instead of those lamps, that a row of young beauties
> Shed light from their eyes between us and the pit "—

except that in this case the young beauties and the candles
were combined.

The floor of the hall was thronged with dignitaries glittering
like goldfinches and chattering like magpies, and the great
variety of costumes, the civilians with their stars and garters
and gold sticks, and military officers in every variety of
uniform, with the ladies in the latest Parisian toilettes,

furnished a constantly shifting succession of rich and striking
pictures. The most picturesque figures were the officers from
the various Asiatic provinces of Russia and from the regions of
"frosty Caucasus." The Circassians with their keen eyes,
black beards and white caftans, showed their purer descent
from the original stock of the European race, and were well
contrasted with the Cossack officers, some of whom looked as if
they might have served in Attila's army. While I was
lounging about and talking to a few acquaintances, a strain of
solemn music announced the arrival of the Imperial family,
and immediately the Emperor and Empress marched in hand-in-
hand, like Adam and Eve, followed by their whole family. The
Empress was looking better in her ball dress than in her
ceremony robe, and the Emperor was as fine as possible in a
red coat and green ribands and jack boots. Next there came
the Grand Duke Michael, the brother of the Emperor, with his
wife, a pretty woman blazing in diamonds and emeralds, and
then the Grand Duchess Olga, the daughter of the Emperor,
who is a blonde, a stately and magnificent beauty with the
Czar's forehead and eye—

> "Who stepped as doth a Spanish barb
> Or Andalusian girl from mass returning."

And then came the Héritier and his pretty wife, and then all
the other little Grand Dukes and Duchesses, down to a little
Grand Duckling of seven or eight years, looking like Puss in
Boots in a cavalry uniform, and who is the youngest but two
of the Emperor's children. They marched round the hall in
a solemn polonaise, followed by about a third of the company,
while the rest looked on for an hour or two to the tune of
slow music; and after this had continued quite long enough,
quadrilles were formed of the *haute volée*. At first and afterwards there was "still vaulting by the whole company," till
we went into supper. This was served in the great banqueting-
room (which is about 200 feet by 120), where the four or five
hundred guests sat down without the least crowding.

The effect was very fine, and the banquet, with the brilliant
lights, the sumptuous furniture, the dresses of the guests, the

elaborate liveries of the countless servants and the pillared and vaulted architecture of the hall, resembled a colossal picture of Paul Veronese. The supper was of many courses and very good. After it was over we all rose and marched back through a long suite of rooms to the Salle Blanche, where dancing was resumed for a little while; but at twelve the Imperials retired and dismissed us. I was very glad that it broke early, for I was constantly thinking "that it was a most excellent piece of work, would it were over;" and I daresay you are willing to say the same thing of this interminably long letter. I know you are fond of details, but I think I have given you enough of them for the present.

I am going to write to mother by this opportunity. Tell Stackpole that I am much obliged to him for his letter, and that I shall write to him by the next courier. Tell him it will be a real charity in him to write often. You have no idea of the absolute and dreary solitude in which I live; and as to hearing anything about what goes on in America, it is entirely out of the question here; and if he had known this, I am sure he would have given me a little more information about what is going on in public matters. Not that I take a very great interest therein; but still, as he wrote after the Massachusetts election, I should like to have known whether the loco-focos[1] carried the State or not, as they seem to have done every other. We know nothing about it here, and shall not perhaps these three months. The only channel of information is private letters, as our newspapers come very irregularly and are always as old as the hills.

Ever your
J. L. M.

---

[1] The Democrats were so called from an incident in 1834, when a meeting, at which the lights had been suddenly put out, was re-illuminated by loco-foco matches.

To his Mother.

St. Petersburg,
December 26th, 1841.

My dearest Mother,—I have just finished a long letter
to Mary, and am going to spend part of this day and solitary
evening in writing to you. It seems hardly right that I
should communicate a part of my dulness to you and to her,
and I feel that I necessarily must, or not write at all; but
still I will do what I can to amuse you, although I am quite
sure that my letters must be as stupid as the place they are
written from. The fact is, I find that I have undertaken a
task almost beyond my strength—that of coming away and
leaving all my home behind me. Still I do not regret
having come, because nothing but my own experience would
have satisfied me upon the subject, and now, being fully
satisfied upon every point, I have nothing to do but to look
forward to a not very distant meeting. I have also one
constant consolation—that I did not bring Mary with me and
my little darlings,

> " Whose breath was given
>   By milder genii o'er the deep."

For say what you will of the American climate, there is none
which has more sunshine or is more cheerful; while here in
this morass, although that well-known person, the oldest inhabitant, has repeatedly declared that he never knew so mild
a winter as this has been thus far in St. Petersburg in the
whole course of his life, the sun has not shone but three days
out of the thirty-nine I have been here. The weather has
not been extremely cold to be sure, the average temperature
having been very much the same as that of Boston for the
same months last year; but the shortness of the daylight
(between five and six hours) and the constant gloom of the
atmosphere make it excessively disagreeable.

I have given Mary a long and tedious description of the
ceremony of presentation to the Emperor. To-day I have
been to see the Grand Duke Michael, the brother of the
Emperor, having received a note from the Grand Master of

the Ceremonies yesterday stating that 2 o'clock to-day was the hour appointed. I found waiting in the ante-chamber the same people who were presented at the diplomatic circle the other day, among whom was my travelling-companion Elliot and some other acquaintances. We were received only on the lower floor, in very ordinary rooms, so that I did not have a chance of seeing his palace, which is said to be very fine, and which the Emperor built and presented to him upon his marriage some years ago. However, next Sunday I shall probably receive a summons to be presented to his wife, the Grand Duchess Helena, for such is the ceremonious style of doing things at this Imperial Court, always reminding me of Dogberry's observation, " Were I as tedious as a King, I could find it in my heart to bestow it all upon your Worship." And such is the number of the people to whom one has to be trotted out, that it will probably be a month or two before I have got through my presentations. Next Sunday, then, I shall probably see the show-rooms of the Michaeloffsky palace, and I suppose they give balls occasionally during the winter.

This week the first of the *bals de la noblesse*, a series of assemblies, commence, to which I have received a ticket through Prince Basil Dolgorouki, a gentleman whom I don't know by sight, but whom I shall investigate next Tuesday; and there is another on Thursday at the Countess Woronzow's, the wife of the Grand Master of Ceremonies, who, as his title indicates, is a grand and rich seigneur. She is a pretty, graceful woman, very much admired at St. Petersburg, and has a very splendid house, where she gives balls once a fortnight. I was there at the last one. The party was given in the " small rooms " of the house, consisting of a suite of six, averaging about thirty feet each in size, of great height, with the ceilings all painted in fresco and encrusted in gold. The principal rooms on the lower floor were not opened.

The prettiest house I have yet visited is that of Count Levachoff, whither we went to a ball a few nights ago, and of which I will now send you the last of my upholsterer's descrip-

tions. We entered through a small vestibule with the usual
arrangement of treble doors, padded with leather to exclude
the cold, and guarded by the "proud young porters" in severe
cocked hats and formidable *bâtons*, into a broad hall, threw
off our furred boots and cloaks, ascended a carpeted marble
staircase, in every angle of which stood a statuesque footman
in gaudy coat and unblemished unmentionables, and reached
a broad landing upon the top, thronged as usual with servants.
Thence we passed through an ante-chamber into a long, high,
brilliantly lighted, saffron-papered room, in which a dozen
card-tables were arranged, and thence into the receiving-room.
This was a large room with a splendidly inlaid and polished
floor, the walls covered with crimson satin, the cornices heavily
encrusted with gold, and the ceiling beautifully painted in arabesque. The massive fauteuils and sofas, as also the drapery,
were of crimson satin with profusion of gilding. The ubiquitous portrait of the Emperor was the only picture, and was
the same you see everywhere. This crimson room had two
doors upon the side facing the windows. The innermost
opened into a large supper-room, in which a table was spread
covered with the usual refreshments of European parties, tea,
ices, lemonade and etceteras, and the other opened into a ball-
room, which is a sort of miniature of the Salle Blanche of
the Winter Palace, being white and gold, and very brilliantly
lighted with ormolu chandeliers filled with myriads of candles.
This room (at least forty feet long by perhaps twenty-five)
opened into a carpeted conservatory filled with orange trees
and japonica plants, covered with fruit and flowers, arranged
very gracefully into arbours, with luxurious seats under the
pendent boughs, and with here and there a pretty marble
statue gleaming through the green and glossy leaves. One
might have almost imagined oneself in "the cypress and
myrtle," instead of our actual whereabout upon the polar
banks of the Neva.

Wandering through these mimic groves, or reposing from
the fatigues of the dance, was many a fair and graceful form,
while the brilliantly lighted ball-room, filled with hundreds
of exquisitely dressed women (for the Russian ladies, if not

very pretty, are graceful and make admirable toilettes), formed
a dazzling contrast with the tempered light of the Winter
Garden. The conservatory opened into a library, and from
the library you reach the ante-chamber, thus completing the
giro of one of the prettiest houses in St. Petersburg. I waltzed
one waltz, and quadrilled one quadrille, but it was hard work;
and as the sole occupation of these parties is dancing or card-
playing, conversation apparently not being customary, they
are not to me very attractive. The lady of the house and her
daughters are nice people, and so are some of the guests.
But Russian society to a stranger is freezing and formal, and
it seems to me to a person of my reserved habits it would take
a great deal longer to become intimate here than to thaw the
Baltic.

One of my acquaintances here is Miss Porter, the authoress
of ' Thaddeus of Warsaw.' She is staying here this winter with
her brother, Sir Robert Ker Porter, who is British Minister at
Venezuela. She is a very agreeable, sensible person, and so is
he. He was aide-de-camp to Sir John Moore at the battle of
Corunna, and has been seventeen years in South America.
I like them both, for there is something frank and expansive
about them, which is refreshing after these frigid and rigid
Russians.

Last night I went to see Taglioni in a new ballet. The
subject seemed to be something about Montezuma and the
Spaniards; but the play-bills are in Russian, and pantomime
is panto-Hebrew to me, so that I don't know the name, and
could only guess at the subject. I have seen her a good many
times, and Mary will never forgive me when I say that she
is decidedly more graceful and a better dancer than Fanny
Ellsler. Nothing can equal her swimming, sweeping, whirl-
ing, floating motion; her dancing is a perfect abstraction or
emanation. Ellsler has more *espièglerie*, is prettier, dances
with more elasticity and power, and I dare say excels her in
pantomime—which I hate and don't understand—but she is
not so graceful as Taglioni. The charm of Taglioni's dancing is
its absolute freedom from effort. Her most difficult steps and
postures seem to produce themselves without any volition of

her own, and the most graceful, and in reality the most
elaborate movements, seem as artless as those of a "three-
years' child."

Ever your affectionate son,

J. L. M.

To his Wife.

St. Petersburg,
January 10th, 1842.

MY DEAREST MARY,—The English courier goes to-morrow,
and you will not be surprised nor disappointed, I hope, to hear
that I have already written to Fletcher Webster, announcing
my resignation.   I have had a talk with Colonel Todd, and he
has consented that I should leave whenever it suits my convenience.   As there is not an earthly thing to do at the Legation,
I have no hesitation in resigning a sinecure whenever I please,
and, as the Minister has made no objection, I shall leave this
some time in March.

I shall leave this in March for Berlin, go to Hamburg, and
from there to the Netherlands, where I wish to pass a few
weeks, and then, if you decide to remain at home, I shall
cross to England, and take passage about the end of May for
Boston.

Todd has been perfectly kind and considerate towards me
ever since we have been here, and I have stated this in my
letter to Webster explicitly, mentioning that we have never
had a word of difference on any subject, and that therefore my
reasons for leaving were unconnected with any disagreement
with him.

I dined a week ago at the British Ambassador's, and two days
ago at Sir James Wylie's, where there was a large and pleasant
company.   The Prussian Minister, the English, and several
other notables were present.   Count Nesselrode was to have
been there, but received orders to dine with the Emperor on
the same day.   I don't know whether I have ever described to
you the great bureaucrat of the great autocrat.   He is a small
man, with a hooked nose and spectacles, of affable and supple

manners, and apparently gifted with ubiquity, for I have seldom been where he was not. I have been honoured by several short interviews with him, and I regret that I did not take down his conversation in shorthand, that I might transmit it to you. The topics have usually been the state of the weather, the heat of the rooms, and a comparative view of the state of the thermometer this year and this time last year. Upon all these subjects of general and exciting interest he seemed full of general information, and delivered his opinions with decision, and at the same time with a frankness hardly to have been expected of a man so deeply versed in the wiles of diplomacy.

Sir James Wylie is a remarkable man. He has been in the Russian service fifty-two years, and is now "Inspecteur-Général du Service des Armées," with the rank of Major-General, having emigrated originally from Scotland as an apothecary's apprentice, I believe. He is a hearty old gentleman, upwards of seventy, and goes out bear-shooting in winter with the ardour of a youth. There has been nothing at Court since last I wrote. The day after to-morrow is the Russian New Year's Day, and we are bidden to what is called a *cercle* at the Palace, which is a showy, formal, and most insipid ceremony. There is to be a ball the same night at Count Woronzow's; but I believe there are to be no more at the Palace this winter, of which I am very glad. I have been driving round occasionally in my sledge to look at some of the churches, in the hopes of seeing something worth describing to you. Some of these, with their graceful cupolas and clusters of turbaned minarets of green and gold, have a pretty, fantastic effect on the outside, but internally they are mostly bare and barren. I have been young lady enough to keep a journal (for your amusement when I return); but on looking over it I find it to be so meagre and so impregnated with my own dulness that I fear to communicate a portion of it to you if I transcribe from it, and, after all, there is nothing worth transcribing.

There are no fine buildings here, although there are many large and showy ones, and the architectural effects of some

of the streets and squares are very imposing from their vastness and regularity.   The best thing in St. Petersburg is
the statue of Peter the Great.   This, in my opinion, is the
finest equestrian statue in Europe.   There is something uncommonly spirited and striking in the action of the horse
and the pose of its rider.   He waves his hands as if, Scan-
dinavian wizard as he was, he had just caused this vast
collection of palaces and temples, this mighty swarming city,
to rise like an exhalation from the frozen swamps of the Neva
with one wave of his hand.   Peter the Great was a great man
unquestionably.   He was addicted to drinking, murdering his
son, beating his Prime Minister, and a few other foibles, to be
sure, but still he was a wonderful man.   He alone raised
Russia out of the quagmire of barbarism, just as he raised
St. Petersburg out of the morass; but it seems to me that
just as this city may at any moment, by six hours too long
continuance of a south-west wind, be inundated and swamped
for ever, so may Russia at any moment, through a succession
of half-a-dozen bad Czars, be submerged in its original barbarism.   The present Emperor is unquestionably a man of
great energy; but how can one man uphold this mass, even
in the state of crepuscular civilisation to which they have
reached?   What is really admirable in the construction of
St. Petersburg are the quays and walls along the Neva and
the canals.   These are all of granite, of great extent and
most massive and admirable architecture, and, with the many
bridges of the same material, are really Cyclopean works, and
worth all the gilt gingerbread of all these stucco streets and
palaces.   These latter, compared to the marble halls of Venice,
Florence, and Rome, are most tawdry and insignificant, although
of great size, and ornamented, like Job Johnson's coat, with
the most lordly indifference as to taste and expense.

Your own

J. L. M.

To his Wife.

St. Petersburg,
February 6th, 1842.

MY DEAREST MARY,—I shall take this letter as far as Berlin myself. My previous letters will have prepared you for hearing that I am now upon the point of leaving St. Petersburg. A good opportunity has presented itself, which I should make a mistake not to seize.

I have been to half-a-dozen parties and a dinner or two since I wrote; but as I have already described the general appearance of St. Petersburg balls in my letters, I have really nothing to add about them. There was to have been a great ball at Princess B——'s two or three nights ago, given to the Empress; but just as we were dressing, we received notice, that in consequence of the death of a near relation of the Princess, the ball was put off for *nine days*, so that I shall not have the honour of assisting at it. I have likewise been going the rounds of the various public institutions and things— hospitals, for instance, which are admirably arranged in every respect as far as meets the eye, although I hear great complaints about the insufficiency of the attendance upon the patients. To give you an idea of the character of the climate, there are 50,000 beds in all the hospitals for a population of about 475,000, and yet there are not nearly enough, and it is with great difficulty that a sick person can obtain a place.

I have also visited the Academies of Sciences and Arts, the Mining School, the Engineer Corps; some of their factories of cotton, linen, playing cards, etc., etc.; the picture gallery of the Hermitage, which is very rich in Flemish paintings, containing the best collection of Wouvermanns and Teniers that I have ever seen; the great Foundling Hospital, which has in its capacious nurseries 18,000 children, which is, however, not much more than half the amount of those in the Moscow institution, which numbers 30,000. Understand, however, that these immense numbers are not all in the building itself. The St. Petersburg Hospital contains accommodation for 1000 infants and 1000 nurses, for each infant is provided with a nurse. This building is the receiving house, and it receives to the tune of 7000 infants per annum. We met two well-dressed women bringing in each a baby as coolly as a bundle, and depositing it without any mystery in the porter's lodge. The infants are kept six weeks or so in the building, and then sent with the nurses to the country, where they are brought up and apprenticed as they become old enough to different trades. A great many of them find their way to the Alexandroffsky Imperial factory, where they are supported, and receive trifling wages besides. From a third to a half of the whole number, however, die in infancy.

Monday, February 7th.—I have just returned from an unsuccessful expedition to Casimir Périer's, the French *Chargé d'Affaires.* I was invited to a *soirée musicale* there, to hear Chinti Damoreau sing; but the father of Vicomte Ferronays (attached to the Embassy) was just dead, and the *soirée* deferred. There was also to have been a ball at Madame B——'s, also given to the Empress, but that also has been deferred, owing to sickness or death of somebody. It really seems to me that I carry destruction and devastation wherever I go. So sure as I dress myself to go to a party, somebody or other makes a point of dying. This is the third case within three days.

Speaking of Casimir Périer, I daresay you have not taken the trouble to read in the newspapers the farcical quarrel between the Courts of France and Russia, which has furnished the main topic of conversation lately in this place. Count Pahlen, the Russian Ambassador at Paris, left his post unquestionably to avoid making the speech to the King on New Year's day—a duty which devolved upon him as senior ambassador. Louis Philippe retorts by ordering his *Chargé* (the Ambassador being already away on leave) to be taken ill upon the day of the Emperor's fête (or day distinguished both as the name's-day of the Czar and the epoch of my presentation), but at the same time to exhibit his convalescence immediately afterwards in the most public manner. Accordingly, Périer abstains from the Court circle on the plea of indisposition, and the next day appears in the Nevskoi Prospect, and the same evening at the theatre. The Czar, in a great huff, immediately despatches

a courier to Mr. Kisseleff, Russian *Chargé* at Paris, ordering
him to be immediately taken ill, in order not to go to Court on
New Year's Day.   Mr. Kisseleff accordingly excuses himself
and *his aunt* at the same time; makes his appearance at various
salons, announcing himself "*indisposé par ordre.*" This com-
pletes the first act of the farce.   The second act opens at St.
Petersburg, with the countermanding of the Court circle on
the Russian New Year's Day, which luckily for the successful
development of these operations is twelve days later than that
of the rest of Christendom, and with the appearance of the
French *Chargé* at the Court ball on the following evening.
The Court circle was (probably) postponed because the Emperor
would at that ceremony have been obliged to converse with
Périer, while at the ball he was able to cut him in the sublimest
manner.   The act closes with the appearance of the Russian at
a Court ball at Paris; the reconciliation is, superficially at
least, effected, and the curtain falls. The whole thing, however,
is chiefly interesting in so far as it illustrates the character of
Russian society.   Since the beginning of the affair, the whole
St. Petersburg nobility have discontinued all intercourse with
Périer.   Dinners, etc., were countermanded, because he happened to have been invited before the plot was discovered, and
their whole course displays the entire and abject dependence
of the whole fabric of society as well as of government upon
the will of the Czar.

Yours ever,
J. L. M.

To his Wife.

Berlin,
February 13th, 1842.

MY DEAREST MARY,—I am going to open the letter which I
wrote just before leaving St. Petersburg, in order to slip in this
note.   I have but half a moment's time in this apology for a
letter to tell you that I left St. Petersburg on the 8th, and
reached here last night at eleven o'clock. I travelled with
Colonel Townley, the English messenger. He has a comfortable carriage, and as we had most singularly fine weather, and

still more extraordinary fine roads, with hard, frozen rivers, we made the journey of 1200 miles in exactly six days and six nights, not having stopped at all on the road.

This is very good travelling, and although this is a pretty long journey, yet by far the worst part of my journey to Paris is over, and the consciousness of being 1200 miles nearer to you, dearest, makes me feel quite happy. I shall leave Berlin by the railroad by Leipzig to-morrow, I think, but possibly may be obliged to stop till the next day; thence I go to Weimar, where I shall probably stop a day; thence to Frankfort and Paris.

I have been fortunate in my travelling companions over the dreary and monotonous route I have just finished.

Townley is a frank, amiable, and agreeable fellow as ever was; and by the way, in your last letter, you asked me about Elliot, who was my companion on my first journey. He is a very nice fellow indeed, manly, unaffected and intelligent, and if it had not been for the immense distances at St. Petersburg and the shortness of the days, which altogether make all social intercourse such a labour, I should have found the three months hang less heavily. He was at my lodgings just before he went away, and quite without any request on my part, offered me letters of introduction to his family, which the next day he brought, namely, one to his brother, Lord Melgund; one to his sister, Lady John Russell; and another to a friend of his in Paris, *attaché* of the Embassy, Mr. Howard, brother of Lord Morpeth. These letters I shall deliver, if I can be in London long enough to make it an object.

To his Wife.

Paris,
February 17th, 1842.

I am very glad to find, my dearest Mary, from the tone of your letters which I had the happiness of receiving on my arrival here, that you will not be dissatisfied or disappointed at the step I have taken, or rather stride, from St. Petersburg to Paris. But as I have nothing very interesting to tell you of this place, where I only arrived day before yesterday, I may as well tell you how I got here. My last letter was from Berlin. I stayed there two days, and went by railroad to Halle. At Halle, where I arrived at 5 P.M., I found by some ingenious blundering upon my part that I was obliged to stop till the next afternoon. However, I did not object to wandering about once more in one of the most quizzical of old-fashioned towns of quizzical Germany.

I had never happened to pass through Halle before, although I have seen hundreds of just such towns; and it was amusing enough to poke about through those narrow, tortuous, entangled streets, which look as if laid out by an *ignis fatuus*, and look up at the tall, toppling, crazy old houses, crowned with gables like cocked hats, reeling against each other till their heads knock together, looking like rows of tipsy spectres, although this was an amusement which would have been soon exhausted. The Square of Halle, with its fountain guarded by two grim lions in the centre, a clumsy and most Gothic statue of a non-descript French Prince Roland made of painted stone stuck up on one side; its fine old church with its needle spires and weather-beaten towers, whose bells have rung out many an alarm in the days of Tilly and Wallenstein; the rickety old Rath-Haus, its narrow thread-like streets (arteries almost too slender even for the slow and torpid circulation of its population) emptying themselves at all corners into the great Square, is just such an old-fashioned Gothic picture as I like occasionally to look upon.

In the evening I ordered dinner, and was regaled with a sumptuous repast, which was so perfectly German that I will describe it to you exactly. It would be easy by borrowing a little from the imagination to concoct a much more absurd description; but I give it you literally and unembellished. First, soup, of course; then course first, beefsteak and fried potatoes; then course second, boiled pork and cabbage; then course third, slices of sausage swimming in a sad-coloured sauce, sprinkled with capers and thickened with flour to "make the mixture slab and good"; then course fourth, roast venison with a sauce of stewed gooseberries and a salad of water-cresses;

then a piece of cake with four apples, then bread and butter
and three kinds of pestilential and uneatable cheese, the whole
irrigated with a pint of Médoc and concluded with a tumbler
of wooden toothpicks.

In the morning, to kill the time, I engaged an ingenuous
youth as a *valet de place*, and began grubbing up the anti-
quities. I went first to the Moritz Burg, or Maurice's Castle.
This is a mixed fastness of which the guide related to me this
legend :—Prince Maurice (of some Saxon House or other, he
did not know which) laid a bet with his sister that he would
build a church, now existing, and called the Maurice Church,
in less time than she could build a castle. They set to work
accordingly, but the sister gave two hellers a day to the workmen and he but one, and so she finished her castle soonest.
Whereupon Prince Maurice was wroth and very naturally
murdered her. The ghost may be seen at any time by apply-
ing at the ruins of the castle. The Burg is a grey old ruin
with swallows' nests in the heavy mullioned windows and fruit
trees in the fosse. The remains of the chapel are picturesque,
and the view from the rampart over the boundless plains of
Saxony is rather striking. The vault under the castle, and
which extends under a greater part of the town, is occupied as
a storage place by a respectable manufacturer, who will be
happy to furnish you with any quantity of starch at reasonable
prices. In the interior of the Maurice Church, which, like all
the churches in Protestant Germany, has been stripped of its
monuments and escutcheons, there is nothing of interest except
a quaint painted old statue of the desperate Maurice. He
appears, if his portrait be correct, to have been a short duck-
legged man, with the grimmest of beards, and is represented
with a girdle of bells about his waist ; which he is said to have
always worn during his architectural operations, to apprise the
workmen of his coming that they might be diligent.

It was certainly good-natured of the cat to bell himself, and
he must have been an excellent person after all. He was
called "Schellen Moritz," or Maurice with the bells, in consequence of this part of his costume.

At 2 p.m. I left in the diligence and reached Weimar the

next morning at daybreak. In spite of the railroads, upon
which one gets an occasional lift, travelling in Germany by
the public conveyances is exceedingly slow and disagreeable.
The German world, like the ancient world, rests still upon the
back of the tortoise. You must travel day and night as a
matter of course, the diligences are carefully constructed to
prevent you seeing anything, and to pass night after night
pent up with six frowzy travellers who will have the windows
shut, is anything but exhilarating. Still "'tis not quite so bad
as going to sea," and that is the best that can be said about it.
I went by way of Weimar to see Madame de Goethe. She
was glad to see me, and the two days I passed in Weimar were
spent principally at her house. She is the same lively, agreeable and intelligent person that she was eight years ago; but
she has grown much older, her hair is entirely grey, and I fear
she is in a decline.[1] She thinks so herself, and is going
to Italy in the spring. Her sons are neither of them in
Weimar. I gave her my article on Goethe, which she read and
was pleased with; but I refused to tell her even the name of
my unfortunate novel, of which she had heard and about which
she was curious. I also passed an evening with my old acquaintance Mr. de Froriep, and another at Madame de M——'s, a
pretty little woman. Her husband is the Russian *Chargé* at
Weimar, and brother to the one who married William Lee's
sister, who is *Chargé* at the Hague. Mr. Froriep wished me to
go and see the Grand Duke; but I thought it not worth while
to go through the presentation as I was going away immediately. Weimar is not what it was in the old Duke's
time, a little Athens inhabited by all the most illustrious
literati of Germany. Of that splendid army of genius, the
coffins of Goethe and Schiller are all that remain.

I left Weimar with regret, and proceeded by way of Erfurt,
Gotha, Eisenach, Fulda, etc., to Frankfort-on-the-Main. The
road is pretty, and the weather was delightful, the last patches
of the winter's snow melting rapidly in the sunshine. In fact,
the weather has been as mild in Northern Europe as by your
letter it seems to have been with you, and while south of the

[1] She was living at Vienna in 1861 when Mr. Motley arrived there as Minister.

Alps I hear this winter has been unusually severe. I passed a day and night at Frankfort. Having nothing to do I tied myself to the heels of a *valet de place* and allowed myself to be dragged through the town. I looked at Goethe's house and at the Ariadne, a celebrated statue by Danneker. It is spirited certainly; but it is not so fine as I thought it was when I first saw it eight or nine years ago. I went to the square in the heart of the old town called the Römerberg, which is one of the most picturesque places in Germany. Gable ends are my weakness; but I spare you any further descriptions after what I have given you, although the Römerberg in Frankfort is far worthier being described than the market of Halle. It was across this square that the Emperor and his train walked after the coronation had taken place in the Cathedral, a few yards off, to the Rath Haus, where a great banquet was provided for the courtiers, while an ox roasted whole in the square, and the fountain in the centre spouted red and white wine for the populace. The old dining-hall contains portraits of all the Emperors of Germany, and it is singular that the picture of Francis II., who was the last Holy Roman Emperor of Germany, occupies the very last space that was left. In the old Cathedral is a clock placed there in the year 1470, which is a model of time-keeping to this day. I looked with something like awe at the grim face of this venerable chronometer, whose pendulum had thus been swaying for near four centuries, and whose pulses were beating their loud and healthful music over the escutcheoned tombs of the devout Barons who are recorded as having placed it in the cathedral, and who were ashes before the country of the respected individual who has been trampling upon their graves had been discovered. A part of the church dates from Charlemagne, the rest is five or six centuries later. It contains a few crumbling monuments of families long since extinct, and a picture by Albert Dürer.

The next morning I packed myself up in the *malle poste* which transported me first by railroad to Mayence, where I crossed the Rhine and proceeded by way of Forbach, Metz. Chalons-sur-Marne, etc., to Paris. On crossing the Rhine, I took leave of frost and snow. The weather here in Paris is spring weather, shower and sunshine, capricious, but most delightful after the death-like monotony of St. Petersburg weather, although the winter there has been milder than for forty years before.

I don't know exactly what my plans are yet, whether I shall stay here a few weeks and then go to England, or go there immediately. I begin to talk seriously of returning in a sailing ship. I am rather skittish, to say the truth, with regard to the steamers. There has one just put back after being at sea seventeen days. However, I shall not return certainly before April, and perhaps not till the middle of it, so I have time enough to consider.

To his Wife.

London,
April 15th, 1842.

A few days before I left Paris I went with General Cass to one of Guizot's *soirées.* I was introduced to him, and "huge Plinlimmon bowed his cloud-capped head," but said nothing, for just as he was going to observe that the weather was very cold for the season, somebody else was announced to whom he was obliged to repeat his bow, and upon whom he probably bestowed his atmospheric observation. Guizot has a fine monastic sort of face, and a short uncourtly figure. Unfortunately, though I went several times to the Chamber of Deputies, I did not hear him speak. However, on one occasion I heard several of the Ministers speak, besides several of the Opposition.

The only person, however, of those whom I heard who is really an orator, is Thiers. The others were merely lecturers (Laplague, Hermann, Duchatel, etc.), who take their speeches (apparently written out in full) into the Tribune, and drone away like preachers in a pulpit. But Thiers had very few notes, and spoke almost without recurring to them. The subject was a very uninteresting one to a stranger, being a debate upon the project of a new law for the assessment of

direct taxes, submitted by a member of the Opposition.
Thiers hopped up into the Tribune after a recess, rubbing his
hands and smirking about with the most delicious *aplomb*.
The House would not come to order for a great while, and he
looked down upon them with the most provoking *sang-froid*,
while the President was ringing his bell like a dustman, and
the *greffiers* (or whatever they are called) were bawling " En
place, Messieurs, en place ! " like so many diligence conductors.
At last, when order was restored, he leaned over the Tribune
and began to squeak, not to speak ; and yet, in spite of his
funny voice, every word that he said was distinctly audible,
and his style was so fluent, so limpid, and so logical, his
manners so assured and self-possessed, that, in spite of the
disadvantages of his voice, his figure, and his great round
spectacles, which give him the appearance of a small screech
owl, I thought him one of the most agreeable speakers I had
ever heard. The Chamber is evidently afraid of him without
respecting him, and his consummate brass, added to his ready
wit, makes every one of his speeches gall and wormwood to
his enemies.

I left Paris on the 10th April.

Travelling alone, and by the abominable public conveyances
of the Continent, is such a tedious business that I gave up the
regular tour through the Netherlands which I had at first
proposed, and contented myself with taking a flying look at
the three or four most interesting towns in Belgium. The
old history of Belgium is so picturesque, the towns where its
most striking and stirring tragedies were enacted—Brussels,
Antwerp, Ghent, Bruges—are so picturesque with the cobweb
tracery of their architecture, the colossal filigree of their town
halls, the transparent and fantastic lace work of their cathedrals, in which stone looks as if it had been spun by spiders,
the elaborate quaintness of their old burgher palaces, with
their gables fashioned like Spanish galley sterns, or Jacob's
ladders, or any other massive whimsy, and all in such admirable keeping with the turbulent history of the Hanseatic
republics gradually changing into Spanish provinces, and with
the showy actors, whose portraits painted by so many immortal

painters, from John of Bruges to Vandyke, still with their
point lace ruffs and gold chains and velvet robes, harmonizes
so well with the scenery, that a loitering tour made at one's
ease through their towns might be a very pleasant summer's
amusement. But to do this one should remain long enough
to learn something of the history of the towns and their
monuments, and to study their painters, some of whom are
wonderful. John van Eyck, or John of Bruges as he was
called, was the inventor of oil painting, but when you look at
his pictures, remembering they were painted nearly a hundred
years before Pietro Perugino, the invention seems like a
revelation. His colour is not only as vivid and beautiful as if
painted yesterday, but it really seems as powerful and as true
as any of later date. His flesh is almost as good as Vandyke's,
and although there is of course great stiffness and ignorance
in the drawing, yet he has much feeling, much sentiment and
ideality—more than the earlier Italians. There is a Madonna
at Ghent by his brother, Hubert van Eyck, and there are two
or three heads by himself, both at Ghent and at Bruges, which
for mere sentiment and perception, and expression of the ideal
beautiful, may be compared with the works of Leonardo da
Vinci and even Raphael, while the colouring is inferior to that
of scarcely any later painter.

I went from Paris to Brussels, swallowed up, like Jonah in
the whale's belly, in the interior of the diligence, and of course
obliged to travel day and night. I saw nothing, and know
nothing of the road. I got to Brussels the morning of the
second day. The next morning I despatched Brussels in the
most summary manner, throwing myself into the lion's den
with the vigour of a Daniel. I left Brussels at 1 o'clock the
same day by the railroad for Bruges, where I slept, and the
next day I executed Bruges and Ghent (a few miles further
on) with matchless rapidity. That evening I went to Antwerp,
and the next morning swallowed the cathedral and its contents, the town hall, the church of St. Paul and a gallery of five
hundred pictures all at a single mouthful, and at 12 o'clock noon
of the same day found myself on board the Antwerp steamer
for London—delightful and improving work, travelling against

time, is it not? I reached London the following morning at
9 o'clock, and here I am, wishing I could annihilate time and
space and find myself with you. I shall certainly sail in the
Patrick Henry from Liverpool 25th April, and hope to be
not much more than thirty days, but it may be sixty, you
know. Still a steamer is so crowded and uncomfortable that
I cannot make up my mind to put myself on board one again.
I shall leave a letter for you to go by the steamer of the 4th
May, which will of course arrive before.

Ever your own
J. L. M.

Extract from Diary.

St. Petersburg, November 28th, 1841.—Shopping in the
Gostivoi Dvor, or the Great Bazaar or market, as they call
it, in the Nevskoi Prospect. This, a triangular, two-storied,
arcaded building, with one apex or angle obliquely striking
the Prospect, and one running along the side. Three hundred
and forty shops inside, or rather booths in rows one above the
other. Shops are like cells; no fire being allowed in them,
the shopkeepers are walking about in the arcade wrapped in
their furs. As you walk along, every one officiously makes a
bow, or rather salaam, and invites you to enter his cell—to be
fleeced most unmercifully. The safest way, accordingly, for
a stranger is to take a shepherd with him, in the shape of an
interpreting servant, who will allow no shears to be applied
to you but his own. The appearance of these fellows in their
caftans and caps, moving about the long corridors of their
bazaar, and popping in and out of their cells, is peculiar—
a combination of Mount St. Bernard monastery and an
American penitentiary.

Shaft says butter is about equal to 2 roubles paper at present.
The pot I bought to-day cost 20 kopecks copper, equal to about
6 kopecks silver. I should think it was about the tenth part of
a pound, but will inquire the next time I send. A roll of bread,
two of which make my breakfast, cost 1½ kopecks silver. Tea
(which comes overland, and therefore better and dearer than

ours) costs from 100 rs. R. N. down to 9 or 10, which I
pay, and somewhat lower, I suppose. Beef is about 3d. English
now. Pork 4d. (because the Germans eat so much pork, he
says). Veal and mutton, sold by the quarter, dearer in proportion. Fowls the pair, about a silver rouble. These things
all dear now, because they have to be brought from the neighbourhood. In the winter (which it should be now) the frozen
things are brought from all parts of the empire at a much
cheaper rate. As no fire nor light is allowed in the Gostivoi
Dvor, they shut up at dark, which is now about 3 P.M. (I
shave by candlelight every morning about nine). The doors
are first locked; then they are sealed with a lump of shoemaker's wax and an impression, for the Russian burglars are
supposed to have an objection to breaking seals—a superstition, unfortunately, not shared by their superiors at the post-
office; a rope is then run along the outside pillars of the
arcade to prevent the drunken from falling in, and a dog is
then turned out on a swivel and string to guard the whole.
Imagine an English burglar being stopped by shoemaker's
wax and a dog on a swivel! How much might have been
saved by Gilbert, Davis, and Palmer, and the other victims
of the English swell-mob deputies, if superstition, instead of
the schoolmaster, was abroad in England and America. The
length of the Gostivoi Dvor on the north prospect is 1015 feet.

Thursday, $\frac{\text{November 27th}}{\text{December 9th}}$—. . . Take a long solitary walk,
nearly the length of the Nevskoi, as far as the bridge where
are the new bronze horses by Baron Kloth. They are very
spirited, though faulty. The effect is good, and the bridge is
splendid—the pedestals of the statues, the masonry. These
bridges are, in fact, the finest things in St. Petersburg. Call to
see Mr. G——. Long Socratic conversation with him, I cate-
chising. Results: First, very difficult to obtain any information here. Source carefully sealed up. He has tried for years
to obtain an account of the annual revenue and expenditure
of the Empire, the source whence the revenue is derived, and
the way it goes. By paying a 1000 rouble bribe to some
employé one might get it, but the Budget is not published, nor

to be got at. As to the sources of the revenue, they can be
conjectured, though, of course, neither the gross nor the
relative amount. An enormous tariff (protective for Russian
tobacco-growers, sugar-refiners, linen-makers, cloth-makers,
etc.) upon tobacco, refined sugar . . . must defeat itself to a
degree, and lessen the consumption. Still, as the production
of articles of consumption is not sufficient for the demand, the
customs must still furnish a large amount of revenue. There
is a high duty, and to be increased (they are hammering out
a new tariff), on cotton twist, for they have been establishing
cotton-mills and manufactures in this neighbourhood, which
are thriving, and the quantity of cotton and twist imported is
increasing. High duty upon tobacco, sugar, coffee, linen,
woollens (teas?), and in general, I should think, all manufactures; but everything is taxed in Russia immensely.

The tax paid by the first Guild merchants is about 4000
roubles per annum; by the second, about 2500; and the third
about 500, say. Then there is a lower class still, the shopkeepers, for instance, in the Gostivoi Dvor. They are too low,
for the Guilds form a class by themselves. But all pay a tax
to Government, and a heavy one. The Guilds are nominally
divided according to amount of property in its members, but,
in point of fact, the payment of the tax to Government is the
test. A first Guild merchant has a right to own a house, to
drive a carriage-and-four, to carry on the foreign trade; while
a second Guild merchant can have but a carriage-and-pair,
and confine himself to the inland trade and manufactures.
The first Guild merchant is exempted from the quartering of
soldiers upon him. No trade or calling, from highest to
lowest, can be practised without some emolument, and the
emolument is heavily taxed. Everybody is taxed in his
calling. There is high tax upon the transfer of real estate,
10 per cent. The foreign trade has been for a long time confined to foreign merchants, but the Russians are coming into
it now. The inland trade confined chiefly to Russians.

The nobles have not only the right of refusing to sell a
serf his freedom, but they often do. Prince —— has a slave
(a Russian merchant) who is worth two or three million

roubles, and who has repeatedly offered his master a million roubles for his freedom, who refuses it. All the property in reality belongs to the master, and there are some (though rare) instances of the master really enforcing his right to the acquired property of his slave. The serf is allowed to work three days in the week, upon land allotted to him by his master. . . .

I cannot admire the vastness and length of the squares and streets. To be sure, the architectural effect of some of them, particularly the part of Isaac's Square, where the column of Alexander stands, is imposing, and reminds one of some of Martin's architectural fantasies, representing imaginary views of Nineveh, Babylon, etc.; but, on the whole, the want of proportion ruins the effect. Perhaps it is because I am near-sighted, and so lose all details in attempting to take in the whole picture; but it seems to me that the breadth, the enormous and incredible breadth of the streets, and parti-cularly of the great square, dwarfs the houses and diminishes the grandeur of the whole. To be as imposing as it ought or was intended to be, the heights of all the houses should have been doubled; the statues, already colossal, should have been magnified, and the whole enclosed in a panoramic building, so that one might have looked at and taken in the whole at one *coup d'œil*, by means of some telescopic arrangement. But the effect would have been the same if merely the distances had been lessened. Peter the Great's statue, one of the finest things in Europe, is lost sight of in the dim distance before one reaches the other end of the square which it ornaments; and so with the column of Alexander, the Church of St. Isaac, and the entrances to the three great perspectives.

$\frac{December\ 7th}{December\ 19th}$. . . . The Legislative, the Executive and the Judicial departments are all, of course, embodied in the Emperor, who is, like "Cerberus, three gentlemen at once." He is also the head of the Church; and as the nobility all take rank, not according to birth or title, but by seniority in his service, the whole society of Russia, through all its myriad links, dangles like a great chain from his

aristocratic thumb.   He is Jupiter Juvans, and he looks the
character and fortunately is equal to it.   Social rank in Russia
has an entirely military organization.   There are fourteen or
fifteen ranks of nobility.   An ensign is *ipso facto* noble, and
transmits nobility to his children, and this is the lowest or 14th
order.   A captain is of a higher class, a colonel of course still
higher, and so on.   There are corresponding grades in the civil
service, but here it requires a relatively higher rank to match
the military order.   Thus a major in the civil service, that is
to say, an *employé*, who by seniority in his profession ranks
as high therein as a major would in the army, is only equal
to an ensign in the army, and belongs to the 14th class of
nobility ; and so on up and through all professions, including
physicians and clergymen.   It is in fact a sort of horizontal
tariff struck through all classes of society and rating them
into different categories *ad valorem.*

According to this rule, for instance, an archbishop is equal
to a general-in-chief; that is to say, they both belong to
the same (the 1st or 2nd class of nobility); and by the
same formula of social algebra, the relative proportions of
admirals, archbishops, ambassadors, field-marshals, judges,
cupbearers, cabinet ministers, theatre directors, masters of
ceremonies, clerks, cornets and middies are assigned.   This
artificial arrangement was first invented, I think, by Peter
the Great (*vide* Voltaire's ' Pierre le Grand '), and was most
admirably contrived by that sagacious despot to break down
the power of the Russian nobility and to strengthen the
autocracy on the ruins of the aristocracy.   His principle
that rank should be assigned according to merit, and not
according to birth, carried with it the necessary corollary
in a despotic Government that rank should be assigned
according to the Imperial favour; and the whole system has
been fully developed and carried out by all his successors.   It
needs a strong hand, however, to hold all these powers, and
the autocrats accordingly are as apt to get murdered here
as in Turkey.   Peter the Great disbanded and annihilated
the Strelitz or Russian janissaries, but the nobles retained
strength enough to murder his descendant Paul.

It would require a long residence and very close and strict attention, to acquire accurate information with regard to the structure of the Russian executive and judiciary departments, and it certainly would not repay the trouble or time expended ; the barbarous, the arbitrary, the confused, the contradictory and the mysterious are the prevailing features. The more I see of other countries, the more I like America. The faults, the blemishes, which are so apparent and so magnified when we are close, diminish wonderfully as we recede, while at the same time the simple and just proportions, the literal and open structure, wide open to the daylight of truth of the American Republic, present themselves more boldly and strikingly to the view. . . .

Thirty million pounds of food (Lebensmitteln) are brought in two months (mid-winter) to St. Petersburg—frozen meats, oxen slaughtered by thousands of hecatombs. All other animals (fish from the Volga), game, vegetables, etc., are brought from a distance of 2000 wersts [1] to the capital—which itself is built upon a morass, and utterly helpless so far as regards its own resources. The direction is taken by compass, and away they go over thousands of miles of frozen snow, without road or railroad. In summer, the water communication by canals is very admirable, connecting the Caspian with the Baltic.

The Russian soldier is reckoned to cost 118 francs a year, and is the cheapest soldier in Europe. A lieutenant gets about 600 roubles paper a year. A colonel very often makes his fortune ; but as he is always supposed to have his regiment full and fully accoutred, with horses, men and equipments, a sudden demand is very apt to ruin him ; still the post is very lucrative. A private soldier may be promoted to a lieutenancy, in which case he acquires nobility ; but the choice of promotion or retreat with a pension is given him, and he almost always prefers the latter. A soldier serves fifteen years, then at home five, then five years more, and then is free. In point of fact, however, the conscript is a soldier for life. The peasants are furnished for the army upon requisition made by the Crown upon their owners, according to the proportion

---

[1] A werst is 3501 English feet.

of ownership. There are certain rules by which the proprietors exempt some peasants. There are not many poor in Russia; generally the law requires each proprietor to take care of his own poor. As the means of life are cheap, and the Russian wants of food, raiment and lodging are very few, there ought not to be a great deal of poverty. Black bread costs at St. Petersburg seven copper kopecks to a cent and a half of our money a pound; and wheat flour in Moscow is about a penny and a half or three cents. Wood, of which they require a good deal, is abundant and generally cheap. Very often, in a season of bad crops, there is literally famine, and very often the peasants die literally of hunger. The crops are sold standing by the proprietor, who is often head-over-ears in debt, carried off, and the peasants who planted, sowed and reaped it are left to starve, while the fruit of their toil pays the debts of their owner in St. Petersburg or Moscow. The prisons and jails I know nothing about. The hospitals (under the immediate and efficient superintendence of the Duke of Leuchtenberg) are admirable, particularly the military hospitals, and I shall go to see them as soon as I have contrived some means of seeing them to advantage.

The policy and pride of the Russian Emperors, from Peter down, have been to encourage and protect domestic manufactures by enormous and constantly increasing tariffs. Moscow is the great seat of the Russian factories. Lord Stuart says it looks like Birmingham. In St. Petersburg there are immense factories of looking-glasses, of porcelain, of cloth, of cotton—in short, in spite of Storck's book written expressly for the use of Alexander and Nicholas when they were youths, and which advocates free trade, they have gone on in the same dull protective career, which all nations begin now, at least in theory, to repudiate. . . .

Friday, December 31st.—Thermometer 28° (Reaumur). Snowing slightly all day. At twelve go to a rehearsal of the *chanteurs de la cour.* In the Greek Church, there is no instrumental music, but the effect of this admirable harmony and variety of voice must be very fine. I have not yet been at mass. These are the singers of the Royal Chapel (in the Palace). It

is in fact a living organ ; the thin, clear pipes of young boys,
mixed with the deep and sonorous bass and thrilling trebles
of men, produce all the volume and all the variety and all
the swelling and sinking cadences of an immense organ. . . .

Wednesday, $\frac{December\ 31st,\ 1841}{January\ 12th,\ 1842}$.—Thermometer 18°. Drive
at 12 o'clock to the annual sitting of the Academy of Sciences,
to which we received cards of invitation. Went in uniform.
Members of Academy, behind a horse-shoe table, all in uniform
(something between a military and diplomatic dress). Handsome hall, portraits of Alexander and Nicholas, Catherine I.
and II., Elizabeth and Paul. Bust of Peter the Great on granite
pedestal. Brazilian Minister and Sir R. Porter only diplomats present. Archbishop of Moscow sat in front of me
—blue caftan with a white napkin on the head, grizzled beard,
altogether as reverend a figure as any of those most venerable
individuals the Russian coachmen. All his acquaintances
kissed his hand. Ceremonies consisted in the reading of the
'Compte Rendu,' by the perpetual Secretary, Dr. Frys, in
French, and by an oration or memoir in Russian by the Vice-
President, Prince Dondoukoff Korsakoff. Introduced to
Admiral Ricard and the Vice-President. As we were
coming away, Prince Dondoukoff gave us each a copy of the
printed Acts of the Academy of last year.

Thursday, January 1/13, 1842.—Thermometer 10° all day.
A frozen fog filled the air, the trees were frosted all over with
silver, ditto the beards of the venerable coachmen and the
manes of the horses. The effect on crossing the Isaac's Place
through the mist, as I took my noonday walk, was singular.
Peter's colossal statue dilated through the mist into gigantic
and spectral proportions. The towers and domes of the
Isaac's Church behind him, loomed up in shadowy grandeur,
and the sun hung like a globe of half-extinguished fire, round
and rayless in the centre of its low arch, and apparently but a
half-hour above the rim of the horizon. The day was cold,
but one did not feel it through one's furs because it was so
still. It has been judiciously said that at St. Petersburg " *on
voit le froid mais on ne le sent pas.*" Still this is not what is

called cold weather.   Everybody says that 25 degrees, day
and night, for a week or ten days together, is the usual state
of the weather at this season.

Dine with Colonel Todd.   In the evening go to the ball at
Woronzow's.   Observe for the first time the Duke of Leuchtenberg, Josephine's grandson, who is son-in-law to the Czar—a
tall, slender, common-place looking man, in a Hussar's uniform.   The only other members of the Imperial family present
were the Grand Duke Michael, and the Hereditary, "the
Perpetual Grand," as Dick Swiveller would call him, for he
is at all the parties perpetually, and perpetually dancing the
mazurka.

Tuesday, January 6/18.—This being the fête of the blessing of the waters, go by appointment of Count Woronzow to
the apartments of Prince Wolkowsky at the Winter Palace,
where one of the Palace servants conducts us into the great
banqueting-room, filled with military, at one of the windows
of which we took our station, directly opposite the pavilion
where the ceremony takes place.   As to effect, it makes no
difference in a procession whether the material be velvet,
satin, or fustian; the arrangement of the colours, grouping,
drapery, etc., may be equally produced in coarse materials.
Here go two or three notes to serve as memoranda.

1. Square space in the ice of the Neva, lined and thronged
with multitudes of spectators, say fifty thousand.   Their bearded
faces agitated like a strong sea, particularly when they crossed
themselves all in a mass at the appearance of the procession.

2. The pavilion, a gaudy affair of wood, painted and gilded,
open all round, and carpeted with red cloth, on a platform
ascended by some dozen steps.

3. The procession, which was of course not very large,
coming only from the Palace gate across the quay to the
edge of the Neva, where the pavilion stood.   First, a double
line of popes, in yellow satin and white robes, their long hair
streaming on their shoulders (bareheaded), and their long
beards, three deep; behind them a row of pages, all bareheaded.
Between this open line of clergy, the procession of archbishops,
bishops, in rich embroidered cloth of gold robes, bearing

banners and emblems, marched; then the principal archbishop, then the Emperor, followed by his suite of great embroidered functionaries, all bareheaded, walk up the steps, and then descend the interior ones leading to the hole cut in the ice. Then the archbishop blesses the water, which of course we could not see, and then a salute of artillery from the fortress announces the fact. Then they return, the archbishop with a little mop or swab twirling water on all the dignitaries from the Emperor down. As soon as they have left the place, general rush from the ice to dip into the water. Came home, and was raised to fever-heat of happiness by finding dear, dear Mary's letter. I shall now begin a letter to her to thank her, although it can't go until next Tuesday.

Thursday, January 8/20.—Passed out of the citadel and went a few rods farther to the house of Peter the Great. This fœtus of St. Petersburg is a one-storey log hut, painted red, and enclosed lately for protection in a brick case. The interior consists in a small room on each side of the entrance (low studded, so that you may touch the rafters of the ceiling with your hat or hand), and a smaller bedroom. One of these is now consecrated as a church, and filled with frippery of all sorts, gold and silver pictures, arms and legs tied up with satin ribbons, and other votive offerings from devout invalids cured of every bodily ailment by the virtues of the throne. In the other room, which was Peter's audience-room, is an old wooden armchair, upon which throne Peter received the foreign ambassadors.

Wednesday, January 14/25.—Thermometer 8°—10°. Dr. Cavill came and we went a round of military hospitals. It is certain that the soldier is taken good care of in Russia. We visited four hospitals—The first—that of the Ismaisoffsky regiment—small, 120 patients—very clean—polished floors— about ten or twelve in a ward—well dressed and with clean bedding—over the head of each patient is a board containing his name, regiment, disease, and diet. . . . There are 3000 men in each regiment and three physicians. There is a physician night and day in the hospital, and the patients are visited morning and evening. It is reckoned that the food costs about eleven silver kopecks for each inmate of the hospitals, the medicine two or three, making about thirteen, and the cost of wood, attendance, etc., etc., make it up to about thirty silver kopecks *per diem* for each patient. The food is pretty good—white bread for the sick, rye bread for the convalescents. They are allowed two pounds of bread, and one pound of meat *per diem*, but Wednesdays and Fridays are always fast days, when they get cabbage soup. They have quassia and a sort of drink made of rye and meal and small beer. It is not known exactly what all these hospitals (of which there are seven in St. Petersburg for the thirteen regiments, and a proportionate number of equally good ones all over the Empire) cost the Government, at whose expense they all are, but an approximation may be made out of the cost of each patient. They are economically arranged, for the overseer told me there was no waste, everything was consumed.

From the Ismaisoffsky we went to one occupied by three regiments—here were 283 patients, a very small number for 9000 men. The arrangements were similar to the last. Thence to the Prebazensky Hospital—this the oldest hospital, having been founded by Peter the Great—very clean, pure, and regular, but no difference between it and the others. The officers of the regiment have a library in the same building, which they showed us—a good collection of history and travels —about 6000 volumes, and they subscribe a fund of about 1500 roubles *per annum* to add to it. There were two Russian newspapers. They showed also the collection of MS., including a book full of the notes, orders, etc., of Peter the Great, Catherine, and Alexander—all written in Russian. From this we went lastly to what is called the great hospital, not appropriated by any one regiment, but receiving patients from several. This was built by Nicholas. Nothing peculiar, except being on an immense scale. There were 800 patients in it—there are beds for 1300, besides 20 for officers. There are three stories, and water forced up to reservoir on top, and let into various washing places for the patients along the corridor. There is an internal and external corridor opening to each ward. Each ward contains eighteen

beds. Good ventilators. Fire-places, as well as an equal
warmth all over the building by Russian stoves. . . .

Thursday, January 15/27.—Thermometer 10°—12°. Visit
the Hermitage Gallery. This is one of the best collections in
Europe. I know of none which has fewer bad pictures. . . .
One room is full of exquisite Wouvermans—battle pieces,
hunting and hawking pieces—fights of banditti and all the
favourite equestrian subjects of that great painter of life in
action—of wild, tumultuous, thrilling action. Another room
is full of Teniers—boors, banquets, village dances, cottage
interiors—many of them masterpieces. Strewed about here
and there are several most delicious Ruysdaels—with their
dark masses of wood and bubbling brooks, cool valleys, and
embowered church spires. One of these pictures, representing
a grove with the trees up to their knees in water, was a
perfect portrait of a maple swamp in Massachusetts. Several
fine Breughels and Berghems—Paul Potters and Cuyps, and
one room full of Rembrandts. Unfortunately the sun was
shining so powerfully upon the best of these that I could not
see them, and only remember one or two grim portraits in his
very best and strongest manner. There are two or three
Raphaels in his early Perugino manner. . . . In one room are
the pictures forming part of the Houghton Collection, em-
bracing some of the best Vandykes in the world—Charles I.,
his Queen—portrait of Sir J. Wharton and the Earl of Danby,
and a most delicious picture of William II., Prince of Orange,
at the age of twelve, in which I think the flesh and blood has
been put upon canvas more perfectly than I remember in
any picture—one of the most difficult things in painting is to
hit the exact colour of the human face. The rich olive of the
boy's cheek with an undertone of vermilion is the *ne plus
ultra* of complexion painting. . . .

Monday, January 19/31.—Thermometer 10°—4°. Visit the
institution for the education of female orphans of officers.
Large, splendid building, of course, connected with the Enfants
Trouvés. The two institutions together are well endowed, so
that although the expense exceeds eight millions *per annum,*
they lay by something every year. In the orphan institute

there are 1123 pupils, divided into six classes. They are taught all the " humanities," reading, writing, history, music, three or four languages, in short, everything, and the institution constitutes a great manufactory of governesses which supplies the whole Empire as far as it can—but the demand is so great that every scholar of good capacity is certain, on completing her education, to obtain a situation as governess. Those whose want of capacity condemns them to a humbler sphere are finished off as *ouvrières*, *brodeuses*, sempstresses, washerwomen, servants, and some of the *enfants trouvés* are at present among them, but it is not intended in future that they should mingle with the others. We went through all the class rooms—examined the best class in Russian, much to their edification and ours—saw their kitchen, dormitories (iron bedsteads and clean bedding, but too many in a room), and saw them come into their dining-hall. They marched in two by two, with merry little faces trying hard to look sedate, but with smiles stealing out of all the corners of their mouths and seeming very happy, into the hall, where they all sung (as is the universal custom of all the institutions) a Russian hymn, devoutly crossing and sometimes prostrating themselves the while—and then all sat down to table chattering and laughing. The effect of the chorus of small, sweet voices, piping out a thanksgiving was delicious, and they certainly ought to be thankful—for how many young ravens are fed who but for this institution would necessarily drag through a life of misery and starvation!

This, like all the noblest charitable institutions of Russia, was originated by the late Empress-mother. Baron Stachelberg, the Director of the Enfants Trouvés, was with us—a very gentlemanlike and intelligent man—of whom the children were evidently excessively fond—thronging round him with smiles and all sorts of caresses, "and plucked his gown to share the good man's smile." The "Enfants Trouvés" has been so often described that there is nothing for me to add. There are about 18,000 at present belonging to it. and 30,000 to the one in Moscow. There are in the house at St. Petersburg about 1000 infants and a nurse to each. They keep them here six weeks, and then if well send them with their nurses to the country—where they are brought up to trades, etc. There are received 3000 or 4000 *per annum*. Two or three had already been brought in the morning that we were there. We met, in fact, two well-dressed women, each bringing in a child. The mothers, if they choose, can come in as nurses. The children are brought openly and deposited in a little room below stairs. After the depositor is gone, the child is washed, ticketed, and delivered to a nurse—the food of the nurses is good—each child has its cradle, which is clean and good—about one-third of the whole number die.

CHAPTER V.

COMMENCEMENT OF THE 'HISTORY'—RESIDENCE AT DRESDEN.

Commencement of the 'History of the Rise of the Dutch Republic'—Arrival in
Europe—The Rhine—Holland—The duel with the sea—Polders—The Dutch
Masters—Dresden—Its climate—The Opera—Sontag—A picnic excursion —
Prospects of the Presidential Election—The Madonna di San Sisto—The
Green Vaults—Progress of the 'History'—Prince John of Saxony—Death
of Daniel Webster—'Uncle Tom's Cabin' and the Slavery Question—The
King and Queen of Saxony—The Court and its etiquette—Marriage of
Princess Vasa and Prince Albert—Court festivities.

[Mr. Motley returned to America in 1842, and in 1844 he
took an active interest in politics. In 1845–47 he contributed
historical and literary papers to the 'North American Review,'
and began to collect materials for a history of Holland. In
1849 he served for one term in the Massachusetts Legislature,
and in the same year he published his second novel, 'Merry-
Mount.' In 1851, finding that he could not properly write a
history of the Dutch Republic without consulting archives
and libraries in Europe, he threw aside all that he had written,
and sailed with his family for Europe.]

To his Mother.

Ship *Parliament*, off Point Lynas,
July 4th, 1851. 1 A.M.

MY DEAREST MOTHER,—Mary has just been writing a
hurried line to Susan to announce our safe arrival at the pilot
ground, and I thought you would like a single line from me at
the same time. They have just been burning blue lights and
firing off rockets on board the ship to celebrate 4th July, and
the pilot has come on board. We expect to reach Liverpool

by six or seven o'clock in the morning. Our plans are still
indistinct; but I am afraid we shall find it difficult to avoid
London, as all the roads seem to tend in that direction. We
shall, perhaps, remain there for a few days, a very few, and
then cross to Holland. I shall, however, write to you again
very soon, and the only reason for my sending this most
unsatisfactory scrawl is, that I am unwilling that the first
steamer after our arrival should sail without taking to you an
expression of my affectionate remembrance. I am determined, however, not to allow myself to be home-sick yet,
although it is very hard to think of Riverdale and all which it
contains with anything like composure. I feel, however, very
grateful that the children have been so well. Susie [1] has never
acknowledged any difference between ship and shore, proved
herself the best sailor from the very first, has exchanged locks
of hair with the captain, and has been the especial favourite
of both the mates.

Good-night, my dearest mother. You will hardly derive
much satisfaction from this note, except that it assures you
that we are well and that our first thought on reaching a
foreign coast is of you and of home.

Ever your affectionate son,
J. L. M.

To his Mother.

Königswinter,
August 11th, 1851.

MY DEAREST MOTHER,—I write from a little village some
half-dozen miles above Bonn, with the castled crag of Drachenfels over my head, and the wide and winding Rhine under
my nose, so that the situation is as romantic as nature and art,
history and poetry can make any spot in the world.

Much to my satisfaction, Mary decided to give up visiting
Paris this year. I was very glad, for the idea was anything
but agreeable to me, and we are now (having left the bulk of
our luggage at Cologne) making a slow and easy tour on the

---

[1] His youngest daughter, now Mrs. Herbert St. John Mildmay.

Rhine. We came to this place from Cologne three days ago, and shall leave to-morrow for Coblenz. We could loiter away a much longer time here, for it is a quiet, dreamy place, lying at the gateway of the Rhine glories and full of natural beauty and romantic associations. I am glad to have Mary wait a little while here till she can form a definite and clear idea of the stream which we are about to ascend. It is striking enough for me, having just come from Holland, where I saw the noble river in its feeble old age dribbling languidly by Leyden, and suffocated at last on its dull Dutch death-bed on the Katwyk sands, to witness the copious and exulting flow of its waters here. It was a melancholy sight enough in Holland. The river, after having commenced its career by a magnificent summersault over the precipices of Schaffhausen, and having pursued its winding and fertilising course through so many romantic regions in Germany, subsides into the most stagnant imbecility in the Netherlands, hiding itself in quicksands and miseries, and forgetting its identity and even its time-honoured name, which is changed and extinguished before its waters are lost in the sea. I believe I alluded in my last letter to this inglorious termination of its career. The river actually becomes too feeble even to die, and is pumped out of existence by artificial means at Katwyk. It had lain strangling there one thousand years, its mouth having been choked with a vast mass of sand driven up by a tempest in 840, till at the commencement of the present century it was helped into the ocean of eternity or the eternity of ocean by means of windmills. Up to that period it was lost in nameless bogs and quagmires. What a dreary termination to its Swiss childhood and its picturesque and impetuous career through the Land of Song! Here the stream is beautiful. Probably no river in the world has been so lavishly endowed by nature and by art, by poetry and truth. Its written history extends with unbroken links from Cæsar to Napoleon, the two notorious individuals whose names are the two greatest epochs of recorded time. Across that chasm of two thousand years, the embroidered belt of the Rhine is flung, emblazoned all over with historical emblems and hieroglyphics.

How different from the silent and solitary course of our own beautiful but deaf and dumb rivers! Great events, thick as the stars of heaven, have illuminated almost every day of its existence, and ten thousand charming fables from the misty and legendary mythology of the middle ages have lent a charm to every rock on its banks and to every brook that mingles with its waters. Here, where we are at present, is the first but one of the most enchanting spots which engage your attention as you ascend the stream. This village is at the foot of the Drachenfels, and one of the renowned seven mountains. These hills are all of volcanic origin, having been spouted up by craters long since extinguished, and consist of basaltic crags broken into fantastic and jagged outlines. Cornfields and vineyards grow now in deep hollows, which are very visibly volcanic craters whose lips were closed long before those of history were opened. Each one of these crags has its vineyards on its lap, its crumbling baronial ruin on its brow, and a little white village at its feet. The Drachenfels, or Dragon's rock, is the most picturesque although not the highest of these cliffs. . . .

To his Mother.

Brussels,
August 6th, 1851.

MY DEAREST MOTHER,— . . . Holland is a stranger and more wonderful country than I had imagined. I did not think that you would so plainly observe how it has been scooped out of the bottom of the sea. But when travelling there you see how the never-ending, still-beginning duel, which this people has so long been waging with the ocean, remains still their natural condition, and the only means by which their physical existence as a nation can be protracted a year. They are always below high-water mark, and the ocean is only kept out by the most prodigious system of dykes and pumps which the heart of man ever conceived. It is like a leaking ship at sea after a tempest, the people are pumping night and day for their lives. Tell the governor that the low land at Riverdale would be an excellent miniature Holland. He has only to dyke out the Charles as the Dutch do the Rhine and the Meuse, cut twelve or fifteen canals at right angles, and keep them dry by a series of mighty pumps worked by twenty or thirty windmills. Such an apparatus would add very much to the picturesqueness of your place, and would improve the value of the land incalculably. We could cut up an immense quantity of English grass and pasture the cows afterwards.

By the way, this is the universal system in Holland. The country is one meadow, and it is strange enough to witness thousands of cattle grazing quietly as it were in the bottom of the sea, usurping the ancient feeding ground of the cods and haddocks. I visited the great polder of all. A polder is the designation of a drained lake or pond converted into arable land. The one I mean is Haarlem lake, which, within the last two years, has been nearly drained. The task, which seemed Herculean, has been talked about for centuries, but at last the danger of inundation which seemed impending over the whole of Holland caused the job to be seriously undertaken. The lake is about seventy square miles in extent, and about sixteen feet deep. By means of three colossal suction pumps, worked by three engines of 350 horse-power, they have drained three-fourths of the depth. They expect to finish it in another year. I doubt it, however, for the hardest seems yet to come. Still, the wonderful feat will be accomplished within a very short time. I had, of course, but little time to see the pictures in Holland.

The collections at the Hague and Amsterdam contain some of the most wonderful paintings of the Dutch and Flemish schools. I could only, of course, look at them for a little while and see how much one loses by travelling in a hurry. It is strange that those two amphibious, half-submerged republics, Venice and Holland, should have instructed the world in colour. Nothing certainly can exceed the brilliancy and profound mastery of colour possessed by Rubens, Rembrandt, and Van Der Helst. You see these masters nowhere in such profusion as in their native land. The landscapes, too, the Ruysdaels and Berghems, you would be delighted with. After your eyes have been put out by the effulgence of their great historical pieces and dazzling portraits, such as Rembrandt and Van Der Helst and Rubens only could paint, they are refreshed by those cool, calm, rural scenes, with shady groves and gurgling brooks, such as only their landscape painters could produce. They seem to have had a deeper sentiment for landscape, and a greater power in reproducing natural beauties, than any people.

How strange that this genius should have risen out of the very bottom of the sea, that a people should have so faithfully and poetically represented on canvas those charming pastoral scenes, of which they could have only dreamed among their native dykes and ditches, without ever seeing them in their own land! The Dutch have certainly done many great things. They have had to contend with two of the mightiest powers in the world, the ocean and Spanish tyranny, and they conquered both. Neither the Inquisition nor the Zuyder Zee was able to engulf them, and yet it is very funny to see a people after having achieved such triumphs seat themselves so contentedly in their summer-houses over their very ill-savoured canals. Every country house has its garden, every garden its canal, and every canal is always creaming and mantling like no other standing pool in the world out of Holland. Nobody knows how stagnant water can be till he has visited this country. The canals smell of anything but Araby the Blest, and yet every summer-house is always planted directly over it. There sit the placid burghers, pipe in mouth, and inhale the odours, hanging over them as if increase of appetite did grow by what it feeds on.

Ever your most affectionate son,
J. L. M.

To his Mother.

Dresden,
November 17th, 1851.

We live in the most profound solitude. We have exchanged calls with the British Minister and his sister, and with this ceremony our acquaintance with the society of Dresden is likely to have begun and ended. I certainly do not regret this on my own account, nor much upon Mary's, because I think that we have become so very much addicted to solitude that we adorn it more than we should society. We should feel like Shadrach, Meshach and Abednego if we should ever venture into the fiery furnace of fashionable life, and mightn't get out of the scrape as respectably as those excellent and unsinged individuals are said to have done.

Our autumn is drawing to a conclusion, but everything is very deliberate in this paternal government. I suppose the weather is regulated, like the price of meat, by the police, in consequence of which we have never very good or very bad weather, as we certainly have never anything but most indifferent beef and mutton. The first frost was, I think, about ten days ago, or say about the 10th of November. The month of September was very cold and rainy. The sun hardly shone once, and the rain was not omitted in more than three out of the whole thirty days. The glass was never so high as 70°, and generally was at about 58°. The month of October was very fine, and fine nearly all the time, as our best October, which is saying a great deal, as that is the month we brag the most of. Even till the last week of that month the glass was for many days in succession as high as 67°, and was hardly ever 20° lower. Since the beginning of this month it has not been higher than 40°, and rarely lower than 30°, although for the last two or three nights it may have been as low as 26°. I talk by the thermometer on purpose because all other talk about the weather means but little. Figures in this respect don't lie, for they have no interest to do so, that I know of. The horse-chestnut trees in our garden were full of leaves, which were almost green until about a week since, when the first sharp frost stripped them. The acacias (rose acacias) under my window and the other shrubbery in the garden are not yet leafless or yellow. The dahlias and roses have been dead about ten days, the grape vines were laid down last week. The grapes here are Sweetwater, and are plentiful, but this year they were not sweet. They are cheaper than isabellas, but I think not much better. We have already had two trifling snow-storms.

Good-bye, my dearest mother. Love to all, for I am closing in great haste.

Ever your affectionate son,

J. L. M.

To his Mother.

Dresden,
April 13th, 1852.

MY DEAREST MOTHER,— . . . As for Mary,[1] she will of course write, but the serious labour of selection will probably devolve upon me. She continues to retain her epistolary mania, which she sometimes wreaks upon me, not rarely addressing upon me billets and even lengthy letters while I am in the same room with her. Poor little thing, both she and Lily have had a somewhat severe illness, a kind of catarrhal fever or influenza, which kept them in bed and their mother in a worry for a few days. They have now recovered, but have not yet been out of doors, and will not if the sun declines to show his face so resolutely. I don't know where he is, probably engaged elsewhere, starring it in some more profitable region; at any rate he is rarely visible here now-a-days, not at home to company at all events. Still the season is about three weeks in advance of our spring, and there is at least much more tacked to autumn's skirts, so that the vegetable year is from six weeks to two months longer. Nature, death and resurrection being brought just so much the nearer. Your accounts of winter, however, remind me that in the American, that is New England, sense there is no such thing as winter here. We have had an absence of warmth rather than the presence

---

[1] His second daughter, now Mrs. Sheridan.

of cold.   Once or twice, but that very rarely, we had the glass
as low as 10° or 15° Fahrenheit above zero, but generally
the temperature in the coldest months hovered about the
freezing point, not going much up or down.   The grass has
been green two or three weeks, and the shrubbery is now in
leaf.   We have no blossom yet, however, and as the cherry and
plum trees are usually in bloom with you by the last week of
April (if I am not mistaken), you see that there is no very
great difference after all.   Thus far I am disappointed in the
spring.   We have had one or two warm days, and thought
spring, that genial season of which you read, and of which we
considered ourselves to have been defrauded in America, had
arrived.   We get occasionally a bright shiny, silvery spring
day, fine as fourpence, but we are sure to have to take the
change for it afterwards in at least six coppery and cloudy
ones.   Still the blackbirds whistle away under my windows
every morning as merrily as any other little niggers, in spite
of the fog and general grimness of the landscape, and there
is a "glory in the grass," and our gardener has dug up
his half-hardy roses, multifloras, and monthlies from their
temporary graves and erected them again on their respective
Ebenezers, and lettuce is already two cents a head, while
asparagus, owing to the sunless atmosphere, remains obsti-
nately at a groschen a spear.   Strange to say, however, the
east wind seems as natural here as if it blew from the end of
Long Wharf, and it has as bad a character almost as with us.
It's very odd, but entirely true, that in spring an east wind
is detestable and disreputable in every part of the world
where I have ever been.   As the Englishman discovered
in Paris, that although the French had no *bread*, they had a
substitute called "pain" which could be used in the same way
and which answered the purpose, so I have always found
almost everywhere a very good imitation of Boston east wind;
not quite equal to the original, but sufficient to answer the
purpose, a fact I leave to the meteorologists, at the same time
boldly affirming that a Boston winter cannot be equalled
anywhere in Europe so far as I know, and out of Russia not
even imitated.

Since Sontag departed we have had nothing at the Opera. She played seven nights here, of which we went six, the seventh being a repetition of a part in which we did not admire her the most (Rosina). The best tickets, the best places (and we had always the best seats in the house, owing to a small douceur judiciously administered to the box-keeper) cost three thalers (two dollars and fifty cents) each. You will probably pay much more. It was rather an extravagance, but Mary has not much amusement here and she is very fond of music. I think you cannot help being pleased with Sontag, and advise you to go very often. La Fille du Régiment is her best part, but she is quite charming in all. She is very pretty at forty-seven, looks twenty-seven, is an uncommonly good and graceful actress in light parts, and her voice, although it is of course faded, and indeed effaced as to some of the notes, is exceedingly sweet, and she possesses to perfection the flowery, arabesque, decorated style of singing, which is so rarely heard. Of course it is not equal to the passionate and tempestuous style of the Italians, of Malibran, Pasta, Grisi, but it comes next to that, and is at least perfect of its kind. She was much admired here, and the house was always brimming over, a thing which I have not seen before or since, although the prices of the seats were tripled. She is to go to America this summer. Lady Adelaide Forbes told me the other day that she had informed her, she should be afraid to say what immense offers she had received from America, for fear she should not be believed. This reminds me that we had a dinner-party at Mr. Forbes's, the British Minister, a few days ago. The party was in a manner given for us, I believe, at any rate he led Mary into the dining-room while his sister Lady Adelaide and I brought up the rear. The dinner was very elegant, and Mr. Forbes and his sisters were very attentive and polite to Mary, but they receive company very seldom. My dear mother, I have now come to the end of my paper.

Good-bye, and God bless you, dear mother,

Your affectionate son,

J. L. M.

K 2

To his Mother.

Dresden,
June 22nd, 1852.

MY DEAREST MOTHER,—I really believe that your letter of
May 10th has not been answered.   I am sure you will soon
write again and not punish me for my negligence by silence.
In truth the time, now that our course of life has subsided into
a monotonous current, goes by so quickly that I forget one
post day after another.   I can't say " how happily the days of
Thalaba went by " as an excuse for negligence; rather flows
the stream of time so muddily, that but little gold seems to
sparkle in the sand as it goes by.   At any rate, when I try to
sift out a few events that may be worth the postage (fortunately, however, you don't have to pay it), nothing seems to
turn up but copper and lead.   Spring has gone by and
summer has come.   The spring was very like an American
one, and at the end of May we were surprised by a week of full-
blown summer weather, just as you seem to have been at
home.   It was not quite so hot here, the glass hardly rising
much above 80° or 81° Fahrenheit in the shade.   Since the
month of June came in, it has rarely been much above 70°, and
there has been rain very frequently.   I am afraid a cold and
rainy summer is the rule here, because I find that those who
have been long resident, complained bitterly of the heat,
during the few days of summer weather, as something they
were not used to, and didn't intend to put up with.   In consequence it has been frigid enough ever since to satisfy an
Esquimaux.   The summer is generally improved, by people
who remain in town here, in making excursions into the
country in small squads.   We have been on one or two.   The
Noels got up one a little while since, a picnic to an unin-
habited chateau on the banks of the Elbe.   I am not much of
a hand at chronicling this sort of small beer, which is apt to
get very stale when it has been once uncorked, and I had
hoped that it would furnish Lily or Mary with a topic for
a letter or two, seeing that we all complain so much of the
want of topics.

The excursion had been projected for a long time, and at last on the day when it was finally to come off, it naturally rained in torrents, so of course it was countermanded, and as soon as that was done the weather naturally began to clear. So Lily's friend, O. Paget, who did duty as an aide-de-camp, general and chief clerk to the weather. department, after one or two missions, again announced that the Gesellschaft's wagen or company's waggon would soon be at the door. Accordingly an enormous and wonderful Noah's Ark soon appeared at the corner of the street. "Six doors off the carriage staid," not so much for fear that men should say that we were proud, as because our street was narrow, and the machine could by no possibility be insinuated therein. It had places inside for eighteen human beings, and outside for three quadrupeds—rather a liberal allowance of humanity you will think. The precious souls all agog to dash through thick and thin, but who were obliged to dash rather moderately, as you may suppose, consisted generally, besides ourselves, of the Forbes's, the Noels, the Pagets, and her daughter-in-law and husband, Countess and Count Bethlen from Hungary, and an English family. On reaching the old *chatee* (as Mary used to pronounce the word), we were joined there by some young ladies of the family to which it belongs, the daughters of an old General von Miltitz. whose ancestors have inhabited the spot for nine centuries, as stated in a tablet on the courtyard. Their present residence is a few miles further down the river, where they have a very beautifully situated and baronial residence. The young ladies were very pretty and agreeable, as agreeable as they could be considering that there were none but middle-aged beaux provided for them, and those all married. The table for a miscellaneous entertainment was spread in the courtyard of the castle, and just as each of the company held a potato on his or her respective fork, down came a magnificent thunder-storm, which had been saving up for us all that time. Everybody clasped his potato and plate in agony and rushed upstairs. In *moins de rien*, as we say in French, the tables were spread in "the banquet hall deserted" of the ·

old chateau. Everybody having held on to his own plate as aforesaid, was reinstated in his original rights on taking up the new position, which in my opinion it would have been much better to occupy at first.

I don't know that anything else very remarkable has occurred. We met one evening at the Forbes's Lord Wynford and his daughter. The next day they were kind enough to call upon us. A few days afterwards they invited us to dinner, when besides his family there were nobody but the Lady Paulett, the Secretary of the English Legation, and another youth belonging to some Spanish Embassy. Lord Wynford is an uncommonly agreeable and unaffected person, and Miss Best is also very agreeable and intelligent. They have certainly been very friendly to us, and insist that we shall visit them at their country place as soon as we come to England. I believe these are the only new acquaintances we have made of late. The Forbes, I fear me, will go before long. We shall certainly go to Scotland some time or other merely to visit them. Good-bye, my dearest mother. Excuse this hurried scrawl. I will write soon again.

Love to all, and believe me

Most affectionately your son,

J. L. M.

To his Mother.

Dresden,
September 13th, 1852.

My dearest Mother,—I have not answered your very kind and acceptable letter of 3rd August, the last letter which we have received from anybody. I take it for granted that General Pierce is destined to win next November in a canter; at any rate, to my unsophisticated judgment out here in the Teutonic wilderness, I don't see how it is to be prevented. I shall look anxiously, however, for the next intelligence to see whether there is anything in the contemplated Southern movements for Webster. When, however, I remember that the Southern aristocracy is always democratic, with the ex-

ception of one or two States, I confess I don't see much room
for hope.   Perhaps the governor will enlighten me on the
subject.

Our general life here is very calm and solitary, infinitely
more so than yours in Dedham.   Our acquaintances are almost
all departed, some few to return, others for good.   Our
garden is very beautiful, and I wish daily that you could see
it once in a while, for you would appreciate it.   We have had
a constant succession and profusion of every flower known
to horticulture—I mean to hardy horticulture.   The roses in
their season were uncommonly fine, and now there is a wilderness of dahlias, asters, gladioli, and day lilies, geraniums,
fuchsias, and countless others.   In the midst of the garden is
a sandbank, and in the midst of the sandbank may be seen
burrowing, at any hour between noon and night, Susie and
Mary, with their friends Adolf and Lulu, children of Madame
de Rumohr, the lady who occupies the other part of our house.
I regret to say that she leaves Dresden before the winter.
Our young Prince is going to Prussia to enter the army, and
Captain de Rumohr accompanies him to Berlin.   We shall
miss them all very much, for they are very amiable, kind-
hearted people.   The Prince is quite a nice-looking, good-
tempered young man of twenty, with very agreeable manners.
The Captain is a very intelligent and amiable man about my
age.   The eldest brother of the Prince has just assumed the
government of his principality on attaining his majority.
Waldeck is the name.

The gallery remains as much a resource as ever.   I find that
I have (and Mary also) a most sincere and unlimited love for
the fine arts, and particularly for painting.   I am pretty well
persuaded that the ' Madonna di San Sisto ' is the first picture
in the world.   I don't think any painter has ever so well hit the
exact combination of the supernatural with the natural which
is always attempted in the face of the Infant Saviour.   The
expression, without ceasing to be that of an infant, has still
something infinitely imposing and majestic.   The Madonna is
faultlessly beautiful and very human, yet there is an expression
beyond humanity ; not elevated, for it is humble ; not trium-

phant, for it is sad ; but prophetic and wondering, as of a face
gazing vaguely but earnestly into the depths of the future, and
dimly conscious of the coming struggles of humanity.   There
is a sentiment that the child in her arms is the Saviour and
the Judge of unborn millions; there is the submission of a
mortal to a superhuman destiny ; there are tenderness, patience,
pathos, and transfiguration above the clouds of common
emotions ; everything, in short, which painters have from the
beginning of Christian art endeavoured to typify by that mysterious image, the Madonna.   I don't think that it is possible
to exaggerate the beauties of this picture with regard to its
suggestive effects.   It has no fault as a composition, which
is a great virtue, for even Raphael often has something which
jars upon the mind, even in his most harmonious pictures.
But here there is nothing discordant—everything is musical.
The Madonna and Child are inexpressibly beautiful and
lofty, the venerable figure of the kneeling pope is full of
piety and fervour.   The Barbara is a model of grace and
modesty, and the two cherubs at the base of the picture are
exquisite expressions of innocence and infantine devotion.

As you are perfectly familiar with the composition by the
engraving, I do not apologise for speaking of the picture,
otherwise I should do so, for I hold that to have to listen to
the description of a painting of which you have never seen any
copy or sketch is an infinite nuisance.   I said that this picture
was the best in the world, and I have tried to explain why I
think so.   Because it is the highest flight into the regions of
the sublime and beautiful to which the mind of Raphael ever
attained.   I never wish to criticise it.   It hushes criticism.
It is the only picture which awes me into silence.   When I
go away I readily admit that there are many paintings much
superior as works of art.   It does not compare to the 'Transfiguration,' nor to Titian's 'Ascension,' nor to Rubens'
'Descent from the Cross,' as a finished exhibition of colour
and handling and technical power.   There is in truth but
little colour, and that is fading.   It looks almost like a fresco
already.   The body of the Child is a mere smooch of lamp-
black, the shadows are generally without transparency, except

in the drapery, which has been retouched. The face of the Virgin, however, is exquisitely coloured, and that of the Child, although by no means strongly painted, has still warm, life-like tints. The truth is, the picture is a sketch wholly from the hand of Raphael, and dashed off in a moment of enthusiasm. It is thought that it was painted *for a banner to be carried in a procession.* Only imagine a wonder of the world originating in such a way. Of course a standard is only a peg above a sign.

Nothing is known of its history. Contemporary writers don't speak of it. I don't know that there is any historical proof that Raphael painted it. Ten or fifteen years ago they found that the top of the picture behind the frame was closely rolled, and the canvas cut into such a shape as to make it probable that it had been fastened on a pole. This idea seems to explain the thin, sketchy, and slight manner in which the whole was executed   Raphael, having dashed it off at a few heats (some people talk most ridiculously of eighteen hours as the whole time occupied upon it), probably thought it good enough for a banner, and gave it to the monks of Piacenza without thinking more of the matter. And in the refectory of the jolly friars it remained till the middle of the last century, when it was purchased for $20,000. I suppose it would be worth a king's ransom now if offered for sale, and kings have risen lately as well as Raphaels.

The engraving by Müller gives a very good idea of the composition. Even that old thing which we left at home, which you have often seen, an impression taken after the plate had been retouched over and over again, and was almost worn through, is worth looking at. It is, perhaps, the best engraving which was ever made of any picture. Of course you can form no idea of the. value by looking at one of these worn-out impressions. Ours has nothing left of the original power or beauty of the engraving, it serves only as a memorandum of the composition. It cost $5. The value of a copy before the letter, when it can be found, is 1000 thalers, say $750. I don't mean to purchase one even if I find it.

The King has got six, but I have not heard that he thinks of sending one to me! Müller's engraving is really a work of genius. Yet one would think the engraver's profession must make a man of genius frantic. To work upside down, scratching away upon a half-covered plate of copper with a kind of cobbler's awl, producing no effect from day to day, being obliged to wait so long before an opinion as to the result can be formed, must be a severe trial to the nerves, and seems enough to drive an impatient person mad. And by the way Müller did go mad over this very engraving. Poor fellow! he was so excited, exhausted, and used up after finishing it that his brain was turned. He jumped off a precipice and broke his neck.

Besides the gallery, there are a great many other remarkable collections in Dresden. These and the beautiful environs of the city have made its fame. The engraving cabinet is perhaps the best in the world. It contains four hundred thousand prints, comprising a full history and exemplification of the progress of the art, and of course a large supply of all that is most masterly and curious and celebrated among its achievements. Then there is the collection of rarities and *objets de goût* and jewellery, called the Green Vault, the name given to a series of rooms in the royal palace where the remarkable museum of trinkets is kept. All sorts of beautiful toys, statuettes, drinking cups, carved in ivory; exquisite cabinets and caskets of every age, of mother-of-pearl, agate, amber, ivory, buhl and ormolu, adorned with topazes, emeralds, rubies, carbuncles, sometimes of very considerable value; magnificent goblets and basins of silver, carved, engraved, embossed by the hands of the most eminent jewellers of the sixteenth and seventeenth centuries; beautiful paintings in enamel, splendid vases, clocks in Louis XIV. style, and in style much earlier and much richer than that of Louis XIV., with numerous puppets once bobbing about and performing all sorts of antics in obedience to the same machinery which moved the hands, but now silent and motionless, run down and worn out, used up for ever; splendid tables of Florentine mosaics, jars and obelisks of jasper, sardonyx and chalcedon ; drinking horns, baptismal fonts, lavers and wine coolers, all of beaten gold ; caskets of elaborate workmanship crusted all over with beryls, sapphires, diamonds, and rubies as thickly as Aaron's breastplate or ephod, or whatever you call it, which contained all the precious stones in the world, besides others ; bushels of intaglios and cameos, both antique and modern ; curious cuttings in wood and alabaster, two small and very singular landscapes or hunting pieces in waxwork, so minutely done that the leaves on the trees, the nails in the horses' shoes, the lace on the riders' ruffles are distinctly finished.

Perhaps, however, the most remarkable part of the collection is the complete department of the works of Dinglinger, the Saxon Benvenuto Cellini, a man who wasted a good deal of real genius and the whole of his life in the production of these curious and exquisite, but, after all, somewhat tasteless toys. There are whole rows of monster pearls, some of them as large as a pullet's egg, but so mis-shapen and imbedded in their shells as to be inseparable from them. These, according to the taste of the seventeenth century, have been made use of as caricatures, legs and arms, heads and wings having been ingeniously fitted to them, so that they furnish counterfeit presentiments of little niggers, Dutch women skating, cobblers and pedlars, humpbacks and cripples, dragons, goblins, and chimeras dire with tails and without, and a whole wilderness of monkeys, lizards, toads, and other oddities, as curious and expensive a collection of gew-gaws as could well be found in Christendom, and a most wonderful baby house, not without beauty, and even utility, in its way, but one not likely to be formed again by anybody. Perhaps the most curious thing in the whole museum is a representation of the Court of the Grand Mogul Aurengzeb, who sits on his throne in the centre, and is surrounded by hundreds of figures in every variety of costume known to that region as described by travellers. This is Dinglinger's masterpiece. It occupied him seven years (from A.D. 1701–1708), and he received for it 59,000 thalers, about $45,000. Certainly an expensive toy. Ask the governor to calculate how much

the money would have come to if kept in the savings bank
to this day. For his behoof I have given the date as above.
The 'Madonna di San Sisto' was a better speculation viewed
in that ignoble light, but I doubt if Dinglinger's *chef d'œuvre*
would bring much if offered for sale now.

The old Electors of Saxony had a turn for the magnificent.
I could fill a dozen more sheets by telling you of the different
museums which they have here. The armour collection is remarkably fine, for example—one of the first in Europe. The
Elector Christian II., who died at the close of the sixteenth
century, had no less than ten suits of armour, of which one
was by the most celebrated armourer of Germany, Holman of
Augsburg, and another was by the world-renowned Benvenuto
Cellini. This last is a most interesting object of art, and
stamped throughout with the genius of that remarkable personage. It is a complete panoply for the horse and rider, is of
hammered steel, and is covered all over with the most exquisite
sculpture or *alto relievo*, representing the wars of the gods, the
combats of centaurs, and other mythological battles, all pour-
trayed with the boldness, accuracy, and beauty which always
distinguishes the hand of the man who made the statue of
Perseus at Florence. After all, it is a luxury to have your toys
by Dinglinger, your Madonnas by Raphael, and your coats of
armour by Benvenuto Cellini. Those Saxon princes, obscure
as they were, except in the Lutheranism which they have
since repudiated, certainly knew how to spend their money
like gentlemen.

And now add to the advantages here enumerated a magnificent library of 450,000 volumes, and very excellent opportunities for education, besides a very beautiful and picturesque
country surrounding the city in all directions, and you will
understand why Dresden is so often selected as a residence.
It is a dull little place no doubt, but I like it the better for
that. It is better for dull little people like ourselves. If I
could get the hang of it, I could live as well for $2500 as in
Boston for $5000. Unfortunately it always takes as much
time as you can spare for a place to learn to live in it. The
children and Mary are all well, and send much love to you

and the governor, and to all. Susie's mind is beginning to
expand. She told me last night that when she was a thousand
millions years old she should know how to sew, and should be
as big as the washerwoman. Rather a commonplace result to
contemplate through so long a vista. Good-bye, my dear
mother. My paper is exhausted, and your patience.

Ever affectionately your son,

J. L. M.

To his Father.

Dresden,

May 18th, 1852.

MY DEAR FATHER,—My last despatch was, I think, about a
month ago, and included a letter to Tom, and another to
mother. Since that time we have had the pleasure of receiving a letter from Susan and another from Lodge. There has
literally been nothing on our side of the world to communicate. Political events and general news reach you from the
great centres of intelligence quite as soon as they do us.
There is so little active existence, and so little interest felt, or
allowed to be felt, in what is going on in the world around,
that one soon finds the old-fashioned drowsy Rip Van Winkle
feeling coming over him, and begins to think on the whole
that it is better to be governed than to govern, to accept a
paternal government as ordained from heaven, and to behave
as good boys should, go to bed at ten, shut the door after you,
smoke a pipe, drink a pot of beer, listen every day to a
groschen-worth of instrumental music, never allude to politics,
nor to anything which interests grown-up men, but leave all
that to your betters, and rely for your personal and political
rights on the Emperor of Russia, and Austria, and the police,
and so "easy live and quiet die," as comfortable burghers
should.

There is something almost refreshing in the utter inanity
which seems to form the atmosphere of these peoples' lives,
which is refreshing for a time, after the noisy splutter-
ing politics which constitute our vital elements. I don't

think I should like it always, but now occupied as I am ten
hours a day, with folks who lived three centuries ago, it is
rather a convenience than otherwise not to have my attention
taken off by anything that is going on about me. It is a
comfort, as I can't make speeches or write articles in the
newspapers (if I wished) against General Haynau, or Emperor
Nicholas, or President Bonaparte, to be able to pitch into the
Duke of Alva and Philip the Second to my heart's content.
It is quite satisfactory to express sentiments, which if I had
the advantage of living three hundred years ago, and had had
the audacity to express myself as freely, would have entitled
me to be burned alive on an average twice a day, and to
know that the only martyrdom I am likely to experience is
that of not finding a publisher for my treason, for fear that it
won't pay; the only rack that of being roasted on the gridiron
of some singeing, scorching, red-hot review.

I have just finished volume No. 2, begun since I was established here, that is about a seven months' child. A year more
will carry me as far as I mean to go alone, particularly as the
expense of publishing three volumes at my own risk, which
perhaps I shall be obliged to do, will be as much as I shall
choose to venture. I don't fear much of a loss, although I
shan't stand much chance of making a fortune. At the same
time I don't care to venture much more. Money is a thing
of which I haven't quite as much to spare as time and labour.
These I am very profuse with. Time they say is money. No
doubt of it, only I never could get mine into active circulation.
Labour is the foundation of all value. Equally certain it is,
then, that I have been digging a cellar big enough, and laying a foundation extensive enough, for a most valuable edifice,
if one would only brings his pigs to market. Still there is
something very healing in these portable maxims. You can
always stick one like a piece of court plaster over the wounds
of your vanity. Moreover it should never be forgotten that
Milton's ' Paradise Lost ' was sold for £5, that Samuel Johnson's
' Dictionary ' brought him in about as much for his labour as if
he had been sawing wood or sweeping a crossing. Further-
more Galileo confessed before the Inquisition that the earth

didn't move, and Harvey was laughed at for circulating a
story about the circulation of the blood; so whenever a char-
latan can't find any to believe in his tricks of mesmerism or
biologism, or whatever may be the latest neologism, when a
literary blockhead can't sell a book, he has only to call from
the vasty deep the spirits of Milton and Galileo and Harvey,
Dr. Johnson and Dr. Jenner, and all the rest. They are sure
to come when called for, being no doubt by this time quite
used to the business; though they probably think that their
last condition is worse than their first, being thus obliged to
console and sanction so much mediocrity. So if a man can't
make anything of his writings, it proves nothing but that he
is probably a second Milton in disguise.

I wish you would say to Mr. Ticknor, with my particular
regards, that I should have written to him before this, as
a slight acknowledgment of the friendly interest he took in
providing me with introductions and advice before starting,
but that I was really ashamed to write so very uninteresting
a letter from Europe as mine must necessarily be at present.
To one's immediate family one can write about oneself, but
it is a most disagreeable and barren topic to me, and we
live so retired, and see so little, that beyond the incidents
of our family circle there is nothing to state. We might
as well be on the Charles as on the Elbe; at the same
time I have enough time to do my work, and the children,
particularly Lily, who is really making progress, are very
well disposed of. I have not (as Mr. Ticknor knows, I believe), presented myself at Court. Mr. Forbes and his
sisters, owing to the letters given by Mr. Ticknor and Mrs.
Ritchie, have been very friendly, invited us to a dinner, and
offered all that we can require whenever we wish to go into
general society. Moreover please say to Mr. Ticknor, that
after the Court festivities were finished, I thought it proper to
pay my respects to Prince John of Saxony,[1] who is a regular
correspondent and friend of Mr. Ticknor. I called in company with my friend Noel on Baron O'Bryan (not an Irishman,
but of Irish distraction), the head chamberlain of the Prince.

---

[1] Subsequently King of Saxony, father of the present King.

A few days afterwards the said Baron called on me in a friendly way, and said the Prince would be happy to receive me the next day informally. I went accordingly, and had an interview of half an hour with his Highness, who received me with great kindness. Mr. Ticknor had been good enough to mention me to him, and he hoped therefore, as I purposed staying another year, to cultivate my acquaintance, etc., etc. He spoke with much affection and respect of Mr. Ticknor, and alluded in terms of high praise to his History. He also spoke of Prescott's works, particularly the 'Conquest of Mexico,' with admiration. Please also by the way to inform Prescott, that if I meet with anybody, prince or plebeian, who don't ask me about him, I will be sure to write and let him know. It will be rather refreshing than otherwise. I find by the way that his Highness had just that morning received a fresh letter from Mr. Ticknor, which he had not had time to read, but of these matters of course there is no need of my writing. As Mr. Ticknor by the way has so good a correspondent at Dresden, it would hardly be necessary for me to apologise for not troubling him. You are perhaps aware that the said Prince John would have been a distinguished professor, if he had not happened to be born in the purple. It is not as a Prince merely, that his acquaintance was worth cultivating. Mr. Ticknor might have said to him, as Voltaire did to Congreve when he was disposed to sink the shop and put on the fine gentleman, "If you had only your genteel birth, it would have been long before I should have sought your acquaintance." Prince John's translation of Dante's 'Divina Commedia' has really great merit. The notes and illustrations, furnishing a running commentary on that great poem, have been translated and are much esteemed in Italy. He certainly received me with great politeness, and I beg you to express my thanks to Mr. Ticknor for having taken so much trouble about us, which our inclination for retirement and obscurity has prevented our turning to so much account as we should have done.

Our society consists principally of the persons already introduced to you in previous letters. The Noels (Mrs. N.

by the way is a near relation and friend of Mr. Ticknor's friends, the Counts Thun, she is a Bohemian and a very amiable person), the Pagets, the Mellys (Americans) and the Forbes's. These last, a mother and two daughters, are distant relations, and intimate acquaintances of the Minister here. They are the most affectionate people in the world. Lily speaks French certainly as well as I do, and begins to speak German very tolerably, and in general matters she is in quite a satisfactory condition of mental health and improvement. Mary has not yet found a school. We have sent her to a kindergarten (child's garden), but this is nothing more than an infant's school, and she already reads German better than the little children there. Speaking, too, she can practise with her little Rumohr friends and neighbours, and the *bonne* is quite competent to give her lessons. As for Susie she is as sweet and saucy as ever, much the most amiable of all the children, and therefore much the more spoiled. She takes a great deal of spoiling, which I consider high praise. Lily and I took a long walk yesterday in the Grosser Garten, or Park. When we got back about seven in the afternoon she said : "This is just the time I used to go and sit with grandmamma on the piazza, I wish I could go to-night." You may be sure I echoed the wish most heartily, though hopelessly.

Most affectionately your son,

J. L. M.

To his Father.

Dresden,
December 23rd, 1852.

MY DEAR FATHER,—Our life is as usual monotonous, furnishing few topics for letters. I am working as hard as a wood sawyer, and am of course as independent as his clerk. I find the atmosphere congenial to literary labour, or perhaps because my time is so wholly my own, I have it more in my power to make long pulls without getting out of the traces. I dare say, like the remarkable cab horse immor-

talised by Pickwick, I should fall flat if taken out of the
shafts, and I only keep up because I keep a-going. That
you may see that this is not an idle brag so far as work
goes, I will state that I have written a volume since the 13th
July of this year, one which will make rather a large printed
octavo, and which is the second that I have written since
I came to Dresden. As this labour includes of course the
digging out of raw material out of subterranean depths of
black-letter folios in half a dozen different languages, all
which works are dark, grimy, and cheerless as coal pits, you
may suppose that I am not likely to be a very agreeable
customer when I come out of my diggings. The worst of it
is when a man is smashing quartz with a sledge hammer he
gets paid for his pains; but here am I working away with my
pick-axe or sifting painfully the sand of buried ages over
which the river of Time has so long been flowing, and yet I
don't know whether I shall at last find a few grains of pure gold
in my cradle, to reward me for my labours. Metaphorically, of
course, not literally, for I don't employ myself in writing and
studying history to make money out of it. "Base" as the
"slave who pays" is the slave who pursues money and not
truth in any scientific field.

But I confess that I have not been working under ground
for so long without hoping that I may make some few people
in the world wiser and better by my labour. This must be
the case whenever a man honestly "seeks the truths in ages
past" to furnish light for the present and future track. And
if you only get enough oil to feed a very small lamp it
is better than nothing. A little lantern may help you to
find an honest man or so in the dark corridor of history; but
not if you look for them in the spirit of Diogenes. It is
always much harder to find commendable than accusable
characters in the world, partly perhaps because the world
likes better to censure than to commend. I flatter myself
that I have found one great, virtuous and heroic character,
William the First of Orange, founder of the Dutch Republic. This man, who did the work of a thousand men every
year of his life, who was never inspired by any personal

ambition, but who performed good and lofty actions because
he was born to do them, just as other men have been born to
do nasty ones, deserves to be better understood than I believe
him to have been by the world at large. He is one of the
very few men who have a right to be mentioned in the same
page with Washington.

Christmas, Saturday.—I was interrupted the day before
yesterday, and my letter has lain unfinished in my drawer till
now. . . . I have the greatest sympathy for you and the
country for the loss of Daniel Webster. It is one which
can never be made good to us. He was not only the
greatest living statesman, but the greatest whom we ever
produced in America, so much beyond all of them past and
present in intellectual force, that it is hardly a compliment to
speak of him as first among the political men of the country.
Very little is known of him in Europe. On the Continent few
have ever heard his name. One literary old maid, who has
written and published books, asked me if he was not one of
our principal poets, and then when I laughed, confessed she
had never heard of him. Yet she had lived fifteen years in
England. The English had of course heard of him, and he
was known to the statesmen; but nobody imagines that he was
a personage to be compared to their great men, and probably
not one hundred men on the continent of Europe has ever read
a line of his speeches, if indeed there be as many who knew
that he ever made any. The fact is, no interest is felt in
America or American institutions among the European public.
America is as isolated as China. Nobody knows or cares anything about its men, or its politics, or its conditions. It is,
however, known and felt among the lower classes, that it is a
place to get to out of the monotonous prison house of Philis-
tines, in which the great unwashed of Europe continue to
grind eternally. Very little is known of the country, and
very little respect is felt for it, but the fact remains that
Europe is decanting itself into America, a great deal more
rapidly than is to be wished by us.

When I say that nothing is known about America, I am
wrong. Everybody knows that slavery exists there, for every-

body in Germany has read 'Uncle Tom's Cabin.' I am
glad of it, because I believe the only way the curse is ever
to be taken from the nation is by creating such an atmosphere all round the Slave States, that a slaveholder may
not be able to thrust his nose outside his own door without
scenting that the rankness of his offence is tainting every
wind of heaven. The only way in which the system can
cease to exist is, it seems to me, by working the children of
the present slaveholders. The coming generation in each
of the fifteen Slave States are the people who must grapple
with this question; but the question won't be staved off for a
third. It is all up for your generation or for mine. If one
or two States, like Kentucky and Tennessee, should come to
abolish the system and should succeed, well; afterwards the
great obstacles would be removed. Of course, the black race is
not by nature capable of social or intellectual equality with
the white; nor have they ever desired it so far as I know.
But it is begging the question to say they will be insolent,
and that they won't work after emancipation. Certainly they
are orderly enough and industrious in Massachusetts. Besides
slavery is an immense crime, while refusing social equality is
a matter of taste, and is only denying to the blacks that which
does not exist, and never did exist anywhere with regard to
the whites. But here in Europe nobody knows anything
about the matter, saving only that slavery exists. They have
no idea that America is a confederation of States, each of
which States is competent to establish and abolish slavery at
its pleasure, and that the general government has no power to
do one or the other. I believe everybody in Europe thinks,
so far as he thinks at all, most of them contenting themselves
with bragging, that the President of the United States could
abolish slavery to-morrow by an edict, just as the Emperor of
the French abolished the Republic by half a dozen lines of
proclamation, or if that can't be, nobody goes so deep as to
conceive a doubt that the Congress could abolish it as easily
as it could pass a tariff law.

To revert to Webster. I hope you will send me Hillard's
eulogy, and also his and the other speeches which were made

formally.   I always take great interest in everything Hillard
writes or says, for I have great respect and regard for him.
As for thinking of America without Webster, it seems like
thinking of her without Niagara, or the Mississippi or any
other of the magnificent natural features which had belonged
to her since I grew up, and seemed likely to endure for ever.
You see now why I don't write oftener.   It is absolutely impossible to amuse or edify under my circumstances, and therefore I have no self-reproach to make for being silent longer
than I should be if I had anything to say.   Here I have
written three or four pages of stuff which would have been bad
enough if uttered between sleep and wake at the fireside
corner, but which deliberately put upon paper " is enough," as
Mr. Macaulay says of Bob Southey's printed pleasantries, " to
make a man ashamed of his species."   Therefore I will now
pause for a reply.

Very affectionately your son,
J. L. M.

P.S.—Up to this time we have had no more snow nor cold
weather than we often have at home in October.   The grass is
perfectly green in the fields, which stretch out before my study
window as far as Saxon Switzerland.   Please to say to Mr. Cabot
that his young friend and kinsman, Mr. Higginson, presented
himself not long ago to us.   He is a very honest, ingenuous,
intelligent lad, who is taking a vacation on account of his
eyes.   He comes and dines whenever he chooses, which is
generally once a week, and he dines with us to-day, Christmas.
Please tell his father I am happy to have made his son's
acquaintance.

To his Mother.

Dresden,
February 3rd, 1853.

MY DEAREST MOTHER.—We jog on as usual, the days and
nights succeeding and certifying each other with the regularity of your kitchen clock.   The monotony of our life was
interrupted a little while ago by our going to Court, and

perhaps you will think that I ought to send you a minute description of the ceremony. But to tell you the truth, these things are to me so insipid that I am unable to extract juice enough out of them to flavour a letter with. I wish I could tell you anything that would entertain you concerning our presentation on New Year's Day, and the Court ball which followed the succeeding week. But I do lack something of the gamesome spirit which enables one to be amusing on such topics. Besides I prefer to leave the details to Mary, who will wake from her slumbers one of these days and send, either to you or to S—— or A—— L——, an account of her achievements. The palace here is a rambling old barrack externally, but within, the rooms are spacious and sufficiently elegant. The principal apartments have been recently painted in fresco by an artist called Bendemann, who is thought by the Germans to be inferior only to Raphael and Rubens. The frescoes have certainly considerable merit as far as drawing and grouping are concerned, but in grace and colour they are not above mediocrity.

The King and Queen receive masculine friends on New Year's morning. His Majesty is a mild old gentleman, wadded and bolstered into very harmonious proportions. He has a single tooth worn carelessly on one side, which somewhat interferes with his eloquence. I do not think that I took notes enough of his conversation to be able to give you a report. He was glad to hear in answer to a question that I proposed passing the winter here. And as I felt how much unalloyed satisfaction the circumstance must really cause to his bosom, I internally resolved not to change my plan. The Queen is very tall and very queenly. Nothing can be more elegant or more winning than her manner. She is, I believe, very benignant in character, and certainly her address is perfectly in accordance therewith. I am not at liberty to mention her conversation with myself. Indeed I did not understand a single word she said, and was entirely ignorant in what language she was speaking, but I have since ascertained that it was probably French. This is a general observation. She speaks in so low a tone and with such a

kind of gentle *roucoulement* that it is almost impossible to catch
her words with any distinctness except after considerable
practice. The King and Queen have no children. The heir
to the throne is Prince John, whom I have already described
to you. He made many inquiries of me again about
Mr. Ticknor, for whom he certainly entertains a sincere
friendship. He is more fortunate as a *père de famille* than
his brother, his progeny sing, "We are seven." Two of the
princesses (Anna and Sidonie) are very pretty. The ball was
not particularly brilliant. The costumes of the gentlemen
were slightly shabby. Those of the ladies were not remarkable. The royal party were of course well dressed. The
Queen wore a magnificent tiara of diamonds. The Princess
Augusta was in a green blaze, being covered with the most
gorgeous emeralds I ever saw. Some few of the high Court
ladies were well jewelled also, but the rank and file were
rather ill-dressed so far as I could judge.

Turning from the fair women to the brave men, it was
funny to observe the profusion of orders and decorations with
which every other person was covered. There were the statesmen of world-wide reputation, the sages and law-givers on
whose accents the world hangs with enthusiasm, the generals
of a hundred stricken fields in which the fate of empires has
been decided, whose names I cannot yet give you, because I
have not ascertained them, but they must all be as eminent
as Metternich or Talleyrand, Wellington or Blücher, Marshal
Ney or King Murat, to judge from the trophies on their
bosoms. Each manly chest, like the spacious firmament on
high, was covered with stars innumerable. I am quite
satisfied that they are all destined for immortality. As I
before observed, there is something like constraint in the
general atmosphere of one of the balls. The etiquette is
perhaps more formal since the reaction after '48. I suppose
it is thought necessary to effect thorough repairs in the
divinity which hedges kings, the said hedge having had so
many gaps made in it by irreverent poachers in latter days.
So the good people all fall back, opening to the right and left,
standing (not at ease) on both sides of the ball-room, when

it is understood that their Majesties and the august family
are approaching. After a little preliminary flourish and
flutter, you hear two or three mysterious raps (something like
your spiritual knockings, I suppose), and then enters the
royal *cortége*, headed by an old chamberlain with a gold stick
in his hand, the personage who, from his high rank or great
services or his imposing bald head, is supposed to be the
most " fit and desartless man " for Court Constable. After this
Dogberry in high life come a few Court cards, whose costumes
look a deal like those of Tommy Crehore's after the pack has
seen a little service. Then come their Majesties with the
rest of the family, bowing to the right and left with great
benignity, and making happy " the upturned wondering
looks " of the mortals who fell back to gaze on them. They
pass, and the solemn hush is succeeded by a chatter of relief.
The ducks, who have been rolling their eyes as the thunder-
storm was passing (as is their well-known nature), now begin
to quack again and to waddle about and to expatiate generally, till another rap and another gathering cloud in the
distance makes all silent once more.

This is thought very good fun in Dresden and in many
other places, and no doubt some amusement may be extracted
from such scenes, but then you must have more inclination
and more time to make acquaintances than I have. I work
like a mule all day long, and I am therefore not equal to the
fatigue of requesting introductions and making myself agreeable to the big-wigs. You will naturally ask why, having
these dispositions or indispositions, we take the trouble to go
out at all. My reasons are twain—one furnished by Lord
Bacon, the other by some anonymous philosopher of almost
equal wisdom. The sage of Verulam enumerates among the
things for a traveller to see and study, " the courts of kings
and princes." As Mary has never been in Europe before,
and as we could go through the kindness of Mr. Forbes with
very little trouble, I thought it best that she should take
the opportunity.

Your most affectionate son,

J. L. M.

Tell Uncle Edward that my next letter will be to him. I am ashamed that I have not written to him for so long, because I know it gives him pleasure, and I should like to give him all the amusement in my power. I have been so dull myself, and at the same time working so hard, that I have let a long time slip by without writing anything but my book, which will be finished this week, that is to say Part I., in three or four volumes, and all perhaps that will ever be written, unless its publication gives me encouragement to continue. Part I. is a complete whole in itself, therefore posterity will not be injured by a total stoppage.

Affectionately your son,

J. L. M.

To his Mother.

Dresden,
June 30th, 1853.

MY DEAREST MOTHER,—We have, contrary to my expectations, been obliged once more to turn out at Court. We have been marrying the Princess Vasa to the eldest son of Prince John, and heir eventually to the Saxon crown, or throne rather, for there is no crown. This young lady was, as you may have read in the papers, the object of Louis Napoleon's aspirations. The Princess Vasa is of a family which was sovereign for three centuries, having risen from obscurity in the early part of the 16th century, in the person of Gustavus Vasa, a man of great talents and very humble birth. This is but a brief pedigree to brag of, particularly as the be-all of the end-all is already arrived at, and it must be confessed that in any historical or philosophical sense the house of Bonaparte is more illustrious *per se*, according to the common notions of illustrations, than that of Vasa.

The Swedish family is however connected by numerous alliances with all the potentates of Europe, and is a recognised party to the family compact which unites all the Lord's anointed into a band of brethren and sisters. The present marriage was one of affection, a rare thing among people in their line of life. Prince Albert, a fine, manly young man, fell in love with the young lady, a pretty, pleasing, gentle young damsel of eighteen. The reception in the town was early in the forenoon of the 18th of this month by a cavalcade of burghers, peasants, and military. The streets were very prettily decorated, the houses being hung with garlands, and triumphal arches as smart as paint and gilding could make them, and the citizens all putting on their best attire and culling forth a holiday in the most approved fashion.

The nuptials were solemnised in the Catholic church. All persons who had been presented at Court were invited to the wedding. It was also intimated that the ladies were to go in trains, and be presented to the bride afterwards at a drawing-room to be held at the palace, between which and the church adjoining there is a gallery of communication. Mary had however already turned her train into a gown, and was not inclined to buy another, and you may suppose that I was most happy to escape the drawing-room. It was well known that many people would go to the marriage and to the ball a few days afterwards without going to the presentation. We sent an excuse therefore, like many others, and received tickets for the body of the church instead of the gallery, where the ladies in full dress were accommodated. In the nave below, the ladies, all much dressed, of course, but in morning costume, were arranged on one side, and the gentlemen, all in uniform, military, civil, or diplomatic, on the other. The day was fine, the hour about noon. The church is spacious but modern, and of no great beauty of architecture or richness in decoration. The grand altar was a blaze of light. Numerous candles, glittering sacramental furniture, and the splendid robes of the priests made a very effective show, at the end of a long vista, formed by a vast tulip bed of gaily dressed ladies thickly planted in rows upon one side, and by a noble army of fine gentlemen, gorgeous as hollyhocks, on the other.

At the appointed moment, the bishop, with his mitre on his head, his crozier in his hand, an effulgent gown of brocade embroidered with gold on his back, and a lackadaisical simper, intended to be a general benediction for the world at large, heretics excepted, upon his pumpkin face, set forth from the high altar, followed by a string of highly-bedizened ecclesiastics. The procession passed close to me, as I was fortunate enough to have a place at the end of one of the benches or pews directly upon the principal nave. (Mary on her side of the church was equally fortunate.) The clerical procession went forth to the main door in order to meet the bridal party, which was now advancing through the gallery above, and which, though invisible to us, was sufficiently manifest in its effect upon the serried ranks of the ladies in the galleries. A general rustle and flutter of the whole throng, a simultaneous bending of feathered heads like the swaying of a field of ripe corn when the summer breeze passes over it (my similes seem to be very agricultural this morning), made it obvious that the glorious presence was revealing itself to them, although it was yet hidden to the upturned eyes of mortals who were gazing from below. Directly afterwards the two streams mingled at the church door. The bishop received the royal party and countermarched them all to the altar. So the whole procession advanced through the aisle for our gratification. First came the said bishop, his head bobbing from side to side with an expression of "goneness." Then came the mob of ecclesiastics. They were followed by a long train of menials in brand-new clothes. The royal livery being a most intense yellow, this swarm of lackeys looked like a flock of gigantic canary birds. After these came a troop of underlings in sky-blue habiliments, a set of officials occupying a middle position between servants and gentlemen, household divinities of one kind or another, ushers, inspectors, or what not. Then the grand dignitaries of the kingdom, in fullest fig, made their appearance, chief marshals, lord chamberlains, ministers of state, gold sticks and silver sticks, equerries and cup bearers, all "fine" as Adam, Ralph, and Gregory.

Thus heralded came the King and Queen, followed by the young and pretty bride, wearing a wreath of diamonds and orange flowers on her head, and walking between her mother and her future father-in-law, Prince John. Her train was held up by her future sister-in-law, young Princess Sidonie, who is very good and very handsome. Her train again was held up by her lady of honour who came behind her. Various princesses and grand duchesses followed in like manner, all staggering under loads of diamonds and all strung together by their long satin tails. Then came the bridegroom with his friends and relations of the masculine gender, looking as little sheepish as could have been expected under such trying circumstances. In due time the party were arranged round the altar, the two sufferers got themselves comfortably on their knees, and the ceremony began. The good bishop, thinking it necessary in compliment to his company to be as "tedious as a king," held forth at a most unmerciful length. But as all things come to an end, so did his exhortation, and at last the booming of cannon and the rattle of musketry outside, with a magnificent *Te Deum* thundered forth by the organ within, announced to the world that the marriage was complete. Soon afterwards, the same procession again moved down the aisle, and up through the galleries into the palace. Those who had chosen to go to the drawing-room went upstairs after them. The rest of us went home to dinner.

On the following evening there was a very general and effective illumination of the town. On the next evening there was an opera at the theatre, to which no tickets were sold, all being distributed by the Court. To this " *théâtre paré*," as it is called, because everybody must go in full Court dress, we received tickets, but could not go as it was on Sunday. On the next was the Court ball, at which we made our appearance, and which was a particularly brilliant one by reason of the numerous foreign princes and dignitaries who were present. Among these the observed of all observers was the Duke of Genoa, brother of the King of Sardinia. He is very handsome and picturesque in appearance, looking like a knight of old, such as Titian might have painted, having the chevaleresque air which befits a man who has fought well in the field for Italian nationality against Austrian tyranny, as becomes a son of Charles Albert, and a scion of a house which, almost alone in Europe, recognises the possession of political liberty by its subjects.

I had hoped that Mary would have mustered up energy to send you a description of these fine doings. It would have been a topic which she would have described with much more vivacity and emotion. I am not good at these gauds. In truth, they weary me beyond measure, but I think Mary would have made a grand mistake not to have improved the opportunity of seeing what she could for once in a way of the humours of a Court. This ceremony of a royal marriage too (and a Catholic one) does not often turn up for outsiders, and she was very much pleased and interested. As for me, I am Mackintoshed into impermeability and such things all descend upon me, and run off leaving me as dry as ever.

Ever your affectionate son,

J. L. M.

CHAPTER VI.

PUBLICATION OF THE 'RISE OF THE DUTCH REPUBLIC.'

The Hague—Residence at Brussels—Mr. Motley's daughters—Letter to O. W.
Holmes—Daily life at Brussels—Companions of past generations—The
River Senne—The Archives—Literary silkworms—Rubens and his art—
The Shakespeare of painting—Arrival in London—Mr. Forsyth—Prelimi-
naries of publication –John Murray—English and American politics com-
pared—Preparations for publication—Mr. Prescott—Frankfort—Basel—Visit
to Herr von Bismarck—His character and career—His family life—Return to
England—An English hotel—Florence—Theodore S. Fay—Paris under
Louis Napoleon—Americans in Florence—Miss Alexander—Thomas Ball—
Mr. Motley's constitutional melancholy — Description of Florence — Her
brilliant past—Her achievements and her feuds—Her present condition—
Publication of the ' History of the Dutch Republic '—Mr. Prescott's praise of
it—Criticisms in the English and in the American press—Sorrento—Letters
about the History from T. S. Fay—O. W. Holmes—C. C. Felton—Letter to
O. W. Holmes on his poem — Letters about the History from G. Bancroft
and Washington Irving.

To his Mother.

Brussels,
November 20th, 1853.

MY DEAREST MOTHER,—The six weeks we passed at the
Hague were pleasant for Mary and the children, and useful
for me. The children were ducked in the North Sea, and
I was buried in the deep bosom of the Dutch Archives,
much to the invigoration of all. The Hague is a mild,
stagnant, elegant, drowsy, tranquil, clean, umbrageous little
capital smothered in foliage, buried in an ancient forest, with
the downs thrown up by the North Sea surging all round it,
and the ocean rolling beyond. We made a good many
pleasant acquaintances at the *Tables d'hôte,* where Susie was
the observed of all observers. The hotel where we stayed had
its dinner at 5 P.M., and as there were not many foreigners
staying there, the company were principally of the natives
and of the very best class. Many members of the Chamber

of Deputies and of the Senate, Ex-Ambassadors, and Cabinet Ministers were constantly there and all were exceedingly cordial, affable and agreeable.   A very warm attachment sprang up between Susie and an old gentleman named Donker Curtius, the Minister of Justice, who was exceedingly diverted with her talk and her comicalities at table.

Our *Chargé d'affaires* there, Mr. Folsom, and his wife, were very polite to us.   Mary drove out with them almost daily, and the children were all very intimate with each other, and got on very well together.   Since we have been here they passed through the town, where they dined with us and spent the evening.   They have now gone to Italy to spend the winter.   Our friends, the Forbes's, of whom you have heard us speak so often and with whom we have been intimate so long in Dresden, came here as much as anything to visit us, and have just terminated their stay here, having left for England by the way of Antwerp two or three days ago.   We are now entirely alone, and we do not wish to make any acquaintances. Of course I came here to study in the Library and Archives. It is, however, as good a place as we could find for the children to learn French.   Paris would be out of the question from its dearness, but we have found a most excellent little day school, kept by a lady from Paris.

You asked me to tell you of the children when I wrote.   To begin with Lily.   She is improving very much in character and is much more willing to be gentle than she used to be. Mary is constitutionally irritable, but she is one of the most single-hearted and disinterested children that ever lived.   She is always thinking of something to do for other people.   She is singularly industrious, I never saw her a moment idle.   She is, like her mother, very handy with her fingers, and is already very distinguished in rugs, and crotchets, or whatever you call them, and furnishes all her friends in parlour or kitchen with caps and pinafores.   Moreover she has long since constituted herself almoner-general of the establishment, and for years has always confiscated every piece of copper money that her mother or I may be in possession of for the benefit of the poor of the parish.   And as the poor we have always with us, you may suppose that she has always recipients for her bounty. If her means were as large as her heart she would feed and clothe the whole continent. She often thinks and talks of home, and has a most tender remembrance of her dear grandpapa. I am sorry to say that she is about as feeble as ever. She is complaining, and has been for some days, of a pain in her side. Sometimes she has a cough. At the same time I don't believe but that she may turn out right after all. I don't want to go to a doctor and have him tap her all over and hint suspicions of tubercles, for then we should never dare to look her in the face again, for fear of reading confirmation of his doubts. Moreover I really believe that she will yet conquer a constitution for herself.

As for Susie, she is the light of our eyes and the sunshine of our lives; she is perfectly good, amiable and gentle. Coming so recently from the hand of God she has lost nothing yet of her innocence and happiness, and has all the freshness of daybreak still about her. I never saw such insolent happiness, as if she had been put into this prison house for no other purpose but to sing and chatter all day long. She has brought a good phial full from the fountain of perpetual youth, and she means it to bubble and sparkle as long as possible.

Poor creature! she will find out soon enough that the world was not made for singing and laughing, but in the meantime she is happy. She speaks German quite as fluently and correctly as she does English. Of course she makes mistakes, as she does, and all children do, in whatever language they speak, but it is quite the same as her mother tongue to her, and nothing can exceed the swiftness of her jabber in either language. She observed this morning at breakfast, "that very few people had seen so much of the world as she had," and then began to enumerate the places she had visited, beginning with Dedham, and ending with Brüssel, as she always calls Brussels.

Your affectionate son,

J. L. M.

To Dr. O. W. Holmes.

Brussels,
November 20th, 1853.

MY DEAR HOLMES,—Most certainly both Mary and myself felt deeply your kindness in writing to us, for although your letter was addressed to me personally, she assumes a joint and several character with regard to it in all respects except in the responsibility of responding, and if I could have merely taken up my pen (style of the earlier part of this century in which you and I began to flourish) and acknowledged the kindness, and so rendered you my debtor instantly for another letter, you may be very sure that you would at this moment be writing to me your sixth or seventh. Honestly and most warmly I asseverate that my delay in answering was only because I felt unable to write anything that would be worth your reading. I was too conscientious to think that one sheet of paper with a post-mark was equal to another sheet of paper with a post-mark, and I hoped not to be forced, as I am at last, to tender a pound of lead in payment for a pound of gold. Do, however, be merciful, take your pen and write four score as if I had really discharged the debt. If you knew how often we have read your letter, and how much pleasure it has given us, and how often Mary has been goading me into answering in the mere sordid expectation of getting a second, till at last even the incrustations of time and self-conscious stupidity have penetrated, you would I am sure be willing once more to write to us. You may be sure even if I have myself "no more wit than a Christian or an ordinary man," that I am quite able to appreciate and to treasure yours.

I do not really know what to say to you. I am in a town which for aught I know may be very gay. I do not know a living soul in it. We have not a single acquaintance in the place, and we glory in the fact. There is something rather sublime in thus floating on a single spar in the wide sea of a populous, busy, fuming, fussy, little world like this. At any rate it is consonant to both our tastes. You may suppose, however, that I find it rather difficult to amuse my friends out of the

incidents of so isolated an existence. Our life is as stagnant
as a Dutch canal; not that I complain of it, on the contrary
the canal may be richly freighted with merchandise, and be a
short cut to the ocean of abundant and perpetual knowledge,
but at the same time few points rise above the level of so
regular a life, to be worthy of your notice. You must therefore allow me to meander along through the meadows of
common-place. Do not expect anything in the impetuous
and boiling style.

I do not know whether you ever were in Brussels. It is a
striking, picturesque town, built up a steep promontory, the
old part at the bottom, very dingy and mouldy, the new part
at the top, very showy and elegant. Nothing can be more
exquisite in its way than the Grande Place in the very heart of
the city, surrounded with those toppling, zig-zag, ten-storied
buildings, bedizened all over with ornaments and emblems so
peculiar to the Netherlands, with the brocaded Hôtel de Ville
on one side, with its impossible spire, rising some three hundred
and seventy feet into the air, and embroidered on the top with
the delicacy of needlework, sugarwork, spiderwork, or what you
will. I haunt this place because it is my scene, my theatre.
Here were enacted so many deep tragedies, so many stately
dramas, and even so many farces, which have been so familiar
to me so long, that I have got to imagine myself invested with
a kind of property in the place, and look at it as if it were
merely the theatre with the *coulisses*, machinery, drapery, etc.,
for representing scenes which have long since vanished, and
which no more enter the minds of men and women who are
actually moving across its pavements than if they had occurred
in the moon. When I say that I know no soul in Brussels I
am perhaps wrong. With the present generation I am not
familiar. *En revanche* the dead men of the place are my intimate friends. I am at home in any cemetery. With the fellows of the sixteenth century I am on the most familiar terms.
Any ghost that ever flits by night across the moonlight square
is at once hailed by me as a man and a brother. I call him
by his Christian name at once.

When you come out of this place, however, which, as I said,

is exactly in the heart of the town, the antique town in the modern setting, you may go either up or down; if you go down you will find yourself in the very nastiest and most dismal complications of lanes and *culs de sac* possible, a dark entanglement of gin shops, beer houses, and hovels, through which charming valley dribbles the river Senne (whence I suppose is derived senna)—the most nauseous little river in the world, which receives all the outpourings of all the drains and houses, and is then converted into beer for the inhabitants—all the way, breweries being directly upon its edge. If you go up the hill instead of down you come to an arrangement of squares, palaces, and gardens, as trim and fashionable as you will find in Europe. Thus you see that our Cybele sits with her head crowned with very stately towers, and her feet in a tub of very dirty water.

My habits here for the present are very regular. I came here, having, as I thought, finished my work, or rather the first part (something like three or four volumes octavo), but I find so much original matter here, and so many emendations to make, that I am ready to despair. However, there is nothing for it but to penelopise, pull to pieces and stitch away again. Whatever may be the result of my labours, nobody can say that I have not worked hard like a brute beast; but I do not care for the result. The labour is in itself its own reward and all I want. I go day after day to the Archives here (as I went all summer at the Hague), studying the old letters and documents of the sixteenth century. Here I remain among my fellow worms, feeding on those musty mulberry leaves of which we are afterwards to spin our silk. How can you expect anything interesting from such a cocoon? It is, however, not without its amusement in a mouldy sort of way, this reading of dead letters. It is something to read the real *bonâ fide* signs manual of such fellows as William of Orange, Count Egmont, Alexander Farnese, Philip the Second, Cardinal Granvelle, and the rest of them. It gives a "realising sense," as the Americans have it. However, you see how insensibly I fall into talking about myself, and yet no topic is more distasteful to me. I hate myself, and am bored by myself, and I

rarely commit the sin of egotism. Yet I feel as if it were in
writing to so old and kind a friend as you, whose good opinion
I so highly value, and to whom I feel grateful for thinking
that I am really industrious and capable of being useful. I
feel, I say, bound to say something of my occupations, and
feel that it would be affectation to be altogether silent on the
subject. At the same time I am, in German slang, rather
objective than subjective, and would rather entertain my
friends with anything than with myself.

There are not many public resources of amusement in
this place if we wanted them, which we do not. I miss the
Dresden Gallery very much, and it makes me sad to think
that I shall never look at the face of the 'Sistine Madonna'
again, that picture beyond all pictures in the world, in which
the artist certainly did get to heaven and painted a face
which man never saw on earth, so pathetic, so gentle, so
passionless, so prophetic, "half of earth, and half of heaven"
—you see I cannot break myself of quoting you to your
face. There are a few good Rubens here, but the great wealth
of that master is in Antwerp. The great picture of the
'Descent from the Cross' is free again, after having been two
years in the repairing room. It has come out again in very
good condition. What a picture! It seems to me as if I had
really stood at the Cross, and seen Mary weeping on John's
shoulder, and Magdalen receiving the dead body of the
Saviour in her arms. Never was the grand tragedy represented in so profound and dramatic a manner. For it is not
only his colour, in which this man so easily surpasses the
world, but in his life-like flesh and blood action, the tragic
power of his composition. And is it not appalling to think
of the large constitution of this man, when you reflect on the
acres of canvas which he has covered? How inspiriting
to see with what muscular masculine vigour this splendid
Fleming rushed in and plucked up drowning Art by the locks,
when it was sinking in the washy sea of such creatures as
Luca Giordanos and Pietro Cortonas and the like. Well
might Guido exclaim, "The fellow mixes blood with his
colours!"

He is certainly the Shakespeare of painting. I did not say that originally: I wish I had. It is worthy to have been said by you. How providentially did the man come in and invoke living, breathing, moving men and women out of his canvas! sometimes he is ranting and exaggerated as are all men of great genius, who wrestle with Nature so boldly. No doubt his heroines are more expansively endowed than would be thought genteel in our country, where cryptogams are so much in fashion; nevertheless with all his exaggerations there is always something very tremendous about him, and very often much that is sublime, pathetic, and moving. I defy any one of the average amount of imagination and sentiment to stand long before the 'Descent from the Cross' without being moved more nearly to tears than he would care to acknowledge. As for colour, his effects are as sure as those of the sun rising in a tropical landscape. There is something quite genial in the cheerful sense of his own omnipotence which always inspired him.

There are a few fine pictures of his here, and I go in sometimes of a raw foggy morning merely to warm myself in the blaze of their beauty.

I have just read over your letter again, rather well thumbed by this time, in order to see whether there was anything especially requiring an answer. I find no interrogations, but you speak of Thackeray and his lectures. Of course I know nothing of them, but I heard here that he was very much delighted *with you*—not the citizens of the U.S.A., but with O.W.H.

Mary sends you an infinite deal of the kindest remembrances. I wish you could come in and enliven our silent fireside (silent after the children have been got to bed) for one evening. My children are all very well and none the worse for their European experience.

Most affectionately yours,

J. L. M.

To his Wife.

Long's Hotel, New Bond Street, London,
Monday morning, May 8th, 1854.

MY DEAREST MARY,—You see I have arrived at my desti-
nation safe and sound. I reached the hotel last night about
11 P.M. The journey was not fatiguing to me. The trains
were not crowded, so that I was able to sit in a corner and
read quietly all day. We got to Calais at about 2.30, I think.
It blew pretty fresh, and there was a nasty chopping sea, so
that the deck was very wet. Almost every passenger was
sick. I was not, but should have been much better if I had
been. My head was so twisted about, that it will take
another four-and-twenty hours to put it straight again. If
I had been turned inside out, I should have been all right
to-day. Instead of which, I am sorry to tell you I am
suffering from one of my worst headaches at this moment,
so that I feel almost unable to write coherently. I knew you
would wish to hear of my safe arrival, and as my first and
last thought is you, I could not set about anything to-day
till I had sent you a line. I have a decentish kind of room
here, and I think I shall stop. I was certainly very fortunate
in the weather yesterday. The day was perfect for travelling
—no rain nor dust, nor too much sun. There was no rain in
crossing, so that I was able to go on deck the whole time. If
I had gone into the hospital below, I don't believe I should
have emerged alive. The groans which occasionally ascended
seemed as from a Gehenna. The vessel shipped so many seas,
however, that I was completely drenched; but as I never catch
cold, you know, that was of no consequence. You will be sorry
to hear that my great-coat, which you think shabby, was
almost entirely ruined with dust and salt-water commingled,
so that I bashfully requested the porter of this hotel this
morning to accept it, and was afraid that he would answer that
he did not like to deprive me of it. However, he thanked me
and took it. I am afraid when he looks at it he will return
it. My dear, dear Mary, I can't tell you how forlorn I am at

being separated from you. It seems to me that I can't go along through the day without seeing you. I have become, I fear, altogether too dependent upon you. I hope that you will not be melancholy. My company is not very lively; but in the evenings it is better than nothing, perhaps. You have the dear children, however. I hate to think of them now. Dear little Susie, she looked so wild yesterday morning sitting up in bed half-awake, wondering at my going. Kiss her twenty-one times for me, and give as many to my dear Lily and to my dear little Mary. I hope they will all be good children, and not give you any trouble while I am gone.

Ever thine,
J. L. M.

To his Wife.

Long's Hotel, Bond Street,
May 10th, 1854.

MY DEAREST MARY,—I wrote to you day before yesterday under the influence of a most ferocious headache, the natural consequence of my journey. That letter was all that I was capable of accomplishing that day. I called at the Sturgis's to-day, but all were out. Gardiner Hubbard and his wife are staying there. Gardiner called to-day upon me, but I was not at home. Yesterday I made an ineffectual attempt to see Mr. Forsyth. To-day I was more fortunate. I found him at his chambers in the Temple—a most intelligent, agreeable, gentleman-like barrister, about my own age I should guess. He was kind enough to look up for me all the English law of copyright as regards foreigners, and there is no doubt that the property of the American author is protected if he publishes *first*, by however small an interval, in England. We talked over the whole matter very thoroughly. He decidedly recommended my trying Murray first; gave me a note to him, with which, and with that from Dr. Thompson, I forthwith proceeded to the renowned publisher's door. Murray received me most civilly, and impressed me very agreeably. He seemed interested in my subject, and entertained the question of

publishing as favourably as I could expect. When I went
away, his porter accompanied me to my hotel, which is only
one street from Albemarle Street, where Murray resides, took
away the whole of the MS. in his bag, and it is at present
in the publisher's possession. Murray is to give me an answer
in a fortnight at farthest. So, at any rate, I have made one
step forward, and I don't see that I can take another. If
Murray refuses it after all, there will not be time to offer it
to another, and to wait for the decision. Therefore I shall in
that event try to make some arrangement to have it offered,
and have the answer sent me by letter. If Murray declines,
however, I shall doubt very much whether anybody will accept,
because history is very much in his line, and as I have been
particularly recommended to him, he would be more likely to
treat with me than anybody else. I must, therefore, pause
for a reply. Of course, I shall let you know as soon as I hear
from him.

Meantime, Mr. Forsyth came to see me here to-day; invited
me to dine next Monday; and is going to take me to the
Courts to-morrow, and to the House of Lords, before a Com-
mittee of which he is to argue a case. In the evening I mean
to go, if I can get a ticket, to the Opera—'Don Giovanni,'
and Bosio as Zerlina. But it makes me so sad to think that
you will not be at my side, that it will destroy all my
pleasure. I went at four o'clock to-day to the Noels'—found
Mrs. Noel at home. She received me in such a warm-hearted,
affectionate manner that I felt very much delighted. I called
yesterday at the Legation, and was introduced by Bigelow
Lawrence to Mr. Buchanan. He has obviously no intention
of returning my call, but he hoped I would call again. I shall
probably omit "calling round," however. I went to-day to see
Bigelow Lawrence's new wife. She is very pretty and pleasing.
By the way, I forgot to tell you that Arthur Forbes called on
me yesterday. I had called on him in the morning, found
him out, but was fortunate enough to be at home when he
called. He is just like them all—frank, agreeable, kind-
hearted. There, my dearest Mary, I have said all I have to
say. The amount is meagre enough. I am dreadfully home-

sick, and long to be in your arms. My dear children—it
seems impossible for me to exist the rest of the month without
them and you.   To-day the weather has been fine but cold.
Monday and Tuesday it poured pitilessly all the time.

Ever thine,

J. L. M.

To his Wife.

Long's Hotel, Bond Street,
Wednesday morning, May 18th, 1854.

MY DEAREST MARY,—As it is three days since I wrote last,
I am sitting down in my den before going down to the coffee-
room for breakfast, in order to scratch you hurriedly a few
lines merely to say that I am very well, and to thank you for
your dear letter, which I found upon the table the day before
yesterday morning.   I like Mr. Forsyth very much.   He is a
very good advocate.   I heard him argue an appeal case
yesterday before the House of Lords, that is to say before the
Lord Chancellor, two ex-Chancellors, and one or two otner
peers, sitting as a High Court of Appeal.   He spoke very well,
as did his colleagues in the case, although they are sure to
lose it.   By the way, I had also an opportunity of hearing the
Lord Chancellor, Lord Brougham, and Lord St. Leonards
deliver judgment successfully upon another case, and that was
about the most interesting thing I have seen in London.
Brougham is much flattered in *Punch*, the actual physiognomy being much more quizzical, but his manner is
impressive, and the old man has still much blood in him.
The present Chancellor, Lord Cranworth, is charming, presiding with most unaffected grace and suavity of manner,
courteous, smiling, gentle, with a constant attention to everything said by the counsel, and making all his interlocutory
observations in a most musical voice.

I dined on Sunday at the Sturgis's.   She is certainly
extremely handsome, much more so than she ever was.
Mrs. Hubbard and Gardiner made a thousand most affectionate inquiries about you.   After dinner, Mr. Cabot's health

was proposed by Sturgis.   Yesterday, in Bond Street, I came
plump upon Lord Wynford.   He was passing, but half looked
at me.   When I accosted him and told him my name, he was
extremely cordial, shook me warmly by both hands, hoped I
could come to see him, etc., etc.   We talked five or six minutes
in the street, and separated affectionately.   He made the most
earnest inquiries after you, for whom I am sure he has a
sincere liking.

Ever your own
J. L. M.

To his Mother.

. . . I went last Friday night and heard a long and dull
debate in the House of Commons.   Such speakers as Webster
and Choate are not to be scared up in England just now.   I don't
say this in glorification of our free and enlightened Republic.
Don't suspect me of too much patriotism.   I have vastly more
respect for the Government of England than for our own—
the nation I can't help considering governed by higher principles of action, by loftier motives.   They at least try to
reform abuses and admit their existence.   We love our diseases, and cling to them as the only source of health and
strength.   When you look at America from a distance, you
see that it is a great machine for constantly extending the
growth of cotton and expanding the area of negro slavery.
This is the real motive power of our whole political existence,
and such a principle can only carry us over a precipice; yet all
who lift their tongues and voices against the course, or who
express their disgust at the hypocrisy of a nation prating of
freedom when its whole aim is to perpetuate slavery, are
esteemed mischievous and malignant.   England is just now,
with the most tremendous naval armament which ever existed
in the world, engaging reluctantly in a war of duty to oppose the
encroachments of the Eastern despotism; and we are playing
the part of Russia in the West, and seizing the opportunity,
while France and Great Britain are otherwise occupied, to

pick a quarrel with Spain, and so steal Cuba, and annex half a million more negroes.   However, I don't see the use of my boring you with all these profound reflections.   If the governor abuses me for want of patriotism, he ought to recollect that his patriotism took root and grew up when General Washington, Alexander Hamilton, John Jay, George Cabot, and others, were the guiding spirits of the country.   We are now in the epoch of . . . . and it is hard to revere such creatures, or the country which looks to them for guidance.

To his Father.

Vevey,
March 3rd, 1855.

MY DEAR FATHER,—In answer to your P.S. to Susie's letter received yesterday, I would say that I am quite aware of the dictum of Lord Cranworth to which Mr. Prescott alluded.   I am not able to take advantage of it, however, as the expense of going a second time to England would be more than the copyright is worth.   I suppose the time of publication will be about Christmas, at which season I should be in Italy.   To leave my family and go to England and return again, would be very expensive, and hardly worth while to secure a copyright which I could not sell for £100.   It may be very well for Mr. Prescott to do so, as he can sell his books for £1000 a volume or more.   Please tell him, by the way, with my particular regards, that I have been upon the point of writing to him every day for the last four years, that I have not done so is because I cannot overcome my repugnance to writing and talking about myself, and I have nothing else to talk about, leading such a recluse and obscure existence.   We had a perfect understanding about our respective plans before I went away.   I remember that he thought that it might be better if we should arrange to publish at somewhat different times, as the works are a good deal upon the same subject.   As this is a consideration, however, which only affects me, as my work can't interfere with the sale of his, I have never thought it a

matter of great consequence, particularly as I don't know, and
never shall know, when I ought to publish.

Now I am on the subject, however, I wish you would add
that my work (that is to say the portion of it which is really
for publication) stops at the year 1584, with the death of the
Prince of Orange. This was unavoidable, as it was quite impossible for me to speculate in more than three volumes at
once; and although I have cut away at my MS. with a broad
axe in order to reduce it, I can't squeeze it into less. If I
receive enough encouragement, which I don't expect, to finish
this work, I shall write three more volumes, in order to bring
my history down to the Peace of Westphalia, 1648. Philip
the Second, although he is, of course, the *Deus ex machina* in
much of my present work, is not my head devil, and he will
have still less, and almost nothing, to do in the continuation.

I still mean to write to Mr. Prescott, but I thought I
would send him this message through you, for I would not
have him think me forgetful of the many acts of kindness
and friendship which I have received at his hands, and it
is possible that he might wish to hear my plans. With
regard to my time of publication, I am inclined to leave that
to you.[1] You, in the most generous manner, have constituted yourself my fellow-victim, and you shall choose the
time of immolation. I suppose by the time this reaches
you, or very soon afterwards, the two copies of Volume I.
will be received. I have already mentioned in my letter to
Annie[2] all that I have to say thereanent. I should not like
Mr. Cabot to see it till it is finished, because I know he
would feel an interest in it, and it will seem so flat taken in
piecemeal. The same principle applies to Uncle Edward. I
should not like him to read it till he can do it all at once, and
make a job of it. At the same time it is, of course, quite at
his service if he chooses to do so. I am afraid that he will be
a good deal of the opinion of the old gentleman to whom
Jedediah Cleishbotham showed the first series of the 'Tales of
My Landlord.' The friendly critic informed the author, you

---

[1] Mr. Motley's first historic work,   was published in 1856.
'The Rise of the Dutch Republic,'   [2] His sister, Mrs. Alfred Rodman.

know, that he has lately been reading a work which gave him
no peace at all, that he had not been able, however desirous,
to lay it down till he had read every line of it. On the other
hand, he congratulated Jedediah that his work had no such
defect, but that it was one which could be laid down at any
moment with the utmost tranquillity. This would be rather a
reason for the sage of Fort Hill[1] to begin upon the ponderous
task at the earliest opportunity. At the same time I advise
him not to do so. I shall write again before long, before it will
be necessary to square our accounts, which won't be till the
autumn, I suppose, when the job will have to be paid for. My
love, and all our loves, to my dear mother, as well as yourself.

Ever yours affectionately,

J. L. M.

To his Wife.

Frankfort,

July 27th, 1855.

MY DEAREST MARY,—The waiters have brought me a tremendously large sheet of paper, but I am afraid that I shall
hardly be able to fill it up in a very interesting manner. My
journey to Basel, notwithstanding the rain, was pleasant
enough. The road is not at all interesting, all the beauty
being in the Minster Thal, in the other direction. My companion in the *coupé* was an old *épicier,* or something of the
kind, from Berlin, who appeared to have been making the
first journey of his life. He had been up the Rigi, the Wen-
gern Alp, etc., and although he seemed about seventy-five, he
assured me he had suffered no fatigue. He had no teeth, but,
en revanche, had a bouquet of Alpine roses in his hatband. His
artless prattle was very refreshing for a little while, but when
he began to put the usual questions about my intentions,
objects in life, occupations, etc., he became a bore, and I took
refuge in a novel. . . . The journey to Basel only occupied ten
hours, the last hour on the railway, so that you get to the
hotel soon after five. . . . The next morning I started from the

---

[1] His uncle, Edward Motley, a most kind friend.

railway terminus (the railroad is finished to Basel) at 7.30, and reached Frankfort at 4.30. As soon as I was dressed I started for Bismarck's house, having previously learned that Keyserling,[1] to my great regret, had not arrived.

When I called, Bismarck was at dinner, so I left my card, and said I would come back in half an hour. As soon as my card had been carried to him (as I learned afterwards) he sent a servant after me to the hotel, but I had gone another way. When I came back I was received with open arms. I can't express to you how cordially he received me.[2] If I had been his brother, instead of an old friend, he could not have shown more warmth and affectionate delight in seeing me. I find I like him even better than I thought I did, and you know how high an opinion I always expressed of his talents and disposition. He is a man of very noble character, and of very great powers of mind. The prominent place which he now occupies as a statesman sought *him*. He did not seek it, or any other office. The stand which he took in the Assembly from conviction, on the occasion of the outbreak of 1848, marked him at once to all parties as one of the leading characters of Prussia. Of course I don't now go into the rights and wrongs of the matter, but I listened with great interest, as you may suppose, to his detailed history of the revolutionary events of that year, and his share in them, which he narrated to me in a long conversation which we had last night. He wanted me to stay entirely in his house, but as he has his wife's father and mother with him, and as I saw that it was necessary to put up a bed in a room where there was none, I decidedly begged off. I breakfasted there this morning, and am to dine there, with a party, to-day. To-morrow, I suppose, I shall dine there *en famille*. I am only afraid that the landlord here will turn me into the streets for being such a poor *consommateur* for him, and all I can do is to order vast quantities of seltzer water.

The principal change in Bismarck is that he has grown

---

[1] Count Hermann Keyserling, a fellow-student at Göttingen.

[2] It was the first time they had met since leaving the Universities of Göttingen and Berlin.

stouter, but, being over six feet, this is an improvement.
His voice and manner are singularly unchanged. His wife
I like very much indeed—very friendly, intelligent, and per-
fectly unaffected, and treats me like an old friend. In short,
I can't better describe the couple than by saying that they
are as unlike M. and Madame de —— as it is possible to be.

In the summer of 1851, he told me that the Minister,
Manteuffel, asked him one day abruptly, if he would accept
the post of Ambassador at Frankfort, to which (although the
proposition was as unexpected a one to him as if I should
hear by the next mail that I had been chosen Governor of
Massachusetts) he answered, after a moment's deliberation,
yes, without another word. The King, the same day, sent for
him, and asked him if he would accept the place, to which
he made the same brief answer, " Ja." His Majesty expressed
a little surprise that he made no inquiries or conditions,
when Bismarck replied that anything which the King felt
strong enough to propose to him, he felt strong enough to
accept. I only write these details that you may have an idea
of the man. Strict integrity and courage of character, a high
sense of honour, a firm religious belief, united with remarkable
talents, make up necessarily a combination which cannot be
found any day in any Court ; and I have no doubt that he is
destined to be Prime Minister, unless his obstinate truth-
fulness, which is apt to be a stumbling-block for politicians,
stands in his way. . . .

Well, he accepted the post and wrote to his wife next day,
who was preparing for a summer's residence in a small house
they had taken on the sea coast, that he could not come
because he was already established in Frankfort as Minister.
The result, he said, was three days of tears on her part. He
had previously been leading the life of a plain country squire
with a moderate income, had never held any position in the
Government or in diplomacy, and had hardly ever been to
Court. He went into the office with a holy horror of the
mysterious nothings of diplomacy, but soon found how little
there was in the whole " galimatias." Of course my politics
are very different from his, although not so antipodal as you

might suppose, but I can talk with him as frankly as I could with you, and I am glad of an opportunity of hearing the other side put by a man whose talents and character I esteem, and who so well knows *le dessous des cartes.* M. de Veh is here, but goes back to Vevey, I believe, to-morrow. Bismarck has invited him to dinner to-day. He is as surprised as I not to find Keyserling, and can't account for his absence. Good-bye, my dearest Mary, I have got to the end of the sheet without saying a word about you and my darlings. . . .

To his Wife.

Frankfort,
Saturday, July 28th, 1855.

I have just consented to wait here until Wednesday morning. . . . I send the despatch from Bismarck's house, and I have just come back to write you this hurried line, as I must go back to dine with him at four. Madame de Bismarck begs me to convey the kindest messages on her part to you, and to say that she depends upon the pleasure of making your acquaintance here this autumn or the end of the summer, and I have promised that we will stop a day or two in Frankfort on our way to Paris. I am perfectly sure that you will like her—you could not help it. She is so amiable, gentle and agreeable in every way, that I feel as if we had been ten years acquainted. She and her mother have both assured me over and over again that Bismarck was nearly out of his wits with delight when he saw my card. *I should certainly not say such a thing to anybody but you,* but you and I are not so overburdened with self-esteem but that we may afford to tell each other the truth in such matters, and it really gives me pleasure to know that a man of whom I think so highly has such a warm and sincere friendship for me. · I am sure that you will like him, and I only regret that we can see so little or nothing of each other for the rest of our lives. There are three children—a little girl named Marie, as sweet as Susie, to whom I gave this morning a little locket in

Susie's name, and told her that Susie would give her a lock
of red hair to put in it when she saw her. She put her arms
round my neck and kissed me, and trotted off in the greatest
glee to show it to her grandpapa and grandmamma.

I feel as much at home already as at Mr. Cabot's, and I should
have almost as little fear of wearing out my welcome here as
there. At the dinner yesterday were some strangers—Prus-
sians—Count Roedern, brother of the Prussian Minister in
Dresden, and his wife and sister. M. de Veh was there, and
as friendly and agreeable as ever. He is off this morning to
Schwalbach, and to-morrow returns to Vevey. After dinner,
Bismarck and his wife, myself, and a youthful *attaché* with
the terrific name of Baron Schreckenstein, took a long ride
on horseback in a beautiful forest on the other side of the
Main, and on our return found M. de Veh and the father-in-
law still deeply absorbed at the chess-table where we had left
them. At eleven o'clock we tried very hard to eat supper,
but nobody succeeded very well, and at twelve I came home.

To his Wife.

Frankfort,
Monday, July 30th, 1855.

. . . . The Bismarcks are as kind as ever—nothing can be
more frank and cordial than her manners. I am there all day
long. It is one of those houses where every one does what
one likes. The show apartments where they receive formal
company are on the front of the house. Their living rooms,
however, are a *salon* and dining room at the back, opening
upon the garden. Here there are young and old, grandparents and children and dogs all at once, eating, drinking,
smoking, piano-playing, and pistol-firing (in the garden), all
going on at the same time. It is one of those establishments
where every earthly thing that can be eaten or drunk is offered
you, porter, soda water, small beer, champagne, burgundy or
claret are about all the time, and everybody is smoking the
best Havana cigars every minute. Last night we went to the

theatre to see the first part of 'Henry IV.' The Falstaff was
tolerable, the others very indifferent. By the way I was glad to
find that both Bismarck and his wife agree with me that Emil
Devrient was a very second-rate actor. I must go out directly
and buy a brooch for my dear little Mary. Little Bill, as the
Bismarcks call their youngest boy of two years, was born on
the same day, and I am going to buy him a trumpet. A
thousand kisses to Lily, Mary and Susie, and accept for
yourself the fondest and deepest affection of

Your own
J. L. M.

To his Wife.

Long's Hotel,
Thursday morning, October 18th, 1855.

MY DEAREST MARY,—I write these few lines merely to tell
you that I arrived *sain et sauf* in London yesterday forenoon
at half-past ten. I crossed the Channel at three. The weather
was very good, and the sea very smooth. The ladies on board
were all desperately sea-sick, much to my astonishment, such
demonstrations being entirely unauthorised by any of the
circumstances. I stopped at Dover for the night, finding it
very ridiculous to hurry up to London at midnight, as everybody in that metropolis was likely to get on very well without
me till the following morning. The inn, the "Lord Warden
Hotel," is one of the best in England. My washing-stand in
itself was enough to inspire one with veneration for the whole
British nation; two great water jugs as big as those in the
'Marriage of Cana,' by Paolo Veronese, a wash basin big enough
to swim in, celestial slop jars, heaps of clean towels, etc., and
more water than was ever seen in one place in Paris, except
in the Écoles de Natation, all made one feel very comfortable.
A Frenchman would have been wretched, however, for there
were not two clocks or even four mirrors in the chamber, but I
solaced myself with the remembrance of the splendour I had
left in Paris, and with the potentiality of being clean a few
brief days in England. I am sorry, however, to say that I am

not as well off here. I have a good enough bachelor chamber,
but it looks like a hospital for invalided or incurable furniture.
The bed is as wide as Oxford Street, it is also quite as hard,
the mattresses being evidently stuffed with paving stones
from that classic and stony-hearted step-mother. I stopped at
Chapman's on my way up from the railroad, so commenced
business sooner than if I had not slept at Dover, filled up the
form of application for the copyright, and in short did all that
was necessary before coming to Long's. We have decided of
course to defer actual publication till the other (American
edition) is ready. . . .

Ever your own

J. L. M.

To his Mother.

Florence,

November 18th, 1855.

MY DEAREST MOTHER,—We have arrived at the only stopping place which we shall have for a long time to come,
having taken lodgings for three months in a quiet house with
the southern sun upon it. . . . You have been aware of our
whereabouts by the letters which Mary has occasionally
written, and by the notes which have been dropping between
the governor and me from time to time. I can't omit
this opportunity of expressing my deep gratitude to him for
his most efficient and generous assistance in the matter of
my history. I am highly gratified with the pleasure which
the work seems to have afforded to him, to you, to Uncle
Edward, and other members of the family, and I beg you to
thank Tom for the great trouble he has taken in regard to the
matter. I fear very much, however, that the governor and
the rest are doomed to much disappointment in regard to
its success. It cannot take in England, and moreover the war,
Macaulay's new volumes, and Prescott's, will entirely absorb
the public attention. I am extremely gratified that Hillard
has been so kind as to write an article upon the book. I
think that the governor quoted his opinion, as upon the

whole favourable, and certainly nobody could be more competent to review it, or can write more brilliantly. I think something was said about his only having time to write a short
article. I would rather he should take time and defer it to
the April number, than not have ample room and verge
enough allowed him. The book is so ponderous that it
ought to sustain a weighty article. Of course the governor
will pay heed to this suggestion, and so no more of this
subject. We left Vevey after more than a year's residence
(very profitably employed for the children) towards the end of
July. We passed some little time in Berne, at which place I
left my family in charge of the Fays, in order to make a visit
to an old University friend of mine, Baron Bismarck, with
whom I was very intimate twenty years ago in Göttingen and
Berlin, and who is now almost the most important statesman
in Prussia.

During my absence, Mary and the children have passed
the time very agreeably in Berne, owing to the constant and
unremitting attentions of Fay [1] (our Minister to Switzerland)
and his wife. I believe I have mentioned them often in my
letters. If not, I will only say that he is almost the best man
I ever knew, one who is never thoroughly happy unless he is
conferring a favour upon some one else. You may judge of
the pain which was caused to all of us a few weeks afterwards,
by our hearing at Interlaken of Mrs. Fay's death. Fay wrote
to me repeatedly during her illness, and telegraphed to me at
its melancholy termination, and I went immediately to Berne,
and was with him till after the funeral. She was a very
honest, frank, kind-hearted, devoted person, and is an irrepar-
able loss to her husband and her only child. They came
afterwards to Interlaken for a little while. He bears the loss
very well, being, fortunately for himself, the most believing
and devout Christian I ever knew. I have not heard from him
since we left Switzerland, but I shall write to him to-morrow.

Upon leaving Switzerland, we passed a month in Paris.
I don't like to say much about that episode in our history,
because the immense fatigue and expense of passing four

[1] Theodore S. Fay.

weeks in that place so entirely counter-balances all satisfaction which can be derived from it, that I cannot speak
upon the subject without injustice and exaggeration. At
the same time, there is no doubt that the city itself is the
most beautiful in the world. Most of the works of improvement going on there now are very extensive and expensive, and many of them have been carried on at a sacrifice of much that was striking and picturesque in ancient
Paris. They are occasioning vast outlay, for which a heavy
debt has been created, partly by the State, partly by the
Municipality, to defray the interest of which the taxes are
rising daily. It is also very difficult for small tradesmen and
mechanics to get houses and shops, all having been pulled
down in many quarters to make room for lengthening lines of
palaces and arcades, which yield no lodgings for poor devils.
Yet it is the custom to say that Louis Napoleon is doing
wonders in providing work for the poor people. I suppose if
the Massachusetts Legislature and the Boston City Government should create a debt of $40,000,000, in order to build
a palace, reaching from the old State House to Roxbury Line,
for Governor Armstrong and his descendants to live in, and if
they should create a further debt, in order to knock down all
the town between Park Street Church and Copp's Hill, and
put up in the place of the demolished buildings a series of
granite, eight-storey palaces with continuous arcades, it would
be considered an act of great wisdom and benevolence, considering the number of Irish hodmen and other labourers who
would be sure to get employment, and yet this is pretty much
what is going on in Paris.

After leaving Paris, we took the train to Lyons, stopping one
night in Dijon. At Lyons, we found by appointment an Italian
vetturino, with whom we had made many journeys in Switzerland, and who has four very good horses and a comfortable
carriage. With him we went to Chambery, over the Mont
Cenis to Turin, and then by rail to Genoa, where we resumed
our *vetturino*, and came with him to Florence, for a *vetturino's*
horses are like " the pampered jades of Asia," which, according to Ancient " Pistol," cannot go but " forty miles a day."

We found Frank Boott here, who had kindly saved us much trouble by looking over the vacant lodgings, so that our work was much simplified. . . . We spent an evening with Mr. and Mrs. Putnam last week. The Alexanders were there, and we saw a large quantity of Fanny Alexander's drawings, and I assure you they are really wonderful.[1] She draws entirely with pen and ink, composing out of her own imagination or from her recollection. But her facility and grace and purity of style are unequalled by any modern drawings which I ever saw. She has the good taste to form her artistic education in the school of the wonderful Quattro Centisti of Florence, the painters, I mean, of the fifteenth century, whose works have spread such a halo of glory around this city, and which heralded the extraordinary effulgence which was to illumine the world in the early part of the fifteenth century. In these pre-Raphaelite productions Florence is very rich. Miss Alexander has not tried her hand at painting yet, although she believes herself to have more feeling for colour than for any other department of Art. She draws outlines, human figures, Madonnas, peasant girls, saints in endless variety, and illustrates old Italian songs, of which she furnishes herself very pretty translations. She is a young person of unquestionable genius, and as simple and unaffected as she is clever. There is also a sculptor here named Thomas Ball, who came out here a year and a half ago, and who is now going home again. He has modelled a very admirable statuette of Washington Allston, and would like very much to have an order to execute it in marble. I wish you would go with the governor to see it when he arrives, which will be in spring or early summer. Ask Mr. Frank Gray to look at it. I should not have written you to-day, my dear mother, feeling that I have nothing to say which can possibly amuse you, had I not received a letter from Chapman yesterday, in which he says he is to publish my History forthwith.

Ever your affectionate son,

J. L. M.

---

[1] Miss Alexander still lives at Florence.

To his Uncle, Edward Motley.

Florence,
December 13th, 1855.

MY DEAR UNCLE EDWARD,—I have been intending day after day and week after week to write to you. I am sorry that your last generous present of £100 arrived before I had written, because it looks almost now as if I proposed to make payment by a few sheets of notepaper, and I am afraid that even your indulgence would hardly consider my letters as cheap at such a price. I don't pretend to thank you for all your generosity. I have already told you that your constant kindness has made me a bankrupt in the means of repaying you even in words just now; I feel as it were overwhelmed by the liberality with which I have been treated both by you and the governor. I am sure I don't know how I should have extricated myself from my printing and publishing difficulties but for the timely and most generous assistance which I have received.

I wish I knew how I could make a letter interesting or amusing to you. The truth is that I am so oppressed by a constitutional melancholy, which grows upon me very rapidly, as to be almost incapacitated from making myself agreeable. You know how to sympathise with this frame of mind, and I should apologise to you for talking about my blue devils, when I know that you are yourself haunted, except that I thought by sending a swarm of them across the Atlantic, they might have an encounter with the legions there, and mutually destroy each other.

Florence is thought in many respects to be the most beautiful town in Europe, yet I suppose few people ever look about them at first without astonishment that it should ever have attained such a reputation. The reason is that the city itself is but the central point of a vast periphery of palaces, villas, castles and villages, which extend over the large basin of the Arno. The city itself is compact—the gates are narrow; the houses vast, massive, and sombre, with fortress-like walls, narrow windows, and huge butting cornices; the churches

heavy, stern, and gloomy. The territory in the midst of
which the town has been standing one or two thousand years
(to be precise) is singularly beautiful. The City of Flowers
(for that is its fragrant appellation) is built upon a garden.
A flat, verdant, luxuriant plain of three or four miles in width
is encircled by a chain of gently flowing mountains; and if
there ever were any little hills which "clapped their hands
and skipped like lambs" according to the Psalmist, these are
the ones to do it. The character of the environs is as jocund
as that of the city is sombre. All the hills are sown broadcast
with palaces and castellated mansions, monasteries and villages
gleaming whitely through silvery forests of olives, luxuriant
vines and solemn cypresses. The town itself, with the towers
and belfries in its centre, is but the heart of the vast flower;
the stamens and pistils and inner petals are here, while the
beautiful and vast corolla unfolds itself far and wide as far as
the eye can reach. To feel this, one has but to ascend any
steeple of any height outside the town, and see how Florence
is wrapped up and encircled by a series of little Florences.

The Arno is not much of a river in appearance, yellow and
shallow and full of gravel banks, yet it serves to keep green
the velvet cushions upon which the luxurious city lies extended like Cleopatra on a couch. The river is however capable
of much mischief, and in times past has produced inundations
very like the deluge. Five hundred years ago the whole town
was laid under water to the depth of ten feet. Since the
canalisation of the river to Leghorn, however, such pranks have
become impossible; but even last year the whole country
round was overflowed, and it was almost as bad this autumn.
It is not used, I need not say, for purposes of navigation, and
it would be quite impossible now for a city placed as this is
to attain to a tithe of the commercial and political importance
which it enjoyed in the 14th and 15th centuries. If one
subtracts from the list of articles of commerce such trifles as
tea and coffee, sugar, tobacco and cotton, which make up
pretty much the whole bulk of the world's merchandise just
now, one can understand how a city which from its position
could take no part in such traffic, could rise to eminence at a

time when those necessaries of life had not been invented.
Before compasses, Capes of Good Hope and Horn, Californias
and Hong Kongs came into fashion, it was easy for a few
cities to monopolise the business of the world's little inter-
changes of commodities. Genoa had its factories in the Crimea
and received the caravans from the North and East; Venice,
its colonies in the Levant, and Florence, with its great banking
houses and manufactories, its large capital, its sound metallic
currency, its corn and oil, received the golden streams as they
flowed from the urns of its sister cities, and conducted them
northward through the marble aqueduct of a few splendid cities
in Germany and the Netherlands. All this is changed now.

Moreover the trade and the enterprise of the city flourished
only during its republican organisation. I think the advocates of a democratic system had better rest their case on the
achievements of two cities, Athens and Florence. I doubt if
either, in the day of their greatness, were very comfortable
places to live in, but there can be no question that the
amount of intellectual vigour displayed by both at the
epoch of their utmost turbulence, was superior to anything
ever heard of in history. The fierce rivalries and passions
of Florence—the constant conflicts of mind with mind,
man with man, and mass with mass—the never-ceasing
human attrition, brought out intellectual electricity enough
to make the whole world vibrate so long that its throbs are
still distinctly felt and traceable to their cause—intellectual
flame enough to light the torches of civilisation over the earth
after they had been extinguished in the Gothic deluge—
intellectual names brilliant and numerous enough to people
the whole firmament with immortal constellations. We are
proud of Boston as the Athens of America, but we shall be
prouder when she has produced, even with Portland and
Newburyport to back her, such names as Dante, Petrarch,
Boccaccio, Cimabue, Giotto, Arnolfo, Brunelleschi, Leonardo
da Vinci, Michel Angelo, Macchiavelli, and Galileo; and I
only mention names such as rise spontaneously like spirits
when the magic name of Florence is pronounced—names
which have echoed for centuries everywhere in the world

where the progress and the triumphs of the human intellect in the various fields of the Arts and Sciences are looked upon with sympathy. Hundreds of other names might be mentioned, known not only to scholars but to the world at large ; and it must be confessed that no satisfactory reason can be given for such splendid corruscations of genius around one single spot but the vivifying presence of political liberty.

The period of this liberty was a short one and a turbulent one. It was coincident, however, with the revival of letters and of civilisation. It was in Italy that the spirit of municipal liberty first roused itself, after it had been crushed by Rome, and buried under Roman ruins by the brutal, blundering but juvenile energies of the German races. Five centuries after the fall of the Western Empire—until nearly a thousand years from the birth of Christ—lasted the syncope, the comatose trance of Europe, and with her first struggles after awaking from her lethargy, the little, now almost forgotten Republics of Amalfi and Naples became visible. Here the elements of Greek, Roman, Byzantine, and Saracen civilisation are preserved and combined—and transferred to the more vigorous municipalities of Pisa and Florence. A couple of centuries of fighting between the Emperors of Germany and the Popes of Rome succeed, during which the cities of Italy seek a shield against imperial oppression in the assistance of the Church. Here was the fatal flaw by which the vase of Italian liberty was cracked when it was first moulded. To go for liberty, human progress, intellectual development, and to expect these things by fighting under the banner of the Church was a delusion to be sure, but it was a fiction which, like many other poetical fables, did good work. The Church party, the Guelphs, were in reality a phalanx of intellectual opposition to imperial and brutal dominion. Papal Rome, even while inventing the Inquisition and the mendicant orders, was the champion of Cities against Kaisers ; and this is the principal good that the Church has ever accomplished.

With the downfall of the Suabian dynasty, at the close of the thirteenth century, Florence, which has long had a republican but aristocratic organisation, while alternatively resisting and acknowledging the sovereignty of the Emperors, is strong enough to set up for itself. Thirty years the noble families of the place have been at feud, fighting like Kilkenny cats till nothing is left but their tails, calling themselves Guelphs and Ghibellines, but ranging themselves on one side or the other solely according to their relationship to one of two families which had been set by the ears in consequence of a young gentleman jilting a young lady whom he was to marry thirty or forty years previously. Thirty years of this kind of work have weakened the pugnacious capabilities of these families, and their result is that the tails as aforesaid—all that is left of this very quarrelsome species—are thrown out of the place altogether. It is a curious fact that not only were the nobles deprived of political power, entirely disfranchised by the Florentine Republic, when at this epoch it first "made the people," as its early statutes express it, but it became a mode of punishment, and one often inflicted, to degrade individuals and families by making them noble. In a single year five or six hundred persons have been chastised for political offences by seeing their names enrolled in the lists of the nobility; and this example was followed by the municipal authorities of other cities governed or controlled by Florence.

No doubt this was a stupid as well as a virulent proceeding. It kept an organised band of powerful, disaffected, and dangerous brigands ever ready to pounce upon the democratic city which had provoked their hatred and their vengeance, while it established in time a second class of nobility, an office-holding oligarchy of mere vulgar origin, without purer motives, by which the liberty of Florence was eventually overthrown. The duration of this liberty was, after all, wonderfully short. The democracy was established at the close of the thirteenth century, and at the beginning of the fifteenth the Medician oligarchy had succeeded. By the middle of the sixteenth the Medici were made into Grand Dukes of Tuscany, and there is an end of Florence. That family died out before the middle of the eighteenth century; and as there happened to be a poor king going about at that time without a crown to his back—one Stanislaus Lecszinski, whose daughter had married the respectable Louis XV. of France—it was thought desirable to make him Duke of Lorraine. There being, however, a Duke of Lorraine, who objected to being unduked, he was pitchforked into Florence, much to his disgust, and was very much astonished afterwards to find that the degrading step had ended in making him Emperor of Germany. Francis of Lorraine, Duke of Tuscany, married with the Empress Maria Theresa, and saw himself and family established on the throne of the Cæsars. Thus Tuscany is a sort of appanage for the younger sons of the Hapsburg family. One reigning Grand Duke has already succeeded to the imperial throne, and transferred the duchy to a younger son; and the present Grand Duke, who has reigned for many years, was naturally set up in business again, after the general smash in 1848, by his powerful relations at Vienna.

Florence is, however, freed at present from the Austrian occupation, and things seem to go on peaceably. Provided a man does not talk politics or read the Bible, he gets on well enough. This would be somewhat of a deduction from the daily habits of New Englanders, but the Tuscans have been so long having their skins taken off that they like it. Of the present aspect of the place, therefore, in a political point of view, I shall not discourse. Florence is a dead city—a splendid tortoise shell, from which the living animal has long since disappeared. The shell will, however, be long an object of wonder. There is no town in the world of its size which contains such a profusion of works of art. There are three large galleries of pictures. All of them together would, perhaps, be equal to the gallery at Dresden, which singly, however, surpasses any one of them. The best gallery, that of the Pitti Palace, is exactly opposite our doors, so that it is easy for us to look at the finest pictures in the world from 9 A.M. to 3 P.M., quite enough to satisfy any reasonable person. I shall not begin to you about pictures, however, because nothing could be more *jejune* than any description of masterpieces which I could send. A catalogue is an extremely convenient thing to have in one's pocket when in a gallery, but the dullest of literary performances would be a running commentary from me to you about pictures which you never saw, and never intend to see. At the same time I feel sure that if you were here you would enjoy them as much as I do. Hillard has written the best book upon Italy which I have ever read. The charms of style and of word-painting can go no further, and his pages have the effect of finely coloured photographs of the scenes he has visited. It is so difficult to fix the fleeting impression produced in one's mental camera obscura by an object seen but for a moment, that I quite wonder at his success. I have saved reading the book till on the spot, and am glad of having done so. At the same time it indisposes me to send home Italian descriptions. Nothing can be more scholarly and elegant than the whole expression of his book; and, although I should occasionally dissent from some of his criticisms upon the old masters, yet I admire it on the whole very much. I shall say no more, because, as I have already had the pleasure of receiving a kind word of approval from him in a postscript to the governor's kind letter, you will think I am trying to get into the Mutual Admiration Society.

Perhaps you would like to know a little of prices, if I have not already bored you sufficiently by my historical and political disquisitions. Before you condemn me, however, for lengthiness on those topics, think what you have escaped. Florence, according to one of its oldest chroniclers, was built by the great-grandson of Noah, who came to Tuscany "to escape the confusion growing out of the Tower of Babel." That being the case, it has probably grown up, little by little, to its present size, just as Calais did, according to the theory of Tristram Shandy; and I might have given you a much larger dose of history if I had taken up matters at the fountain head, that is, at the Deluge.

A good house, or lodging as large as a house, without furniture, and on a lease of two or three years, could be had for $300 a year. Beef and bread, the two staves of life, are 10 and 5 cents a pound respectively. A respectable turkey, such as would not be ashamed to see himself roasted on

Thanksgiving Day in Portland, costs 50 cents. A pair of
fowls, 30 to 40 cents. A cauliflower, as big as your head,
3 cents. Celery, and such things, pretty much nothing at all.
Groceries, however, are comparatively dear. Tea, coffee, and
other colonials, as they call them, rather dearer than with us.
Cotton is dearer; ladies' apparel dearer; men's clothing much
cheaper. Lessons of all kinds (except first-rate musical
instruction, which is $1 a lesson) average about 30 cents an
hour, whether for one or half a dozen pupils. You see that
for a resident Florence is, as compared to Boston, fabulously
cheap. A passing stranger gets no great advantage, however.
I hope to be able to write you again very soon, if you have
not had enough of this. Meantime Mary and the children
desire to be most affectionately remembered to you.

Believe me, yours affectionately,

J. L. M.

To his Mother.

Florence,
April 1st. 1856.

MY DEAREST MOTHER,—We decided to pass the winter in
Florence, principally because the children would have the
benefits of instruction at a cheaper rate. We shall probably
go from Rome to Naples early in May, and return by steamer
either to Genoa, and thence over the Simplon, or direct to
Marseilles, a voyage which I dread, and hope not to make.
Our plans, however, are somewhat foggy. I have heard nothing
from Chapman touching the sale of my book, and suppose that
very few copies have been sold.[1] It has been very favourably
received in the *Athenæum*, the *Press*, and some other papers,
and Mr. Froude's article in the *Westminster Review* for April
is uncommonly well written and extremely flattering. I
have heard of nothing more, and if the edition is eventually
sold, it must be a long time first. It takes a good time to
read such a long work. We parted with Frank Boott and

---

[1] Seventeen thousand copies were sold in England during the first year of
publication.

L—— with great regret. We have seen them constantly
since our arrival here, and have passed much time very
agreeably together. He has the same excellent and sterling
qualities and truthful character which he always had, and she
is a very interesting and intelligent child.

Your affectionate son,
J. L. M.

From Mr. W. H. Prescott.

Boston,
April 28th, 1856.

MY DEAR MOTLEY,—I am much obliged to you for the copy
of the 'History of the Dutch Republic' which you have been
so kind as to send me. A work of that kind is not to be run
through in a few days, particularly by one who does his reading chiefly through his ears. I shall take my own time therefore for going thoroughly through the book, which I certainly
shall do from beginning to end, notes inclusive. Meantime I
have yielded to my impatience of seeing what sort of stuff it
is made of by pitching here and there into various places,
particularly those with which I am most familiar myself and
which would be most likely to try your power as a writer.
The result of a considerable amount of reading in this way
has satisfied me that you have more than fulfilled the pre-
diction which I had made respecting your labours to the
public. Everywhere you seem to have gone into the subject
with a scholar-like thoroughness of research, furnishing me
on my own beaten track with a quantity of new facts and
views, which I was not aware it could present to the reader.
In one passage I remember, the sack of St. Quentin, you give
a variety of startling and very interesting particulars, and
when I envied you the resources at your command for
supplying them to you, I found they were all got from a
number of the 'Documentos Ineditos' which slept harmlessly
on my shelves from my own unconsciousness that it contained
anything germain to the matter. Your descriptions are everywhere graphic and picturesque. One familiar with your

romances, will not be surprised at your powers in this way.
But yet after all the style for history is as different from what
is required for romance as that of a great historical picture is
from a scene-painting for a theatre. You prove that you
possess both. Your portraiture of character is vigorous and
animated, full of characteristic touches, from a pencil that is
dipped in the colours of the old masters.

You have laid it on Philip rather hard. Indeed you have
whittled him down to such an imperceptible point that there
is hardly enough of him left to hang a newspaper paragraph
on, much less five or six volumes of solid history as I propose
to do. But then you make it up with your own hero, William
of Orange, and I comfort myself with the reflection that you
are looking through a pair of Dutch spectacles after all. As
to the backbone of the work, the unfolding of the great
revolution, I am not in a condition to criticise that, as no one
can be who has not read the work carefully through. But I
have conversed with several, not merely your personal friends,
who have done so, and they bear emphatic testimony to the
power you have exhibited, in presenting the subject in an
original and piquant way to the reader. Indeed you have seen
enough of criticism probably from the presses of this country
and of England, to satisfy you that the book has made a
strong impression upon the public mind and that it must be
entirely successful. There is one little matter which I have
heard quarrelled with, and which I must say I think is a
mistake, but which relates to the *form* not to the *fonds* of the
work—that is the headings of the chapters, and the running
titles of the pages. They are so contrived as to show the
author's wit, but nothing of the contents of the book, and have
the disadvantage of giving a romantic air which is out of
place in history. But this sort of criticism you may very well
think is like praising one for his intellectual, his moral, and
all that, and then taking exception to the cut of his waistcoat.
You have good reason to be pleased with the reception the
book has had from the English press, considering that you
had no one particularly to stand godfather to your bantling,
but that it tumbled into the world almost without the aid of

a midwife.   Under these circumstances success is a great triumph. . . .

With my kindest regards to your wife, believe me, dear Motley,

Very sincerely yours,
WM. H. PRESCOTT.

To his Father.

Rome,
May 13th, 1856.

MY DEAR FATHER,—I perceive that the Harpers have published the 'Dutch Republic' at last.   No doubt they are the correct judges of the correct time; but I must say that I should have liked to have had it published in time to allow a review in the April number of the *North American.*   You say nothing of this in your letter.   Have you observed in one of Mary's letters a request to send a copy to Sam Hooper and to E. P. Whipple?   The latter is one of the most brilliant writers in the country, as well as one of the most experienced reviewers. I am glad you received the *Press.*   Some of the papers have been decidedly disagreeable; a weekly, called the *Saturday Review,* and the *Literary Gazette,* for example.   The *Examiner,* too, is very censorious as well as patronising.   The warmest article is in a weekly called the *Nonconformist,* date April 30th, and if Chapman has not sent it to you or to Harper, I wish you would send for it, as it would be desirable to have it republished.   I don't know who the editor of the paper is, nor the author of the article.   The Forbes also sent me a very flattering notice of the book from the Edinburgh paper, *The Scotsman.*   On the whole, it has been treated as well as an unknown production could expect in England, where success belongs to those only who have already succeeded.   I have heard nothing from Chapman since the book was published, but I feel sure from the silence that very few copies have been sold. I shall be surprised if a hundred copies are sold at the end of a year.   I directed that a copy should be sent to Mr. Bates with

your regards. I suppose you have retained the list of persons
to whom I wished copies sent. One person in particular I beg
may receive one, if he has not already done so, Thomas G.
Bradford. Have the kindness when you next write to look
over this letter, and answer these various matters propounded.
I repeat that the greatest satisfaction which I have derived
from the writing of the History is the pleasure and occupation
which it has given you, and were it not such a very expensive
matter to both our pockets, I should like nothing better than
to write another immediately; but I think it safer to pause
upon the road to ruin.

I remain, yours affectionately,

J. L. M.

P.S.—I am glad you sent a copy to Mr. Deblois. My
regards to him as well as to his "guide, philosopher, and
friend," the sage of Fort Hill.

To his Father.

Castellamare, near Naples,
June 6th, 1856.

MY DEAR FATHER,—I repeat what I have more than once
said already, that the principal pleasure I have received in
publishing my History is the great satisfaction which you and
my dear mother have derived from it, and the warm expressions
of sympathy which I have met with from my friends. I always
knew that Mr. Cabot and William Amory were my friends,
but I confess that I had not expected even from them such
enthusiastic approbation, the echo of which from beyond the
Atlantic has touched Mary and me most deeply. I shall be
most grateful to them as long as I live. I was, of course, much
pleased with Tom's last letter containing a copy of that article
from *Harper's*. I ascribe the necessity of printing the second
edition to Cabot's and Amory's tremendous cornering operations in the first. I have received Mr. Prescott's very kind and
hearty letter, and will answer it at my first moment of leisure.
Mr. Ticknor's I cannot answer because he is already in Europe.
Please to thank Hillard most warmly for his article in the

Courier. I could not be otherwise than extremely grateful to be made the subject of such very high and elegantly expressed commendation, although I feel at the same time that I am far from deserving such praise. Will you take an opportunity to present my compliments to the editors of the *Boston Post*, and thank them sincerely for the handsome and very flattering friendly manner in which they have noticed my labours? I feel very sensibly any commendation coming from my native place now that I have been so long resident in foreign lands. Don't forget, too, to give my regards to Epes Sargent, and to thank him for the warm and friendly interest which according to the extracts sent me he has manifested so constantly in the work.

By the way, will you tell me what arrangement has been made about the *North American Review?* I suppose, as a matter of course, that Hillard has not written two reviews of the book; but I should be very sorry to lose a regular article in the *North American Review*, to which I think the book is fairly entitled, and it would be a pity to leave it to the chance mercy of the editor whom I don't know and who may be unfriendly. I read the article in the *Tribune*, and was satisfied with it. It is curious that everybody who has censured me severely either in England or America has attacked the headings of the chapters, and it would be amusing if my letters to Chapman could be found and printed, to see how vigorously I remonstrated against, and how reluctantly I consented to making these kind of titles, thinking the summary at the head of each chapter quite sufficient. If I had the opportunity, which I have not at present, of making alterations, perhaps I should do so on this point, although it looks rather sneaking to back out in consequence of criticisms.

We made a very pleasant excursion to Sorrento yesterday. An old friend of mine, Baron Canitz, who is Prussian Minister here, and whom I knew twenty years ago in Germany, has been extremely cordial. He came down here with his Secretary of Legation yesterday, and we all went together. He invited me to dine to-day with him with the Prince of Saxe Meiningen, and a dozen bigwigs of the *corps diplomatique*, but the weather is too warm for such efforts on my part, and I insisted on declining. I shall write as soon as we have crossed the Simplon, and Mary will probably write next week from Genoa. Meantime, with the best love of all of us to my dear mother and yourself, and with kindest remembrances to every member of the family, never forgetting Uncle Edward, of whose health I wish you would give me a little better account, I remain

Most affectionately your son,

J. L. M.

From Mr. Theodore Fay.

United States Legation, Berne,
June 18th, 1856.

MY DEAR MOTLEY,—I am afraid to tell you what I think of your History! It is one of the finest I ever read. You need be under no apprehension. It is destined to immortality. It is a noble painting largely done, the delineations of character not only by a master hand but from a heart that sees right through the souls of men and means to speak the truth. I do not know that there could be found a period of grander interest, or a historian more able to represent it with all the force of truth. The drama is opened and conducted with superior power. The figures rise upon the mind in fearfully vivid colours but without exaggeration. There is a rare union of simplicity and strength, of poetry and truth. The style is limpid, forcible, unaffected, and eloquent. Many of the descriptions eminently beautiful, as, for instance, that of the cathedrals. The author has received from nature a high historic power, and the marks of conscientious study and reflection are felt in all the details. No library will be complete without your work. I congratulate you upon what must prove a complete success, and I only hope all men may read, mark, learn, and inwardly digest the meaning of such a character as Philip Egmont, and the grand and noble William of Orange. For my part I shall consider forwarding your manuscript as one of the honourable distinctions of my life. It was a higher act than you supposed, for I did not suspect how proud I should be of it. We are well. My daughter, who is my reader, as my beloved wife would have been, owes her first ideas of history to your pen, and joins in all my praise and kind regards to you and yours.

As ever your friend,

THEO. S. FAY.

From Dr. O. W. Holmes.

September 23rd, 1856.[1]

MY DEAR MOTLEY,—I welcome you and all yours back to your country and your friends, among whom I know you count me as not the newest or the least attached. I should have been to see you before this, but for reasons of little consequence in themselves, but just enough to keep me at home for some days, and perhaps for the rest of this week. There are many things I should love to talk over with you, but chiefly your own labours and experiences in the pursuit of your noble object, the fruit of which it is not too much to say is spoken of everywhere among us with admiration rather than common praise. Your wife and children, too—have I not known one from girlhood, and the others from infancy, and shall I not have a prattle with them as soon as may be?

So you expect my bodily presence shortly for an hour's talk —this week if I can, but next week whether I can or cannot. Until then, and always thenceforth,

Believe me, truthfully yours,

O. W. HOLMES.

From the same old *habitat*, 8, Montgomery Place, September 23rd.

From O. W. Holmes.

8, Montgomery Place,
January 9th, 1857.

MY DEAR MOTLEY,—I promised you a glass of wine one day, and you must let me redeem my promise by sending you

[1] Mr. Motley passed the winter of 1856-7 in Boston.

these half a dozen bottles. They are marked in Judge Jackson's catalogue " Essex Madeira, bought and imported through Mr. Isaac P. Davis in 1818," and have been commonly called " Essex Junior." Mr. Parker (of P. & Codman) says the wine is well thought of, and I remember Mr. Isaac P. wanted to purchase all the Judge had in his cellar at one time. But good or bad, there is a bouquet of old friendship under every cork, and to borrow the words of a poet of the nineteenth century, an admirer of your genius, and a near relation in the ascending line of the youth who brings you the friendly tribute (or would have brought it if not too heavy)—

> " It is not the sunset that glows in the wine,
> But the smile that beams over it makes it divine."

Don't answer this note, but nod your acknowledgments over the next glass of wine we drink together.

Yours faithfully,
O. W. HOLMES.

P.S.—Washington Irving [1] says " reliable," and Worcester credits the word to Sir Robert Peel.

From Mr. C. C. Felton.

Cambridge,
April 17th, 1857.

MY DEAR MOTLEY,—Some days ago I received a copy of your 'Dutch Republic,' which you have the great kindness to send me. I assure you there are few things which could have given me so much gratification. Instead of acknowledging your kindness immediately I sat down to read the book, and have occupied myself with it all my leisure moments since. Fast-day was thus converted into a most delightful feast-day, and I am still under the magician's spell. It so happens that I have before only had time to read here and there a chapter—enough to form an idea of its characteristic merits. I had intended to take it up in the summer vaca-

----

[1] ' Life of Washington,' ii., 240.

tion and study it carefully; but, having it on my table, I cannot resist the temptation nor postpone the gratification so long.

I congratulate you very sincerely on your good fortune in having added a permanent and precious contribution to the historical literature of our age. I consider him the happiest of mankind who, having a taste for letters and the genius requisite to accomplish great work, is so favoured by his outward fortunes that he can follow his tastes and give free scope to his genius. This happiness you have, and you have shown yourself to be worthy of it by the great achievement you have accomplished with the freshness of glowing and vigorous early manhood still upon your spirit.

May your future career in letters correspond to the auspices of the present, and may I live to refresh my mind, wearied with daily labours, by many a brilliant page of picturesque eloquence, sustained by love of truth and ethical justice, fearlessly and forcibly expressed, from you.

Ever, my dear Motley, your obliged friend,

C. C. FELTON.

To Dr. O. W. Holmes.

18, Boylston Place,
May 3rd, 1857.

MY DEAR HOLMES,—I do not believe that my affection for you has led me astray while endeavouring to form an impartial judgment upon your poem. I have read it a great many times, and I have admired it more at each successive reading. Each of the episodes has freshness, strength and beauty, and the whole fabric is simple and noble. What gives me particular pleasure is, that the more lofty the strain, the better and grander becomes the poetry. The episode of the young Roman is handled with much classic elegance, as well as with great tenderness and truth. The best portion, however, is that which embodies the mother's secret. The pictures are finished with an artistic delicacy of touch, and a piety of feeling, which remind me of the Florentine painters of the fourteenth and fifteenth centuries. The Webster photograph is bold, shadowy and imposing, but would probably elicit more hearty applause from a public audience than from some of us who have perhaps pondered too much the unheroic and the unpoetical elements which constituted so much of that golden-headed and clay-footed image.

The same remark I should be inclined to make upon the fraudulent banker. You have painted a very vigorous picture, but there is something in the details which are too inharmonious with the ideal. I suppose that you will not agree with me, and very likely it is some narrowness on my part, or over squeamishness, but the particulars of a modern dinner-party will refuse to make poetry to my imagination. The more lifelike they are (and nothing can be more vivid than your sketch), the more does my mind rebel at them. At the same time, I beg you to believe that I feel as warmly as anyone can do the genial glow of the atmosphere, and the genuine ring of the verse, even in the passages which I put below the other parts of the poem in comparison. Indeed, the description of the ruined home on Apple Island is almost the best thing in the poem. I have taken the liberty to say exactly what I think, because, although you may not accept my criticisms, I am sure you will accept the spirit in which they are written. If I thought that you had said your *dernier mot*, and that you were not likely in future to excel yourself, I should then, as one of your warmest admirers, as well as one of your oldest friends, have poured out for you, what Miss Edgworth says will alone satisfy an author, "large draughts of unqualified praise." I could have done that, too, with a clear conscience. But as I believe you to have it in you to write a great poem, and as I consider everything which you have hitherto written only as stray nuggets, golden pledges of the unfathomed and unsunned ore below, I am the more inclined to be critical.

As I said before, the loftiest passages in this, as in your other poems, are much the best. One of your tendencies, not a bad one if properly understood by you, is to rise above your subject. Therefore, if you will select a grand,

earnest, heroic theme, and put your whole soul and strength
into it, I believe that you can accomplish what has not yet
been done in this country. You have strength of mind
enough to rise to the highest imaginative regions, and to
sustain a long and measured flight therein. You have at
your absolute command the difficult but noble measure which
will always ring in our ears with the true heroic clang until
Dryden and Pope are forgotten. But you cannot do what I
wish you to do except upon two conditions : one, devotion of
your faculties and of your time to the one great object; the
other, cotton-wooling your ears absolutely to all hand-clapping
and greasy mob applause of mercantile lecture-rooms. Discard
from your verse every word and every thought that has not
the ring of the pure metal. To the *morally* pure and noble
there is no need of my exhorting you. To that you are always
instinctively and unerringly true. To the intellectually
beautiful and sublime you are equally loyal. I have marked
with parallel lines (as Channing used to do our themes) the
passages which please me most. You will see that I have
marked a very large part of the poem. I have also ventured
several criticisms, generally verbal ones, on the margin. Do
not be vexed with me if you think them stupid, and reject or
accept just as many of them as you think proper. Meantime,
I remain, as ever,

Sincerely your friend,

J. L. M.

From Mr. George Bancroft.

Newport, R.I.,
July 14th, 1857.

MY DEAR MOTLEY,—You can make me but one compensation for having missed your visit in New York. Come down
and pass a day, or two days, or three or more as your time may
warrant. Come next Friday in the morning train and boat;
you will be here at eleven. On Thursday I may possibly run

up to hear Mr. Everett, though I doubt. Next week I may
go to New York to work, for work here is impossible.

Yours of the 9th I received yesterday morning. I shall
value very highly, I assure you, the copy of your History from
its author. You send it at least to a house where it is valued.
Mrs. Bancroft has read every word of Harper's three volumes,
and was among the earliest to take her place as one who does
full justice to the work; and, of course, my self love is pleased
with this, for you may suppose I have trained her to good
judgment on such matters. Indeed there is but one opinion
on what you have achieved. My friend Ripley, whose judgment in this case was unbiassed by personal friendship or
acquaintance, and whose judgment under such circumstances
I think the best of any one in New York, has always in private
conversation and in public given you the tribute you deserve,
and I believe thinks in his heart that you have excelled
us all.

But come on Friday in the morning train and stay as long
as you can, and we will talk of all sorts of things before you
put an ocean between us.

Ever yours,

GEO. BANCROFT.

From Mr. Washington Irving.

Sunnyside,
July 17th, 1857.

MY DEAR SIR,—Mr. Cogswell apprises me of his having
received at the Astor Library a copy of your work which you
have done me the honour to send to his care for me.

A short time since on reading the first volume of your
History I was so much struck by its merit that I was on the
point of writing to you to express my admiration of this great
literary achievement and my delight at such a noble accession
to our national literature; but I checked the impulse, lest it
should be deemed an intrusive assumption on my part. You
may judge therefore how sincerely and deeply I appreciate the
proof you give me of your favourable consideration. I am now

on the third volume of your History, reading it with unflagging interest and increasing deference for its author. The minute and unwearied research, the scrupulous fidelity and impartial justice with which you execute your task, prove to me that you are properly sensible of the high calling of the American press—that rising tribunal before which the whole world is to be summoned, its history to be revised and rewritten, and the judgment of past ages to be cancelled or confirmed. I am happy to learn that you are about to return to the field of your labours—an ample field it is—and the three teeming volumes you have so suddenly laid before the public show how well you know where to put in your sickle.

With warmest wishes for your continued success, I am, my dear sir,

Most truly your obliged friend and servant,

WASHINGTON IRVING.

J. L. Motley, Esq.

CHAPTER VII.

To Dr. O. W. Holmes.

Walton-on-Thames,
September 16th, 1857.

MY DEAR WENDELL,—This is not a letter, not even an
apology for one. I only wish to say to you that I intend to
write very soon, and that I hope to hear from you as often as
you can overcome your avaricious tendencies. I am myself
excessively miserly at this moment, for I am almost distraught
at the circumlocution and circumvolutions of London. To
try to do anything in a hurry here is to "hew down oaks with
rushes." Sisyphus with his rock was an idle, loafing individual
compared to the martyr who is doomed to work up the precipice of English routine. I have been in London a month,
and my rock has just come down upon my toes for the fourth
or fifth time. I have not yet got into the State Paper Office,
where I expected to have effected my entrance after the first
day or two succeeding my arrival. I thought to have done a
great deal of work there this time. But the American Minister,
and the Minister of Foreign Affairs, and the Minister of the
Interior, and the Master of the Rolls (who by the way is not a
baker, as Lowell would probably suggest), and various other
dignitaries have all to be made aware (in a Pickwickian sense)
that an insignificant individual like myself is desirous of
reading some musty and forgotten old letters which not one
of them could read or would wish to if they could. A friend

of mine once went into a soda-water shop in Boston on a very
hot day, and was told by an elderly individual behind the
counter that his son John, proprietor of the establishment,
had gone to Portland, but that upon his return he would
undoubtedly be very happy to prepare him a glass. This is
exactly my case. The Earl of Clarendon is absent with the
Queen at Balmoral. Panizzi of the British Museum is in
Turin. Dallas is at the Isle of Wight, and others are hiding
themselves in other corners or pretending to be absent, even
if actually here, because in September it is disreputable to be
in London. No moral or religious person therefore would
acknowledge himself to be here. When these illustrious personages all get back, they will unite to prepare my glass of
soda-water. By that time I shall be in Paris. I have also
had time during the last two or three weeks to go over a mass
of MS. in the British Museum. *Mais il faut casser des œufs
pour faire une omelette.*

Routledge tells me that your poems (particularly the *Punch-
Bowl*), are familiar to everybody in England. I have been a
recluse till now. We are at present staying at this magnificent place, Mount Felix, near Walton-on-Thames, enjoying the
princely hospitality of our friends, Russell Sturgis and his wife.
I wish you were here too. Remember me kindly to Lowell and
Agassiz and Felton, Longfellow, Tom Appleton, and all the
members of our Club, which I hope you have regularly joined
by this time. My wife joins me in warmest remembrances
to you and your wife and children. I am provoked that I
have been writing all about myself. I shall write to you ere
long again, and will not use this horrible paper. *Nec tenui
penna* is a good motto, but *Nec tenui charta* shall henceforth
be mine. Do write me occasionally, if only a single sheet of
notepaper, and pardon the detestable stupidity of this.

Ever most sincerely your friend,

J. L. M.

An English admirer of yours, Mr. Synge, *attaché* in Her
Majesty's Foreign Office, who is staying in this house and who
has heard much in your praise from Thackeray, asks to send
you his respects.

To his Mother.

Nice,
December 13th, 1857.

MY DEAREST MOTHER,—Mary and Susie were charmed with your letters to them, and with your account of your Riverdale wedding festivities. I tell them I hope you will celebrate your one hundredth jubilee in the same way and place, although I suppose it is rather a longer prospect than any of us would care to look forward to just at present. As I have never been in the tropics, I cannot get used to this constant flood of warm sunshine, cloudless and almost oppressive day after day, in what certainly are not generally considered the genial last weeks of the year. We have been here about six weeks, and there have been but two or three cloudy days, and those were warm rainy ones, all the rest as warm and as fine as our best days in early October. Warmer than those, because there is always a lump of ice stirred in at night into the American Indian summer. Here we have had no signs of frost as yet; green peas are about as cheap as in July in Boston, and red roses are as plenty out of doors at Christmas as red noses are in Winter Street at the same season. The consequence of this satisfactory condition of the atmosphere is that Lily is almost growing fat. She has improved during six weeks more than we had dared to hope, though I am sorry to say her condition is far from being completely satisfactory. She is still languid, and unable to take much exercise, but she can breathe the fresh air and sunshine all day long, by merely opening the window and going out on the balcony.

Nice is in itself an insignificant little town, with about 40,000 inhabitants. The chief productions of the place, as the school geography would say, are oil, perfumery, and beggars; the latter article being rather too strong a combination of the two first. It is placed along a crescent-shaped bay, formed by beautifully and boldly outlined mountainous headlands, with a little lighthouse at the tip of each horn, and with a background of high, solid, warm rocks, with orange and olive groves crammed into all the interstices. It unfolds itself to the sunny Mediterranean on the south, and shelters itself under the

mountains from the north wind.   For these reasons it has,
perhaps, the best and brightest climate in Italy.   Our apartment fronts the sea, having as bold a marine view as the Nahant
hotel.   The murmurs of the tideless ocean upon the shingly
beach are never silent under our balcony, the profiles of the
mountains which encircle the place are always seen through a
golden and purple haze, which is peculiar to Italy, and the
windows on the opposite side look over whole acres of orange
orchards, just now golden with fruit, and fragrant with blossoms,
in addition to which three miles of shirts and chemises can be
seen drying any day upon the beach in front, gracefully flutter-
ing and displaying their raggedness along the whole sinuosity
of the bay.

You must not suppose that I am idle.   I certainly should
not have chosen Nice for a family residence, except on Lily's
account.   Nevertheless, being here, I can occupy myself
for a long time with several hundredweight of books, which
I have brought with me, and which I must devour and turn
into chyle before I can do much in the way of writing.   My
time in London was not lost for a single day, and I have
now two persons employed there in copying for me, according
to my mapping out when personally in the State Paper Office
and British Museum.   I was also hard at work in the Archives
in Paris during the few weeks that we were there.   I have,
however, much to do in the subterranean way in Brussels,
the Hague, London, and Paris.   I do not write at all as yet,
but am diving deep and staying under very long, but hoping
not to come up too dry.   My task is a very large and hard
one.   My canvas is very broad, and the massing and the composition of the picture will give me more trouble than the
more compact one which I have already painted.   Then I have
not got a grand central heroic figure, like William the Silent,
to give unity and flesh and blood interest to the scene.   The
history will, I fear, be duller and less dramatic than the other.
Nevertheless, there are many grand events and striking characters, if I can do justice to them.   If I could write half a
dozen volumes, with a cheerful confidence that people would
read them as easily as I write them, my task would be a com-

paratively easy one. But I do not know where all the books are to go that are written now-a-days. And then my publishers have failed, and Heaven knows what may be the condition of the market when I take my next pigs there. In short, I cannot write at all, except by entirely forgetting for the time that there is such a thing as printing and publishing.

Nice, I am very much disappointed to say, is very dear, being a kind of watering-place, where the six lean months of winter are made to swallow the six fat ones of summer. If you should stay a year, and get the fat and lean both, the average would be respectably low.

To his Wife.

Hôtel du Rhin, Paris,
January 15th, 1858.

MY DEAREST MARY,—I wrote you a brief note from Marseilles just before leaving that place for Paris. I made the journey comfortably enough, getting about as much sleep out of the *coupé* of the railroad as I usually do out of a bedstead, arrived here about seven o'clock of a dismal sloppy morning, and installed in a garret on the courtyard of the inside house. When I got home I found that old —— had been looking for me, and wished much to see me before I departed. So I went to the " Hotel du Louvre " and found him. Mrs. —— was of course on hand, mending her stockings, and the children were bivouacking as usual upon the floor and skirmishing about the room. She informed me that the atmosphere of Nice was very cold and foggy; which statement was so very like that respecting the Correggio in the Manchester Exhibition that I could only bow meekly in deference to her superior wisdom. Poor —— seemed more oppressed by her than ever. We got into a corner, and I tried to make him forget his misery. But Mrs. —— was constantly hovering over us like a vulture, and at last pounced upon him bodily, insisted on discussing the point whether she might go and make her visits in a fiacre with one horse, or whether she ought to have two. She then screwed herself up to asking me to dinner, and looked radiant

when I told her I was engaged. I did not tell her I never
dined in the dark, and as there is a very brilliant row of
gas-lights in the street opposite their windows, I suppose
they never indulge in candles.

I think I have chronicled small beer enough for you for the
present. I leave to-morrow morning at eight for Brussels. I
have not yet heard from Van de Weyer, but I have written to
him to send his letters to Brussels. I can do nothing here.
Kiss my darlings a thousand times. Tell Susie I hope she has
begun to miss me a little bit, even in spite of my scoldings.
Tell Lily that when she has finished what she is reading,
I recommend her to get Sismondi's 'Précis de l'Histoire de
France,' which is very readable and in but three volumes. If
it is not in the Library, I think she will be able to buy it at
Visconti's; I should like her also to read Lingard's 'History
of England.' He is a Roman Catholic, but honest enough,
and at any rate more respectable than Hume. She had better
read also Bancroft's 'History of the United States,' and
Thierry's 'Conquête de l'Angleterre.' All these books are in
the Library. I wish she would find time, too, to study Italian
a little. If she wants a teacher no doubt plenty are to be
found at Nice.

As for my little Saint Mary, I only wish I had her always
with me to take advice and example from. I have none to
give her.

You see I do not bore you with the *Attentat*, for I know
nothing that is not in the newspapers. I have made no call
either upon Guizot or Madame Mohl or anybody. As I am
only passing through, it would be nonsense.

Ever affectionately yours,
J. L. M.

To his Father.

Brussels,
January 24th, 1858.

MY DEAR FATHER,—Finding my family so well and comfortably established at Nice for the winter, and Lily's health
so much improved as to be no longer a source of anxiety,

I was unwilling to delay any longer making a move towards the land of my labours. Although the books that I took with me would have given me employment for several months at Nice, yet I wanted to set about as soon as possible the work which can only be accomplished here and at the Hague.

I came to this place intending to make an effort to see the MS. copies made long ago by order of the Belgian Government of a very important correspondence of Philip the Second and his Ministers with the governors and other important personages in the Low Countries. This correspondence is in course of publication by Mr. Gachard, Archivist of the Kingdom, and an acquaintance of mine. At the rate at which the publication proceeds, however, I shall be dead and buried before it reaches the epoch at which I wish to use it. M. Van de Weyer, with whom I spent a day and night at his house at Windsor, when I was last in England, promised me to use his best efforts to obtain the permission for me to read the correspondence in MS. We agreed that when I was ready to proceed to Brussels, he should write letters to Mr. Gachard, to the Minister of the Interior, and others, urging my claims, etc. Accordingly the other day before leaving Nice, I wrote to M. Van de Weyer, asking for those friendly offices. I did not reflect, however, that I had stumbled exactly upon the moment of the marriage of the Princess Royal, when the whole Belgian royal family were on Van de Weyer's hands, and when he could hardly be expected to think of anything else.

In consequence of that, I hardly expect to hear from him at all at present; but as I shall be here again in the summer, I shall have plenty of time to attend to the matter then. Meanwhile, as I had come so far, I thought I had better make a slight invasion of Holland, and so a week ago to-day I went to the Hague. My reception there was very cordial. All the newspapers announced my arrival with a good deal of flourish. The two gentlemen whose opinion I most value (as they are themselves leading authorities in all matters of Netherland history), Mr. Groen van Prinsterer, who has the charge of the private or family archives of the House of Orange-Nassau, and who is well known as an author, besides being a prominent member of the States-General, and Mr. Bakhuysen van der Brink, the Archivist-general of the Kingdom, the most learned man and the cleverest writer in the country, both spoke of my work in the strongest terms of approbation. They assured me that almost everybody in Holland had read it, and that there was but one opinion about it, that it had made a very deep and general sensation. A great many things were said to me which it would not be becoming to repeat. The book very soon after its appearance was reprinted at Amsterdam, and has had a large sale, not to the benefit of the author's pocket, however, but I am very glad to have it circulated. The edition is quite a pretty one, and sells for about three-and-a-half dollars. I think that you are already aware that a French translation is preparing under the auspices of the distinguished Mr. Guizot. I had a kind invitation to visit him in a few days when I return to Paris, and I suppose the translation will appear before long, but have no recent news on the subject. The whole work has also been translated into German, and has been published at Leipzig and Dresden. I have not yet seen the translation, but I mean to get a copy in Paris.

But the most satisfactory thing on the whole to me is that a translation into Dutch is now appearing (published in numbers), under the superintendence of Mr. Bakhuysen, of whom I have already spoken. He has written a preface, and adds a good many notes and comments. The book is very handsomely printed, and I regard its publication as a very satisfactory testimonial to the permanent value of the work. I think it is something better than vanity which causes me to take an honest pleasure in finding my labours appreciated and commended by the persons most fit to sit in judgment upon them. I own that I should have been deeply mortified on arriving in Holland to find that nobody had heard of my book. Yet previously to last week I had no reason to suppose that it had obtained any currency. Nobody had ever told me of the translations and republications, so that I was quite taken by surprise at finding myself so well-known here. The best results of these favourable views regarding my work is the facility which it gives me for the one with which I am at present occupied. Mr. Groen and Mr. Bakhuysen both take the greatest pleasure in aiding my researches in every possible way, and a great mass of unpublished documents will be laid before me when I come back in June.

I shall doubtless find letters to-morrow at my bankers here. Lily, thank God, is so much better that we are no longer anxious about her. Mary and the other two children are very well. There was never anything like the atmosphere of Nice. We came to that place in the first week in November, and till the 12th of January, when I left, there had been but three days when there had not been cloudless sunshine and balmy airs. The windows of our apartment were open all day long, and sometimes it was even necessary to shut the green blinds just as if it were mid-summer instead of mid-winter. Here in the Netherlands we have generally lowering and rainy skies, and great-coats and fires are indispensable. Still there is neither frost nor snow, nothing like winter as we understand the word in America. Give my love to my dear mother. I do hope and trust that she will send me with her own hand a better account of herself.

In order to gain time and to lighten my labours, I have already engaged a very competent person to make certain preliminary researches and copies during all the time I am absent from the Hague. I expect on my return thither in June to find a considerable progress made. The same is doing for me in the State Paper Office and the British Museum of London. Alas! I am not making much money by such operations; but I believe in the long run that even in a pecuniary point of view I am doing right to make thorough work. It will be impossible for anybody to deny a permanent value to labours which have been conscientiously carried out, and have obtained the unqualified approbation of those most competent to pronounce upon them. When my two works are both finished, I cannot help thinking that they will have a considerable value even in the money market. But at the same time it is impossible for me to do anything at all unless I discard all such ideas from my mind when I am writing. The moment a man begins

to write for money, it is apt to be all over with his true reputation. Meantime, with my love to all both great and small at
home, I am

Affectionately your son,

J. L. M.

To his Wife.

Brussels,
January 24th, 1858.

I have been working pretty hard in the short time I was at
the Hague, and I feel that I have made a good deal of progress. I should have stayed a little longer, but for a reason
which seems a ridiculous one enough to state, but you know
me well enough to acquit me of affectation—I could hardly
have remained longer without going to see the Queen. Our
old friend, Count Louis Bylandt, told me she was the first
person to speak to him of my book, telling him that he must
read it, and using very complimentary language on the
subject.

He told me that I ought to send to Count Randwyk (from
whom, by the way, you remember that I received a very civil
message through Sir Charles Lyell), and be presented to her
at once,—that she would be much pleased to see me, etc., etc.,
and that he should tell her that I was in the Hague as
soon as he saw her,—that her small tea-parties are extremely
agreeable. There is also a great ball at the English Ambassador's, and Count Bylandt wanted to send word to him
that I was there, saying that he had had a great deal to say
to him about me, and would at once send me an invitation.
The Groen van Prinsterers were also very urgent that I
should go into society, telling me that I should find that
everybody was acquainted with me already. Under these
circumstances, finding that I should be obliged to abandon
my beloved solitude, you will think it very natural that I
should decamp. If I had been twenty-three instead of forty-
three I daresay it would have been very jolly to go to the
Queen's tea-parties and get a few sugar-plums, but my

appetite for such diet is gone. I enjoyed my twilight walks under the leafless branches of the magnificent oaks and beeches of the great wood, musing and moralising like the melancholy Jacques in the forest of Arden, and once I took a long stroll on the sands at Scheveningen. The winter sky was wild and lowering, and for miles seaward the waves of the stormy North Sea were rolling in vast sheets of foam over the breakers. It was a grand and gloomy Ruysdael, a good counterpart to the golden Claudes which you have daily from your windows at Nice.

I had not much time to enjoy the "rapture of the lonely shore," but I remain of the opinion that the Hague is in winter the prettiest town in Europe. It is so clean, and orderly, and elegant, and so embowered in foliage. I could not well have remained longer without making visits, etc. The newspapers, both of the Hague and Rotterdam had announced my arrival with a great flourish of trumpets (fortunately not till the day before my departure), so upon Saturday morning (day before yesterday) I returned to this place.

Count Bylandt has sold the Murillo to Mr. Aspinwall for something less than the price he asked when we were at the Hague ($16,000), Mr. Aspinwall had also bought the Claudes, and I am glad that one rich American has bought some good pictures as a set off to the Leonardos and Titians of the ——'s gallery and other similar collections. I am quite disgusted. I have been writing two sheets and a half about myself. But how can I help it? You will want to know about my visit to the Hague, and it would be a silly affectation not to say what I had to say, and what I suppose will interest you to hear. Nor is it as if I had been talking from the housetops or in the newspapers. Still if I had any other topic to entertain you with I would do it with pleasure, but I have been completely alone ever since I left Paris, and I dread going back there where there are such a lot of people. This is Sunday, and I have therefore not been able to get my letters, which I ordered Monroe to send to my bankers here. To-morrow I shall of course have news of you, dear Mary, and

of my little darlings.   Tell Lily I think she may find the
stories of Henri Conscience interesting.   I bought two or three
to read while travelling, but as they are in Flemish, they
would be of little use to anybody else.   They have all been
translated into French, however, and I suspect you will find
them at Visconti's.   They are something like Auerbach's
stories, generally of the Flemish peasants and artisans, and
contain many pleasing quiet Gerard Dow-ish incidents and
quiet, gentle unfoldings of sentiments and affection very
different from the highly charged romances of the Satanic
schools.   The moral tone is unexceptionable, but they are
perhaps a little flat, too little cayenne for your taste, but still
you might fancy them.   Has Susie begun to miss me yet?
How is her handwriting?   I am in daily expectation of seeing
some remarkable result of the method so much approved by
Tomkins of London.   Has she curled the *père* C.'s hair
as she proposed?   What is my little angel Mary doing?
Taking care of everybody but herself, as usual, I suppose.   It
seems to me as if I had been gone a year, and that nobody
would know me if I should walk into the Maison Donaudy.
I shall write soon again.

Affectionately your own,
J. L. M.

To his Wife.

Brussels,
March 2nd, 1858.

MY DEAR MARY,—I hardly know whether I have written to
you within the last few days or not.   My days and nights
succeed each other and certify each other so monotonously
that they seem to be all stuck together in one piece.   It is
like one long sentence without punctuation, like the interminable Spanish despatches which I am reading every day,
and which run sometimes for fifty pages without a period or
even a comma.   I am at the Archives every day before ten,
and generally till five, as Gachard, when he stops, invites me
into his cabinet after the regular hour of closing, which is

three. Then, *la nuit tombante,* I take a grim crepuscular walk
round the shabby little *boulevards,* after which I go to the
reading-room for an hour. At half-past seven I dine alone in
the large *salle à manger,* lighted by one candle, with two waiters
looking at me, so that I always feel like Warren in the farce
which we saw at the Museum. After this I work till twelve
or one o'clock, burning a good deal of midnight spermaceti,
which, at the rate charged for it, comes, according to my
calculation, to about one whale a month. Thus you see that
I have always a pickaxe in hand, and am working my way
pretty steadily into the bowels of the land. At the same time
I do not see that I have anything amusing to communicate to
you. I have a fine opportunity for cultivating my talent for
silence, but that does not enable me to be very agreeable in
conversation, even by letter. I am attacked by very frequent
fits of the *à quoi bon* disease, and am constantly asking myself
why I should condemn myself in this absurd way to *travaux
forcés à perpétuité.* Here I go *trainant ma boule,* and it does
not do me any good, or anybody else. I am getting disgusted
with the word "history," and yet I go boring on merely
because it seems to be my destiny *faute de mieux.*

I went again to see Madame Metivié yesterday, and found
her at home, together with the other one. Miss le Strange[1]
was there, too, with her father, and was delighted to hear of
Lily and Mary, whom she recollects very well, and begged
to be kindly remembered. She is quite a pretty, pleasing
girl.

March 15th.—I have pretty nearly finished in Brussels for
the present. I have gone through nearly the whole of the
Simancas correspondence, twelve hundred letters, many of
them sixty pages in length, and after all they are rather a
seccatura. I suppose I shall go to Paris by the end of the
week.

Ever yours,

J. L. M.

[1] Now Mrs. Waller, who, with her sister, afterwards Mrs. Laurence Oliphant, had been fellow-pupils and friends of his daughter.—ED.

To his Daughter.

Paris,
March 26th, 1858.

MY DEAR LITTLE MARY,—Your sweet, beautifully-written letter of February 26th gave me a great deal of pleasure, and I did not intend to have left it so long unanswered. But I am always very hard at work, and besides, I have usually at least a dozen letters on hand, generally to persons I care very little about, which is the most disagreeable labour of all to me. It would be a great pleasure to me to write to you now if I could say anything that would interest or amuse you. My darling child, you have always been a blessing and a consolation ever since you were born. I never can express the tenderness and gratitude I feel towards you.

Your mamma gives me a much longer period for staying in Paris than I intend to spend here. I am rather tired of work, and not very well. After I have got through a little job at the Archives, which will not take me a great many days, I wish to come and see you all once more. As for Paris, " *c'est la mer à boire* " in respect of work, and I do not like to look at the Archives or the Library, for they show me how much labour there would be for me if I stayed longer. I have been to see Mrs. Crowninshield, but did not find her, and shall go again to-day. I went to see Mrs. Brooks last evening. She made many kind inquiries after mamma and Lily. I have seen Mrs. Amory and S——, who seem satisfied with their winter's work. Mr. Frank Lowell goes to-day to Italy. Good-bye, my dear little Mary. Give my love to mamma, Lily, and Susie, and believe me,

Your affectionate little
PAPA.

To his Wife.

Frankfort,
Monday night, May 3rd, 1858.

My DEAREST MARY,—According to my promise I write you
a single line before I go to bed that I may inform you of my
safe arrival in this place, notwithstanding the numerous
dangers of flood and field which beset the venturer on such
unfrequented paths. I slept the first night at Yverdun, an
unsophisticated place, where they have not yet learned how
much to charge for their indifferent accommodation, an ignorance which will soon fade before the advancing railroad
system. The next day I left by the boat at eight, and crossing
the two lakes of Neufchatel and Brienne, took the rail at 6 A.M.
There is a tunnel eight minutes long on this road, which had
just been opened the day before yesterday. From Bale to
Frankfort I came to-day, and reached this place at half-past
four. After dinner I went to the Bismarcks, and received as
affectionate a welcome from them both as I knew I should,
and like them if possible better than ever. Keyserling and
Wanda were there, and are staying at this hotel. His wife
died in Venice in March, after much suffering. Behr, his
brother-in-law, is also here, but goes to Curland to-morrow.
I suppose I shall stay through the week. The Bismarcks,
however, are in great confusion, as they are exactly in all the
agonies of changing their residence. The house which they
have inhabited for the last six years they have been obliged
to give up to the owner thereof, who has just inherited seven
million guldens, and is disposed to go into his house on the
strength of it. They are therefore just now sitting on two
stools, and as comfortable as people generally are in such a
position.

May 4th.—I wrote you a short note the night of my arrival.
Since then the Bismarcks have got pretty well established in
their new house. I have dined there every day, and spent
most of my time with them. They are entirely unchanged,
frank, cordial, and affectionate as ever, both of them. Their
new house has a large garden, as large as Eichlers' in Dresden,

with a magnificent view into the country, and the Taunus Mountains.   I shall leave to-morrow for Cologne, and the next day go to Calais, and the third to London.   I am urged to stay, but I must get to work or I shall get rusted irrevocably, and as so considerable a part of our revenue has to come out of the inkstand, I have not much time to lose.

The weather is horrible—cold, windy, and dusty, with occasional snow squalls by way of variety.   The genial month of May is always atrocious anywhere on this side the Alps.   It makes me shiver to think of the dismal voyage down the Rhine, and across the Channel, where there is no keeping tolerably comfortable, except by going down into those diabolical cabins, where perpetual eating is being perpetrated by the ever-hungry Germans.   I am sorry that the weather is still so disagreeable with you.   I feel very anxious about you all—but, as you say, I can always be with you very soon in case of necessity.   Do keep well yourself, dear Mary, and keep my darlings well also.   I am very glad to hear my sweet little Mary is well again.   Believe me always

Most affectionately yours,

J. L. M.

CHAPTER VIII.

LONDON SOCIETY.

To his Wife.

London,
May 13th, 1858.

I reached this place this morning, Tuesday. I was just
ready to start from the "Hôtel d'Angleterre at Frankfort," at
about 9 A.M. My luggage was all packed into a fiacre, and I
was just getting into that vehicle myself, when Madame de
Bismarck made her appearance, and as I was bidding her
good-bye, she insisted upon it that I should not go—that my
room was quite ready at their house, and that I must proceed
there instead of to the railroad.

While I was expostulating, she gave a sudden nod to the

cocher of my fiacre, and before I could stop him he was on
his way to her house with my trunks. She then whisked me
off in her carriage to the *embarcadère* to see Keyserling and
Wanda, who were taking their departure in another direction.
After we had seen them safely started, we proceeded to her
house. . . . I was, however, considerably indisposed, and did
not care about being invalided in their house. I remonstrated
so earnestly therefore, that she agreed to let me go to the
Bureau to make inquiries. I only mention this incident to
you to show the perfectly frank and cordial way in which
they treat me, and would treat you if you had accompanied
me. She is so kind-hearted, amiable, and jolly. She is
very desirous that you should spend a winter at Frankfort,
and wishes to bring Lily out. Bismarck is unchanged to me ;
his wife says he seems twenty years younger when I am
there, which is the real reason why she likes my society so
much. She is devotedly attached to him and he to her. It
seems ridiculous to me that any one should be enlivened by
my company, but this is a very good reason. His time is so
much occupied with that most tedious of all *seccaturas* the
politics of the German Confederation, that it is no wonder
when a middle-aged gentleman is transformed temporarily into
a stripling of eighteen, with deportment conformable, his
family are satisfied. I make these remarks exclusively that
you may not suppose that it is my important individuality
which makes my presence agreeable to them, but that I am
important only as her husband's friend. . . .

I came accordingly, as above remarked, to Cologne on
Tuesday. The day was a fine one—the only fine one for many
days, and the voyage down the river was not so tedious as I
had anticipated. I enjoyed not so much the ruins and the
river as I did looking at the spot where we were together
so long ago. The " Hotel du Lis " at St. Goar, where the
waiter threw down the dishes to look at the steamboat, the old
" chatee " at Braubach, and the house at Königswinter, from
whence dear little Mary's letter of " We are now at Rhine "
was composed—were all visible before the mists settled down
upon the landscape, and made it dimmer than the memory
of it, which is still so fresh. It was ten in the evening when

we got to Cologne, and on the following morning at eight
I was on my way in a pelting rain to Ostend. The weather,
however, very civilly cleared up at sunset. I decided to cross
from Ostend because it saved nine hours of rail, and only gave
three and a half hours more of boat. The sea also was not
very rough, and I had no sea sickness, but, as you may
suppose, was rather bored. I reached Dover at one in the
morning, slept there, and took the eight o'clock train for
London. I had the pleasure of getting your kind, affectionate
letter on my arrival.

To Dr. O. W. Holmes.

London,
May 16th, 1858.

MY DEAR WENDELL,—Your most agreeable and affectionate
letter ought not to have remained so long unanswered. That
such has been the case is not the fault of my heart, but my
head. You, whose reservoir is always filled from the perennial
fountains thousands of feet above the heads of *nous autres*, so
that you have only to turn the plug to get a perpendicular jet
straight into the clouds, must have compassion on those
condemned to the forcing-pump. I do not mean, God forbid,
that I have not written because I despaired of being witty or
amusing. Certainly I do not look upon a friendship such as
ours as requiring any demonstrations beyond those of sincerity
and steadfastness. At the same time, I have got of late to be
affected—"but why I know not," as Hamlet says—with such
a constant and chronic blue devilry, that I am ashamed to
write to any one. Unfortunately, the disease with me takes
the form of pure and unmitigated stupidity, so that it is not
in the least interesting or romantic. *You* do not know what
it is to re-echo daily poor Sir Andrew Aguecheek's pathetic
complaint, "Sometimes I have no more wit than a Christian
or an ordinary man." All this is intended, not as an apology
for my silence, but an explanation thereof. I have been
doing my best. I bought six months ago a memorandum-
book, as big as a ledger, to take notes of my own conversation,
in the manner recommended by the original autocrat who

reigned over us, *consule Planco,* and I have been patiently
hoping to catch myself saying or even thinking a good thing,
in which case down it would have gone in black and white
for your benefit. In vain I have placed myself in the attitude
of Sterne's portraits, with my forefinger on the bump of
ideality, in which attitude, he says, he verily believes he has
often intercepted ideas which were intended for somebody
else's brain. It is all no go.

By the way, your letter had various adventures before
reaching me. I was then in Brussels. My address was, and
always is, Baring Brothers and Co., London. You had the
original conception of addressing me to the care of *Brown*
Brothers and Co., London. Now it is rather a remarkable
fact, that although there are several persons rejoicing in that
name in London, the only Browns who have anything fraternal
about them in the whole town are some chairmakers in Piccadilly. They declined receiving your letter, and then it somehow went back to Liverpool. Some weeks later I heard from
home that you had sent the letter, and I wrote to Russell
Sturgis (of the Barings) to help me if possible to it. He very
kindly wrote to the General Post Office, and also to Brown,
Shipley and Co., Liverpool, and eventually the letter was extricated and sent to me, covered all over with very funny hieroglyphics illustrating its various adventures. I might have used
this as an excuse for my delay in answering, had I not preferred
making a confession rather than an apology. Your letters,
fortunately, are not like eggs, telegrams, and things of that
nature, good for nothing except fresh, and therefore I enjoyed
it the more in consequence of the difficulty in getting it. I
was much obliged for your kindness in mentioning the favourable opinion concerning me expressed by Mr. Dorsheimer,
and the fact gave me great pleasure. I regret to say that
I have seen of the *Atlantic Magazine* only the first two
numbers. The reason for this is that I have been for the last
six months, with hardly an interval, in very out-of-the-way
and obscure places, where light never comes that comes at all.
Nice at first, and Brussels afterwards. I took my family in
November to the former place on account of Lily, whose

health was very delicate, but I rejoice to say she has very
much improved, and after establishing them there, I departed
to spend the most solitary winter I ever spent in my life in
Brussels. I was all day in the Archives, and nearly all night
in my chamber. I hardly ever spoke except to exchange a
few brief signals with my fellow worms, who were feeding like
myself on the carcase of the buried centuries, and the con-
sequences of such a solitary and Ghoul-like existence, was to
subdue my nature to the condition of the carrion I had been
consuming.

I find your 'Autocrat' (the first two numbers of which, as
stated, are all I have yet seen) as fresh and poignant in flavour
as those of twenty years since, which is sufficiently high praise
as to manner. As to matter, the substance is unquestionably
stronger, sterner stuff than in those days, and will endure long.
You must always have an eye to their subsequent appearance
in volumes by themselves, when of course you can leave out
what you think of transitory interest, and give them the last
polish. I have but just arrived in London, but as this is
Sunday and I shall be immersed in hard work from to-morrow
forward, in the State Paper Office and British Museum, I
thought I had better sit down and have a little talk with you
when I was sure of perfect solitude. To-morrow I shall get all
the numbers of the *Atlantic* and devour with immense greedi-
ness first the 'Autocrats,' and then Lowell and Emerson and
Longfellow and others, as doubtless I shall know them all by
the "twinkling of their eyes." If I meet any literary men,
I shall not fail to call their attention to it, as unquestionably
the best magazine in the language. I hope when I next write
I may have something amusing to tell you. As I said before,
I have but just arrived. A young friend of mine who is in
Parliament is going to take me to his club to-night, where I
hope to hear not logic chopped but politics discussed, as
they are at the very culminating point of a crisis; the debate
of Friday having been adjourned over till to-morrow.

À *propos* of the Atlantic, not the magazine, but the ocean,
I happened to find this paragraph the other day in the
commencement of articles on some subject, I forget what, in

the *Allgemeine Zeitung*, and since you have become a German scholar, I hope you will laugh at it as heartily as I did. " Seit der Entdeckung Amerika's ist die Geschichte nicht mehr thalassisch sondern oceanisch." I could read no more of the article. I was already washed out of existence by such a world of water. I suppose you sometimes are glad of a suggestion or two of topics for your ukases at the breakfast table. I think you might handle the subject of stale metaphors for a page or two with much effect. Take for example the ship of state from the time of Horace's " navis referent in mare," etc., down to the last speech of the member for Milwaukie, there has perhaps never been an oration delivered, or a poem perpetrated, without some reference to that unlucky ship of state, which always *will* be getting on breakers, and to the pilot who always *will* be weathering the storm as freshly as if no such allusion had ever been made. The best of it is the satisfaction with which these metaphors are produced as if perfectly fresh and choice, and the conscientious manner in which they are polished up for exhibition. Then there is the deadly upas tree, which has so long poisoned everybody's young existence, the phœnix, the dying dolphin, and many such fools and fishes, and do say something about that unpleasant Spartan boy, who has been following us about, with the fox biting away his nether integuments from time immortal. Then you may write an imaginary puff on somebody's hair dye, or still better get some living barber to pay you handsomely for it by merely changing a few words in Goldsmith's " when lovely woman stoops to folly," ending of course with " is to dye."

There, I consider I have given you at least $20, for if you cannot beat those golden thoughts into a platitude of two magazine pages, you are not the gold-beater I took you for. Pray take all the credit and all the money yourself. I do not ask a commission. Do not say, " An eminent historian, now running to seed in a foreign land, has suggested the following very brilliant, and at the same time profound thoughts." If you should ever hint at my existence again in the magazine, I will never forgive you. I prefer

to rest upon the verses in the first number, of which both
for the affection, and the generous over-appreciation re-
vealed, I shall be proud all the days of my life, and my
children after me, and I do not wish anything to disturb that
impression. I have been running on with a most intolerable
skimble-skamble. I wish I had anything better to say. Pray
forgive my dulness, and prove it by writing to me very soon.
Give my kindest regards to your wife and children. Also
remember me particularly to Lowell, Longfellow, Agassiz,
Felton, Whipple, and others who may remember me, and
believe me always,

Most sincerely your friend,

J. L. M.

P.S.—This letter was written yesterday, but was not sent.
Meantime, last evening, I dined with a small party at the
Mackintoshes. Thackeray was there, and suddenly in the
middle of dinner he made the following observation, not to
me, but to his neighbour on the other side of the table: " Have
you read the ' Autocrat of the Breakfast Table,' by Holmes,
in the new *Atlantic Magazine* ? " He then went on to observe
that no man in England could now write with that charming
mixture of wit, pathos, and imagination, that your papers were
better by far than anything in their magazines. I expressed
my delight at his warm language, and told him I knew you
would be pleased to hear that he had thus spoken of you. He
said that he had been so much interested, that he had been
about to write to you, and I begged him urgently to do so.
The opening observation had been made by Thackeray, entirely *à propos des bottes.* Not a word had been said by me, or
any one else at table, of the magazine, or of you. After dinner
I had a good deal of talk with him about you, and he spoke
with much warmth and appreciation of your poems ; he praised
particularly the ' Last Leaf ' and ' The Punch Bowl.' I cannot
help thinking that it will please you to hear this, so I have
gone to the expense of a new envelope (price one penny), in
order to mention it, my letter having been already sealed and
directed before I went to dinner.

Always affectionately yours,

J. L. M.

To his Wife.

London,
May 28th, 1858.

MY DEAREST MARY,—I wrote to you last Sunday, and
according to my promise I am now going to send you a few
lines to tell you what I have been about, although it
is nothing very wonderful. The place is so large as to
be an intolerable nuisance to any one who puts the least
value on time, money, or shoe leather. You live in half a
dozen towns at once, and pass ever so many hours daily in
going from one of them to another. Last Sunday, after
writing to you, I went and dined with the Sturgis's, and found
them as cordial and agreeable as ever. There was no company
except I—— and S——. Late in the evening I went with
Arthur Russell to the Cosmopolitan. This is not a club house,
but only a club which meets late in the evenings twice a week,
Sundays and Wednesdays, in a large room which is the studio
of the painter Phillips, in Charles Street, leading from
Berkeley Square. The object seems to be to collect noted
people and smoke very bad cigars. This evening I found
Mackintosh there, and among other men was Higgins, a gigantic individual who writes in the *Times* under the name of
"Jacob Omnium," Layard the Ninevite, Stirling, the author
of the 'Cloister Life of Charles V.,' Monckton Milnes, besides
various other personages connected with literature and
politics. I was introduced to a good many of them, and they
all said civil things to me, nothing worth repeating to you, or
in fact which I remember. It is not considered good taste
here, as you know, to throw a man's writings very hard in his
face. The formula is, "We know you very well in England,"
"Your name is very familiar to us," "Your fame has preceded
you," or words to that effect. It is however a convenience to
observe that one's name is more or less known, whether they
have read a word of you or not, because, as Tristram Shandy
observes, a man is always puzzled if asked to say who he is.
I liked Stirling, with whom I had a long talk. He is mild,
amiable, bald-headed, scholarlike, a Member of Parliament

and a man of fortune.   He is at present engaged, he told me, in a work upon Don John of Austria.   He is a great friend of Prescott's, but we both agreed that his Philip was altogether too mild and flattered a portraiture of that odious personage.

Milnes is a good speaker in Parliament, a good writer of poems, which have been praised by critics who have roosted on his mahogany tree, a man of fashion, and altogether a swell of the first class.   Layard is short, square, hirsute and taurine of aspect, as befits the Nineveh bull, but he is the bull without the wings.   Not that he is slow in reality, for the world knows well enough the indomitable energy and rapid intelligence of the man.   Moreover he has rushed all over India in an impromptu manner and incredibly short time, for the sake of investigating matters there and tossing the Ministers with his horns when he returns, and he is now delivering lectures upon the subject. He told me that he came from Alexandria with a countryman of mine, Mr. Sturgis.   This is a brother of Russell, who has just arrived (yesterday) in Southampton.   Monday I passed at the State Paper Office, and I made my first dive this season into the dead sea, in which I have so long laved my youthful limbs. I find my secretary (I have three secretaries for foreign affairs, you know—one resident at Her Majesty's State Paper Office, one established at the British Museum, and one in the Kingdom of Holland ; and when the salaries of all three are paid, the balance for the Home Department will be somewhat diminished)—I find, I say, my secretary quite satisfactory ; he is intelligent and writes a good hand.   The price paid is 4*d*. for what is called a folio, which is seventy-two words.   This makes exactly nine words for one cent, which is the highest price paid for copying anywhere.   I have just consoled myself by writing out a page of the *Atlantic Magazine* in folios, and I find that to copy that amount would be worth about eighty cents. Therefore, if I am forced to penny-a-lining, I can get about thirteen times as much for writing a page as for copying one.

There is an enormous lot of documents both in the S. P. O. and the British Museum ; but I shall soon begin to see land. However, I will not bore you with these details, which are

about as interesting to an outsider as it is to look at the
paddies digging the cellar, the cartloads of bricks and the
great puddles of mortar out of which somebody or other is
going to build a house. When it is finished, and you can walk
in at the front door, and the hod-carriers and carpenters have
all vanished, it is time enough for your friends and the public.

In the evening I dined at Mackintosh's. The party consisted of the Sturgis's, a Mrs. ——, of whom I know nothing,
except that Thackeray kept saying, as I learned afterwards, all
dinner-time to Sturgis, "I hate that woman!"—why she was so
odious I have not yet been informed, as she seemed as harmless as a dove if not as wise as a serpent. The others were
Thackeray, Lord Carlisle, and myself. I believe you have
never seen Thackeray. He has the appearance of a colossal
infant, smooth, white, shiny ringlety hair, flaxen, alas, with
advancing years, a roundish face, with a little dab of a nose
upon which it is a perpetual wonder how he keeps his
spectacles, a sweet but rather piping voice, with something of
the childish treble about it, and a very tall, slightly stooping
figure—such are the characteristics of the great "snob" of
England. His manner is like that of everybody else in
England—nothing original, all planed down into perfect
uniformity with that of his fellow-creatures. There was not
much more distinction in his talk than in his white choker or
black coat and waistcoat. As you like detail, however, I shall
endeavour to Boswellise him a little, but it is very hard work.
Something was said of Carlyle the author. Thackeray said,
" Carlyle hates everybody that has arrived—if they are on the
road, he may perhaps treat them civilly." Mackintosh praised
the description in the 'French Revolution' of the flight of the
King and Queen (which is certainly one of the most living
pictures ever painted with ink), and Thackeray agreed with
him, and spoke of the passages very heartily. Of the Cosmopolitan Club, Thackeray said, " Everybody is or is supposed
to be a celebrity; nobody ever says anything worth hearing;
and every one goes there with his white choker at midnight,
to appear as if he had just been dining with the aristocracy.
I have no doubt," he added, "that half of us put on the white

cravat after a solitary dinner at home or at our club, and so go
down among the Cosmopolitans."

I have strung these things together, not with the idea that
the observations are worth sending (except for peculiar
reasons, the last one), but because in your solitude I think that
both you and Lily may be as easily amused as the friends of
Mr. Peter Magnus were. This is what mainly occupies me
when I go out; the thought that perhaps I may suck out
something out of the somewhat flat and gravelly soil of London
society, which may flower into a letter for your gratification,
is about the only one which gives me much satisfaction.
Therefore I beg you to find the bouquets very fragrant and
very brilliant, although they are in truth about as rare as
dandelions.

Thackeray invited me to dine next Sunday (that is to-day),
and he went off very soon, as he confessed, to work at the
'Virginians.' Lord Carlisle was excessively civil to me. I
think you have seen him, although I never did. He is tall,
awkwardly heavy featured, but much better looking now than
as a young man. His hair is snow white, parted over a prodigious bump of benevolence. He has been Lord Lieutenant
of Ireland for the last three years, having just gone out with
the advent of the Derby Administration. He begged me to
give him my address, saying that he was at present absent
from town, but hoped to have the pleasure of cultivating my
acquaintance on his return. On Tuesday I worked at the
State Paper Office. After my return, Sir Charles Lyell called
on me, and sat a good while. He is the eminent geologist,
you know, and has been often in America. He was very agreeable, and as Mackintosh came in while he was there, who knows
him very well, we got on comfortably. By the way, they have
had me admitted to the Athenæum Club during my stay in
London. This is a fine building on the corner of Pall Mall
and lower Regent Street, and you get all the papers and
journals, and have the run of a library of thirty thousand
volumes, and can breakfast or lunch and dine there, very well,
and at a cheaper rate than at any hotel. In the evening I
dined again at the Sturgis's. There was a large party of

Americans.   Afterwards I went very late to a small party at
Mrs. Warre's.   It was a kind of bridal party, and there was a
great lot of very pretty girls in bridesmaid costumes.   I was
introduced to about twenty-five of them.   But I am unable
to inform you of the name of one of them.

The party was about breaking up when I arrived.   Froude
(whose wife, you know, is Mrs. Warre's sister) is not in town,
and I am sorry to say has got an alarming affection of the
eyes.   I am going to write to him to beg him to come up
while I am here.

Wednesday morning Mackintosh came to my quarters again.
I never saw such a fellow—it seems as if he could not do
enough for me.   He is half the time apparently in a brown
study and oblivious of your existence, when he suddenly
wakes up and you find he has been turning over in his mind
what he can do to oblige you.   I hardly knew him in America,
never met him but once or twice, and that a hundred years
ago, so I never knew what a good fellow he is, full of humour
and a great deal of talent and character.   Well, he came down
to persuade me to go down to the Derby that day.   This, you
know, is the most famous race in England or the world.   The
Derby stake is the prize for which once a year the best
trained three-year-olds in the country contend, and the horse
who wins it is for ever famous, is worth no end of money, and
puts fabulous amounts of it into the pocket of his owner.   The
races are on the Epsom downs, about fifteen miles from
London, and the Derby day is the one holiday which is
religiously kept by every one great and small, from peers to
pickpockets, throughout London and its neighbourhood.   No
better proof of its precedence over all other sublunary affairs
could be given than by the spectacle which was presented by
the House of Commons adjourning over two days on account
of the Derby, in the very midst of a Ministerial crisis and of
an unfinished debate, the result of which was to determine
whether the Government should be overthrown, and if overthrown, whether it would dissolve Parliament.   The funniest
thing was that the leading favourite for the race was Lord
Derby's horse, Toxophilite, and it was very generally believed

that the Premier was much more anxious to win the "Derby,"
which Dizzy long ago termed "the blue riband" of the turf,
than to keep his post at the head of the Empire.

I shall not bore you with a description of the race. We
had a very good position, and saw it very well. The scene was
sufficiently amusing—the horses for the Derby Cup all ran so
close that you might have covered them with a handkerchief,
and it was only by the signal at the winning post that the
spectators could be sure that Beadsman had won, and that
Toxophilite was done, coming in only second; but I was told
that the owner of Beadsman, Sir Joseph Hawley, pocketed
£30,000 as the result of that race.

We came up to town and went to the Opera together. I
did not care much to go particularly, as the price of a stall
is *only* one guinea, but I did not like to refuse, and was
willing enough to see the opera-house, which I had never
seen. The opera was the 'Barber,' and it was very mysterious
to know where and how Alboni as Rosina had been able to
bestow her mountainous masses of flesh within the bodice and
the vest of the *costume obligé* of the young maiden of Seville.
She did not look exactly monstrous, and she sang magnificently. There was afterwards an act of the 'Fille du
Régiment,' Piccolomini as the heroine. She is pretty, *petite,*
piquante, and with most exquisite hands and arms, vindicates
her rights to the illustrious name she bears. She is rather
too fond of looking captivating and winning, and grinning in
front of the foot-lights, and her style is altogether, I should
say, *petit genre.* After the Opera we went to the Cosmopolitans, it being Wednesday night. There I had some talk
with Layard, Thackeray, Milnes, and also with Kingsley, who
seems to have a stuttering way with him which one would
think would interfere with that eloquence of preaching for
which he is celebrated. He is tall, rather thin, with commonplace features, neither handsome nor the reverse, but seems
a good fellow, and entirely unparsonical. He had not heard
of Froude's attack of ophthalmia, or whatever it may be, as
he is only passing through town. Another young man of
some eminence was introduced to me—Lord Goderich, a rising

member of the House of Commons, who made the night before
last a very neat and telling speech against the Government.
He was very civil to me, and paid me some very handsome
compliments on the D. R.

On Thursday, according to express and very urgent invitation, I went with Mrs. Amory and S—— to call at the
Lyndhursts'. As soon as I got into the room Lady L.
opened upon me such a torrent of civilities that I was nearly
washed away. I certainly should not repeat, even to you, and
even if I remembered it, the particular phraseology. Once for
all, too, let me say that I only mention such things as these
in conformity to your urgent request. I would no more write
such things to any one else, even to my mother, than I would
go and stand on my head in the middle of Pall Mall. I feel
like a donkey, and am even now blushing unseen, like a peony
or any other delicate flower, at the very idea of writing such
trash, and I beg that you will thrust my letter into the fire at
once. Moreover, I assure you, with perfect honesty, that if
you had not been so very desirous that I should put my head a
little while out of my shell, I should certainly keep it in and
pass all my time at work, which, by the way, is getting these
few days past somewhat behindhand. She then took me in
and presented me to Lord Lyndhurst. I liked him very much.
Although he is eighty-six years of age, his intellect is un-
dimmed. He has almost lost the use of his legs, and is wheeled
about in a chair; but he goes down to the House every day, and
he occasionally makes a speech, which is neater, more concise,
and more elegant than any that are delivered there. He must
have been very handsome, with a decided resemblance to his
sister, Mrs. Greene. He wears a brown wig; has regular
features; is not very unlike Mr. Otis[1] in appearance. His
manner is very gentle and winning. He said some very kind
things to me about my book, and talked very agreeably on
other topics. They urged me to dine there that day, but I was
engaged at Mr. Reeve's. Reeve, you know, is the editor of the
Edinburgh Review—a good-humoured, tall, large Englishman;
Mrs. Reeve is intelligent and literary. There were one or two

[1] Harrison Gray Otis.

Members of Parliament present, but none known to fame, unless Mr. Lowe [1] be an exception. Friday I made a call at the Russells'. Lady William Russell, a high-bred dame, among other things, informed me that she was very intimate with the Queen of Holland, and that she wished to give me a letter of introduction to her. I dined this day at the Mackintoshes, with the Amorys, two Englishmen—Mr. Darwin and Mr. Phillips—and Felton, who has suddenly turned up here on his way to Greece.

Saturday I went down with Felton by rail to Chiswick House to lunch, by invitation, with Lord Carlisle. He is going, I believe, into Yorkshire for some days; but as Felton was only passing through London, he was desirous that we should make a brief visit to Chiswick. This is a very beautiful Italian villa, with fine grounds, trees, gardens, and conservatories, which was lately bequeathed to Lord Carlisle's mother by her brother, the Duke of Devonshire. There was no company there; but we passed a few hours very agreeably, looking at the house and grounds, and talking wisdom. Lord C. is excessively amiable and friendly, and says he wishes when he returns to London to cultivate my acquaintance, which he is at liberty to do if he chooses; but as I again repeat to you, if it were not for your particular request, I would go nowhere, for my time is frittered away into nothing.

By the way, I dined by myself at the Athenæum Club, and rather enjoyed my own company. Sunday, I lunched with Sir Charles Lyell, who invited me and W. Greenough of Boston, who brought him a letter, I believe, to the Zoological Gardens. I have done my duty to that eminent institution, and although when one has plenty of leisure no better morning lounge could be found, yet as I have, unhappily, no turn for zoology, and more work to do than I could accomplish if every day had forty-eight hours, I could have dispensed with the beasts on this occasion. I was glad, however, to improve my acquaintance with the Lyells. He is a most distinguished man of science, and very companionable; and she is an

---

[1] Lord Sherbrooke.

extremely pleasing and just ceasing to be a very pretty woman. Afterwards, I went to call at Lady Byron's, who is living at her house near Primrose Hill, in Regent's Park. She is still very delicate in health, but has got through the winter tolerably well. She is as kind and earnest as ever, and seemed very glad to see me. I was much pleased to hear that the Noels were in town for a few days, although they had at that moment gone out. In the evening I dined at Thackeray's. There were fifteen or sixteen people. I do not know any of their names. I sat between Thackeray's two daughters. They are both intelligent and agreeable. The youngest told me she liked 'Esmond' better than any of her father's books. Thackeray, by the way, evidently considers that kind of thing his forte. He told me that he hated the 'Book of Snobs,' and could not read a word of it. 'The Virginians,' he said, was devilish stupid, but at the same time most admirable; but that he intended to write a novel of the time of Henry V., which would be his *capo d' opera*, in which the ancestors of all his present characters, Warringtons, Pendennis's, and the rest should be introduced. It would be a most magnificent performance, he said, and nobody would read it. After the ladies had left the house, we went downstairs and smoked cigars till into the small hours. One of the company I discovered to be Blackwood, the present proprietor of *Blackwood's Magazine;* another was the Secretary of the English Legation at Frankfort. He knew Bismarck, of course, and said there was no doubt he was the cleverest man in Germany, and that everybody hated him in consequence, and was afraid of him.

The Thackerays are to have what they call a "drum" or a tea-fight to-night (Monday). I accepted an invitation to it, but I do not think I shall go, for I am to dine late to-day at Mackintosh's, to meet Lord Carlisle and Milman.

This letter, begun yesterday (Sunday), has been concluded to-day (Monday). I shall write again next Sunday. I do not think, dear Mary, you can complain of a scarcity of details in this epistle. I only hope you may not be bored by them. My next will be very different; for although you may think from this that I am a good deal in society, it is not at all the case,

and after a day or two, I shall be entirely alone again, which
I shall only regret on your account, and rejoice for on my own.
God bless you, dearest Mary; kiss my darling children, and
believe in the love of

Your affectionate
J. L. M.

To his Wife.

London,
May 30th, 1858.

MY DEAREST MARY,—On Monday I dined with the Mackintoshes. Macaulay, Dean Milman, and Mr. and Mrs. Farrar
composed the party. Of course you would like a photograph
of Macaulay, as faithfully as I can give it. He impressed me
on the whole agreeably. To me, personally, he spoke cour-
teously, respectfully, showed by allusion to the subject in
various ways that he was quite aware of my book and its
subject, although I doubt whether he had read it. He may
have done so, but he manifested no special interest in me. I
believe that he is troubled about his health (having a kind of
bronchial or asthmatic cough), and that he rarely dines out
now-a-days, so that it is perhaps a good deal of a compliment
that he came on this occasion on purpose to meet me. His
general appearance is singularly commonplace. I cannot
describe him better than by saying he has exactly that kind
of face and figure which by no possibility would be selected,
out of even a very small number of persons, as those of a
remarkable personage. He is of the middle height, neither
above nor below it. The outline of his face in profile is
rather good. The nose, very slightly aquiline, is well cut,
and the expression of the mouth and chin agreeable. His
hair is thin and silvery, and he looks a good deal older than
many men of his years—for, if I am not mistaken, he is just
as old as his century, like Cromwell, Balzac, Charles V., and
other notorious individuals. Now those two impostors, so far
as appearances go, Prescott and Mignet, who are sixty-two,
look young enough, in comparison, to be Macaulay's sons.

The face, to resume my description, seen in front, is blank, and as it were badly lighted. There is nothing luminous in the eye, nothing impressive in the brow. The forehead is spacious, but it is scooped entirely away in the region where benevolence ought to be, while beyond rise reverence, firmness and self-esteem, like Alps on Alps. The under eyelids are so swollen as almost to close the eyes, and it would be quite impossible to tell the colour of those orbs, and equally so, from the neutral tint of his hair and face, to say of what complexion he had originally been. His voice is agreeable, and its intonations delightful, although that is so common a gift with Englishmen as to be almost a national characteristic.

As usual, he took up the ribands of the conversation, and kept them in his own hand, driving wherever it suited him. I believe he is thought by many people a bore, and you remember that Sydney Smith spoke of him as " our Tom, the greatest engine of social oppression in England." I should think he might be to those who wanted to talk also. I can imagine no better fun than to have Carlyle and himself meet accidentally at the same dinner-table with a small company. It would be like two locomotives, each with a long train, coming against each other at express speed. Both, I have no doubt, could be smashed into silence at the first collision. Macaulay, however, is not so dogmatic, or so outrageously absurd as Carlyle often is, neither is he half so grotesque or amusing. His whole manner has the smoothness and polished surface of the man of the world, the politician, and the new peer, spread over the man of letters within. I do not know that I can repeat any of his conversation, for there was nothing to excite very particular attention in its even flow. There was not a touch of Holmes's ever bubbling wit, imagination, enthusiasm, and arabesqueness. It is the perfection of the commonplace, without sparkle or flash, but at the same time always interesting and agreeable. I could listen to him with pleasure for an hour or two every day, and I have no doubt I should thence grow wiser every day, for his brain is full, as hardly any man's ever was, and his way of delivering himself is easy and fluent.

At first, in deference to me, there was a good deal of talk about Holland, Maurice of Orange, Oldenbarneveld, the Archives of the Hague, the State Paper Office, on all which subjects I spoke myself as little as I could, because I wished to hear Macaulay and Milman converse, to both of whom I listened with great pleasure, although neither said anything very new or striking, or which would in the least interest you. Then Macaulay talked of an old acquaintance of his, Basil Montagu, who was a commissioner of bankruptcy, before whom he argued cases when very young, and also an editor of Bacon's works. "Bankruptcy and Bacon," said Macaulay, "were the only things which Montagu cared for in the world." This was the nearest approach to an epigram which he made. Then there was a talk about the clubs, and he said that Burke, when these were first instituted in London, denounced them solemnly as pernicious in their tendency. Having his head full of the Jacobin clubs of Paris, he foretold the subversion of the English institutions as a consequence of such establishments. A club house still existing, said Macaulay, inspired Burke with especial horror. It was set up by some returned East Indians, was called the Oriental Club, and may still be seen, "a gaunt, yellow, bilious, mulligatawny-looking building, now in the last stage of decrepitude," yet this concern has been considered, by so great a statesman, as brimful of danger to English liberty.

Something was said of Bulwer Lytton's project for a guild of authors. Macaulay ridiculed it. Lytton, he said, has constantly wished to interest him in it, but he had been obstinate. Why, he asked, should there be a society, or guild, to support and pension authors who were unsuccessful? It was offering a premium for dulness. If a man wrote a book which nobody would read, why should he be rewarded, therefore, with a maintenance for life? The most extraordinary part of the scheme, too, was that Lytton had given lands in his own grounds at Knebworth for these destitute *literati*, so that he was always surrounded, when at home in the country, with a transplanted Grub Street. Moreover, said Macaulay, these people, if they have merit, are very apt to get some place or pension. There is James, for instance; he has a consulship, has he not? I do not know how deserving he may be; I never read but one of his novels. "He never wrote but one," said Mackintosh, in his dry way, which was the best thing said that day at table. Milman I liked very much. I had always been told by Sir Charles Lyell that he had read and approved my book very much, and desired to make my acquaintance, so that I felt quite at ease with him. He is the Dean of St. Paul's (which is the next thing to being a bishop), the author of the 'History of Latin Christianity,' but better known to you as the author of the famous tragedy of 'Fazio,' with a good deal more poetry of merit. He is now about sixty-five, or even seventy. He is singularly bent, but not, I think, with age, so as to give, at the first glance, the appearance of extreme decrepitude. This seems, however, purely a local affection, for his manner is bright, and youthful, and genial. He has a long, large, rather regular face, with thick hair, and very black, bushy eyebrows, under which his eyes flash like living coals.

Mrs. Milman is a tall, handsome—and has been very handsome—woman, very cordial and agreeable in her manner. They invited me to go, Thursday of this week, to a famous anniversary in St. Paul's—the singing of the charity children, several thousands in number—a ceremony which Thackeray declares in one of his lectures to be the most interesting spectacle which Christianity can furnish, far more impressive than any of the sights and shows of Holy Week at Rome. A ticket of admission into the Dean's pew will give me a very good facility of witnessing the affair. Afterwards the invited guests are to have luncheon at the Deanery.

After dinner Macaulay had a pretty severe attack of coughing, and went home early. The Thackerays had a "drum" in the evening, and as the Milmans were going, as well as myself, they kindly gave me a lift in their carriage. I found at the party, of my acquaintance, Mrs. Reeve, the Synges, Mrs. Sturgis, Russell and Colonel Hamley. I was also introduced to Mrs. Procter (alias Barry Cornwall). I do not know whether the illustrious Barry was there himself or not. Mr. and Mrs. Blackwood, whom I met the day before at dinner, were also of the party, and there was a tremendous screeching lady, who stunned the company with Italian music, with a voice which wanted elbow room as much as it did melody.

Thackeray introduced me to Lady Stanley of Alderley, at whose house he is to read the lecture to-morrow of which I told you, I think, in my last letter. She is a tall, fair, agreeable dame, with blonde hair and handsome features, apparently thirty-five, yet one of those wonderful grand-mothers of which England can boast so many, and who make one almost a convert to the "delicious women of sixty."[1] Not that she is in any proximity to that famous epoch, but she astonished me by suddenly saying that her daughter, the Countess of Airlie, wished very much to make my acquaint-ance, for I had taken the mother for quite a young woman. The daughter, Lady Airlie, is a very pretty woman, with a rosy face. Both of them overwhelmed me with compliments about my book, which, they said, every one of their family had read with delight from beginning to end. Lady Stanley begged me to be sure not to fail to come the next day to the lecture. There were also the two —— girls, who visit at Walton, of whom you heard Tom Appleton and the Sturgises speak. I was introduced to them, and they seem lively young things enough. The Sturgises brought me home.

Next morning I went up to Lady Byron's, to lunch with her and the Noels, and we had a long, quiet talk about Dresden times. They all made very kind inquiries about you and Lily. The Noels left London the same day, but are to return after a week. I believe Lady Byron is rather feeble, but no worse, I should say, than two years ago. By the way, it will amuse you to hear that Noel told me she had talked a great deal more about that likeness,[2] which

---

[1] Mrs. Harrison Gray Otis said that while comparatively young women were socially neglected in America, in Europe she had known "delicious women of sixty."

[2] Mr. Motley's resemblance to Lord Byron.

she speaks of as "most wonderful." At five o'clock I met
Thackeray by appointment at the Athenæum Club, and we
went together to Lady Stanley's. The lecture was in the
back drawing-room of a very large and elegant house, and
the company—not more than fifty or sixty in number—were
all comfortably seated. It was on George III.—one of the
set of the four Georges, first delivered in America, and which
have often been read in England, but have never been
printed. I was much impressed with the quiet, graceful ease
with which he read—just a few notes above the conversational
level—but never rising into the declamatory. This light-in-
hand manner suits well the delicate, hovering rather than
superficial, style of the composition. He skims lightly over
the surface of the long epoch, throwing out a sketch here,
exhibiting a characteristic trait there, and sprinkling about
a few anecdotes, portraits, and historical allusions, running
along from grave to gay, from lively to severe, moving and
mocking the sensibilities in a breath, in a way which I should
say was the perfection of lecturing to high-bred audiences.
I suppose his manner, and his stuff also, are somewhat
stronger for larger and more heterogeneous assemblies, for
I have no doubt he left out a good deal which might jar upon
the ears polite of his audience on this occasion. Still, I was
somewhat surprised at the coolness with which he showed up
the foibles and absurdities of kings, and court, and court
folks in a former but not remote reign, before a small
company, which consisted of the cream of London cream.
They seemed to enjoy it, and to laugh heartily at all the
points without wincing. If he had shown up Democracy or
Southern chivalry thus before an assemblage of the free and
enlightened, he would have been tarred and feathered on the
spot.

After the lecture was over, I expected to slip away un-
noticed, but Lady Stanley came to me, and talked with great
kindness, and introduced me to several persons, all of whom
said I was no stranger, or words to that effect. One of the
persons was the Marchioness of Londonderry, a tall, fair,
very handsome woman, apparently young, but having a son,

just of age, by a previous husband, Lord Powerscourt. Then
Lady Airlie said to me, Mrs. Norton wishes to make your
acquaintance. I turned and bowed, and there she was,
looking to-day almost as handsome as she has always been
described as being. I know that you will like a sketch. She
is rather above middle height. In her shawl and crinoline,
of course I could not pronounce upon her figure. Her face is
certainly extremely beautiful. The hair is raven black—
violet black—without a thread of silver. The eyes very
large, with dark lashes, and black as death; the nose straight;
the mouth flexible and changing; with teeth which in themselves would make the fortune of an ordinary face—such is
her physiognomy; and when you add to this extraordinary
poetic genius, descent from that famous Sheridan who has
made talent hereditary in his family, a low, sweet voice and
a flattering manner, you can understand how she twisted
men's heads off and hearts out, we will not be particular how
many years ago.

    She said to me, as I made my bow on introduction, "Your
name is upon every lip." I blushed and looked as much like
a donkey as usual when such things are said. Then she
added, "It is agreeable, is it not?" I then had grace enough
to reply, "You ought to know if any one;" and then we
talked of other things. There was no time for much conversation, however. Presently it appeared that a Miss ——,
a young lady belonging, I believe, to the fashionable world,
but who rejoices in a talent for the stage, was to recite;
so she recited. It was a passage from 'Phèdre' (I believe).
Her accent was very good, and she certainly declaimed
very well. Afterwards she recited Tennyson's 'Charge of
Balaclava.'

    As I was going away, Lady Airlie invited me to a dinner
for the following Tuesday (which is now the day after
to-morrow). Mrs. Norton told me she should be happy to see
more of me. A day or two afterwards accordingly I went to
call on her. She received me with great kindness, and was
very agreeable. She has a ready, rapid way of talking—
alludes with perfect *aplomb* to her interminable quarrels with

Mr. Norton. She spoke of her two sons, one of whom is heir to a peerage, and the other to beggary. She showed me a photograph of this second one, who is evidently her darling, and who, by way of improving his prospects in life, married a year ago a peasant girl of the island of Capri. Mrs. Norton does not even think her very handsome, but says that he imagines her perfection, particularly in her fancy costume. She knew Webster when he was here, and admired him very much. She is also very intimate with the Queen of Holland.

I do not know that I have much more to chronicle of her conversation. She was always animated and interesting. My impressions of what she must have been were confirmed; certainly it was a most dangerous, terrible, beautiful face in its prime, and is very handsome still. Her two sisters, the Duchess of Somerset and Lady Dufferin, were equally celebrated for their beauty, and the latter for her talent also. Mrs. Norton told me that she wished me to dine with her, and to ask some people to meet me, and is to appoint the day very soon. She wishes me particularly to know Lady Dufferin.

On Saturday, along with fifty of my compatriots, I was Peabodied. The good old gentleman, according to his wont, had made a razzia among all the Americans now in London, and swept them all off down the river in a small steamboat to see the Leviathan, and afterwards to dine at Blackwall. I was glad of the opportunity, for I am sure that I should never have had energy enough without assistance "to put a hook in the nose of the Leviathan," and I rather wished to see it. The company was of course as miscellaneous and as uninteresting as might be expected. The Leviathan was visited, and is certainly a most astonishing object. I suspect, however, that the shareholders say with Christopher Sly, "A most excellent piece of work, would it were done," for I believe they are at a standstill for want of funds; and if it cannot be finished till the sale of tickets to visitors can float it on to fortune, she is likely to remain a torso as many centuries as the Cologne Cathedral, and the one just now looks as likely to make a voyage to Australia as the other. I shall not describe

R 2

the ship. You have only to imagine a Cunarder doubled, or trebled for aught I know, in all its proportions, and you have the vessel.

Nothing is finished of the state rooms or cabins. It is all in a clutter, the engines are not in, and in short you get not a much better idea of it from a visit than from reading a description in the newspapers. The dinner was at the hotel at Blackwall. Mr. Peabody had organised his dinner very well, having arranged the way in which his company should pair off, and having sent the men into the dining-room beforehand to find out where each name, together with that of the partner of his toil, was inscribed. He assigned to me a nice English girl, who knew the Sturgis's, Thackeray, Dickens, and others, who was lively and disposed to make herself gene- rally agreeable, so it was much better than the rather dreary festival which I had anticipated. On my other flank was Mrs. Charles Amory. She and S—— came into the hotel at the last moment from the country, where they had been staying a few days at Lord Hatherton's with no end of swells, and find everything as rose-coloured as usual. They are very jolly, and desirous of pleasing everybody and being pleased. S—— promised me faithfully to write immediately to Lily, and I think she will keep her promise. She is a very good girl, frank and unaffected, and very good- humoured. Joshua Fisher and his wife and daughters were also of this party.

Hurlbert has turned up here. He was at this dinner. He is staying in the country with Hughes, the author of 'Tom Brown's Schooldays,' a book which has had a great run. He informed me that Hughes wished to make my acquaintance very much, that he was about, with other *literati*, to establish a new review, in the first number of which an article on my book was to appear, etc. I go to a party at Lady Lyell's to-morrow. Tuesday I dine at the Airlies'; Wednesday, at the Warres'. Thursday I go to a luncheon with the Dean of St. Paul's.

P.S.—*Monday, 31st.*—I broke off here yesterday, dear Mary, not as my angelic little Mary used to say, because I wished to add a postscript, but because I had promised to make a call at Lady Stanley's. I went, and had a very pleasant visit. She is an agreeable person, with plenty of talk and fond of literary people and literature. Her youngest daughter[1] was there, and was very glad to speak to me, because she had read every word of the 'Dutch Republic,' not from compulsion, but from choice. I said I considered it one of the highest compliments I had received, because if so young a person could read it, I felt that I was not a bore. She said, Oh! no, it is just like a novel; and the others said the same. I feel that if old Lord Lyndhurst, who was eighty-six day before yesterday, and a very young girl, can both read three solid volumes without being bored, they cannot be so very heavy, for two such individuals may be considered representative persons. I do not say excuse this egotism, because I write it on purpose to please you. To utter such things to any one else would be the height of absurdity. Lady Stanley, as I went away, asked me if I knew Lady Palmerston. I said "no;" and she told me she would inform her that I was in town, and would see that I was invited to her next party.

Good-bye, dearest Mary. If I have bored you unmercifully, at least you will admit that it is with the best intentions of amusing you. I know you like details, so there are a lot for you. Kiss my dear, dear, darling children a thousand times, and accept the love of

Yours most affectionately,

J. L. M.

To his Wife.

London,

June 6th, 1858.

MY DEAREST MARY,—It is a great pleasure to me to sit down and try to amuse you every Sunday morning with a record of what I see, for I most sincerely assure you that it is almost the only real satisfaction which I derive from this

---

[1] Now Hon. Mrs. George Howard.

going up and down like Beelzebub in the world of London. I must retract what I said in my last letter of not being in society. My only difficulty now is in keeping out of it a little, so that I may not entirely neglect my business in the Archives.

On Monday evening I went to a small party at Lady Lyell's. The Amorys were there, and Mackintosh, and the Mrs. ——, hated of Thackeray, of whom I spoke to you in my last. Beyond these and Dean Milman and Mrs. Milman, I do not think that there was anybody that I knew by sight, and we came off before 12 o'clock.

Just before going to this party I received a very kind note from Lady W. Russell, of which this is an extract—" Lord and Lady Palmerston are anxious to make your acquaintance, and I have taken upon myself the responsibility of venturing a short notice of an invitation to dinner, as they have but that day disengaged and do not like to delay the meeting." The day then proposed by them was Wednesday, and Lady William Russell was to call for me to take me to Cambridge House. Unluckily, I was engaged to dine at ten days' previous notice with ——, so of course I was obliged to decline, which was a disappointment to me, because I knew it would be one to you. I had never mentioned the name of the Palmerstons anywhere, nor have I in any case since I have been here gone one inch forward to any one, so that when civilities are offered me, I can at least have the satisfaction of knowing that they are spontaneous, and that if I prove a bore, people have nobody to blame but themselves.

Tuesday morning early I received a very nice note from Mrs. Norton, enclosing a card from her sister the Duchess of Somerset, inviting me to a breakfast party at her villa at Wimbledon Park. The breakfast hour was from 1 till 7 P.M. The occasion of the party, as Mrs. Norton informed me, was " the marriage of the second daughter of the Duchess with the brother of the Marquis of Bath, Lord Henry Thynne." As I know you are fond of " high life, with pictures, taste, Shakespeare, and the musical glasses," I thought I would put in this statement. I took the rail accordingly from the

Waterloo Station at two, and after twenty minutes stopped
at Wimbledon, where a fly conveyed me to the Villa. The
house is a modern, not very extensive building, placed in the
midst of a little garden of Eden, brimful of flowering plants,
with a spacious lawn dotted with magnificent cedars of
Lebanon, ilexes, and other trees, while a stately park encloses
the whole domain. Beyond and from every point there are
views of the lovely pastoral scenery of English wood and dale
and hill, like which there is nothing in the world, the very
perfection of the commonplace. The day was cloudless, and
would have been hot for August even in America. You may
judge if the English complained of the heat, and whether or
not I was satisfied with the temperature. I found Mrs. Norton
looking out for me to introduce me to the Duchess of Somerset.
This lady was, as you may recollect, the famous " Queen of
Beauty " at the Eglinton tournament a good many years ago.

Her daughter, Lady Ulrica St. Maur, is a very beautiful
girl, closely resembling her mother, and obviously reproducing, perhaps in an inferior degree, what the Queen of
Beauty of the tournament must have been in the blaze of her
beauty.   Lady Dufferin I hardly saw, although I was presented to her, for at the same moment the two sons of the house
came up to me and began to talk. One of them, apparently
about twenty, had just returned from India, where he had
been, not with the army exactly, but a kind of spectator or
volunteer. He seemed intelligent and very handsome. The
other, Lord Edward St. Maur, was a very bright, good-
humoured lad of about fourteen. He said he had never travelled, but the very first tour he made he was determined
should be to America. I then went with Mrs. Norton into
the *salle à manger*, and while we were there, a plain, quiet,
smallish individual in a green cutaway coat, large yellow
waistcoat, and plaid trousers, came in for some luncheon, and
Mrs. Norton instantly presented me to him. It was Lord
John Russell. He was very civil to me, and we talked together for some time over the drum-stick of a chicken. His
face is not the least like the pictures one sees of him. No one
would suppose him the man of large intellect and indomitable

ambition, which he unquestionably is, by looking at him or
hearing him talk in a breakfast room. I do not mean of
course that a statesman is always to emulate Burke, of whom
Dr. Johnson said a man could not accidentally stop under a
shed with him to escape a shower, without discovering that he
was in the presence of a great man. There is also something
preferable in this easy nonchalant, commonplace manner to
the portentous aspect on the commonest occasions of many of
the "most remarkable men in our country, sir," which is apt
to characterise transatlanticism as much as the customary
suit of solemn black " in which they are pleased to array
themselves."

I can hardly report to you much of Lord John's conversation. He talked a good deal of Dizzy's famous speech at
Slough. You ask me by the way to give you occasionally a
touch of politics. I would gladly do so; but if I chronicle,
what I know you will like better, the little details of persons
and things that I purchase with my own pennyworth of observation, I know you will be better satisfied. And I really
should not have time to go into what after all you can read a
thousand times better in the *Times*, which I should think
you might contrive to get in Vevay. Suffice it that the
Derby-Dizzies, after it was thought certain that they would be
upset on the Cardwell motion of censure regarding the Ellen-
borough despatch business, have got a little fresh rope. The
withdrawal of that motion was a *dénouement* expected by
nobody the day before. Lord Lyndhurst, who at eighty-six is
not "passion's slave" nor party's, told me that the Government would be in a minority of eight or ten, and that then
they would dissolve Parliament, and have a general election.
The truth is that this threat of a dissolution is exactly what
saved the Ministry. Parliament has been but a year in
session, and there are so many members who were so excessively disgusted at the idea of the risk, trouble, and expense
of unseating themselves, and clambering back into their seat
again, or failing to do so, that they were glad to let the
Ministers off, knowing them to be reckless and desperate
enough to try the hazard of a general election.

Accordingly down goes Dizzy for the Easter holidays to Slough, and after a constituency dinner, seems to have absolutely been made drunk with the unexpected chance of retaining power a few months longer. He then delivered to the farmers and graziers and gentlemen there assembled, one of the cleverest, wittiest, most mendacious, most audacious, most besotted speeches that was ever made. He clapped his wings and "crowed like chanticleer an hour by the dial," without apparently remembering that electric telegraphs and stenography had been invented. In a day or two afterwards, Parliament came together again, and Dizzy recoiled in secret horror " e'en at the noise himself had made." Palmerston gave him two tremendous dressings in the House of Commons, and then Lord Clarendon in the Lords administered a most serious fustigation. In short, never was a Chancellor of Exchequer so belaboured since such officials were instituted. The lie was given to him as flatly as the Pickwickian rules permit by Palmerston and by Clarendon, and although Dizzy defended himself at first with adroitness and impudence, he was fairly obliged to eat his own words.

Well, Lord John touched lightly and slightly on these matters in his still small voice. I said it was a severe strain upon an English statesman to remember that every word he uttered in public was instantly and for ever to be recorded even as it fell from his lips. He said if a man did think of that he would not be able to open them. He spoke a little of the row about the Cuba slave trade and the American skippers, said that the American and English naval officers were the best people to settle that kind of embroglio, that they always respected each other and fraternised if the thing were possible, that the idea of war with America could never enter an Englishman's head. The triangulation of England may be considered complete as long as he and Palmerston are both alive. Both mean to be First Minister of the Whigs. Meantime the Tories, without any real principle of action, keep the provisional government by the equilibrium established between the large body of independents and the respective forces of Palmerston and Lord John.

I was introduced to a good many ladies, some of them pretty
and young. There is no doubt that the English aristocracy
has much beauty. When I say how handsome the women are,
the reply is invariable—that is a great compliment from an
American, for everybody knows that the American women are
the handsomest in the world. On the whole I think that the
grandmothers of England are the most miraculous race. There
are the Duchess of Somerset, Lady Dufferin, and Mrs. Norton,
then Lady Stanley, of whom I have spoken several times, the
Marchioness of Londonderry, and various others, all exceedingly handsome women still. I can hardly remember the
names of the many persons I was presented to. I remember
one, a lively, agreeable person, whose name was Lady Edward
Thynne, a daughter of Mrs. Gore the novelist. She was
apparently a young woman, and I dare say she is capable of
having at this moment ten grandchildren for aught I know
to the contrary.

Nothing can be kinder than Mrs. Norton. She takes me
under her especial convoy, and seems to think she can never
do enough for me. I feel as if I had known her for years, and
I am satisfied she does not dislike me, or she would not be
presenting me to everybody worth knowing. While I was
talking with her at another time she said, "Oh, there is my
lover, I must go and speak to him." She then went up to a
plain-looking benignant little old gentleman in a white hat
and a kind of old-world look about him that seemed to require
a pig-tail and white top boots. She whispered to him a
moment, and he came forward, beamingly saying, "Delighted,
I am sure, to make Mr. Motley's acquaintance," and shook me
warmly by the hand. This was the old Marquis of Lansdowne,
late President of the Council. He told me he was deeply
interested in my book, and that he had been much instructed
by me, and was much obliged to me. He said he was obliged
to go away immediately as the debate on the Slough business
was to come up in the Lords that afternoon, but he hoped
soon to see me again. My friend Lady Stanley and her
daughter, Maude Stanley (a pretty name, is it not?) were
there, also the Baroness Rothschild, who seems a very good-

humoured personage, and a great friend of the Amorys,
through the Lyndhursts, and a lot of other people were
there. I returned by the rail at six, and was tremendously
tired, to dress for dinner at eight at Lady Airlie's. She is
a very pretty, fresh, rosy woman, daughter of Lady Stanley,
and married to a handsome, good-humoured and unaffected
young Scotchman, the Earl of Airlie. The dinner was not
very large. There were half a dozen Members of Parliament
there and their wives. The lady next me was rather pretty ;
opposite was a bright, lively young woman, with an intelligent, sparkling, piquante face, and a merry laugh, who was
Lady Goderich. I was introduced to her before dinner, and
she went away after the coffee and ballad singing were
finished. I am however invited to dine at her house next
week. She was prettily dressed, with a head-dress of gold
coins, and a great string of pearls round a very white neck.

Lord Goderich, whom I have met once or twice, and who is
a rising man in politics, did not come on account of business
in Parliament.

In the evening came Lady Stanley and Miss Stanley (her
sister-in-law), who knew Washington Irving and other veterans.
Wednesday morning, before I was out of bed, I received a note
requiring an answer. It was again from Lady W. Russell.
It began : "I hope, my dear sir, that you are at liberty on
Saturday next? For if I fail in this second negotiation I
shall never be employed diplomatically again." She then
said Lord and Lady Palmerston begged me to dine on the
following Saturday, and she concluded : "Pray do not tell me
that you are again indissolubly pre-engaged."

The same forenoon Mackintosh came to me by appointment
to go with me to Mr. Hallam's, who had previously expressed a
wish that I should call. The great historian is long past the
"middle ages" now. He is paralysed in the right leg, the right
arm, and slightly in the tongue. His face is large, regularly
handsome, ruddy, fresh, and very good-humoured. He received me with great cordiality, and we had half an hour's
talk. He begged me to leave my address, and I suppose he
means to invite me to something or other, for I believe he

occasionally entertains his friends. His mind does not seem
essentially dimmed, and there is nothing senile in his aspect,
crippled as he is. He is a wreck, but he has not sunk head
downwards, as you sometimes see, which is the most melancholy termination to the voyage. His mind seems bright and
his spirits seem light. I dined this day at the Warres'.
You know about them. I like them both very much. To my
great delight Froude was there. He had just come up from
Bideford. He looks delicate, has a slight cough, but is mainly
troubled about his eyes. (The result, however, of his consulta-
tion with an oculist the following day, was that the disease
was not an alarming one, but would probably be chronic.)
The party was a pleasant one; the house is a large, elegant
mansion in Belgravia. I do not know who the company all
were. On the other side of me was Mrs. Mildmay, who
seemed an agreeable person. She told me she would see that
a ticket for the next "Almack's" was sent me, which balls it
seems are revived this season after an immemorial desuetude,
as —— might express himself.

After dinner I was introduced to Lady Mary Fielding, who
knew the Sturgis's very well. The next day I received a
message from her that her father (Earl of Denbigh) was too
gouty to call on me, but that if I would waive ceremony and
call there, it would be very kind of me. So I suppose I shall
go this week. In the evening late I went to the Cosmopolitan
with Froude. I had some talk with Layard and one or two
others, and met Lord Goderich, who asked me to dine Saturday
of this week. On Thursday I went to St. Paul's Cathedral, to
witness the ceremony of the singing of the charity children.
This takes place once a year. I had received a card from the
Dean of St. Paul's for a seat in his pew. The spectacle is
certainly very touching and impressive. There are about 4000
children, mostly under the age of ten or eleven. Arranged
in long rows, rising tier upon tier above each other, and all
dressed in dark stuff gowns with white kerchiefs and aprons
and mittens, with quaint old-world starched caps about their
young fresh faces, they have a very unique aspect. Particularly when they all rose and seated themselves as by a single

impulse, the flutter of these thousands of white wings all through the church, with the devout innocent look of the thousands of child faces, and the piping of their baby voices, suggested the choir of the angels in Paradise. I do not know much to say of the charity. It is merely a collection of all the children, some of whom are fed, clothed, and educated by various schools, which are variously endowed. But as an artistic exhibition it is certainly most effective. Thackeray, who was with me in the pew, said: "It is the finest thing in the world—finer than the Declaration of Independence." After the ceremony the luncheon for twenty or thirty invited guests was in the deanery, which is a large comfortable house near the church. I like Milman. He is very quick, shrewd, active of mind, almost a man of genius, a good historian, and apparently a good-hearted, sympathising person altogether. The sermon by a full-blown bishop was remarkably slow. I dined with Thackeray afterwards. The only people I liked and knew were Mr. and Mrs. Blackwood.

Friday morning I went down to the City with the Amorys. I acted as cicerone to show them the Chapter Coffee-house in Paternoster Row, which you and my darling Lily will recollect is the place of all others in the world in London which Charlotte Brontë selected when she came suddenly from Yorkshire to London to make a two days' visit. The place is as gloomy and forbidding as it is described to be by Mrs. Gaskell, and certainly no house in all the town could be imagined more forlorn for any woman to select as even a temporary residence. The alley is so narrow that one can almost touch the houses on both sides, and the whole expression of the locality is disconsolate in the last degree. The inscription is "Chapter Coffee House—Faithful"; and I asked a man who is there to superintend the premises, which are to be let, whether he had ever heard of Miss Brontë. "Can't say I ever heard the name, sir. Was she here in Mr. Faithful's time?" was the only reply. The slender furrow made by little Jane Eyre in the ocean of London had long been effaced.

We went also to the beautiful Temple church and gardens; and I thought of you, dear Mary, and the pleasure it gave you

to see these places when we were together in London. I went
afterwards to the Deanery of St. Paul's, to call on the Milmans,
found them at home, and they brought me back to the West
End, along with Mr. Senior, an ancient writer on political
economy, and a contributor to the *Edinburgh Review*. This
day I dined by myself at the Athenæum. The next day,
Saturday, after a day spent in the British Museum, I went with
Lady W. Russell and Arthur to the Palmerstons. Cambridge
House is one of the finest mansions in London, not far from
Hyde Park Corner. I was received very cordially by Lord
and Lady Palmerston. She is agreeable and well bred in her
manner, but at present without anything striking in her
appearance. Lord Palmerston is not the least like any picture
I ever saw of him. I thought him a tall, slender man. He is,
on the contrary, rather short, and looks older than I expected,
although I knew him to be seventy-four. His face is, however,
handsome, and his address very gentle, soft, and winning.
The features are regular, the teeth, if indigenous, good, but
the eyes are small and rather lack-lustre. He had the broad
blue ribbon of the garter over his white waistcoat, and he
wore, what one rarely sees now-a-days, a blue coat with gilt
buttons. He talked with me a few moments on miscellaneous
topics, and dinner was soon afterwards announced.

I went to the *salle à manger* with Mrs. William Cowper. The
company consisted, besides the hosts, of Lord and Lady Clarendon, their daughter, Lady Constance Villiers, the Countess of
Tankerville, Lady Olivia Ossulston, her daughter-in-law, a very
handsome woman, Lady Victoria Ashley, Monckton Milnes,
Mr. Labouchere, Monsieur Duvergier d'Hauranne (an ex-
minister of Louis Philippe), Lady William Russell and
Arthur Russell, and one or two others whom I have forgotten. The dining-room is large and elegant. The service
was plate, and the dinner and wines very good, but much
like all dinners. I found my neighbour, Mrs. Cowper, a very
pretty and agreeable person, disposed to please and be pleased,
and the dinner went on with the hush and calm characteristic
of these stately occasions. When the ladies retired I found
myself next to Lord Palmerston, and he talked with me a

long time about English politics and American matters, saying
nothing worth repeating, but conversing always with an easy,
winning, quiet manner, which accounts for his great popu-
larity among his friends.   At the same time it seemed difficult
to realise that he was the man who made almost every night,
and a very late hour in the night, those rattling, vigorous,
juvenile, slashing speeches which ring through the civilised
world as soon as uttered. I told him that it seemed to me
very difficult to comprehend how any man could make those
ready impromptu harangues in answer always to things said
in the course of the debate, taking up all the adversary's
points in his target, and dealing blows in return, without
hesitation or embarrassment. He said very quietly that it
was all a matter of habit; and I suppose that he really does it
with as much case as he eats his breakfast.

   After we rose from table, Lord Clarendon came forward to
me, and was introduced, and spoke very kindly to me, saying
that my name was very familiar to everybody in England,
and that it was a great pleasure to him to make my acquaintance. He asked me how I liked the arrangements of the
State Paper Office, and expressed himself with much interest
concerning my proceedings. He talked with me a quarter of
an hour or so very agreeably. Soon after we reached the
saloons, of which there were four or five *en suite*, the company
began to pour in, and they were soon overflowing.

   Baron Brunnow, the Russian ambassador, a tall man, with
an intensely ugly but very shrewd face, the Duke of Malakoff,
a short square figure with a broad white waistcoat and a singularly coarse and brutal physiognomy, and various other
diplomats less known to fame, were there. There were a good
many ladies whom I had met at the Duchess of Somerset's and
other places, Lady Airlie and her mother Lady Stanley, the
Baroness Rothschild and her daughter, recently married to
another Rothschild, Lady Lyndhurst and her daughter, and
various others, with all of whom I had the usual vapid conversation common in the crush of crowded saloons. I was also
introduced to one or two literary and scientific celebrities,
such as Hayward, a celebrated writer in the *Quarterly*, and

Sir Henry Rawlinson, the famous Eastern traveller, and Sir
Roderick Murchison, the great geologist. Lady W. Russell,
on introducing me to the last-named personage, said that she
was as Boswell said of himself with regard to General Paoli
and Dr. Johnson, "like an isthmus connecting two great con-
tinents." But I did not think the grim geologist seemed to
relish having his ancient stratum of reputation placed on a level
with so recent and tertiary a formation as he probably considers
mine to be. I do not know that I have anything further to
record of this evening's entertainment. I forgot to say that
upon the forenoon of this day Lord Lansdowne left his card
for me, together with an invitation to dinner for next Friday.
The difficulty now with me is to reduce my invitations to
order, for as I often have two a day, and cannot eat more than
one dinner per diem, there is often embarrassment of choice.
On Sunday I went to call on Mrs. Norton, and found her as
agreeable as ever. I think she talks about as well as Holmes,
and at the same time has that attractive manner, low, sweet
voice and expressive style of beauty which has made her so
celebrated. While I was there several people came in, among
others, Stirling, the Charles V. man; and presently the old
Marquis of Lansdowne toddled in, and sat drinking every word
she said with great delight. On going away he hoped I should
not decline his invitation, adding that Mrs. Norton's presence
would probably not make me less willing to be of the party.

I dined with the Sturgis's. The company was Frank
Cunningham and his wife, who have just turned up out of
Egypt, and look very fresh and pleased with their perambu-
lations, and Colonel Hamley. Afterwards I went for an hour
to the Cosmopolitan, where I found A. Russell (who begged
me to send his particular regards to you), Reeve, Layard,
Mackintosh, Milnes, and others; and I am now, at 2 A.M., just
finishing this long-winded epistle. So good-night and God
bless you and my darling children, dearest Mary.

Ever affectionately yours,

J. L. M.

To his Wife.

London,
June 13th, 1858.

MY DEAREST MARY,—As usual upon Sunday morning I am
going to give myself the pleasure of sending you a brief
account of my seeings and doings. I do not think that I
have a great deal that will prove interesting. I say also
sincerely that the principal, nay the only, source of gratification to me in being the " favoured guest of many a gay and
brilliant throng," as R. Swiveller might express himself, is
that I can amuse you and Lily with a few sketches of people
and things you may have heard of. Let me, however, thank
you both for your letters of June 6th last Sunday.

The Russells are kindness itself to me. I like Lady
William extremely, and I feel sure she likes me, and is very
fond of introducing me to people she thinks worth knowing.
I visit her occasionally, and she comes and takes me to parties,
etc. I got a note from her last Monday morning, which I
would send you if it were not on such thick paper. I think,
however, an extract from it will amuse you. It begins thus—
" My dear sir, I hope you will break every tie, should you be
entangled, on the 15th, and accept the enclosed invitation from
my friend, who tried with me to find you at Lady Palmerston's.
The dinner will be pleasant, and Lord Brougham, who will be
there, pants to make your acquaintance. I saw him no less
than three times in one day, et chaque fois il était question
de vous," etc., with a good deal more in the same vein. The
card is from Lady Williams (wife or widow, I do not know
which, of one of the judges), and takes place day after to-
morrow.

To resume my week's small beer. On Monday I worked
pretty hard all day (which is very apt not to be the case, my
time is so cut up with breakfasts, luncheons, etc.) at the State
Paper Office. In the afternoon I went down with the Sturgises,
Hamley, and the Blackwoods, to a dinner at Richmond. I
did not care much for it, as I was not much disposed to be
merry, and I feel very unhappy and depressed, more than

tongue can tell, about my dear mother. If I were amusing myself here in London, and if going to dinners were what it is to so many, what it might have been to me at twenty-five, an excitement and a pastime, I should reproach myself. But I do it with deliberation, and at a great sacrifice to my own feelings, because I believe it to be as it were my duty, being here in London, and with every door opened to me even without knocking, to see something and only once for all of English society.

There is nothing to say of this Richmond dinner. The Sturgises and Hamley were as gay and amusing as ever, and the Blackwoods are quiet, simple, intelligent people whom I like very much. I think I told you that he is both proprietor and editor of the famous magazine established by his father. On Tuesday there was a dinner at Lady Stanley's of Alderley. I think it was rather made for me than otherwise. The company was, besides the Stanleys, their married daughter and her husband, Lord Airlie, Lord Strangford, a young man who has been much in the East, and who is a very good Oriental scholar, and son of Lord Strangford, who translated the 'Lusiad' of Camoens, Lady Palmerston, her daughter Lady Shaftesbury, Lord Lyndhurst, Lord Brougham, Lord and Lady Stratford de Redcliffe.

Lord Lyndhurst, who has very much lost the use of his legs, but not of his brains, did not come up in the drawing-room. I was introduced to Lord Brougham before dinner. He shook hands cordially, and expressed himself as glad to make my acquaintance, but he did not seem to "pant" so much as might have been expected. We soon went to dinner, and his place was at the opposite end of the table from mine, so that our acquaintance for the present is limited. I have no doubt I shall see more of him, but to tell you the truth I fear he is a mere wreck. Let me give you a photograph, while his grotesque image still lingers in the camera-obscura of my brain. He is exactly like the pictures in *Punch*, only *Punch* flatters him. The common pictures of Palmerston and Lord John are not like at all to my mind, but Brougham is always hit exactly. His face, like his tongue and his mind, is shrewd, sharp, humorous. His hair is thick and snow-white and shiny; his head is large and knobby and bumpy, with all kinds of phrenological developments, which I did not have a chance fairly to study. The rugged outlines or headlands of his face are wild and bleak, but not forbidding. Deep furrows of age and thought and toil, perhaps of sorrow, run all over it, while his vast mouth, with a ripple of humour ever playing around it, expands like a placid bay under the huge promontory of his fantastic and incredible nose. His eye is dim and could never have been brilliant, but his voice is rather shrill, with an unmistakable northern intonation; his manner of speech is fluent, not garrulous, but obviously touched by time; his figure is tall, slender, shambling, awkward, but of course perfectly self-possessed. Such is what remains at eighty of the famous Henry Brougham.

My place at table was between Lady Stanley and the pretty Countess of Airlie, her daughter; on her right sat Lord Stratford de Redcliffe, and at the other end of the table on each side of Lord Stanley were Brougham and Lyndhurst. I have already described Lyndhurst. When sitting down he appears younger than Brougham, although really six years older (he was eighty-six last week); his voice is silvery and his manner very suave and gentle. The company was too large for general conversation, but every now and then we at our end paused to listen to Brougham and Lyndhurst chaffing each other across the table. Lyndhurst said, "Brougham, you disgraced the woolsack by appearing there with those plaid trousers, and with your peer's robe on one occasion put on over your chancellor's gown." "The devil!" said Brougham, "you know that to be a calumny; I never wore the plaid trousers." "Well," said Lyndhurst, "he confesses the two gowns. Now the present Lord Chancellor never appears except in small clothes and silk stockings." Upon which Lady Stanley observed that the ladies in the gallery all admired Lord Chelmsford for his handsome leg. "A virtue that was never seen in you, Brougham," said Lyndhurst, and so on. I do not repeat these things because they are worth recording, but because I always try to Boswellize a little for

your entertainment. All dinner-time, Lord Lyndhurst's
servant, who came with him, stood behind him, allowing him to
eat only the dishes which he selected for him, and seeming
very much like the Doctor who stood behind Sancho Panza,
when governor of Barataria, and perpetually waved away the
dishes which that functionary was inclined to devour.

Lord Lyndhurst is always very kind and attentive to me.
He called out to me in the old-fashioned way to drink wine with
him at table, and after dinner both he and Brougham addressed
a good deal of the conversation, which turned on American
matters, slave trade, etc., to me, and you may be sure that I
was glad to speak my mind on those subjects. I told them,
however, that the English were doing a great deal of damage
and no good, by the utterly indefensible and insolent conduct
of the petty officers in the West Indian seas. There is no
doubt that all this will be speedily put an end to, for the
English are very anxious to avoid any quarrel with America
as well as not to furnish us with any additional pretext for
taking Cuba. I liked Lord Stratford de Redcliffe very much.
He is the man, you know, who has been so long ambassador in
Constantinople, and doubtless stands at the head of English
diplomacy. He is a tall, thin man, with a handsome, distinguished face, bald and grey, advanced in the soixantaine, with
perfectly simple, unpretending manners. I had imagined,
from the accounts of him, a tremendous swell, with much
pomp and circumstance. He talked with me a good deal
during dinner, and when we went to the drawing-room, he
requested a formal introduction, and conversed half an hour
with me. He had been in former times minister in America,
and among other people he remembered very well John
Quincy Adams and Mr. Otis. He told me he should like to
cultivate my acquaintance while I was in England, and I
suppose I ought to call on him, as he is an ex-ambassador and
as he cannot know where I live. I have not yet done so,
however, as I cannot meet people even half-way. Mrs. Norton
took me severely to task for making old Lord Lansdowne call
first on me, saying that I had no business to give him the
trouble to send word to inquire my address, which he had been

obliged to do. Lord Lyndhurst, on account of his leg-less
condition, did not come upstairs, and Lord Brougham stayed
down with him to talk of some bill, soon to be brought into
the Lords, so that neither came above the horizon that night.

Wednesday.—As I had resolved, according to your wish, to
refuse no invitations to sit at " good men's feasts," I had
accepted an invitation to a *déjeuner* at Lord Carlisle's at
Chiswick House. There was a great flower show at the Horti-
cultural Gardens, which are near Lord Carlisle's house, and
he had taken the opportunity to make a small party. About
thirty people sat down at 2.30 o'clock. I had hoped that the
Duchess of Sutherland would be there; she was not, and unless
Lord Carlisle comes to town I am afraid I shall not see her.
Her daughter Lady Blantyre was there. I went to table with
Lord Carlisle's sister, Lady Dover. There was also the family
of Hamilton Fish of New York. I have a curiosity to see the
Duchess of Sutherland on account of her high reputation, but
I do not like to ask for an introduction, and prefer to wait till
I am bumped in her direction in the general maelstrom of
London society. Mackintosh was there, but not his wife, and
with that exception I cannot tell you the names of the people.
They were doubtless all swells, but I doubt if there were any
celebrities.

On Thursday I worked all day at the State Paper Office,
and dined *en famille* with Thackeray, whom I happened to
meet the evening before at the Athenæum. He has been very
friendly to me; I believe him to be very kindhearted and
benevolent. His eldest daughter I like very much. When I
came home in the evening I found an invitation from Lady
Palmerston for the same night. It had been overlooked or
mislaid or something, and was marked " immediate," but it
was too late for me, fatigued as I was, to go. I suppose there
will be another next Saturday.

On Friday afternoon I went into the Athenæum for a
sandwich, and there I met Milnes, who asked me to breakfast
next Wednesday. He also asked me to go down to the House
with him, which I was willing to do for an hour or two,
although I was to dine at eight. When you are introduced

by a member you are seated in the House itself in some very
good seats reserved for members of the other House and "illustrious foreigners," so that you hear the debates quite as well
as the M.P.'s themselves. For such a brief visit I made rather
a good hit. The testy old Admiral Napier had just been
asking some questions about the defences of England, and
Dizzy then got up to reply. In the course of his speech,
which was about twenty minutes, he made the announcement,
new to most people, that the Cagliari question had been settled
so satisfactorily. This is another piece of good fortune in the
run of luck which the Ministers have been having. It was not
new to me, for we had happened, as we walked down, to meet
Delane, editor of the *Times*, who had mentioned the circumstance. Dizzy's manner was calm on this occasion, statesman-
like and very different from the boisterous and declamatory
style adopted by him the other day in his speech at Slough.
He expresses himself with considerable fluency for an Englishman, the most eloquent of whom are so apt to "stick on conversation's burrs."

Afterwards Bright made a few remarks. He is one of the
favourites of the House, belonging to the branch of that
extreme Liberal party which has taken the present Ministers
under its protection, to annoy Palmerston on the one side and
Lord John on the other. It was quite amusing to see him
patting Disraeli on the head from the Opposition benches.
His manner is easy, conversational, slightly humorous, rather
fluent. The whole style of thing is very different in Parliament from the American way of proceeding in Congress or
State Legislatures. Everything here is toned down to a gentle
business-like mediocrity. The invisible but most omnipotent
demon of good taste which presides over the English world,
social, political, and moral, hangs over the heads of the legislators and suppresses their noble rage. The consequence is
that eloquence is almost impossible. Nobody drinks up Esel
or eats crocodiles, but at the same time a good deal of passion
and rhetoric, which might occasionally explode to advantage,
is for ever sealed up. I doubt whether Sheridan or Burke in
this age would not find the genial current of their soul to be

frozen by this clear cold atmosphere of good taste which coagulates the common talk of Englishmen, however wise or witty.

I was obliged to come away very early to dress for dinner at Lansdowne House. You remember the place which is on the opposite side of Berkeley Square to Thomas's hotel and inside a brick wall. (By the way, the Airlies live next door to Thomas's.) The house for London is spacious and splendid, the reception-rooms and dining-room being on the ground floor. I should think the dining-room was about 50 feet by 25, and well proportioned as to height. There are many statues about it. The hostess at Lansdowne House is his daughter-in-law, Lady Shelburne, who is pretty and pleasing. The company consisted of Mrs. Norton, Dean Milman and his wife, Lord Macaulay, Lady Dufferin and her son Lord Dufferin, Hayward, Miss Thellusson, and a gentleman whose name I did not hear. Rather a small party for so large a room. I had on my left the young lady who declaimed so vigorously at Lady Stanley's, and who is intelligent and agreeable. On my right I had the good luck to have Lady Dufferin, whom before I had hardly seen. She is extremely agreeable, full of conversation, with a charming manner, and has or had almost as much beauty and almost as much genius as her sister Mrs. Norton, with a far better fate. At table by wax-light she looked very handsome, with a wreath of white roses on her black hair; while her son, a very handsome youth of near thirty, sat near her looking like her brother. Hallam's 'Middle Ages' ought to be a classic work in England certainly, for there is no country in the world in which that epoch is so triumphant. The grandmothers of England seem almost as young as the mothers. Lady Dufferin has, I believe, never published, but she is perpetually writing *vers de société*, prologues for private theatricals, songs and impromptus. Mrs. Norton's 'Miss Myrtle is going to marry' and 'So so, Sir, you have come at last,' are as familiar, as you know very well, as Percy's 'Ballads.' Her son told me that Lord Palmerston once quoted a verse of "the charming woman," saying, "as the old song says," which was not particularly com-

plimentary to the woman, however agreeable it might have
been to the poetess.

She made herself very agreeable all dinner-time. I told
her I had just heard Disraeli speak. She said she had always
known him and liked him in spite of his tergiversations and
absurdities. When he was very young and had made his
first appearance in London society as the author of 'Vivian
Grey,' there was something almost incredible in his aspect.
She assured me that she did not exaggerate in the slightest
degree in describing to me his dress when she first met him
at a dinner party. He wore a black velvet coat lined with
satin, purple trousers with a gold band running down the
outside seam, a scarlet waistcoat, long lace ruffles falling down
to the tips of his fingers, white gloves with several brilliant
rings outside them, and long black ringlets rippling down upon
his shoulders. It seemed impossible that such a Guy Fawkes
could have been tolerated in any society. His audacity,
which has proved more perennial than brass, was always the
solid foundation of his character. She told him, however, that
he made a fool of himself by appearing in such fantastic shape,
and he afterwards modified his costume, but he was never
to be put down. She gave me another anecdote of him. "He
was once dining," said Lady Dufferin, "with my insufferable
brother-in-law, Mr. Norton (of course long before the separation), when the host begged him to drink a particular kind of
wine, saying he had never tasted anything so good before.
Disraeli agreed that the wine was very good. 'Well,' said
Norton, 'I have got wine twenty times as good in my cellar.'
'No doubt, no doubt,' said Dizzy, looking round the table,
'but, my dear fellow, this is quite good enough for such
canaille as you have got to-day.' Everybody saw that the
remark was intended as a slap for Mr. Norton, except that
individual himself, who was too obtuse to feel it."

I do not know that I have anything more to record of
this dinner. Macaulay was too far off for me to hear much
of his talk till the ladies retired, although I observed very
few of those brilliant "flashes of silence in his conversation"
to which Sydney Smith once alluded. After dinner, the con-

versation was miscellaneous, but Hayward, who is a Quarterly
Reviewer of some reputation and a diner-out, got into an
argument with Macaulay about sculpture and painting, and
the whole apple-cart of conversation was upset. Milman
was agreeable, as he always is, and so was Macaulay. Old
Lord Lansdowne sat beaming and genial in the centre of
his system, and had evidently acquired a good deal of fresh
warmth and radiance from Mrs. Norton, who sat next him, and
had been looking handsomer than I ever saw her before. She
was dressed in white, and from the end of the table where I
sat it would have required a very powerful telescope to discover that she had passed thirty. Before we went away,
Milman invited me next week to breakfast with Macaulay.
He had again a violent fit of coughing just before he went to
the drawing-room, but it seemed to me of an asthmatic character. He went away early, and I departed about eleven.
Next afternoon I drove out with the Amorys to a breakfast (at
Lady Dufferin's, at her villa in Highgate, about five miles
from London). The grounds are charming ; the villa a
beautiful English house, with lawn and shrubbery, and oaks,
and wide views over the hill and dale, such as are in perfection
in England. The weather was, as it has been for the last ten
days, very summery and sultry. Tea tables and ices were
spread on the lawn under the trees, and there were many
persons of my acquaintance present. The Stanleys, the
Airlies, Mrs. Norton, the Duchess of Wellington, and various
other persons were there. The tone of the party was very much
sans gêne, and Mrs. Norton triumphed over her age and the
sunlight. Both the Amorys looked very well.

I do not know that I have anything special to record of this
afternoon's entertainment. The Countess of Clarendon was
there, and requested Lady Dufferin to introduce me to her,
and was very civil and agreeable. We returned in time for
me to dress, and go to dine at Lord Goderich's at eight.
I think I mentioned in my last that Lord Goderich is a rising
young politician, with a good deal of talent, and very liberal
principles. Of my acquaintance was Hurlbert, who, as I have
before mentioned, has recently turned up here, and A. Russell.

Besides, there was the "young couple" whom we met two or
three years ago at Lucerne.   As I rarely forget faces, I
recognised theirs.   They are a Mr. and Mrs. ——.   He is a
Member of Parliament and a Radical.   She sat on my left,
and I asked in the course of dinner whether she remembered
where we had last met.   She said she had been puzzling over
it (which I do not believe at all); I said, in Lucerne.   Then
she remembered, or affected to remember, and added, "Why
is it that we English, when we meet abroad, are so very
friendly, and when we reappear in London are so very
hedgehoggy?"   I told her that the reason why there was no
hedgehogginess on this occasion was because I was not an
Englishman.   "From which of the sister islands, then?" she
asked.   "From none," I answered.   "Then from one of the
colonies?"   "Yes," said I, "from Australia."   Russell and
Lady Goderich laughed, and I left her to burst in ignorance.
After the dinner, Russell and I retired to the Athenæum at
eleven, to drink soda and water and smoke cigars, which evil
habit I have occasionally resumed late at night, but very
rarely at the Cosmopolitan.

To-day, Sunday—for the last sheet of this letter I have taken
up late this evening—I have done nothing but take a short
drive in the park with the Amorys, and dine with the Sturgises,
and now I am tired, and so I shall say God bless you,
dearest Mary; kiss my darling children, and believe me ever,

Most affectionately yours,
J. L. M.

To his Mother.

London,
June 17th, 1858.

MY DEAREST MOTHER,—I was rejoiced to find by the letters
which arrived yesterday that your health had improved.

It makes me very sad to hear of you as suffering so much
pain, and I trust most sincerely that the change of air and the
quiet of Riverdale will re-invigorate you, and that we may
have the happiness to hear of a still further improvement.   I

am leading rather a solitary life here, for although I go a
good deal into society, this is rather as a matter of duty than
anything else. My own family are all far away from me in
Switzerland; although thank God they have hitherto been
pretty well, I cannot feel perfectly comfortable when the
separation is such a decided one. Moreover, I do not get so
much time to work as I hoped to do. London is such a large
place that an enormous deal of time is spent in getting from
one place to another. If you go out to breakfast or to
luncheon your day is broken in two, and is no longer good for
anything.

Lord Brougham interests me as much as any man. He is
now eighty years of age, but I do not see that he is much
broken. His figure is erect, not very graceful, certainly, but
active. His face is so familiar to every one, principally through
the pictures in *Punch*, as hardly to require a description.
The whole visage is wild and bizarre, and slightly comical, but
not stern or forbidding. Like his tongue and his mind, it is
eminently Scotch, sharp, caustic, rugged, thistle-ish. The top
of the head is as flat as if it had been finished with a plane.
The brain-chamber is as spacious as is often allotted to any
one mortal, and, as the world knows, the owner has furnished
it very thoroughly. The face is large, massive, seamed all
over with the deep furrows of age and thought and toil; the
nose is fantastic and incredible in shape. There is much
humour and benevolence about the lines of the mouth. His
manner is warm, eager, earnest, cordial. I was with him half
an hour yesterday, and he talked a good deal of the question
of Cuba and the slave trade. He was of opinion that the claim
to visit must be given up; that there was no logical defence
for it, but he spoke with a sigh and almost with tears at the
apparent impossibility of suppressing the slave trade, or of
preventing in America the indefinite extension and expansion
of slavery.

I told him that Americans belonging to the Free States
were placed in a position such as no great body of men
had ever before found themselves in. They were forced to
choose between an act of political suicide or connivance at the

steady expansion of the slavery system, which was repugnant both to their principles and to their interests. A man in Ohio or Massachusetts must either be a rebel and bend his energy to the dissolution of the Union, or he must go heart and hand with Alabama and Carolina in acquiring Cuba and Central America, and carving out an endless succession of slave states for the future. He said this was quite true, and that all lovers of progress and liberal institutions could not help being afflicted at the terrible position in which the Free States were placed. Whichever way one looked, dissolution seemed to stare us in the face, for the annexation of the worn-out, effete, mongrel Spanish-American population into our confederation was after all a vitiation, corruption and death to our original and powerful organization. I do not give you exactly his words, but as I agreed in everything he said, and as he seemed to sympathise with all I ventured to express, I thought it would interest you to hear it. No man wishes more good, more glory, more prosperity to the American people than Lord Brougham, but he cannot believe (nor can I) that those objects are to be attained by extending slavery and re-establishing the slave trade. I have got to the end of my sheet, my dearest mother, and so I shall bid you good-bye for the present, meaning to write again very soon. I shall remain about a fortnight longer in London, and then leave for Holland, where I have some two or three months' work. My best love to father, to my dear A——, of whom I am glad to hear so much better accounts, and to all the rest of the family. And believe me, my dear mother,

Most affectionately your son,

J. L. M.

To his Wife.

London,
June 20th, 1858.

MY DEAREST MARY,—Although I go out a good deal, and dine with somebody or other every day, I see no new celebrities, and, indeed, there are very few to see. I doubt if I shall see Disraeli or Bulwer. Both are now Ministers, and

rarely go into society, I believe. Carlyle was to have come
to breakfast at Milnes's, but he was ill, and sent an apology.
Monday I dined with Mr. Darwin, cousin to Mackintosh, and
son or grandson of the man who wrote the 'Botanical Garden.'
Mackintosh was there, and his sister and brother-in-law
the Wedgwoods, descendants of the famous Wedgwood the
potter, and sundry other people, whose names I do not know.
The day was insufferably hot. The weather, the three or four
days of the past week, has been hotter than any one ever
believed it possible to be in England. The glass was near 90°
in the shade, and there was a sense of suffocation in the air,
which was intensified by dining in the inevitable white choker
in close rooms. For once in my life I have known the weather
too warm for my taste, but it has furnished a topic of conversation inexhaustible and providential.

On Tuesday I dined with Lady Williams, the widow of
a judge of some note. The company consisted of Mr Harcourt,[1] a bland old gentleman, to whom I was introduced
on arriving. When I came in with A. Russell (Lady W.
Russell, being taken suddenly ill, was unable to come to the
dinner), Lady Williams addressed me in French. I replied
in that language, thinking perhaps she had mistaken me for
Malakoff, and being unwilling to disturb the illusion. She,
however, soon after presented me to the said Mr. Harcourt,
and after I had turned away, I heard her ask him confidentially if he had read the D. R. As she is very hard of
hearing, he was obliged to whisper in a tremendous undertone audible a mile off, "Not yet, but Lady Waldegrave (his
wife) is reading it at this moment with great pleasure;" all of
which I was *censé* not to hear. Then came Lord Brougham,
looking as droll as ever. There certainly never was a great
statesman and author who so irresistibly suggested the man
who does the comic business at a small theatre as Brougham.
You are compelled to laugh when you see him as much as at
Keeley or Warren. Yet there is absolutely nothing comic
in his mind. On the contrary, he is always earnest, vigorous,
impressive, but there is no resisting his nose. It is not merely

---

[1] George Harcourt, Esq.

the configuration of that wonderful feature which surprises
you, but its mobility. It has the litheness and almost the
length of the elephant's proboscis, and I have no doubt he
can pick up pins or scratch his back with it as easily as he
could take a pinch of snuff. He is always twisting it about
in quite a fabulous manner.

Then there were Lord and Lady Stratford de Redcliffe, the
Earl of Powis, who told me that he knew the Fays when
they lived in Shropshire, some young men whose names I have
forgotten, and a very pretty girl who sat next me, whose name
was Campbell. I can absolutely tell you nothing of this
entertainment. I am not much of a judge of cookery; I really
cannot say whether the cuisine of the various places where I
dine is commendable or the reverse, and I can only say that it
is stereotyped. The same soups, fishes, and dishes succeed each
other in one unvarying procession, just as in a Boston dinner
party or a German *table d'hôte*.

No doubt, too, the society is too large. The wide orbits in
which the higher constellations move, admit but slight possibilities of conjunction, and so in solemn silence, or nearly so,
all move round the vast terrestrial ball. There is not much
chance for anything beyond a slight and formal acquaintance,
however disposed the natives may be to be civil to strangers,
and in my own case I have received a good deal of civility.
Still, the width of society makes it dreary for a foreigner. On
Wednesday morning I breakfasted with Milnes. He is a
particularly good fellow, hearty, jolly, intelligent, rich, and
hospitable, a man of letters, and a Member of Parliament.
His wife is at present in the country, so that he does not give
dinners, although they say his house is one of the best to dine
at in London. A breakfast is in itself an absurdity. At least
I for one hate to talk at breakfast to people with whom I am
not intimate.

It takes at least a few glasses of champagne to thaw the
surface of any general intercourse, but to pour tea upon the
ice is indeed a weakness. To be jolly over muffins is the
most wretched of delusions. There was a Professor from Baltimore, whose specialty seems to be an international currency,

who asked if I happened to be acquainted with my namesake, the author of the 'Dutch Republic,' two or three foreigners, Lord Ashburton, and a Crimean hero or two, *et voilà*. I am sure I cannot tell you anything of the conversation, as there was no celebrity present whose head I can take off for your amusement. . . . I dined with John Forster, formerly editor of the *Examiner*, author of several very clever works. The company consisted of Dilke, editor of the *Athenæum*, Egg the painter, Sir C. Eastlake, President of the Royal Academy, and his wife. The thermometer had been at 90° all day, and you may imagine what the effect of wax candles, steaming dishes, and a parboiled dozen or two of human creatures must have been. For my own feelings I can only say that St. Lawrence on his gridiron was an emblem of cool comfort in comparison. The conversation was not exciting or instructive. Lady Eastlake had been a good deal in Germany and in Courland, and I have an idea that she is the author of a very clever book I once read called 'Letters from the Baltic.' Her husband is a sensible man in his profession of *cognoscente*. On Thursday morning, while I was making a call on Julia Sturgis, in walked Madame Mohl. We fell into each other's arms of course. I do not know how long she is to stay here. It appears that the Queen of Holland has been lately making a visit to the Emperor in Paris. She told Mr. Mohl she wanted to see Mignet, Cousin, and other celebrities. He told her she could not, for nothing would induce such men to go to the Tuileries. The only way it could be managed was for her to come to his house, and he would invite them to meet her. With this she was delighted, so the Mohls gave a luncheon or dinner, I forget which, and had all these celebrities, and her Majesty came and was delighted.

Mme. Mohl said that Count Randwyk told her it was indispensable that I should report myself to him on my arrival at the Hague. He is her Master of Ceremonies. I do not think I shall, however; certainly not if I can possibly help it.

That day I went, according to appointment, to the House of Lords, sent in my card to Lord Brougham, who came out and brought me into the House, and gave me a place on what is called the steps of the throne, where you are separated by a slight rail from the body of the House.

The speaking on the Cuba business was opened by the Bishop of Oxford, in a fervid and impassioned speech. He is the son of the celebrated Wilberforce, and one of the best speakers in England. There is no need of my talking about the matter of this debate. The manner is all which is important, as you have perhaps seen what was said; and if not, it is of little consequence, for the whole matter, so far as England and America are concerned, is settled. The men who spoke were, besides the Bishop of Oxford, Brougham, who was earnest, eager, and eloquent as a young man; Earl Grey, who was very peppery and pugnacious; Clarendon, who was gentlemanlike; Carlisle, who was brief but earnest and almost eloquent. Just before the end of the debate he came over to me to tell me that he had just sent me a note inviting me to dinner on the 3rd July. On the whole the style of thing was very creditable, the elocution was above mediocrity, and the tone was in mortifying contrast to that of the recent debate in our Senate, where each speaker vied with the rest in using violent and abusive language towards England,—I say mortifying contrast, because whatever be the right or the wrong, and I believe that we are right, yet it is detestable to see people without any feeling of the responsibility of statesmen and bragging away about going into a naval war with a power which has got some four hundred ships of war while we have got twenty-five or thirty.

On Saturday I went to a large morning party at the Marchioness of Westminster's. Their residence is Grosvenor House, one of the most splendid palaces in London. There were a dozen or two of people that I knew there. The principal reception room was the great picture gallery, but there was no opportunity of seeing the pictures, and the crowd was so great that there was no chance for anything but to suffer and be strong for a little while, and then to come away. I was obliged to leave by five o'clock, as I was engaged three weeks long, with fifty or sixty of my compatriots, to be starred and gartered by Mr. Peabody at Richmond. I went with the

Sturgis's in their carriage. The day was fine and the drive pleasant, and the dinner less oppressive than I had anticipated. The Amorys were there, both looking handsome and beautifully dressed, the Dallases, Fishers, and a comprehensive catalogue of starred and striped individuals from Connecticut to California, the latter State being represented by a voluminous nuggety lady. I conducted to dinner Mrs. Morell, the married daughter of Mrs. Dallas.

We reached town at about 11.30, at which hour I was deposited at Cambridge House, where there was a party. There is nothing particular to be said of this festival, nobody there whom I have not described. Lord Palmerston came up to me, and talked a quarter of an hour very pleasantly; and there were others whom I like to meet, as Baron Bentinck, the Netherlands Minister; an especially agreeable person, Baroness Rothschild, who invited me to dinner next Thursday.

Affectionately yours,

J. L. M.

CHAPTER IX.

LONDON SOCIETY (CONTINUED).

To his Wife.

London,
June 27th, 1858.

MY DEAREST MARY,—My last letter, rather a jejune specimen, I am afraid, was duly posted on the Sunday. I believe
that the wondrous tale of my adventures on that occasion was
brought up to Saturday inclusive. There are so many individuals in London society, that it is a long time before one
meets, except at a grand evening party, many persons on any
one occasion that one has seen before, and at the same time
those you met yesterday, that it comes to the same thing.
About 8 P.M. I drive daily in a hansom along Piccadilly,
in a white choker, and the colossal and comical statue of the
Duke of Wellington always seems to tower above Belgravia, as
the presiding genius of dinner parties, marshalling his baton
the way that so many thousands are to go to table. Then you
go into a grave-looking mansion of nankeen-coloured brick,
are received by a squad of respectable flunkeys, confide your
name in a modest whisper to one of them, so that he may roar
it up the staircase to his colleagues on the landing. Then you
go into a large salon with a score or so of gentlemen and

ladies.   Then, after the usual remarks concerning the heat of
the weather and the odoriferousness of the Thames, the solemn
procession goes down to the *salle à manger.*   "Slowly and
sadly we sat us down," and precisely the same dishes in exactly
the same order are placed under our noses, exactly at the same
moment.   Then, after the normal lapse of an hour and a half,
the usual struggle of crinolines takes place, and the ladies soar
to the supernal regions.   The male survivors pretend to be
relieved, and to draw nearer and affect to talk politics, although
nothing is ever said, and pretend to drink wine, although not
a pint is consumed.   Then after the normal twenty minutes
are past, the solemn question, " A little more wine ? " is propounded, and the procession with funeral gravity moves
upstairs—as if they had all met to pay the last homage to a
deceased friend, and were glad to have accomplished the rite
in a becoming manner.   After coffee, the party is sometimes
strengthened by a fresh infusion of new company from without,
and the languid circulation is thus improved, and then you
eclipse yourself when you like, or remain till twelve o'clock,
draining the cup to the dregs.

To descend to particulars.   On Sunday I drove out with
A. Russell, by invitation, to Pembroke Lodge, Richmond, to
make a visit to Lord and Lady John Russell.   I have already
described him to you, and I have nothing to add to that
picture.   His manner, especially in his own house, is more
pleasing than I had expected.   His voice is gentle, and his
address is not restrained or even indifferent.   We sat in the
drawing-room till a shower was over, and then we walked about
the grounds with Lord John.   This place is one given, or
rather lent, to him by the Queen for his life, and is built in the
royal park, and has a magnificent view of the Thames scenery,
with all the rich combinations of bosky bourn and sunny
glade, and cottage chimneys, that smoke beneath the ancient
oak Milton so loved to paint.   I think the ' Allegro ' and
' Penseroso ' must have been written on the top of Richmond
Hill.   Lady John Russell looks like her brother, Henry
Elliot, from whom she said she had often heard of me.   They
have several children, the youngest a pretty little girl.   The

cottage is simply and plainly furnished. It was pleasant
enough to see the ex-Premier under his own vine and
fig-tree. He is a very good politician and statesman, and
a model *père de famille*. They wished me to appoint another
day to come out to luncheon. I dined afterwards with
Mrs. Norton. She made the dinner for me, but she was
somewhat disappointed in her company, several of the persons
that she wanted, among others Delane, having been engaged.
The company consisted of the Marquis of Lansdowne; Lord
Dufferin, and his mother, Lady Dufferin; the "young couple"
of whose name I think I have already informed you; Mr. Harcourt; Hayward, the Quarterly Reviewer and universal diner
out; the Earl of Gifford, and Sir Hamilton Seymour, the man
who was Minister in Petersburg at the time when the "sick
man" gave the Czar Nicholas so much anxiety.

I believe I have already described the individuals composing
the troop thus enumerated, except the two last-named individuals. Sir H. Seymour is not especially describable. He is
obviously intelligent, caustic, and apparently good-humoured,
and with a good deal of the *usage du monde* to be expected in
a veteran diplomatist. He is still comparatively young, but
has laid himself up on a pension. Lord Gifford is the eldest
son of the Marquis of Tweeddale, is an M.P. till he succeeds
to his father's peerage, is about thirty-five years old, plain-
looking, intelligent, spectacled, and a sculptor of remarkable
talent. There is at Dufferin Lodge a marble bust of Lady
Dufferin executed by him, which is singularly like and very
beautiful, and another one in plaster of her brother, Brinsley
Sheridan, which is almost as good. I do not remember anything especially worth reporting of this dinner. The conversation rolled on the accustomed wheels. But where two such
persons as Mrs. Norton and Lady Dufferin were present, you
may imagine that it was not slow. Mrs. Norton, however, was
a good deal indisposed, so much so as to be obliged to leave
the table. She recovered, however, and remained till 12.30 in
her salon, at which hour Hayward and myself retired. The descriptions of Mrs. Norton have not been exaggerated. In the
noon of her beauty she must have been something wondrous.

On Monday I got a pretty good day's work in the State
Paper Office, and at seven I drove out to Highgate to dine
with Lady Dufferin. There was no party, except one young
man whose name I forget, and Brinsley Sheridan, with his
wife and two daughters.

Mr. Sheridan has a good deal of the family fascination,
being still very handsome, with a very winning address. One
of his daughters is very pretty, and is just engaged to be
married to the eldest son of Lord Poltimore.

This dinner, although merely a family one, was one of the
pleasantest I have been at. When there is one such person at
table as Lady Dufferin, of course it makes all the difference.
She has known everybody, and tells peppery little anecdotes,
strikes out little portraits, and talks on grave and gay subjects
with the same animation and brilliancy. Then she paints
beautifully, having adorned the panels of her own boudoir with
her own pencil, and is perpetually writing clever verses.
When well dressed, she is very pretty, but she never could
have had the beauty of Mrs. Norton, who has the head of a
classic muse, and the eyes of a sibyl.

I brought Sheridan into town, who asked me for a lift, that
some one else might be accommodated in his carriage, and he
made himself very agreeable during the drive.

On Thursday I went with Mrs. Norton and Stirling by rail
to Cliveden. This is a villa belonging to the Duke of Sutherland, and famous in Pope's verses as " Cliveden's proud
alcove,"—

" The bower of wanton Shrowsbury and love,"

and now in possession of a purer celebrity. I had received an
invitation from the Duchess through Mrs. Norton, entirely
unawares, as I had never been presented to her; but, as I have
already observed, it was probable that I should be drifted in
her direction before I left London. I suppose you will like a
description of her. There is something very plenteous and
bountiful and sunny in her aspect. She is tall, and very
large, and carries herself with a very good-natured stateliness.
Her hair is blonde-silvered, her features are large and well
chiselled, her smile is very beaming, and there is benevo-

lence and sunshine in every look and word. With her ripe,
autumnal, exuberant person, and radiating expression, she
looks a personified Ceres, and ought always to be holding a
cornucopia in her right hand. She welcomed me like an old
friend, shaking hands as if I had known her from the tenderest
infancy; and then we went, being late, to the table, where
about twenty-five people were already seated. The company
consisted mainly of ladies. There was next me Lady C.
Denison, wife of the Speaker of the House of Commons;
opposite was Mrs. Van de Weyer, who was affectionate in her
greetings, and there were various members of the Carlisle
family; Lady Stafford, the daughter-in-law of the Duchess,
Lady Blantyre, and a Count and Countess Potofski, Austrian
Poles, for whom the party was made; Grenfell, a brother of
Mrs. Froude, whom I very often meet in society, and whose
father's place adjoins Cliveden; Miss Weston, cousin of Mrs.
Van de Weyer, who has been several years in Europe, and
seems ladylike and intelligent, and various others whose names
I have forgotten. There was not much done at the party.
The view from the house is wonderfully fine, commanding a
view of the silver Thames, winding through plains of almost
ever green freshness, and masses of ancient foliage, such as
England only has to show.

The house is modern, and a small palace built by Barry,
the painting of the ceiling and panels is by Landseer and
other artists, the service of the table of quite regal magnificence, and the strawberries very portentous in size. After the
"trifling foolish banquet" we loafed about the grounds, but
the whole thing was brought to a rapid termination because
the Duchess, who is not living here at the moment, was to go
to town by the 4.30 train. This house is only one of a dozen
or two palaces, villas, and castles which they possess. Of
course they only reside here a few weeks in each year. She
charged me to make her a visit very soon at Stafford House,
saying that she was always at home about two.

On Wednesday morning I breakfasted again with Milnes.
The company consisted of two or three English Consuls from
foreign parts, Parker the publisher, Mr. Arthur Stanley, cousin

of Lady Stanley of Alderley, a canon of Christchurch and an
eminent divine, whom I had met before at Milman's, Lord Carlisle, Earl Grey and Lord Stratford de Redcliffe.   I sat next
to the two last-named individuals.   I had never met Lord Grey
before, although I had heard him speak.   He told me he knew
me very well through the D.R. and I found him rather an
entertaining person.   He has more talents than many of his
brother peers.   I see no reason to modify my sentiments on
the breakfast system.   If the autocrat of the breakfast table
had been present, the scene would have been changed indeed.
If he could only establish his sway in London, a social revolution would be produced ; and I am quite persuaded that if by
accident, without changing any of his other qualities, he could
have a palingenesis, and appear as a Howard or Stanley of
England, people would gather up his conversation, five baskets
full every time he honoured any mahogany.   As he was not
there I took no notes of anybody's conversation, not even my
own, which I flatter myself would exceed in dulness that of
any of my competitors.   Kingsley gave me a very pressing
invitation to visit him at Eversley.   Milnes, by the way, is
bright, jolly, and amusing, one of the best fellows in London.
If he would only shove his entertainments to the other edge
of the daylight, and give us cups that inebriate instead of
cheering, I should have no fault to find with him.

After breakfast I went down to the British Museum.   I had
been immersed half-an-hour in my MSS., when happening to
turn my head round I found seated next to me Thackeray with
a file of old newspapers before him writing the ninth number of
the 'Virginians.'   He took off his spectacles to see who I was,
then immediately invited me to dinner the next day (as he
seems always to do everybody he meets), which invitation I
could not accept, and he then showed me the page he had been
writing, a small delicate legible manuscript.   After this we
continued our studies.   I can conceive nothing more harass-
ing in the literary way than his way of living from hand to
mouth.   I mean in regard to the way in which he furnishes
food for the printer's devil.   Here he is just finishing the
number which must appear in a few days.   Of course, whether

ill or well, stupid or fertile, he must produce the same amount
of fun, pathos, or sentiment. His gun must be regularly
loaded and discharged at command. I should think it would
wear his life out. This day I dined at Mr. Danby Seymour's.
He is a very good fellow, an M.P., and of the elder branch
of the Seymour family. He descends from the famous protector Duke of Somerset, and a less remote Sir Edward
Seymour ancestor is the one who made the famous reply to
William III., when he landed from Holland. "You are one of
the family of the Duke of Somerset?" asked this king. "No,
your majesty," answered Sir Edward, "he is of mine," which
was true, the ducal branch being the younger one. They have
some fine portraits in the house, one of this same Sir Edward,
another of the protector Duke, and a full length, large as life,
of Harry VIII., by Holbein.

I made the acquaintance of Mr. Seymour the first time I
was at Cambridge House. On being introduced to him he
said, "I know you well, I read your book eight years ago."
To whom I replied that he was my earliest reader, for he had
read it six years before it was published, and we have been
great friends ever since. There were not many notables
present, and the usual sprinkling of lords and ladies, colonels
and M.P.'s. The lady with whom I went to dinner was very
lively and sociable—Mrs. Vernon Smith, wife of the man of
whom you have heard as having been President of the India
Board in Lord Palmerston's ministry. They sent me an invitation to dinner next day for a few days afterwards, but I was
engaged. I eclipsed myself rather early from the evening
party which followed the dinner, and went to the Cosmopolitan.
Among the usual members who were there, there was one Mr.
Venables, one of the Saturday Reviewers, who told me of a personal compliment which will please you and Lily to hear.
He said that he was an intimate acquaintance of Tennyson,
and that Tennyson had recently told him that he admired my
history more than any he had ever read, and that he had rarely
been so much excited by any book. He did not know that
I was in town till the day he went away, or would have liked
to see me, etc. As this is somewhat different from the *banalités*

of every day, I thought I would sink my blushes and let you hear it.

On Thursday morning Dean and Mrs. Milman called in their carriage to take me to Harrow to hear what are called the " Harrow Speeches," to which I had received an invitation from Dr. Vaughan, the head master. This affair is very much like our college commencement. The prize boys speak Latin, Greek, and English orations and poems, and there are also a few scenes from French, German, and English plays acted. The declamation was of a very inferior description. When they acted, however, and so got out of themselves into somebody else, it was quite different, and although their pronunciation of French and German was stunning to unprepared ears, their performance in other respects was rather light and airy. After the exercises were over, the invited guests went to a collation in the head master's house. Lord Palmerston, who rode down, a distance of ten miles, and back, was called on first after the banquet in the usual form. It is not fair to criticize such performances, for certainly there never was a more senseless ceremony than this, of calling men out to make speeches when they have nothing in the world to say.

I went up afterwards to the churchyard of Harrow-on-the-Hill to see the tomb on which Byron used to be fond of sitting when he was at school there. The view is a very extensive panorama and very English and beautiful. We got back to town just in time to dress for dinner. I dined with the Rothschilds. This is the Baron Lionel, about whom the row as to his seat in Parliament has been so long reproducing itself. It seems probable that next week the Bill will pass, and that he will take his seat as member for London, to which office he has been so often elected. His wife is very nice, with much *esprit*, intelligence and cultivation. There was the married daughter of the house, the wife of course of another Rothschild [1] (for the Rothschilds all marry Rothschilds), who is very beautiful and perfectly Hebrew and Oriental. A pale face, arched brows, eyes and hair of the blackest, with a gentle, pretty manner and a *petite* figure, are her character-

---

[1] Baroness Alphonse de Rothschild.

istics. Then there is a younger daughter of their father's house, unmarried, and a son too. Besides these were Hayward, Villiers, brother of Lord Clarendon, the Honourable Geo. Byng, rejoicing in the appellation of " Poodle Byng," and nobody else. I sat next to Mme. Rothschild and so did very well. On Friday I called at Stafford House. The Duchess was at home, and after I had been there a little while invited me to go to luncheon. This is, in fact, a 2.30 dinner as you know, consisting of soup, boiled and roast, pastry and fruit, like any other dinner, is an institution at first devised to keep the strong in awe, for who has the strength to eat two dinners in one day? Of course there was no company, and I only came to make a morning call. There were the Duke, Lady Stafford, and Lady Blantyre.

After the refection the Duchess showed me all over the house. Descriptions of houses are not much. Suffice it to say, that this is the best private palace in London. The double staircase especially is very broad and stately, and the wide entrance hall is ornamented with fine groups of statuary by modern sculptors—nothing very remarkable, but very good as furniture. I think there are few of the palaces in Genoa with so fine an entrance and staircase. The rooms are all very grand and gilded, the "enervating saloons," to get an invitation to which Roebuck complains of the baseness perpetrated by members of Parliament, and the gallery is very handsome. I was disappointed in the pictures. With the exception of two Murillos from the Soult collection, ' Abraham Entertaining the Angels,' and 'The Return of the Prodigal Son,' both of which are treated with a dramatic energy unusual with Murillo, and with his richest and strongest colour—with these two signal exceptions there are hardly any first-rate pictures. After passing a very agreeable hour or two in this way I took my leave. I dined that day with the Sturgis's. By the way, Milnes, the other day, being invited by Lady Palmerston to dinner, declined on the ground of a previous engagement. She begged him to decline the previous engagement. " No," says Milnes, " whatever else I may be, I am an honest diner out." The party at the Sturgis's had few persons that I knew. I went to dinner with Mrs. Mansfield, mother of

General Mansfield, who at the age of forty has already acquired great reputation and rank in India. She is originally from Baltimore, she told me, but has been in England ever since her marriage. Then there were a Mr. and Mrs. Ponsonby; she a very pretty woman and sister to Lady Stanley of Alderley. I do not remember anything worthy of note at the dinner, which, like all those at the Sturgis's, was very good, they have almost the best *cuisine* in London.

At eleven o'clock we adjourned to Lansdowne House, where there was a private concert, to which the Sturgis's as well as myself were invited. The concert room is very spacious and elegantly decorated. The musicians were Viardot, Garcia, Grisi, Mario, Graziani, and others. The room was, however, very hot, and it was difficult to get a good place, so that as a concert I cannot say that I enjoyed it much. It was not a very general party, only several large spoonfuls of the cream of the cream. I do not remember any people of whom I have not spoken, except some members of the Royal Family, the Duke and Duchess of Cambridge, and the Princess Augusta. But to tell you the truth I forgot to look at them, and so cannot describe them to you, saving the Duke of Cambridge, who stood near me about five minutes. I had a good deal of talk as usual with Mrs. Norton, Lady Dufferin, Mme. Rothschild, and other old acquaintances. The Duchess of Manchester was there also, a very pretty blonde, with a wreath of gold scallop shells in her hair. The Marchioness of Stafford was there also, and these two are considered the prettiest women in London.

Next day I worked pretty well at the S.P.O. for a few hours, but there is no doubt that my time is a good deal cut up, and although I shall get through my work pretty soon, yet I could have accomplished it all by this time, and sooner, had I been entirely unknown. Breakfasts, luncheons, and visits, consume valuable hours in this wide wilderness. I went in the afternoon to return a visit to Lord Stanhope, who had called on me the day before. He is better known to the world at large under the name of Lord Mahon, which he bore when he wrote the 'History of England from the Peace of Utrecht,' a work which has a high reputation, and was favourably reviewed on its first appearance by Macaulay. He is a distinguished personage in the way of letters, science and art, and I found him particularly agreeable. He is a slender, thin man, with handsome features, curly hair, and spectacles. He showed me the MS. of Byron's 'Curse of Minerva,' in which almost every word had been altered, so numerous were the corrections ; also a very pretty valentine of some thirty lines, written by Macaulay to his (Lord Stanhope's) little daughter.

Afterwards I drove down to Chiswick, to dine with Lord Carlisle. The company consisted of William Prescott and his wife, who are on their way to America, sailing next Saturday ; a Mr. Calvert, a very entertaining and intelligent Englishman, who is Consul in the East, and has a farm on the ruins of Troy ; Lord Granville ; the Speaker of the House of Commons, and his wife, Lady Charlotte Denison ; Lord and Lady Chichester, Lady Shannon, and Colonel and Lady Louisa Pyne. I give you the names just as they would be given by Jenkins, the reporter of fashionable intelligence for the *Morning Post.* The only notabilities of this party were the Speaker, who is tall, with a good Roman face, which must look uncommonly well in the wig. He seemed good-humoured, and sufficiently reasonable, and I daresay looks very stately in his costume. Lord Granville was Minister of Foreign Affairs in Palmerston's Government, is small, bright, boyish-looking, young, and very agreeable. He has a decided resemblance to Longfellow in manner and visage. Lady Charlotte, the Speaker's wife, is a good-natured, cultivated person, whom I have met several times. The rest of the company were commonplace folks, not worth describing, except that you will like to hear a word of the Prescotts. They came over with the Whartons from Calais, who have gone for the summer to the Isle of Wight, so that you will not see them, I am sorry to say. They speak of Prescott, the father, as very well, and wishing to write, but restrained by the physicians and friends. He is more popular here than ever. After returning to town at eleven, I went to a rather small party at the Palmerstons.'

To his Wife.

London,
July 4th, 1858.

MY DEAREST MARY,—This will be but a short and dull letter. I wrote you an unconscionably long one last Sunday. To-day, and for several days past, I have been very much indisposed. You need not be in the least degree alarmed. It is only my old enemy, difficulty of breathing, but it is so obstinate and unrelenting that it makes me incapable of work or amusement, and depresses me very much. There is not the least need of your worrying yourself, for it is only what I have been suffering from for half my life, and I daresay, after a few days or weeks longer, it will pass away. I should not mention it at all, except by way of excuse for my inability to write anything to amuse you much this week. It does not prevent my daily occupations, but it rather neutralises them. I go to the S.P.O. every day, but it is difficult for me to work, and I dine out every evening, but it is a supplice to talk or to eat. Last Sunday I passed an hour at Mrs. Norton's. Among other persons there was Lytton,[1] the son of Sir E. B. Lytton. I met him afterwards the same evening, and he made me a formal speech about the D.R., saying it was a great privilege to know the author, etc. He is a handsome young man, and very clever, having published some poems, which are good, under the *nom de plume* of "Owen Meredith."

Sunday evening, I drove out to Wimbledon, and dined with Hughes, the author of 'Tom Brown's School-days,' a book which has had a great run, and is generally admired. He had invited me once before, but I was engaged. Hughes is an excellent fellow, very plain, unsophisticated and jolly, of course full of talent. He is not a professional author, but a working barrister. His wife is a pretty and pleasing person, and they live in a pretty cottage near Wimbledon Common. Kingsley was expected, but did not come, which was also the case with Lord and Lady Goderich, who were prevented by illness. The only persons present besides ourselves were Mrs. Phillips, wife

---

[1] The present Earl of Lytton.

of the artist; a gentleman whose name I have forgotten, and a Lady somebody. The dinner was plain, but it was *san gêne*, the conversation less *guindée* and conventional than is customary in London.

Monday I went out with A. Russell by appointment to Hatfield, a celebrated country-house of the Elizabethan period, originally presented to Robert Cecil, first Earl of Salisbury, and now inhabited by his descendant the present Marquis of Salisbury. A part of the house remains as it was originally built, the other portion was burned some years ago, together with the mother of the present proprietor, but has been restored in the same style. It is a rambling, zigzag structure of brick, with gables, turrets, and oriels, a superb dining-room, oak-ceilinged and wainscoted and floored, a fine library, superb views of park scenery and distant hills from the windows, and stately avenues of lime-trees and horse-chestnuts. Then there are various portraits of the great Lord Burleigh and his greater son, Queen Elizabeth, and other historical personages, which have a peculiar interest for me, as I happen to be writing about them. And there are also formal old-fashioned gardens, with clipped yew hedges, and alleys, and fish-ponds, and conservatories. Descriptions of palaces are a bore, and I will not describe. We had luncheon in the antique banqueting-room. There are also in the library some private papers of the famous Lord Burleigh, which I should like very much to have the ransacking of, although I have hundreds of them in the archives; but Lord Salisbury, I have always understood, does not wish any one to see them, so that I did not allude to the subject. I dined this day with Sir Charles Lyell. The Prescotts, whom it is always a pleasure to meet, both on their own account and their father's, were there, and Mr. and Mrs. Lyell. James Lawrence came in the evening. He is just come out alone for rheumatism, and is going straight to the Continent. I regret very much to say that he gives an unsatisfactory account of Prescott. He is kept on a very low diet, and I fear such great precaution is rather alarming.

Next day I had a quiet dinner at Mackintosh's, almost the first time I have dined in London except at a dinner party, and

I was very glad of the repose. I like them both very much and they have been very friendly to me. She always tells me to send her kindest regards to you. I am very weary of sitting at good men's feasts or bad ones. I have dined out about forty days in succession, and I am now inclined to go into the wilderness and fast forty days, but I have about a dozen invitations ahead.

On Wednesday I breakfasted with Lord Stanhope. I think I spoke of him in my last letter. Lady Stanhope is very agreeable, with a very sweet face, one of the persons I like best in London. I have nothing special to say of this entertainment except merely to mention the names of the guests, and I suppose that you will like to hear them. Macaulay did not come, which is the third time I have been disappointed of meeting him at breakfast. Each time he has been obliged to excuse himself on account of illness, and I am afraid that he is in a very bad way. His cough is certainly very alarming, and each time when I have met him at dinner he has had a very alarming fit of it. The persons who did come were Milnes, whom it is always pleasant to meet; the Bishop of Oxford, whom I have met once or twice before at breakfast, and who is a solid, thickset man, agreeable in conversation, and a splendid orator . . . . Lord and Lady Shaftesbury, Lord Powis, and one or two more. Lady Shaftesbury is daughter to Lady Palmerston, and is a fresh, handsome woman, although one of her younger sons has just set forth to make a tour in America. England is certainly the paradise of grandmothers. Lord Shaftesbury has made himself distinguished by promoting all sorts of charities, is strong about Sabbath-breaking, and is in general one of the leaders of the Exeter Hall political pietists. He is very lugubrious about the present aspect of affairs in England, and assured me that he considered the country fast rolling down the hill into the abyss of democracy.

This day I dined with Mr. Nassau Senior, a noted writer on political economy, an Edinburgh reviewer, and an ex-professor. Latterly he has travelled much in Greece, and his MS. journals are lent about London and Paris. He is friendly and hospitable and very *répandu*. His son is a big, burly barrister in spectacles. His son's wife, Mrs. Nassau Senior, junior, is pretty, very fair, with a wonderful profusion of gilt flaxen crinkle-crankled hair, and a remarkably fine voice, with which she discoursed after dinner much eloquent music. She is sister to Tom Hughes, alias Tom Brown. Phillips the artist and his wife, both sensible, agreeable people, were the only ones of the company I knew. On Thursday I went with the Sturgises and Incheses, after an early dinner, to the Princess Theatre to see the 'Merchant of Venice.' It was crowded, hot, and uncomfortable. I had afterwards for the same evening an invitation, which of course I could not accept, from Lady W. Russell to go with her to Covent Garden Opera. This house I have not yet seen, and it is very large and handsome. However, I did not care much more about going to the one or the other. The Queen was there, and of course rather a brilliant crowd.

Friday I dined with Lady Mary Fielding and her father the Earl of Denbigh. They sent me an invitation to dinner for either Friday or Saturday, so I took Friday. The family is distinguished for two things—for claiming to be the elder branch of the imperial house of Austria, calling themselves Counts of Hapsburg, and having the double-headed eagle on their spoons; and for numbering the immortal Henry Fielding among the scions of their house. The party was almost a family one, there being about five ladies, Fielding, and two or three colonels of the same name. Besides these were Max Müller, the famous Oxford philosopher, a very learned though comparatively a young man, and Arthur Stanley, of whom I have spoken to you before. He has asked me to dinner three times, but I have always been engaged. I chronicle these names and very important facts, because I have nothing else in the world to say. Of course you do not care to hear how many "dead letters" I read in the State Paper Office, or any of the details regarding my diggings generally.

Saturday, having a few days before found Noel's card on my table, I went up to Lady Byron's, but found that they were again flown. It is in vain to attempt to see anybody in London except by positive appointment. Lady Byron was at home by a sea-coal fire (for the weather has become as unblushingly cold as it was hot a week ago); she is pretty well for her, and was pleased to see me. This day I dined again with Lord Carlisle. The Milmans were going also, and took me in their carriage to Chiswick House, about five or six miles from Hyde Park Corner. It is always pleasant to go to Lord Carlisle's, he is so unaffectedly cordial and even affectionate, that it would be impossible not to be fond of him. He has been more attentive to me than anybody in London, except the Russells and Mrs. Norton, and I like him extremely (I mean, of course, of my new acquaintances). The company, besides the Milmans, consisted of Mr. Ball, a M.P., who has been an under secretary, and his wife, who is a Venetian, speaking hardly any English, who sat next me, and was quite delighted when she found I could speak French; Macaulay, who came contrary to expectation, but has a very bad cough and looks very feeble; Mr. Labouchere, once Minister for the Colonies, and his wife, Lady Mary, sister of Lord Carlisle; Mr. C. Howard, his brother; Lord and Lady Wensleydale, Sir David Dundas, who is just going to America, and two Members of Parliament.

Nothing very memorable occurred. Macaulay did not talk so much as usual, although he seemed in good spirits enough. He was speaking with me after we went upstairs upon American matters, when he was seized with two or three violent fits of coughing. Soon after he went away, and everybody seemed to feel anxious about him. Lady Mary Labouchere is as kind-hearted and agreeable as the rest of the family. I had never met her before, but she treated me like an old acquaintance, invited me to go out to their country place to-morrow to lunch, and see the churchyard where Gray's 'Elegy' was written, and to dine with her in town next Wednesday. Lord Wensleydale is the Baron Parke about whose life peerage there was such a row a year or two ago. It was finally settled by making him a peer *tout bonnement*, with remainder to his lawful issue, but as he and his wife are about seventy-five years old each, and have no sons as yet, it seems likely enough that it will remain a life peerage. I stopped at Cambridge House coming up, where, as usual, on Saturdays, there was an assembly. Lady Palmerston is always kind enough to invite me; passed an hour or two there, and I returned at one o'clock. To-day I dine at Holland House, which historical mansion I will describe in my next. God bless you, dearest Mary; take care of my darling children, kiss them all three a thousand times, and believe me,

Most affectionately yours,

J. L. M.

To his Wife.

London,
July 11th, 1858.

MY DEAREST MARY,—I am not able to give you any new sketches of celebrities. Having seen nearly all the prominent people in London, chalked them out *tant bien que mal* for your entertainment, I can now do little more than send you, like Jenkins, a list of the nobility and gentry that I meet daily at dinner and other parties. Sunday, I paid my weekly visit to Mrs. Norton, and found her as agreeable and interesting as she always is. Her talent for conversation is almost as remarkable as her beauty, and even superior to her poetic genius. I dined afterwards at Holland House. This is a quaint, antique old manor house belonging to the early period of James I., but having the general characteristics of the Elizabethan mansion. Built of brown brick, with turrets and gables, mullioned oriel windows, terraces, stately staircases, tapestried rooms, and painted ceilings, it is, on not a very large scale, one of the most beautiful country houses that it is possible to conceive. It is approached by a noble avenue of lime trees, is surrounded by an ample lawn, dotted with oaks, pastures, "where the nibbling sheep doth stray," and by a vast park of splendid forest trees, while close to the house are trim gardens, with clipt hedges, sundials, fountains, and statues, and "a lush of flowers" sufficient to gladden the soul of John Keats, and all this in what might be called the heart of London, certainly in its pericardium.

Kensington, near which country village Holland House once stood, is already swallowed into the all-devouring stomach of London, assimilated into the brick and mortar chyle out of which the life of that gigantic organisation is perpetually reproduced and enlarged. "Kensington Gore" is a recognised street of London, and the avenue gates of Holland House open really upon a continuation of Piccadilly. There was a discussion yesterday where I was dining about the value of the place for building purposes. Lord Clarendon said it would bring in an income of £6,000 a year; and Rothschild, who sat next me, said it was worth £150,000 at least. Yet the present Lord Holland only lives here about six weeks in the year, residing the rest of the time in Naples, where he has a fine house, as in Paris. He is a singularly agreeable person in his manners. I went out there this day, having received an invitation on very brief acquaintance, and expecting to find myself rather awkwardly placed among strangers. I got there about eight (having been invited for 7.30, and this is punctuality itself), and there were but two persons in the room. In the twilight I did not recognise them, but presently I observed the familiar proboscis of Lord Brougham wagging in a friendly manner towards me. He and another gentleman, commonly called Bear Ellice, were the only persons there. Brougham was very cross at waiting for his dinner, having been there half an hour, and Lord Holland had not shown himself. Presently he came in and apologised by saying that Lady Holland was taken ill and could not appear. Brougham's wrath was mollified, and he became very agreeable.

Lord and Lady Lyndhurst soon arrived, and with a few others, including the Duc de Richelieu and some persons whose names I did not hear, the party was complete. Lord Holland made me sit next to him, and Lady Lyndhurst was on the other side, so that I felt perfectly at home. Lords Lyndhurst and Brougham were chaffing each other as usual. Nothing can be more genial, genuine, and delightful than Lyndhurst's manner. He is particularly kind and friendly to me on all occasions, made me come and sit with him after dinner, and we talked together for half an hour. He always

expresses much interest in my studies and writings, but it is
not for that that I like his society, but because of the magnificent spectacle he affords of a large bright intellect setting
in " one unclouded blaze of living light," without any of the
dubious haze which so often accompanies the termination of a
long and brilliant career. Everybody looks up to him with
reverence and delight. He is full of fun, always joking, always
genial, and alive to what is going on around him from day to
day. He has made two or three very good speeches this
session, and is going to make another, and there is not a sign
of senility in anything that he says.

The next day I went by invitation to Stoke Park to luncheon.
This is the beautiful country seat of Mr. and Lady Mary
Labouchere. He is a man eminent in politics, of great wealth
and formerly a Cabinet Minister, as Secretary for the Colonies.
She is the youngest sister of Lord Carlisle and the Duchess of
Sutherland, and the most amiable creature living. Indeed
the whole family seems somehow or other to have absorbed
more gallons apiece of the milk of human kindness than
would serve for the average allowance of several hundred
individuals. It is certainly agreeable to see people in high
station and with vast wealth so overflowing with benevolent
virtues. Chill penury could certainly not suppress their
noble rage, but in my experience I have found that luxury
sometimes has as refrigerating an effect upon the "genial
currents of the soul" as poverty itself. These delicious expressions, which you recognise, are bits from that immortal,
monumental poem, the 'Elegy in the Country Churchyard,'
are very à propos at this moment, for the 'Elegy' was
composed on this very spot. It was to see the church and
churchyard that they asked me out to dine. There was no
company except Lord Carlisle (whom I may call now my intimate friend, for he is untiring in his demonstrations of regard
for me), his brother Charles Howard and his mother-in-law
Lady Wensleydale. We walked over the grounds, went to a
bit of the old manor house once the residence of Sir Christopher Hatton, and then round about the churchyard.

It is exactly what it ought to be ; and as almost every line of that poem has lingered in my memory ever since I used to recite it when a small boy to my dear mother, I enjoyed the exquisite fidelity of the description to the actual scenery, which is as remarkable as, on the other hand, its broad lofty and stately moralisation, which would be almost as true in a graveyard in Wisconsin or Connecticut as in Buckinghamshire. "The rugged elm and yew trees' shade" are still there, embowering the little church, which stands on the edge of Stoke Park; and the little enclosures, "where heaves the turf in many a mouldering heap," have been literally ploughed into furrows by the long succession of sowers and reapers in God's acre. The "ivy mantled tower," where the "moping owl doth to the moon complain" is still covered with its luxuriant festoons, but I regret to say that the ivy looks sickly and as if decaying. The church itself is one of the most exquisite of English country churches, and this is saying enough. The only thing I missed was the village. There is none in sight; and (at present at least) there is not much in the stately and sequestered aristocratic park to suggest all those rural pictures which the musing, melancholy poet painted, and the "rude forefathers of the hamlet" driving their teams afield, the busy housewives' evening care, and children climbing the paternal knee. All is very still and silent, and nothing like profane vulgar intrudes upon the calm and exclusive scene. This is what I missed most in the locality. For the rest it is perfect. Gray lies buried in the same grave with his mother, and a plain monument, inscribed with some of the best lines of the elegy, has been erected in the park.

I had to hurry to town because I had to dine out. This day it was at Lady Williams, with whom I dined once before. She is a very clever person, original and rather funny, and receives the best company in London. There is nothing very remarkable to say of the entertainment. Now that I have described to you many dinners, the rest hardly require to be sung. There are the same dishes, the same wines, the same solemn stillness, the same gorgeous flunkeys, and a score of personages of quality, the same even if different, for one lord differeth less from another in glory than do the stars in their courses. To-day were again Lord Brougham and Lord Lyndhurst at dinner, whom I meet so often that I am gradually getting to mistake myself for an Ex-Chancellor, and shall probably be soon caught propounding legal opinions with oracular gravity and expecting my words to be accepted as oracles.

On Tuesday I dined again at Holland House. (I have been invited to dine there four times in a week, so that if they retain their original maternal principle of the Holland House organisation, I have a right to conclude that they do not consider me a bore.) The company to-day consisted of the Duc d'Aumale (one of the sons of King Louis Philippe) and the Duchesse, Lord and Lady Clarendon, Macaulay, Duvergier d'Hauranne, Lady J. Russell, and Hayward. It is always delightful to meet Macaulay, and to see the reverence with which he is regarded by everybody; painful to observe the friendly anxiety which every one feels about his health. Sir H. Holland told me his complaints were bronchial and asthmatic, but I should have thought them more like dropsy. He was obliged to leave the table for a few minutes on account of a spasm of coughing, which has been the case ever since I have met him. I think, unless he is much changed, that Sydney Smith's descriptions or rather flings at him are somewhat unjust. He is not in the least the " colloquial oppressor " he has been represented. On the contrary, every one wishes to hear him talk, and very often people are disappointed because he does not talk enough. To be sure, a mind so brimful as his must spout forth uncontrollably, if you once pull out the plug ; nevertheless he is always willing to shut himself up again, if anybody else wishes to pour himself out. Usually nobody does where he is present. His conversation is, however, rather learned and didactic than *spirituelle*. His " brilliant flashes " are only those of silence, according to Sydney's memorable sarcasm. This is strange, for in his writings he is brilliant and flashing almost to painfulness, but I observe nothing pointed or epigrammatic or humorous in his talk. It is very wise and very instructive, but not the kind to set the table in a roar.

Lord and Lady Clarendon I meet very often; they are very civil to me, and are both among the most agreeable people in London. You are aware that he is one of the most eminent political characters in England, having been a long time a Foreign Minister, and subsequently Minister of Foreign Affairs. He is a tall, thin, handsome, aristocratic-looking person. His wife is a blonde, very young for her age, whatever it may be, with an amiable manner. On Wednesday morning I went out by rail to Cassiobury Park, seat of the Earl of Essex, to which place I had received an invitation to a *fête champêtre* or luncheon party. In the compartment in which I went were Mrs. Norton, Lady Stanley, Lord and Lady Airlie, and Lord Stratford de Redcliffe. The party was brilliant, the park magnificent, the house stately. There is nothing very exhilarating to be said of the party. They are generally somewhat slow these same country festivities. If it were not for Mrs. Norton I should be often bored on such occasions. But she can create an oasis in the most arid place, where one can listen to the constant and musical gurgle of her witty or thoughtful conversation and be refreshed. The luncheon was a kind of brief and somewhat scrambling dinner. The Duke of Cambridge, at the board's end, stolid and manful, flanked by Malakoff, looking like a military Silenus; and at the right of Lord Essex was the Princess Edward of Saxe-Weimar. I cannot give you a list of the other swells who were present, for I forget the names almost as soon as I hear them.

The grounds and the gardens, the park and the lawn, looked very brilliant with the rainbow-coloured petals of the female flowers blooming out so suddenly in all directions, but not to blush unseen, nor to waste their sweetness, and the "whole dream of fair women" was as successful as such things usually are. If I were Boccaccio or Tennyson, instead of a somewhat slow and cynical Dryasdust, I dare say I could paint wondrous pictures of romance and poetry upon such a canvas as was here unrolled; but in my commonplace frame of mind, the scene was commonplace. As usual I had to fidget into town before I was ready, in order to be in time to dress.

To-day Lord Lyndhurst gave me a dinner, the company being invited to meet me. This is a compliment of which I am very proud. The party was a small one. There was Lord Carlisle, Lord Granville, Lord Wensleydale, Mr. Greville, Sir E. Landseer, Lord Ashburton, and Lord Sefton, a youth who reminded me somewhat of W—— O——, being very lively, boyish, and rattling; and it was too funny to hear him speak incidentally of doing something or other in the House of Lords, with the rest of the hereditary legislators. The party was particularly cosy and agreeable, more so than almost any I have assisted at. I consider it a privilege to have known so well and seen so much of Lord Lyndhurst. This day he was even more genial and sunny than usual. Lady Lyndhurst is always kind and obliging. On Friday I dined with Lord Granville. I hardly think it worth my while to rack my memory to give you a list of the twenty persons present. The lady next me was agreeable and handsome, and opposite me was a remarkably pretty woman. I knew their names once, but have now forgotten. On my right was rather an amusing personage who had just arrived from the Cape of Good Hope, and had been in Cuba and the United States. Then there was a gigantic and agreeable Russian named Count Pahlen, and a famous homœopathic doctor, Quin, and a mass of others whom I do not remember even indistinctly.

Next day I dined with Vernon Smith. He was once of the Palmerston Cabinet, as Secretary of the Board of Control for India. He is a handsome man and popular in society. His wife is a very pretty young woman of fifty, a not very rare genus in England, and an agreeable, lively, sociable person. The company were the Rothschilds, Baron, Baroness, and daughter, whom I have already described to you; the Marchioness of Clanricarde and her daughter; Lord and Lady Clarendon, Lord St. Germans, and Mrs. Dyce Sombre. The latter personage was the one whom I escorted to dinner. I had received an invitation to dine the same day with Lady Palmerston, but could not accept it, but I went there in the evening. There were but few persons, not a party —Lady William Russell, Lord Shaftesbury, who invited me to

make a visit to him at his country place, as has also Lord
Stanhope, Lord Carlisle, and many others, which invitations
of course I cannot accept. Kennedy of Baltimore was there
also. I called this morning on them. I have got to the
end of my fourth sheet, dearest Mary. I dine to-day with
Monckton Milnes; to-morrow with Lord Ashburton, and so on;
and there is a ball to-morrow night at the Duchess of
Wellington's, to which I shall probably go. God bless you
and my dear children. Kiss them a million times, and
believe me always,

Affectionately yours,

J. L. M.

To his Wife.

July 18th, 1858.

MY DEAREST MARY,—I came up this morning from Walton,
where I went yesterday, and found my dear Lily's letter on
my table, and was much gratified by it, as also by funny
little Susie's delightful epistle. Thank them both, and kiss
them, as well as my darling Mary, a hundred times. I
also enclose a letter from my mother just received, and you
will be glad to hear that she is decidedly better. I wrote to
her by the last mail, and shall very soon write again. I will
now huddle up very rapidly what I have been doing so far as
society is concerned, premising that I have now finished with
London, and that I have declined all invitations for this
week.

On Sunday I dined with Monckton Milnes. His wife I had
seen for the first time the evening before at Lady Palmerston's.
The dinner was small, consisting of two Frenchmen, one, the
editor of the *Siècle*, who never could hear himself talk enough,
and a Marquis de Ribère, a Legitimist, married to an English-
woman, an agreeable and intelligent person. I have nothing
more to say of this festivity. Next day I dined at Bath House,
the splendid mansion in Piccadilly of Lord Ashburton. He is
the son of the first Lord Ashburton, and the head of the second
branch of the Barings. He is an exceedingly shy, almost

timid, personage, but cultivated and friendly. He has a very
fine collection of paintings in his town house, and still more at
his country residence, the Grange, to which he has given me a
very pressing invitation. The dinner consisted of Lord and
Lady Euston (the niece of Lord Ashburton), Lord and Lady
Dufferin, Sir David Dundas, Mr. Drummond, M.P., and Henry
Taylor, author of 'Philip van Artevelde.' The latter personage, I think, I have not before described to you. He is
tall, apparently forty-five or fifty years of age, with a handsome,
striking face, with regular features, and long grizzled hair, and
a quiet, perfectly English manner. We sat next each other
at table, but his conversation was quite as commonplace as
mine, or any other Christian; it is impossible to chronicle
anything concerning it. I liked him, on the whole, as well as
any literary man whom I have met, always excepting Froude.
I had a good deal of talk with Lady Dufferin after dinner,
whom it is always delightful to meet.

In the evening I went, with the rest of the world and wife,
to the Duchess of Wellington's ball. Apsley House is, on the
whole, the finest private palace in London, except Stafford
House. The staircase, corridors, entrance-hall, are all spacious
and imposing ; a heroic, colossal, and very detestable statue of
Napoleon salutes you in the vestibule, and there are several
portraits of him, as well as of great English generals and companions in arms of the Iron Duke, upon the walls of the various
saloons. The great dancing hall is very large and lofty, hung
in cherry colour, but, being well gilded and gas-lighted, is, notwithstanding, very brilliant, and the other rooms *en suite* are
elegant and palatial. As I know a great many people now, I
amused myself well enough for a couple of hours, although, as
a general rule, I enjoy nothing in London but dinner parties,
not because I want to eat, which you know is not my *faiblesse*,
but because it is impossible to talk with any comfort except
in a *demi-couchant* attitude, and as my toes have ceased to
be fantastic, the dancing hall has no attractions for me, and
makes me rather dismal. "They have dancing shoes with
nimble soles—I have sole of lead," etc. I cannot say, however,
in my capacity of spectator, that the actors in such scenes

seem inspired by any very wild excitement. Their tameness is shocking to me, as was that of the " beasts that roared over the plain " to the late Alexander Selkirk.

On Tuesday I dined with the Sturgis's, a small party of English, among whom were Lord Dufferin and Arthur Russell, and Lady Selina Vernon, a great friend of Mrs. Sturgis, next whom I sat at dinner. On Wednesday I dined by myself at the Athenæum. Thursday afternoon Lord Lyndhurst took me down to the House of Lords, to hear the commencement of the India debate. It is always a great pleasure to me to see Lord Lyndhurst. He is very kind to me, always makes much of me when we meet at dinner (and it has been my privilege to dine very often in company with him), and makes me help him up from his chair, and takes my arm to go upstairs, a distinction I am very proud of. He is a most charming old man, full of fun and wit, interested in everything going on, and, as I am, much occupied with the present as the past, notwithstanding his eighty-six years. His face is very smooth, less wrinkled than mine, so that his brown wig is almost illusory. The debate was rather poor. I heard the Earl of Derby, who was fluent enough and graceful, but tedious as a king. After him came Lord Granville, whom I like so much personally that I was very glad to find him a very good orator, with an admirable sonorous voice, and with some humour in his style of speaking. I was obliged to go off in the middle of his speech, because I had promised to go down to Walton to dine (they moved there yesterday), it being Mrs. Sturgis's birthday.

I came up the following morning, being engaged to dine with Lord and Lady Wensleydale. The party was rather made for me, I believe, as I had the honour of going with Madame to dinner. He is the famous Judge, Baron Parke, a shrewd, keen, quick, lively, jolly personage. She is, not unjustly, vain of getting into the peerage in her old days, and of having her stock mingled with the blood of all the Howards, her daughter, now dead, having been the wife of Charles Howard, brother of Lord Carlisle. He is a very kind-hearted, unaffected person, like all the family that I know. The rest

of the company, so far as I remember them, were the dear old
Lord Lyndhurst, Dr. Lushington, Mr. Pemberton Leigh, a
distinguished barrister (who I believe once refused the Lord
Chancellorship), Mr. Fitzgerald, Under-Secretary of State,
Lady Cranworth, Lady W. Russell, Lady Robert Cecil, and
one or two more. After dinner came in a reinforcement from
without, among others a person whom I always like to meet—
Lady Mary Labouchere.

The next day I had accepted an invitation to lunch with
Lady John Russell, having declined once or twice before. I
went out by rail to Richmond. The weather was magnificent,
and I walked up the hill from the station, and enjoyed the
spacious and far-famed view. There was nobody at Pembroke
Lodge except George Elliot, Lady John's brother, and Sir
George and Lady Theresa Lewis. He was Chancellor of the
Exchequer in the last Administration. Lady Theresa is sister
to Lord Clarendon, remarkably clever and *spirituelle*, full of
talk and cultivation. Lord John was very amusing, told lots
of anecdotes about the Duke of Wellington, George IV., and
other personages with much sly humour and enjoyment. The
popular idea of "Johnny" is that of a cold, cynical, reserved
personage, but in his own house I never saw a more agreeable
manner.

I proceeded afterwards overland to Kingston, whence the
rail brought me to Walton, and the quiet scenery and friendly
welcome which is the lot of those who are intimate in that
beautiful house, is most refreshing.

God bless you, my dearest Mary, kiss my dear children,
and believe me,

Most affectionately yours,

J. L. M.

To his Wife.

Oude Doelen, The Hague,
July 26th, 1858.

MY DEAREST MARY,—Yesterday, Sunday morning, at 10 A.M., I took the boat for Rotterdam, arrived at that place at 8.30 this morning, and by rail at 9.30 reached this hotel by ten. So that twenty-four hours of discomfort and boredom, mingled with a gale of wind, have saved me a long, tiresome and expensive railroad journey, had I gone any other way. It blew very hard indeed in the morning, so that if I had had you all with me I should not have gone, but luckily the wind was very favourable, and as we steamed away directly before it, we were not incommoded. It faded out by nightfall. To go back and very rapidly account for myself since I last wrote. On Monday I went to Walton, to rest a little and breathe the delicious country air, but after two pleasant days, during which Mount Felix and its occupants were as delightful and friendly as ever, went over to Lord Lovelace's. Previously, on the Tuesday, Julia Sturgis and I drove over to Twickenham, where her boys are at a private school, attended and were somewhat amused by the distribution of prizes, two of which fell to little Julian and one to Harry, and then brought them home in a very jolly frame of mind for the holidays. By appointment I went to East Horsley Towers on Wednesday, and stayed till Friday morning. I like Lady Annabella King, the daughter of Ada Byron, very much. She has much talent, very agreeable manners, and a good deal of fun, plays and paints admirably, and has evidently a very sweet disposition. I returned to town on Friday, found there a very kind note from Lady Palmerston inviting me to Brocket Hall for the three days which had just expired (I having been absent all the week, had not received the note). I was sorry to miss this, as Hayward told me that the party was very pleasant and " Pam " in excellent spirits.

Friday, I dined at the Athenæum, along with Hayward, who amuses me with his malicious little anecdotes about everybody who ever is or was in London; Sir Henry Rawlinson, the cele-

brated Orientalist ; the Prince Frederick of Schleswig-Holstein,
one of the deposed family of claimants to the buried Majesty
of Denmark, and a very accomplished and agreeable young
man of much character and talent whom I met very often, and,
fourthly, Kinglake, author of 'Eothen.' I forget whether you
read or liked that remarkable book, but I have read it more
than once, and like it exceedingly. It is full to the brim of
talent and caustic observation, and I was glad to meet him.
There is nothing marquant in his appearance or conversation.
He is blond of beard and visage, fortyish in years, with a good
eye and a pleasant voice, like most Englishmen. He has thus
far made no great figure in Parliament. Good-bye, God bless
you, dearest Mary ; excuse the meagreness of this letter, but I
thought it better to scribble off a dozen lines rather than delay
another day, lest you should be anxious. I am very tired and
stupid, not having slept in that confounded boat. Kiss my
darlings a thousand times.

Ever affectionately,

J. L. M.

CHAPTER X.

THE HAGUE.

Work at the Hague—The National Archives—Presentation to the Queen of
Holland—"The House in the Wood"—A royal dinner party—Prince
Frederick—The American Revivalists—Lord Dunfermline—Family anni-
versaries—A Dutch literary celebrity—The King of Holland—Court *Fêtes*—
Court Ball in Amsterdam—Prince Henry—The Prince of Orange.

To his Wife.

The Hague,
August 1st, 1858.

MY DEAREST MARY,—I wrote you on Monday last, the
morning of my arrival in this place. To-day I resume my
Sunday letters, although I fear they will be rather meagre in
future. This is not so large a town as London. I saw M.
Groen van Prinsterer the morning of my arrival. He is going
away immediately, to my regret, on a journey of some weeks,
and will hardly be back till after my departure. However he
has already published a second volume of his documents from
the private Archives of the Orange-Nassau family, so that I
have no special need of his presence, as everything which I
require in that collection is now printed in a most convenient
and readable form. With regard to the great collection of
national Archives, I have of course immediately plunged over
head and ears in them. My old friend, Backhuyzen van der
Brink is on the spot. It is of great service to have his introduction to the Holland public. Madame Groen, on taking
leave of the Queen the day of my arrival, told her that I was
here, and the same day I saw Count Bylandt. He told me
that the Queen expressed disappointment to him in January
that she did not see me in my visit at that time, so that he
said he was glad to find that I had kept my promise of returning. Count Randwyk called on me, with Bylandt, the evening of
the day of my arrival, and accordingly the next day I addressed

a note to him requesting the honour of a presentation, etc. I
received an answer the same morning appointing the interview
for 3.30 P.M. Accordingly I drove out at that time to the
" House in the Wood " (Huis ten Bosch), in which beautiful
little villa in the very heart of the forest she is at present
residing, the King being at Wiesbaden.

I was received in the large saloon by an elderly maid of
honour, who entertained me with discourse on various subjects,
social, literary, and political, for a few minutes, and then I was
sent for, and she piloted me to her Majesty. The Queen
received me at the door, quite without ceremony, with " I am
so glad to make your acquaintance, Mr. Motley, pray sit down ;"
so she seated herself on her sofa and made me take a fauteuil
near it, and then she conversed with me for about half an hour
in the most unaffected, simple, and agreeable manner possible.
She is tall, very fair, and must have had a great deal of blonde
German beauty. She was very simply dressed, but I am sorry
for Susie's sake that I have entirely forgotten her costume.
Her teeth are beautiful, and her hands small, white, and
exquisitely shaped. Her voice is agreeable and she speaks
English, not only with great elegance and fluency, but almost
entirely without a foreign accent. This by the way was one of
the compliments which she paid me, observing "how beautifully you speak English," adding, "for to tell you the truth we
think we can always tell the difference, and we do not like
American English generally so well, but you seem to me to
speak like an Englishman," etc. She said a great many
things in a very graceful way about the 'Dutch Republic,'
asked me how I came originally to take up the subject, and
alluded to various portions of the work, etc.

She spoke of Lady W. Russell as an old friend for whom she
had much affection, and expressed disappointment that she had
never been at the Hague. We talked a good deal too about
Mrs. Norton, of whom she expressed the most unbounded admiration for her genius and the charm of her conversation. I
hardly remember much more of her conversation. She is certainly very clever, remarkably intelligent, and with a great deal
of information on all subjects, a person who has read much and

acquired much and with much capacity for thought on high
and important matters.

Altogether I have rarely made a morning visit on any lady
where the conversation was more fluent, lively, and interesting.
The best compliment I can pay her is, that one quite forgets
that she is a queen, and only feels the presence of an intelligent and very attractive woman.

The interview lasted so long as to make me think, contrary
to the rule of courts, that I was to take my leave, and I said,
" Your Majesty must send me away if I am tiresome," but she
said, " No, no, do not go, what have you got to do, do you dine
out ? "   I said yes, but that was nothing, and it was a long
time to the dinner hour. I desired nothing better than to stay,
etc. So we talked on some time longer, and then she rose,
saying, " Will you have the kindness to dine with me the day
after to-morrow at 5.30 ? " Of course I accepted, made my bow
and departed. I dined that day with a gentleman, a friend of
Groen van Prinsterer's, M. Elout de Soeterwonde, a man of
much distinction, literary, cultivated, a member of the States
General and a judge. He called on me the day of my arrival,
saying, that every Hollander had a right to my acquaintance,
etc., and I found his family very pleasant. His wife is a very
pretty, pleasing woman, and to my profound astonishment she
informed me that she had seven children. They live in a very
pretty, old-fashioned house on the edge of the wood called the
Huister Noot, not far from the Hotel Bellevue.

It was a kind of family party, brothers and sisters-in-law,
and so on, but they were all friendly and kind-hearted and
intelligent, and I was glad to see something of the interior of
the best Holland families. On Friday I dined by appointment
with the Queen. The company—about sixteen or eighteen in all,
male and female—were received by a tall chamberlain (nobody
was in uniform) and ushered into one of the large saloons.
Here, as usual on such occasions, we were all stuck up in a circular row, like the jars in the "Forty Thieves," and presently
entered the Queen like Morgiana, and went round dropping a
few words into the ears of each.

After this process was got through with (and she talked

to me a good while), we went to dinner, Queen first alone,
then the ladies were all driven in by the master of the ceremonies by themselves, and then the gentlemen followed helter
skelter, each having been previously informed where he was
to place himself at table, something according to the Peabody
system.

I hardly knew the names of the company. The Belgian
minister and his wife, the Danish minister, Count Randwyck,
a professor of botany, and various ladies of honour, etc. The
Queen sat in the middle of the table, the two ministers one on
each side of her, I sat opposite her with Count Randwyck on
my right, and a very chatty agreeable maid of honour on my
left, who had accompanied the Queen last year to England, and
knew a great many people that I knew.

The dinner was very good, better on the whole than most of
the London dinners, and the only fault was the march of the
dishes, which was rapid enough to suit Mr. Cabot. There was
no pausing, and as I cannot talk with my mouth full, I was
obliged either to hold my tongue half the time, or lose half my
dinner. Now strange to say, or very naturally, I have recently
a great appetite produced by going into the North Sea every
morning before breakfast, a system which I shall keep up as
long as I am here, although it costs me two hours and two
francs per diem, all of which I begrudge. After dinner (which
by the way was in the great circular hall built by Amalia de
Solms, wife of Frederic Henry, youngest son of William the
Silent, and adorned by magnificent frescoes by the scholars of
Rubens), we returned and made another circle in the saloon,
had our coffee, and the Morgianic process was repeated. The
Queen stopped and talked with me a long time about English
society, the Palmerstons, Clarendons, Hollands. She also
spoke of Madame Mohl and her husband (of which last couple
she spoke with much kindness). By the way, she observed to
me the day before that she had never been able to make out
whether Madame Mohl wore her own hair or a wig, but I told
her she might set her mind entirely at rest on that subject.
No human intellect could ever conceive, or the hand of man
execute such a wonderful Medusa crop, nor would it be within

the resources of science to manufacture any artificial covering which would stand all the tugging and tossing to which those serpent locks were daily subjected. The Queen agreed with me that there never was a kinder-hearted or more amusing or original little old woman in the world.

The next day I had an audience of Prince Frederic, uncle of the King. He had mentioned me as having been presented to the Queen, and of course it was necessary for me to call likewise upon him. He is a man of sixty, very mild and amiable in character and manners, married to a sister of the King of Prussia, and of the Empress of Russia, and I believe a very noble and unexceptionable character. The interview lasted about three quarters of an hour. He was very frank and cordial, of course made the 'Dutch Republic' the principal topic for a long time, and then discoursed on other matters. I do not think I can recollect anything of the conversation, but he seemed very amiable and simple, and was certainly very friendly. He said at parting, he hoped he did not see me for the last time, and I dare say I shall be invited to dine at his country place, where he is staying, a few miles out of town. These matters are a little interruption, but the place is so quiet and small that I have plenty of working hours, whereas in London the enormousness of all dimensions makes one's time shrivel into nothingness, and each day shrinks into an hour so far as any real work is concerned.

Ever most affectionately yours,
J. L. M.

To his Wife.

The Hague,
August 15th, 1858.

MY DEAREST MARY,—I work every morning at home two hours before breakfast, then go to the Archives till three, after which, in the course of the day and evening, I get a few hours more. I am more than ever desponding about my task. It is very extensive, laborious, and expensive. I am obliged to travel over thousands of square miles of documents followed by a couple of copyists, who will, of course, require treble the time to write which it takes me to read, and, without reckoning the confounded expense of the whole business, there is such an endless amount of time to be consumed in waiting.

I have dined out four times this week, but I do not think I could find much entertainment for you in a description of these festivities. On Monday I dined with Mr. —— —— ——. They are friendly people, intensely religious, and I dare say they think me a violent uncompromising Calvinist like themselves. On this occasion there were some raw Scotchmen, just descended from their native heath and mad with orthodoxy. One of them observed, on some reference to the late revival in America, that the hand of the Lord was most manifest in that great and wonderful development. He then gave an instance of a mercantile friend, who had gone out to New York in the midst of the commercial crisis to collect some money owing to him, but who had naturally, like every other creditor, been referred to the town pump for liquidation. He had brought back, however, something far better than silver or gold, for he had himself experienced religion in New York, and had returned a regenerated sinner, a brand snatched from the burning. These were almost his exact expressions—saving the irreverent allusions to the pump—and I thought the idea of the New Yorkers paying off their Scotch creditors by unlimited draughts upon the treasures of the next world one of the best dodges I have yet heard of. I could hardly sit still in my chair—however, I kept my countenance and looked edified.

The next day I dined with a young couple, de Jonghe. He is a very nice fellow, who is employed in the Archives, but seems to have property of his own, and is of good family. His father was a distinguished man of letters here. His wife is a pretty, pleasing person, talking English—as many of the women here do—perfectly.

The next day I dined with Lord Dunfermline. The party was the same as the last time I dined there, with the addition of Bylandt, and the subtraction of Spanish Minister and his daughter. They (the D.'s) are very friendly, unaffected people,

and I like them very much.   Day after to-morrow I am to dine
with Baron Golstein, the Minister of Foreign Affairs.

Ever yours,

J. L. M.

To his Wife.

The Hague,

August 29th, 1858.

MY DEAREST MARY,—Since I last wrote I have had the
pleasure of receiving your letters from Geneva, and two
from Vevay, also Susie's and Mary's, and a long and very
charmingly written letter from my dear Lily, taking great
pains, and very successfully, to impart to me a portion of the
pleasure which she has derived from the excursion to
Chamouni.   I am so glad you and she were not disappointed,
that you found the Amory party so friendly, and that the
weather was so auspicious.   I am sure I wish you could have
more such amusements.

Before I go any further, let me, after thanking my sweet
little Mary for her letter expressing sorrow that I should
have written upon August 1st, and not have remembered at
the moment that it was her fifteenth birthday.   She knows
how much I love her, and if I did not say anything about her
fête, it was from no want of interest in such a day.   My
darling child !   It seems impossible that she can have lived
fifteen years in this weary world, for she seems as young and as
innocent now as if she had just descended from heaven.   I
never feel as if I had any right to her, and I can never express
half the tenderness and the affection I feel for her.   Since she
has been in the world she has been a blessing and a consolation, and she can never cause you or me any unhappiness,
except she should die, which God in His mercy forbid !   My
little impudent, nonsensical, good-hearted Susie, too, is getting
to be a very good child, and in time, when she can be induced
to talk a little and get up an appetite for her dinner, she will
be all that can be wished for.

Affectionately yours,

J. L. M.

To his Wife.

The Hague,
September 3rd, 1858.

MY DEAREST MARY,—The other day I received a visit, while
I was seated at my solitary breakfast in the *salle à manger*, from
a benignant old gentleman, who came forward smiling, and said,
" Mr. Motley, I believe." " Yes." " Well, I am —— ——."
I looked as conscious as I could, at a moment's warning, of
being in the presence of a celebrity; but as I had rarely or
never heard of the great ——, I was a little embarrassed, not
knowing exactly what his particular line of eminence might be.
He relieved me, however, by seating himself at once at my
table as spectator, not participator, and informing me that he
was the author of many poems, histories, dramas, and political
pamphlets.   He made a slight but handsome allusion to the
D. R., but to my great relief he evidently preferred talking of
his own performances, which he was good enough to do for
about half an hour without cessation.   As his English, which
he insisted upon talking, was imperfect, and his teeth, I regret
to say, still more so, I was not able to enter into the full
current of his conversation.   Moreover, as he took snuff to such
an extent as to make him decidedly unpleasant, I should have
preferred to receive his visit after breakfast.   He observed,
quoting Lord Byron, that " the myrtles and roses of sweet two-
and-twenty were worth all your laurels however so plenty."
From which I inferred that his head was crowned with laurels,
for there could certainly be nothing in common with him and
the other two shrubs.   I am sure I do not know why I am
boring you with the portraiture of this individual, except that
the week is sterile in topics for your entertainment.   Moreover,
it is too bad in me to ridicule a personage who, I have since
been informed, is really a deserving and eminent man of
letters, and who came to see me as a mark of politeness, and
begged me, if I came to ——, to make his house my home.

    The King returned last Friday, and on the following
Monday I had an interview with him at the palace at the
Northend, the one opposite which is the equestrian statue of

William the Silent. I drove thither by appointment at 12.30,
and was ushered into a very small room, where I was left for
a little while in the company of an inkstand and a sheet
of paper, in case, I suppose, that if any reflections suggested
themselves, I might instantly reduce them to writing. Soon
afterwards two young aides-de-camp came in, one a whis-
kered light-infantry man, the other a fierce Hussar, and
after bowing profoundly, they both began conversing with
me on the subject of the D. R., of which I am, without affectation, getting as tired as ever was a wandering dog of a
tin canister tied to its tail. Exactly as the clock struck the
half-hour, the door opened, and a stoutish, youngish, tallish
man, in a blue cut-away coat, checked shirt with a turn-
down collar and grey trousers, walked up to me and said in
English with a loud voice, "Mr. Motley, you have written a most
magnificent work, and I am proud to make your acquaintance."
Whereupon I shrewdly suspected the individual to be his
Majesty, although I had expected to be ushered through six
more rooms at least; but the King is one of those royal personages who has the good sense to leave a gap in the hedge of his
divinity for special occasions. I must say that he made a very
agreeable impression upon me; and you will say, of course, that
this is on account of my susceptibility to flattery. I know it
to be a weakness, but if people are very polite and complimentary and kind to me, whether they are kings and queens, or
only knaves or persons of lesser rank, I am but too apt to
respond—I cannot help it.

The King is forty-one, but looks younger, having thick,
brown, ungrizzled hair and beard, a fresh, smooth, unwrinkled
face, regular features, a clear blue eye, and a tall, erect,
muscular, and graceful figure. He speaks English with a
good accent and in rather a violent manner, as if he was
disposed to tear through all idiomatic difficulties by main
force. He was very cordial and agreeable, and kept me about
three-quarters of an hour, and at departing hoped he should
have the pleasure of seeing me again. Two days afterwards
I received a package containing the twelve volumes of Groen
van Prinsterer's 'Archives et Correspondance de la Maison

d'Orange,' splendidly bound and gilt, with a note from the
King's librarian informing me that it was a present from his
Majesty. On the first page of the first volume, moreover, the
King had written this inscription, which, as I shall be obliged
to pack up the books, you will like me to copy, so excuse the
vanity of the proceeding :—

" A Mr. J. L. Motley, historien consciencieux et éloquent, au
digne appréciateur du 1er Guillaume d'Orange, le plus grand
homme de son époque, est offert de souvenir, comme témoignage
d'estime et d'admiration.

"GUILLAUME III D'ORANGE,
"Roi des Pays-Bas.

"**La Haye, 31 *Août* 1858.**"

Perhaps the chief pleasure that I derive from this present
is the proof which it affords that the King thoroughly
appreciates the grandeur of his immortal ancestor and
namesake, and religiously cherishes his glory and his memory.
I am invited to a Court ball at Amsterdam on Tuesday
night. The *fêtes* of the birthday of the Prince of Orange
(yesterday, 4th) consisted in a dinner to the Ministers of
State, and Chiefs of Foreign Legations, and the ball, day after
to-morrow, to which the foreign ministers are *not* invited, so
that I shall hardly find an acquaintance there. I wrote to the
Maréchal de la Cour that I had no court-dress, the invitation
being to a "bal gala," but I received in consequence an
invitation to come "en frac," and to Amsterdam I must go.
Fortunately the Danish Minister, who is the most kind-
hearted, obliging fellow in the world, is going to stay on after
the dinner at Amsterdam, and has promised to see that I
have a room, a carriage, together with his own servant to go
to the ball with me. His name is de Bille; he was brought up
in America, where his father was minister, and he is the most
amiable creature living. It is my present intention to leave
the Hague for Arnheim this day week, on my way to Vevay. I
may possibly stop one day with Bismarck if he is at Frankfort,
but I think I shall be with you at latest this day fortnight,
perhaps a little earlier.

The weather has been dreary for a fortnight, I hope you have it better in Switzerland.

Good-bye, my dearest Mary. My love to my dear children. God bless you!

Ever affectionately yours,
J. L. M.

P.S.—I forgot to mention that, by a rather odd coincidence, on the same day on which I received the King's present, I took from the post office a letter from one John Hopkins of Chattanooga, Tennessee, informing me that " some weeks since a bookseller, of whom he was making some purchases, insisted until he purchased the D. R.; " he then declares himself highly gratified by the perusal of the work, and expresses a thousand wishes for my happiness.

J. L. M.

To his Wife.

The Hague,
September 11th, 1858.

MY DEAREST MARY,—I have neither time nor topics for anything but a very brief epistle. I leave to-morrow morning early for Arnheim, thence I intend to make a brief excursion to Zutphen for the sake of seeing that town, which was the scene of many events in the period I am to write about, and the neighbouring village of Warmfeld, where Sir Philip Sidney was killed. I suppose I shall sleep at Zutphen to-morrow night, and the next day get as far as Bonn, thence to Mayence, Bâle, and Vevay. If Bismarck is at Frankfort, I shall pass a day with him there, if not I shall not go to Frankfort at all. I may arrive on Thursday. I may not get to Vevay till Saturday. I hope that you got my note from Amsterdam and acted upon it immediately.

The ball at the Amsterdam palace was much like other Court balls, or rather it was much unlike them in one respect, the Hague Society was not there. As Touchstone would have said in respect that it is at Amsterdam, it liketh me well, but

in respect it is not at Court, 'tis a very vile ball. In fact it
was rather a national sort of thing. The marechals and chamberlains of the Court, and other swells were there, and of course
the royal family and their hangers-on, but no other ladies from
the Hague. The royal family were all very civil to me. The
king came up to me very early in the evening, shook hands
very cordially, and after talking with me some time, said his
brother Prince Henry wished to make my acquaintance, and
if I would come with him, he would introduce me. So we
went together to the next room, and I was presented. Prince
Henry is a young, delicate-looking fellow, rather shy, and I
believe quite intelligent. He talked about America, where he
was once, and seemed to have been very much pleased with his
visit. The Prince of Orange came up to me as soon as he saw
me, and the king introduced me. He is rather tall, and very
slight in figure, with a very interesting and amiable face,
resembling very much his mother. I believe he is considered
very kind-hearted, disposed to act well his part, and with very
good talents. The Queen says he is lazy, but she is very fond
of him. His manner is extremely good. I was also introduced to the Princess Frederic, who is an intelligent and
accomplished person, the sister of the King of Prussia and of
the Empress-dowager of Russia, and also of the Princess
Henry, who is very lively, young, and jolly, daughter of Duke
Bernhard of Saxe Weimar, who travelled in America, and was
the hero of the famous story about " Are you the man who is
going in the stage to Baltimore ? " " Yes." " Well, I am the
gentleman who is going to drive you."

I was just going to ask her if she remembered the story,
when the music struck up a tremendous flourish and drowned
the conversation.

I must break off short here, dearest Mary, for I have a
million things to do. Give a thousand kisses to my dear
children, and believe me always,

Most affectionately yours,

J. L. M.

CHAPTER XI.

To his Mother.

Rome,
October 10th, 1858.

MY DEAREST MOTHER,—I write a line in the midst of great
confusion, merely to let you know that we have arrived in this
place for the winter. We are still in the hotel, and our trunks
are still packed, so I cannot get your letter to Mary (which
we had the great pleasure of receiving just before we left
Vevay) to read over again, which I shall be most delighted to
do the first thing after we get established. We have taken a
lodging, very satisfactory on the whole, on the Corso, with
plenty of rooms, new furniture, and sunny. It will be ready
for us in five days, and I hope to get to work very soon
afterwards. The Storys whom we expected to find already
returned from the country are not yet here, but are expected
every day.

I am most happy to hear from yourself such good accounts
of your health. I do entertain very sincere hopes that you
have turned the corner, and that your constitution will prove
itself much stronger than you feared, and that your recovery
will be permanent. Do not fail to write to me as often as you
can. Your letters are inexpressibly delightful to me. I am
sorry to find by your last that my father had not been very
well. By your description of his ailment, however, it seems
obvious that it was but a temporary one, and no doubt it has

long since passed away. I have not yet had time to reply to
two or three notes which I received from him. The reason is
that they came just as I was obliged to pack up everything,
and since that time I have been so much on the road that my
papers have been buried out of sight. I remember, however,
that he enclosed the proof sheets of an extract from Mr.
Allibone's Biographical Dictionary in which honourable mention was made of my labours. Perhaps he will be willing, as
he has been in correspondence with that gentleman, to state to
him that I feel very much honoured and flattered by the very
obliging manner in which he has spoken of my work, and that
I wish every success to the difficult and very important enterprise in which he is engaged. That it deserves to succeed
cannot be doubted, to judge from the strong language of
encomium used concerning it by the eminent gentlemen
whose letters on the subject have been published. As I have
not myself yet seen the work, I am of course not able to express
an opinion of my own.

I feel also very grateful for the warm and hearty commendations bestowed upon me in the letters of Dr. Lieber,
Mr. Everett, Mr. Prescott, Hillard, Sumner, and others.
Nothing can be more encouraging to a writer engaged in the
arduous pursuits of literature, in which he is obliged to
spend not only time and strength but also no inconsiderable
amount of money, than to find his labours smiled upon and
sympathised with by the most eminent minds of his country,
and I shall always feel proud of such approbation. I expect
to be as hard at work as I have been ever since I left home for
a good while to come. I do not know when I shall have a
couple of volumes ready, for I have gone in very deep and
have been striking out wide. I left Holland at the latter end
of August, and, after stopping a couple of very agreeable days
at Frankfort with one of the most intimate friends I have in
the world, Mr. de Bismarck, now Prussian Ambassador at the
Diet, and formerly a companion of my youth, I came to Vevay,
whence, after reposing a fortnight, we took the rail to Lyons
and Marseilles, and thence the steamboat to Civita Vecchia.
Our voyage of two nights and a day was very prosperous, the

sea calm, and the skies bright and warm, so much so that I, in
my own person, passed the night on deck.

I had hoped to have found an opportunity to send the
London letters, which you think will amuse you, before now.
It has, however, been impossible thus far, but I am in daily
hope of finding some one who will take them to London at
least, whence there will be always a chance of getting them
to Boston. I must once more observe that for two reasons
they ought never to go out of the house. First, because they
are *deliberately* full of egotism and vanity. I mean that Mary
and Lily wished to know what people said to me about my
book, and I did so to a certain extent, although I have a
right to say in my defence that a great many things were
said to me which I should blush to repeat even in a letter to
them or to you.

To his Mother.

Rome,
November 27th, 1858.

MY DEAREST MOTHER,—It is several weeks since I wrote,
I believe, but time passes so rapidly that it does not seem so
long ago.

We are now in very comfortable lodgings in the Corso, about
opposite the church of San Carlo, if you happen to remember
it. We are on the third floor, but as the rooms are all sunny
and well furnished when you get there, and plenty of them, we
do not much mind going upstairs.

I have a very good room for my study, and I am hard at
work. I began my first volume about a fortnight ago and
hope to have it done by April. My task is, however, rather a
difficult one, more so I think than in my former book. I have
to spread myself over a wide surface, for after the death of
William the Silent, the history of the provinces becomes for a
time swallowed in the general current of European history.
I do not mean by that that it loses its importance. On the
contrary the Netherlands question becomes the great question
of Christendom. Netherlands history is for a time the only

European history. France, England, Spain, and Holland being all mingled into one great conflicting mass, it is difficult to say who are friends and who are enemies, except as the dividing line is drawn according to religious opinion. I am obliged, therefore, in order to carry out my intention, to go more fully into English and French contemporaneous history than I did in the other book. This obliges me to take much greater care, because I come very often upon fields which have been more trodden before than the historical soil of the Netherlands. I have, however, made very extensive collections of MSS. in England, Holland and France, and whatever may be the success of the merits of the volumes when done, I am sure I shall have plenty of solid work in them, and from original and substantial materials.

You may imagine that it is not a very money-making concern, but history writing must be pursued honestly as a science, if it is to be permanently valuable, and not as a trade. I have not yet succeeded in getting a title for my book. It is in reality a continuation of the other on a little different plan, but I do not mean to call it so, but bring it out as an independent work. All history is of course but a fragment. You may write the history of two centuries, and yet you will give but a slice of the great lump of human history, and I wish each of my histories to stand on their own legs. I suppose I shall eventually think of some brief title. That is the only part of the book of which I hope to take a mercantile view. A telling and selling title is always desirable to attract readers and buyers. The great cause of regret that I have, however, admits of no remedy. There is no great hero. It is difficult to scare up another William of Orange, and whatever success or virtue my other book may have had, is owing to my having discovered one of the great men of the world's history, who was, I think, not generally known or appreciated. I have several lesser lights in the course of my new volumes, and shall make what I can of them in succession, but I feel the difference between them and that radiant character.

I have been talking of myself, my dearest mother, or rather

of what I am about, because I know that it will interest you.
I get up at daylight every morning and begin to work. This
sounds very fine, but you know it is not daylight at this
season before seven. Little Mary and I and Susie have a cup
of coffee at that hour together, the two other females not rising
so early. The French governess comes from nine to eleven
for the two children, and at 11.30 we breakfast *à la fourchette*,
and dine at six. I thus get every day eight or nine hours of
work. The children are very well, and the climate agrees
with them. The Storys we see frequently, and like them
both very much. She is a bright, sweet-tempered, intelligent
person, and he is decidedly a man of genius. His sculpture
is of a very high order of merit. He has just completed an
exquisite statue of Hero holding a torch, as if looking for
Leander, which has as much expression as has often been put
into marble. I wish I were rich enough to buy it, not because
he is in the condition of a poor artist, having money enough
of his own. His statue of his father is admirable. He has
also just finished a Cleopatra, which is highly original in
attitude and design.

The children are very fond of E——, who is about Mary's
age, and they have a dancing class together twice a week,
which is a good deal of amusement for them. Mr. and Mrs.
Charles Perkins, Mrs. Bruen, and Miss Bruen, are also here,
and I believe Edward Perkins and his wife. Mrs. Cleveland
and Mrs. Doane are come, or coming. There are also other
scattering of Americans here and there, but none I think
whom you are acquainted with.

I am, most affectionately, your son,

J. L. M.

From M. Guizot.

Paris,
25 *février* 1859.

Vous avez probablement déjà vu par les journaux, Monsieur, que le premier volume de la traduction de votre
'Histoire de la Fondation de la République des Provinces-

Unies' vient de paraître. L'éditeur, M. Michel-Lévy, a dû, d'après ma recommandation, vous en envoyer deux exemplaires. Je vous prie de me faire savoir si cet ordre a été exécuté. J'aurai mieux aimé qu'on publiât les deux volumes ensemble ; la traduction française en aura quatre ; mais la publication, déjà avançée, d'une autre traduction française en Belgique a décidé M. Michel-Lévy à se presser. Je sais que cette traduction belge a été faite sans votre aveu ; M. Mohl m'a donné connaissance de ce que vous lui avez écrit à cet égard. Je ne doute pas que votre ouvrage n'obtienne, en France, le succès bien mérité qu'il a obtenu aux États-Unis et en Angleterre, et qu'il n'aide efficacement au triomphe de cette grande cause de la liberté religieuse que vous avez soutenu avec tant de sincérité, de savoir et d'éloquence.

Recevez, Monsieur, l'assurance de tous mes sentiments d'estime et de considération très distinguée.

GUIZOT.

To his Mother.

Rome,
March 26th, 1859.

MY DEAREST MOTHER,—We go on here in a very jog-trot fashion. I work pretty hard, but the ditch grows larger with every successive dig. I have nearly finished a volume, but I am not very well satisfied with it. You need not be anxious about my head-aches ; I have them from time to time, but they are by no means so furious or so frequent as they used to be.

The children and Mary are all very well. Last Tuesday I had the honour of dining with the Prince of Wales, who is passing the winter here. The invitation was quite unexpected by me. Colonel Bruce (who is his governor, and a very agreeable person, brother of Lord Elgin) called on me, and said his Royal Highness was desirous of making my acquaintance. The next day I received a note from him, saying that H.R.H. Baron Renfrew would be happy to see me at dinner, etc. Baron Renfrew is the Prince's travelling name. The party was very small; there was Colonel and Mrs. Bruce, the parson, the doctor, the aide-de-camp, the diplomatic representative here, Mr. Russell, Mr. Gibson the sculptor, Mr. Hay, an excellent old gentleman here, formerly an Under-Secretary of State, and myself.

The Prince is about eighteen. His profile is extremely like that of the Queen. The complexion is pure, fresh, and healthy, like that of most English boys; his hair is light brown, cut short, not curly. His eyes are bluish-grey, rather large, and very frank in their expression; his smile very ready and genuine; his manners are extremely good. I have not had much to do with royal personages, but of those I have known, I know none whose address is more winning, and with whom one feels more at one's ease. He has been well educated, and I should think had a good mind; but of course it is impossible to measure his intellect after so brief an acquaintance. I talked to him before dinner. At dinner he sat on one side of Mrs. Bruce, and I on the other, and we talked upon the common topics, the table not being too large for general conversation. After dinner he asked me to take the chair next him, and we conversed for half an hour together. He talked about German literature, Goethe, and Schiller, objects of art in Rome. Altogether the dinner was a very pleasant one, and it is very agreeable to me to have made the acquaintance of the future Sovereign of the magnificent British Empire in such a simple and unceremonious manner. I have left myself no room, my dearest mother, except to say God bless you. Give my love to the governor, A——, and all the rest of the family, small and great, and with the united and kindest affection of us all, I am,

Most affectionately, your son,
J. L. M.

To his Mother.

Paris,
June 5th, 1859.

MY DEAREST MOTHER,—We left Rome Wednesday morning, June 1st, and reached Paris Friday afternoon at 5 P.M. of June 3rd. This is the most rapid travelling we were ever guilty of. The railroad took us in two hours to Civita Vecchia; then the steamer landed us in Marseilles in about thirty hours more. Then the express train, which started at 10·30 P.M. of Thursday evening, brought us to Paris in eighteen additional hours. The weather was very fine, so that the journey, though disagreeable, was soon accomplished. It seems almost incredible that we were breakfasting in our Roman lodgings on Wednesday, and that I am now writing to you on Sunday morning from an apartment in which we have already installed ourselves at Paris.

We were driven out of Italy by the war. My plans have been quite upset by these unforeseen circumstances. It had been my intention to pass most of the summer in Venice, going thither about the middle of June, and staying there till September, after which we should have probably wintered in Florence. There is much very important and interesting matter in Venice which I had reckoned upon, not only for the work which at present occupies me, but for future historical labours; and as Edward Perkins and Lillie Cleveland, whom our Lily is very fond of, thought of passing the summer there also, the project was a very satisfactory one. I could have worked hard all day, and we could have swum about by moonlight in gondolas in the evenings. But—

    "The best laid schemes o' mice and men gang oft a-gley,"

and so there was no staying in Italy. We have come for the present to Paris—a place which we one and all detest. Rome was tranquil enough, but the climate after the middle of June has a bad reputation, and, indeed, there were three cases of fever, one, and perhaps two, fatal ones in the apartment underneath ours in the same house. I believe, however, that it was typhus and not Roman fever, and contracted in another place. We have been all, thank God, very well, and the weather in Rome was exquisitely beautiful up to the moment of our departure, the very perfection of spring—that season which exists only in imagination with us. I can hardly conceive of two things more diametrically opposed to each other in the way of atmosphere than the April and May of Rome and Boston.

It is not very easy for me to give you any news about the war in Italy. The events, as they occur, are of course immediately given in the American newspapers. The telegraph adding, however, its inevitable blunders to the indispensable lies of the bulletin, the confusion is worse confounded than ever. Thus there is no doubt that in all the engagements that have taken place hitherto, in which much life has been squandered without any result, the advantage has been uniformly with the French and Sardinians. Yet in the official accounts, for example, of the action of Montebello the statement of the allies is that there were 4000 French and 400 Sardinians engaged with 18,000 Austrians. The Austrian commander-in-chief, on the contrary, puts the number of French and Sardinians at 40,000.

With regard to the war itself, my sympathies are warmly with Sardinia. Nothing can be more chivalrous, manly, vigorous, progressive, and enlightened, than the King of Sardinia, his Prime Minister, and his whole nation. It seems to me that no man deserves to mention the word liberty, who does not feel the warmest admiration and sympathy with so noble a cause. But of course it is extremely difficult to place confidence in the intentions of the French Emperor—for me it is impossible, and while I do not wonder that Sardinia should have made the alliance, yet it is not easy to be very hopeful as to the result. It is true that the Emperor has hedged himself about with protestations and self-denying ordinances of all kinds, but those who remember his career for the last ten years, can hardly put much faith in such exuberance of virtue on his part, and I do not believe there will be very much gained for liberty and human progress if Prince Napoleon is made into a King of Etruria, and a Murat into King of Naples, and a Bonaparte (I forget his name) made into a pope. Yet the Italian liberals are very sanguine. There are no Italians, high or low, who do not sympathise with the movement (except the reigning individuals of course), and who do not abhor Austria. The position of Prussia with a king who has hopelessly lost his reason, and yet may live many years, complicates matters very much. The German politicians are rapidly tending to an almost unanimous conviction that the interests of Germany require them all to support Austria, and they probably will do so, a result which will make the war universal. They are impelled to this by their hereditary and natural hatred of France, and by the indispensable necessity of keeping a united Germany as a bulwark against Russia.

Yet if there were a young, vigorous, intellectual sovereign in Prussia at this moment, a man like Frederic the Great, or Peter the Great, he would see that the time had arrived for Prussia to secure at last the object of its ambition, the imperial crown of Germany. If the house of Brandenburg, which governs the powerful, wholly German, and progressive Prussia, could become emperors of Germany, to the utter annihilation of a fictitious, artificial sham, which was got up at the Congress of Vienna forty years ago, and baptized the Empire of Austria, in which there are only about seven millions of Germans, shaken up pell-mell in a great bag with some thirty millions or Slavonians, Magyars, Italians, Croats, and Greeks, and the Lord knows what a hodge-podge, which has never had any vitality except in defiance of all laws, divine or human—if such a result could take place, then there might be a real Germany, and a handsome solution to the present European question.

You ask me whether I propose publishing one volume at a time of my book, and that is exactly what I do not know myself. I have written a volume since November last—in Rome. But it will take me some two or three months to get it into publishing shape, and where I shall find a resting-place I know not. Two days in Paris have convinced me that the expense of this town is so frightful, as to make it altogether beyond my possibilities, and we are now thinking a little of England for a time.

My facilities for work are greater there than anywhere, as I have always a copyist or two engaged at work. But we have not yet decided on anything, but have meantime taken a lodging for a month, during which we shall make up our minds.

I do not know that I can say anything more to entertain you, my dear mother. The influences of Paris are very depressing to me. I dislike the place more and more every time I come to it. I like Italy, but there are many drawbacks to a residence there for a literary man. But the climate is most delightful, and spoils you for other atmospheres. I found it favourable to labour, and I do not think I ever got through a greater amount of work in the same time than I did in Rome. My habits in one respect are changed. I have become a comparatively early riser. I got up usually in the winter at seven, and latterly at six. I get more time I find by this system. We are all well.

Most affectionately your son,

J. L. M.

To his Mother.

Mount Felix, Walton-on-Thames,
August 18th, 1859.

MY DEAREST MOTHER,—Your letter of 18th July was welcomed most warmly. I am delighted to find you feeling yourself so well, and I was still more gratified to be informed a few days ago by Mr. Lothrop that he had seen you just before he left home, and that he had not seen you looking so well for years, and that you seemed to him quite recovered. I cannot help regretting a little that you did not carry out your plan of making a visit to Nahant, for it seems to me that a tonic atmosphere like that of Nahant would give you courage and strength to grapple with your enemy, who seems already a retreating one. As to age, I wish you could see some of the people in London society. There is Lord

Palmerston, seventy-five years exactly, Prime Minister in
England for the second time, full of life, bustle, and business
in the House of Commons every night till after midnight, and
making a speech every night, receiving large companies at
dinner, and in the evening every Saturday for the whole
season, and having no more idea of considering himself old
than Lady Palmerston, who is, I believe, of exactly the same
age, and in her way quite as alive and youthful in manner and
appearance, and quite as active, influential, and reigning, and
charming a personage in the great London world as she ever
was. Then there is Lord Lyndhurst, who celebrated his eighty-
seventh birthday last month, whose intellect is as vivid, whose
voice as melodious, and whose interest in the great questions
agitating the world as comprehensive and unflagging, as if he
had fifty years less upon his back than he has.

He made an admirable speech on foreign politics the other
night, and he told me a few days ago that he meant to make a
speech on a subject which he has very much at heart—the
natural necessity of a strong and cordial alliance between the
two great English commonwealths on the two sides of the
Atlantic. England and America together, he says, may defy
the world, and England can have no real friend among the
despotic governments of Europe. The season was too late, he
thought, for him to make a speech on the subject this year,
but he meant to do it next session. So you see that eighty-
seven years do not prevent him from laying out work for
himself in the future. He is very fond of his two nieces, Mrs.
Amory and her daughter, and always speaks of them, as you
may suppose, with the warmest interest and affection. I do not
say anything of our few weeks in London. You have been
recently reading my letters of last year, in which the whole
ground was gone over, and, in addition, Lily has written you
(I hope you have received them, and were not alarmed at the
postage) a detailed account of our proceedings in the form of a
journal, which she kept mainly because she thought it would
amuse and interest you.

I did not care a great deal about going through a second
London season. But as we were obliged to leave Italy (where

I had intended passing a second winter, having sent all my books and papers there), there seemed no other course open, particularly as I had much literary business in England. I thought too that, as Lily was just grown up, and old enough to go into society, and likely to please and be pleased, it was a kind of duty to let her have the advantage which my position as a man of letters gives her, of seeing for once the most brilliant and cultivated society in the world, viz., the highest circles of London in the full of the season. I must say, without meaning to take any credit to myself, except as belonging to a peculiar class, that I cannot help forming a favourable idea of English civilisation when I see the position accorded in this country to those who cultivate art, science, and literature, as if those things were worth something, and were entitled to some consideration, as well as high birth, official rank, and wealth, which on the Continent are the only passports.

I do not like to say much about European politics. A black cloud seems to envelop the Continent. The nations of the earth, in their cowardice or their inertness, have allowed the most dangerous malefactor who ever usurped supreme power to paralyse and stultify them all, and frighten them all out of their wits. The confidence reposed by the whole Italian people at the beginning of this year in the intentions of Louis Napoleon, was as incredible as it was pathetic, and would have converted into a hero any man standing in his position who had been possessed of one spark of virtue or generosity. There is no doubt of two things— that he originated the Italian revolt, and that he has, against the unanimous wishes of the Italians, left them in the lurch, having pledged himself to Austria to restore the archdukes. The firm, moderate, consistent, unanimous, dignified and courageous conduct of the Italians in this tremendous crisis will always remain one of the grand lessons of history. If they are destined to be crushed into submission, after this calm and deliberate expression of their wishes, at any rate a significant chapter in the history of freedom and tyranny will have been recorded, and it will be something that the mask will at last be torn from the face of the French Emperor. The Tuscan Assembly has just voted unanimously that the Hapsburg-Lorraine dynasty shall *never* be restored. They will doubtless vote as unanimously to annex themselves to Sardinia.

Our plans are not yet fixed, although they will be before the end of the week. A furnished house is offered me at the Hague for a year, which I shall either take, or take lodgings in the country in England. I have lost three months, and must get to work again, if my two volumes are to be ready by next fall.

We are all well, staying at this delightful country house of the Sturgis's, where we are always treated with such hospitality that it seemed as if the house belonged to us. Mrs. John Sturgis had a little girl born a week ago, and both mother and child are going on very well. Little H——, the youngest child of Mr. and Mrs. Russell Sturgis, is a most charming little boy. Give my love to the governor and all the family.

Always most affectionately your son,

J. L. M.

CHAPTER XII.

To his Mother.

Oatlands Park Hotel, Walton-on-Thames,
November 24th, 1859.

MY DEAREST MOTHER,—My life is now very much within
the four walls of my study. I am hard at work, but, alas,
my work grows and expands around me every day. I am
like the conjuror's apprentice in the German ballad, who
raised a whole crowd of spectres and demons by stealing his
master's wand, and then did not know how to exorcise them
and get rid of them. The apparitions of the sixteenth
century rise upon me, phantom after phantom, each more
intrusive and threatening and appalling than the other,
and I feel that I have got myself into a mob of goblins, who
are likely to be too much for me. The other day I read of
an eminent photographic artist to whom a ghost appeared.

Instead of being frightened, the photographer was enchanted. "Stop a bit, my dear spectre," said he, while he made a hurried search for the implements of his trade, thinking that the chance of getting a daguerrotype of a *bonâ fide* ghost was a speculation not to be neglected. Upon which the ghost vanished, much disgusted at being converted into an article of merchandise. Well, I am afraid my ghosts will vanish while I am trying to photograph them, and that always keeps me in a state of impatience and excitement. For two or three years, during which I have written almost nothing, I have been collecting a vast quantity of materials in the shape of unpublished letters, and other documents, of eminent historical characters, and I have been reading them so much and so constantly that the individuals seem to clothe themselves with a ghastly kind of life, and seem to haunt me.

The truth is, I have laid out too much work. If I laboured away like a galley slave at the oar, eight hours a day for the next five years, I should hardly fill up the outlines which I have chalked out. However, I hope to get a couple of volumes ready in the course of the next year, although it will only be in the sweat of my brow.

We are living a most retired life. The country here is very rural, cultivated, and pretty. The climate is moderate, the early winter thus far being rarely frosty, but often foggy. To-day, for example, the tall trees, within a hundred yards of my window, are swallowed up in a white gloom, while the big oaks and beeches closer to me are, like Ossian's heroes, vague, misty, and gigantic. I do not object to fog, always excepting a black fog, a London fog. I was obliged to pass the day in town yesterday, and to breathe unmitigated coal-smoke for six hours. When the fog settles down in London, the smoke from millions of chimneys settles down with it. It cannot escape upwards, and so every breathing being is turned for the time into a chimney. I was a chimney all day yesterday, and rejoice that I was not born in that station in life, not finding it exhilarating. London is not attractive in November. I had something to do in the libraries. Just before leaving town I stumbled against Stirling in the fog, and had a walk

and talk with him. He had just got back from Spain. He
tells me that he expects to publish his Life of Don John of
Austria in a few months. Do you know his books? If not, I
advise you to read them. His 'Cloister Life of Charles V.' is
a charming book. So are his Lives of the Spanish painters.
The Life of Don John will, doubtless, be best of all. He is
a man of large fortune and of ancient family, a Member of
Parliament, and, as Dogberry says, "with two gowns, and
everything handsome about him." He has a magnificent
place in Scotland, mentioned in some of Scott's poems as
the "lordly brow of ancient Keir." Last year he invited
me down there, but I left England as soon as the London
season was over. While I have been writing, the fog has been
growing whiter and whiter, and thicker and thicker. My
Ossianic trees have withdrawn themselves deeper and deeper
into the mist, and have nearly all vanished. Only one giant,
whom I can almost touch from the window, is dimly visible, a
shrouded and vegetable phantom. I am delighted to find, my
dearest mother, that you give such good accounts of your
health. I always believed that you would triumph over your
disorders, and now I am convinced of it. Pray accept this
letter for what it is worth, and if you are willing, I will write
oftener, and each one stupider than the other. Give my best
love to my father and all the family great and small, and
believe me always

Most affectionately your son,

J. L. M.

To his Father.

East Horsley Towers,
December 29th, 1859.

MY DEAR FATHER,—I received your kind letter three days
ago, and I thank you very much for the cheque therein contained. You do not say anything as to my dear mother's
health, but as she has always reported very well of herself, and
as the accounts have always been good, I trust sincerely that

she is as well as she has lately been, and that many years of
happy life are in store for her. I always believed that the
strength of her constitution would enable her to surmount her
difficulties, and now I feel convinced of it.

I notice what you say about the map for the siege of
Leyden. I could send a plan or chart cut from a contemporary chronicle, which I used very minutely in writing my
account, and perhaps it might be worth while to have it copied
and inserted. I will think of it, and let you know very soon.
I am glad to hear that General Pierce expressed himself so
agreeably on the subject of the 'Dutch Republic.' We met
several times at Rome, and he seemed a very kind-hearted and
excellent man, and although I differ from him in politics as
far as it is perhaps possible for two persons to differ, yet I was
very favourably impressed by him. I was especially touched
by the gentleness and care which he had for his wife, who
is a great invalid, and also for the warm sympathy which he
manifested for his old friend, and my friend, Hawthorne,
during the alarming illness of his daughter.

I hear, by the way, that Hawthorne is about to publish a
new novel. I know that he wrote one in Rome, and I hope it
will be as beautiful and as successful as his other works. We
liked him very much. He is the most bashful man I believe
that ever lived, certainly the most bashful American, *mauvaise
honte* not being one of our national traits, but he is a very
sincere, unsophisticated, kind-hearted person, and looks the
man of genius he undoubtedly is.

We had a merry Christmas party at Mount Felix. Everybody enjoyed themselves, as they are apt to do at that most
hospitable mansion.

This place is in Surrey, about ten miles from our own
residence at Oatlands Hotel. The only guest here to-day (we
had some others yesterday) is Ruskin, of the 'Seven Lamps'
and the 'Italian Painters.' He is very agreeable company, very
fond of talking, but not dogmatic as in his books.

Most affectionately yours,

J. L. M.

To his Mother.

East Sheen,
February 13th, 1860.

MY DEAREST MOTHER,—I am writing to you from the house
of your old acquaintance Mr. and Mrs. Joshua Bates. Saturday we had a large party of country neighbours to dine, but
there were none of them known to fame, nor any of them at all
interesting, except one lady, who sang and played remarkably
well, and charmed us all at the piano for an hour or two after
dinner. Yesterday we had no one at dinner but a Polish
gentleman whom one often meets in London society, and the
celebrated Professor Owen. This is the great lecturer and
writer on comparative anatomy and on fossil remains, to hear
whom Lily goes up to town every Tuesday, generally passing
the day with her friend, Lady Annabella King, at her grand-
mother's, old Lady Byron. She was, therefore, very glad to
make his personal acquaintance. To-day we are to have more
people at dinner, the Van der Weyers among others. Van
der Weyer is a particularly agreeable person, and a great
favourite with everybody.

Mr. Bates is a most excellent man, kind-hearted, benevolent,
and sensible. He is in very good health, and goes to Bishops-
gate Street every day of his life, which I should not care to do
if I were past seventy, and had a million pounds sterling.

The last house where we were visiting a week ago is a very
different place, belonging to very different persons—Mr. and
Mrs. Grote. I do not know whether you have ever read
Grote's 'History of Greece.' But it is one of the great works
of the age, is fully recognised as such, and will last as long as
Gibbon's 'Roman Empire.' I feel it a great honour to have
been commended and taken cordially by the hand by such a
man. He had been reading my book, and showed me many
passages which he had marked and commented upon. He is
very kind-hearted, and with most genuine, childlike simplicity of manner, not always found in company with such
exuberant and accurate erudition as he possesses. Mrs. Grote
is a character, very firm, decided, clever, accomplished, strong-

minded, tall, and robust, whom Sydney Smith called the most
gentleman-like of women. She is very droll in her dress,
despising crinoline and flounces, and attiring herself, when
going out for a walk, in a shawl thrown over her shoulders and
tied round her waist, with a poplin gown reaching to the tops
of her boots, a tall brown man's hat, with a feather in it, and a
stout walking-stick. She is the best company in the world,
full of originality and humour, has seen and known every
remarkable person in England and France, and is full of
anecdotes about everybody and everything. One of the best
things she ever said was about Sydney Smith's daughter (who
was married to Dr. Holland), in consequence of her husband
being baroneted. Somebody hearing Lady Holland spoken
of, asked if Lord Holland's wife was referred to. "No," said
Mrs. Grote, "this is New Holland, and the capital is Sydney."

I am going to town to-morrow to see John Murray, the publisher, about my new volumes. I do not know whether you
remember that when I was first about to publish the 'Dutch
Republic,' I offered the MS. to Murray, to whom I had a note of
introduction. After retaining the work a fortnight, he declined it
very civilly but decidedly. In consequence, as you remember,
I had it printed and published by Chapman, and the governor
was kind enough to pay the expenses. Well, the other day I
received a note from Murray, expressing in very strong language his self-reproaches for his shortsightedness for having
lost his chance of being my publisher, and his desire, if possible, to repair his mistake if I was not bound to any one
else. . . . So I hope to make an arrangement with Murray,
who is by far the best publisher in England.

Most affectionately your son,

J. L. M.

From M. Guizot.

Paris,
16 mars 1860.

J'ai eu un grand plaisir à vous proposer à l'Académie des
Sciences morales et politiques, comme successeur de M. Prescott en qualité de correspondant, et je me suis félicité de cette

occasion d'exposer vos titres à cet honneur.   J'espère que vous continuerez votre belle 'Histoire de la Fondation de la République des Provinces-Unies,' en la conduisant jusqu'au moment où l'Espagne elle-même a été forcée de reconnaître que la République était fondée.   Le succès de votre premier ouvrage ne vous permet pas de le laisser incomplet, et je serai charmé d'apprendre que vous vous occupez de la compléter.

J'ai bien regretté de ne pas me trouver à Paris pendant le temps que vous y avez passé.

Recevez, je vous prie, Monsieur, l'assurance de ma considération la plus distinguée.

GUIZOT.

To Dr. O. W. Holmes.

Oatlands Park Hotel, Walton-on-Thames,
March 29th, 1860.

MY DEAR WENDELL,—I am not going to make one word of apology for my long silence.   If you will forgive it and write me again at once, I promise faithfully that I will write to you as often as once a quarter if you will do the same.   I cannot do without letters from you, and although I have a special dislike to writing them myself, I am willing to bore you for the sake of the reward.   I really believe that you are the only one of my friends to whom I have not expressed in rapturous terms the delight with which I have read and re-read your 'Autocrat.' We were quite out of the way of getting the 'Atlantic' in our foreign residences—in Nice, Switzerland, and Rome.   But one day after it had been collected into a volume some traveller lent it to us, and we carefully forgot to return it—a petty larceny combined with breach of trust which I have never regretted, for no one could appreciate it more highly than I, in the first place, and then all my family.   It is really even better than I expected it to be, and that is saying much, for you know how high were my anticipations, and if you do not, poor Phillips, now no more, who always so highly appreciated you, could have told you how surely and how often I predicted your great and inevitable success.   The 'Autocrat' is an inseparable companion, and will live, I think, as long certainly as anything which we have turned out on our side. It is of the small and rare class to which ' Montaigne's Essays,' ' Elia,' and one or two other books belong, which one wishes to have for ever under one's thumb. Every page is thoughtful, suggestive, imaginative, didactic, witty, stimulating, grotesque, arabesque, titillating—in short, I could string together all the adjectives in the dictionary without conveying to you an adequate expression of my admiration.

In order that you shall not think me merely a devourer and not an appreciator, I will add that the portions which give me the most pleasure are those, by far the largest, which are grave, earnest, and profound; and that the passages least to my mind are those which in college days would have most highly delighted me—viz., the uproariously funny ones. But, as Touchstone observes, "we that have good wits cannot hold, we must be flouting," and I do not expect to bottle you up. I have not the book at my elbow at this moment, and am too lazy to go downstairs to fetch it, but as an illustration of what I most enjoy, take such a passage as about our brains being clock-work. I remember nothing of the diction at this instant, but the whole train of thought is very distinct to me. Also the bucketful of fresh and startling metaphors which the autocrat empties on the head of the divinity student in return for his complimentary language as to the power of seeing analogies. Also—but I shall never get any further in this letter if I once begin to quote the 'Autocrat,' so I will only add that I admire many of the poems, especially the Voiceless, which I am never tired of repeating. It is scarcely necessary for me to add that it is always with a deep sensation of pride and pleasure that I turn to page 28 and read the verses therein inscribed. Strange to say, I have not yet read the ' Professor at the Breakfast Table.' I tried to buy it the other day at Sampson Low's, one of the chief American re-publishers or importers, but he said that it had been done by —— (gentlemen who have, among others, done me the same favour).

Is there no chance of ever getting an international Copyright Bill and hanging these filibusters, who are legally picking the pockets of us poor devil authors, who would fain become rich devils if we could? Why do you not make use of your strong position, having the whole American public by the button, to make it listen to reason. If I were an autocrat like you, I would issue an edict immediately. Or I would have a little starling that should say nothing but " copyright " and let the public hear nothing else. Let me not omit to mention also with how much pleasure I read your poem on Burns. It is magnificent, and every verse rings most sympathetically upon the heart. So you see we do not lose the run of you, although I have been so idle about writing, and I am promising myself much pleasure from the ' Professor at the Breakfast Table,' which I shall have sent to me from Boston. By the way, I bagged the other day a splendid presentation copy of the ' Autocrat,' which you had sent to Trübner for some one else, and I gave it to Mrs. Norton (of whom you have heard often enough, and who is a poet herself), who admires it as much as I do. I do not know whether I shall like the novel as well as your other readers are likely to do, because the discursive, irresponsible, vagrant way of writing which so charms me in the ' Autocrat' is hardly in place in a narrative, and for myself I always find, to my regret, that I grow every year less and less capable of reading novels or romances. I wish it were not so. However, I doubt not you will reclaim me, but I do not mean to read it until it is finished.

I have not a great deal to talk about now that I find myself face to face with you. We have been, by stress of circumstances rather than choice, driven to England, and we have seen a great deal of English society, both in town and country. We have received much kindness and sat at many "good men's feasts"; and I must say that I have, as I always had, a warm affection for England and the English. I have been awfully hard at work for the last year and a half, with unlucky intermissions and loss of time, but I hope to publish a couple of bulky volumes by the beginning of next year. There is a cartload of MS. already in Murray's hands, but I do not know how soon we shall begin to print.

I wish when you write—and you see that I show a generous confidence in your generosity by assuming that you will write notwithstanding my delinquencies—you would tell me what is going on in your literary world, and also something about politics. One can get but little from the newspapers—but I should really like to know what chance there is of the country's being rescued from the Government which now oppresses us. But I forget, perhaps you are not a Republican, although I can hardly conceive of your being anything else. With regard to my views and aspirations, I can only say that if Seward is not elected (provided he be the candidate) this autumn, good-night, my native land! I admire his speech, and agree with almost every word he says, barring of course the little senti-mentality about the affection we all feel for the South, which I suppose is very much like the tenderness of Shylock—"Kind sir, you spat on me on Thursday last, you spurned me such a day, and another time you called me dog, and for these courtesies," etc., etc. However, if Mr. Seward thinks it worth while to stir in a little saccharine of this sort, he knows best. The essential is to get himself nominated and elected. Now please write and tell me what the chances are, always provided you agree with me, but not if you are for the pro-slavery man, whoever he may be. I have not yet succeeded in suppressing Louis Napoleon, who bamboozles the English Cabinet and plays his fantastic tricks before high heaven with more impunity than ever. Of a truth it may be said now—three hundred years ago it was uttered by one of the most illustrious of her sons—"Gallia silvescit." What can be more barbarous than the condition of a country relapsed of its own choice under a military despot?

Pray remember us most kindly to your wife and children, and believe me always

Most sincerely yours,
J. L. MOTLEY.

Pray remember me most affectionately to all the fellows at the Club.

From Mr. N. Hawthorne.

13, Charles Street, Bath,
April 1st, 1860.

MY DEAR MOTLEY,—You are certainly that Gentle Reader for whom all my books were exclusively written. Nobody else (my wife excepted, who speaks so near that I cannot tell her voice from my own) has ever said exactly what I loved to hear. It is most satisfactory to be hit upon the raw, to be shot straight through the heart. It is not the quantity of your praise that I care so much about (though I gather it all up most carefully, lavish as you are of it), but the kind, for you take the book[1] precisely as I meant it, and if your note had come a few days sooner I believe I should have printed it in a postscript which I have added to the second edition, because it explains better than I found it possible to do myself, the way in which my romance ought to be taken. . . .

Now don't suppose that I fancy the book to be a tenth part as good as you say it is. You work out my imperfect efforts and half make the book with your own imagination and see what I myself saw but could only hint at.

Well, the romance is a success even if it never finds another reader.

We spent the winter in Leamington, whither we had come from the sea-coast in October. I am sorry to say that it was another winter of shadow and anxiety, not on Una's account, however, but my wife's. She had an attack of acute bronchitis, which reduced her very low, and (except for an enduring faith in the energy and elasticity of her constitution) I should have been almost in despair. After a long confinement to her bed she at last recovered so far as to enable us to remove from Leamington to Bath; and the change of air seems to have been very beneficial. The physician feels confident that she will be quite restored by our return to the United States. I have engaged our passages for June 16th, and patriotic as you know me to be, you can conceive the rapture with which I shall embrace my native soil. Mrs. Hawthorne and the

---

[1] Hawthorne's Romance, 'The Marble Faun.'

children will probably remain in Bath until the eve of our
departure; but I intend to pay one more visit of a week or
two in London, and I shall certainly come and see you. I
wonder at your lack of recognition of my social propensities.
I take so much delight in my friends that a little intercourse
goes a great way and illuminates my life before and after.

Are you never coming back to America? It is dreary to
stay away, although not very delightful to go back. I should
be most happy, and so would my wife, to think that Mrs. Motley
and yourself and your daughters were within our reach, and
really you ought to devote yourselves in the cause of your
country. It is the worst sort of treason for enjoyable people
to expatriate themselves.

> Your friend,
> NATH. HAWTHORNE.

From Dr. O. W. Holmes.

Boston,
Avril 29th, 1860.

It was so pleasant, my dear Lothrop, to get a letter from
you. I have kept it a week or two so as to have something
more to tell you, yet I fear it will not be much after all.
Yesterday, the Saturday Club had its meeting, I carried your
letter in my pocket, not to show to anybody, but to read a
sentence or two which I knew would interest them all, and
especially your kind message of remembrance. All were delighted with it; and on my proposing your health, all of them
would rise and drink it standing. We then, at my suggestion, gave three times three in silence, on account of the
public character of the place and the gravity and position
of the high assisting personages. Be assured that you were
heartily and affectionately, not to say proudly, remembered.
Your honours are our honours, and when we heard you had
received that superior tribute, which stamps any foreigner's
reputation as planetary, at the hands of the French Institute,
it was as if each of us had had a ribbon tied in his own

button-hole. I hoped very much to pick up something which might interest you from some of our friends which know more of the political movements of the season than I do.

I vote with the Republican party. I cannot hesitate between them and the Democrats. Yet what the Republican party is now doing it would puzzle me to tell you. What its prospects are for the next campaign, perhaps I ought to know, but I do not. I am struck with the fact that we talk very little politics of late at the Club. Whether or not it is disgust at the aspect of the present political parties, and especially at the people who represent them, I cannot say ; but the subject seems to have been dropped for the present in such society as I move about in, and especially in the Club. We discuss first principles, enunciate axioms, tell stories, make our harmless jokes, reveal ourselves in confidence to our next neighbours after the Chateau Margaux has reached the emotional centre, and enjoy ourselves mightily But we do not talk politics. After the President's campaign is begun, it is very likely that we may, and then I shall have something more to say about Mr. Seward and his prospects than I have now.

How much pleasure your praise gave me I hardly dare to say. I know that I can trust it. You would not bestow it unless you liked what I had done, but you would like the same thing better if I had done it than coming from a stranger. That is right and kind and good, and notwithstanding you said so many things to please me, there were none too many. I love praise too well always, and I have had a surfeit of some forms of it. Yours is of the kind that is treasured and remembered. I have written in every number of the *Atlantic* since it began. I should think myself industrious if I did not remember the labours you have gone through, which simply astonish me. What delight it would be to have you back here in our own circle of men—I think we can truly say whom you would find worthy companions : Agassiz, organising the science of a hemisphere ; Longfellow, writing its songs ; Lowell, than whom a larger, fresher, nobler, and more fertile nature does not move among us ; Emerson, with his strange, familiar remoteness of character, I do not know what else to call it; and Hawthorne and Dana, when he gets back from his voyage round the world, and all the rest of us thrown in gratis. But you must not stay too long; if all the blood gets out of your veins, I am afraid you will transfer your allegiance.

I am just going to Cambridge to an "exhibition," in which Oliver Wendell Holmes speaks a translation (*expectatur versio in lingua vernacula*), the Apology for Socrates ; Master O. W. Holmes, Jun., being now a tall youth, almost six feet high, and lover of Plato and of Art.

I ought to have said something about your grand new book, but I have not had time to do more than read some passages from it. My impression is that of all your critics, that you have given us one of the noble historical pictures of our time, instinct with life and glowing with the light of a poetical imagination, which by itself would give pleasure, but which, shed over a great epoch in the records of our race, is at once brilliant and permanent. In the midst of so much that renders the very existence of a civilisation amongst us problematical to the scholars of the Old World, it is a great pleasure to have the cause of letters so represented by one of our own countrymen, citizens, friends. Your honours belong to us all, but most to those who have watched your upward course from the first, who have shared many of the influences which have formed your own mind and character, and who now regard you as the plenipotentiary of the true Republic accredited to every Court in Europe.

To his Mother.

31, Hertford Street, Mayfair,
May 10th, 1860.

MY DEAREST MOTHER,—I send by this steamer a copy of the *Times* containing an account of the Anniversary Banquet of the Royal Academy. You will see that I was called on to respond to the toast of Literature, and that I was obliged to make a short speech. It was a most awful ordeal. For the company is exceedingly select, which made the compliment very great, but the feeling of trepidation still greater. However, as I knew a day or two beforehand that I was to be called on, I got out of the scrape pretty well, and received much applause and congratulations afterwards. But it was quite impossible for me to enjoy the dinner as I should have done had I been merely a spectator. Fancy being obliged to get up and address such an awful set of swells as the Cabinet Ministers, Palmerston, Gladstone, Lord Russell, the Chancellor, the judges, the Opposition fellows, Dizzy and the rest, the Lord Mayor in all his glory, all the artists, and many distinguished men of letters! It was a horrible moment for a bashful youth like me! The dinner was in itself a very pretty sight. It was in the principal hall of the Exhibition (opened that day and the day before for invited guests only, and made public a day or two afterwards). The leading pictures of the year cover the walls of the room. The dinner begins at six, and as the twilight comes on, after the tables are cleared, the choristers begin 'God Save the Queen.' At the first stave the gas is suddenly let on, and the walls become alive and glowing with the pictures. The effect is very startling and brilliant. There is to be another dinner, that of the Literary Fund, next week. I have accepted the office of steward, one of the twenty of course merely nominal officers, but with the express condition that I am not to be called on for a speech. I wish to have the satisfaction this time of enjoying the dinner and hearing the others, which I cannot do with the knowledge that I am to be served up as a part of the entertainment.

Of course it is unnecessary to add that this is strictly between ourselves. I hardly feel at home here yet, and am discontented and fidgety because I have not yet got to work. I always feel thrown on my beam ends when I am compelled to be idle. However, I have a good, comfortable, little library, with all my books and papers arranged, and it will be my own fault if I do not turn off a good lot of MS. daily so soon as the mill gets going, which will be to-morrow.

Good-bye for the moment, my dearest mother. I pray most fervently that you may continue in good health, and that you will pass a happy summer at Riverdale. Write to me as often as you can, if only a few lines, which gives us always the greatest pleasure. All send much love to my father and yourself, and I remain

Most affectionately yours,

J. L. M.

P.S.—We had one glimpse, but a delightful one, of the Agassizs. They only stayed three days in London. They would have been overwhelmed with invitations had they remained, which I suppose was one reason for their rapid departure.

To his Mother.

31, Hertford Street, London,
June 22nd, 1860.

MY DEAREST MOTHER,—I do so long to see you again, and feel very unhappy that the work which I have given myself to do seems to protract our exile. My two volumes will be published, I suppose, early in November, and I hope will prove interesting, although they do not cover so large a space of time as I expected would be the case when I began them. But my materials have grown so enormously on my hands that I have found it difficult to keep within reasonable bounds. The next two, which will complete the work, will travel over a much longer range of years.

Lily's letter has so well described the " Commemoration Day " at Oxford, when I received my honorary degree of Civil Law, that there is no need of my saying anything about it. It was an honour quite unexpected and unsolicited by me.[1] Indeed, I knew nothing of it until the other morning, when Dean Milman, in inviting me to breakfast, congratulated me. When I went there I told him there must be some mistake, but on returning to my house I found the official communication. The only thing I have to add to Lily's account is a

---

[1] He, with his wife and eldest daughter, were the guests of Rev. Arthur Stanley (afterwards Dean of Westminster) and of his sister Miss Stanley.

slight allusion to the absurd figure the Doctors cut walking
gravely through the streets.

> " A long red gown, well brushed and neat,
>   We manfully did throw "

over the customary suit of solemn black, and then with a vast
black velvet machine on the head, something between the
Doge of Venice's cap and a large coal scuttle, we proceeded
through the rain with as much solemnity as if we were not the
most absurd caricature in the world.   And the best of it was,
that even the street boys, who I supposed would receive us
with jeers and chaff, were evidently very much in awe of us.

Nothing could be more absurd than old Brougham's figure,
long and gaunt, with snow-white hair under the great black
porringer, and with his wonderful nose wagging lithely from
side to side as he hitched up his red petticoats and stalked
through the mud.   Three of the new-made Doctors were
very distinguished personages—Lord Brougham, Sir Richard
Bethell (the Attorney-General), and Leopold MacClintock.
The other three—viz., Swedish envoy, Platen, Count Strzelecki,
and the humble writer of this note—were much less known to
fame. You would know that I am not writing this out of mock
modesty, even if I were capable of such an affectation, if you
could have heard the tempest of cheers and hand-clapping
that greeted Brougham and MacClintock. The others crept
in under a very mild expression of approbation from the gods
in the gallery—*videlicet* the undergraduates—who from time
immemorial make this a kind of "nigger's holiday," and
indulge themselves in all the chaff they can manufacture.

I regretted very much that the weather was so bad that we
could see nothing of Oxford to any advantage. I was also sorry
that on the Commemoration Day we lunched in University
Hall rather than in All Souls', where we were also expected,
because All Souls' was founded by Archbishop Chicheley, in
the reign of Henry VI., of a Northampton family, of which
your grandfather Checkley was no doubt descended. Until
very recently, any one proving kindred with the old archbishop might have claimed free instruction at his college, so
that I might have been educated at All Souls' at small expense,

but the privilege is now done away with. I leave to Lily the task of chronicling our movements, as she does it, I think, very well indeed, and is fond of writing letters, while I, on the contrary, am so fearfully driven for time, being hard at work eight hours a day, when I can secure myself against interruption, that I must confine myself, until my volumes are done, to very brief notes.

Ever your most affectionate son,
J. L. M.

From Lady Dufferin to Hon. Mrs. Norton.[1]

DEAR CAR,—Refuges have been erected at all the expoged parts of the road, pattens are provided for entering the dining-room; water souches and flounders will be the staple of the repast, with ducks, snipes, and other water birds. Beds—water beds—are provided for belated travellers; in short, every aqueus comfort that can be expected.

"Come unto these yellow sands." Three *beaux* await the fair Lily, who must be a water-lily for the nonce, and a warm welcome for the rest. I trust we shall be able to keep our heads above water, and have no doubt the little aquatic party will get on swimmingly.

Seriously, you will all be very welcome; and what signifies the weather to determined souls in waterproof soles?

Your affectionate Naiad,
H. D.

To his Mother.

Dufferin Lodge, Highgate.
August 14th, 1860.

MY DEAREST MOTHER,—It gave me the greatest delight to receive once more a letter from you, and although you do not speak of your health in quite as satisfactory language as I had hoped, I cannot doubt that the Nahant air has been rapidly bringing you up beyond the former level. The governor, in

[1] Who was engaged to dine, as well as Mr., Mrs., and Miss Motley, at Dufferin Lodge, Highgate. The day proved so wet that a note was dispatched to know if the guests were still expected.

his last letter, spoke of you in such sanguine terms that I cannot help feeling entirely encouraged about you. We have
been here at this pretty villa more than a week. I do not know
whether any of us have ever mentioned that we were coming
here. I found myself a little run down at the fag end of the
season, for I have been very hard at work; and so Lady
Dufferin, who is the most kind-hearted and amiable and
accomplished woman in the world, insisted on our all coming
here to make a visit of a week or two. Little Mary, who
was also rather poorly, has picked up wonderfully in the few
days that we have spent here. We return to town to-morrow,
and have hardly time to get ready for our intended visit to
Scotland. We have a great many invitations to country
houses—I hardly know how many we shall be able to accept
—but our head-quarters will be Keir, the place of my particular friend Stirling. His works you are acquainted with, I
know. He is a most accomplished writer, a good speaker in
Parliament, and the most genial and delightful of companions.
His fortune is large, and his family very ancient and distinguished. You will find his place mentioned in the ' Lady of
the Lake,' in the description of FitzJames's rapid ride after
the combat with Roderick Dhu—

> "They saw just glance and disappear
> The lofty brow of ancient Keir."

Our old friends, the Misses Forbes, are going to have the
children for a visit to Aberdeen, which they will enjoy very
much, and meantime we can make our visits and excursions.

Lady Dufferin herself went yesterday to Ostend, whither
she was summoned to make her friend, the Prince Regent of
Prussia, a visit; and she only would go on condition that we
would stay on making use of her establishment here as long
as we could. There is too great a blank left, however, by her
departure, and we shall leave to-morrow morning. Her son,
Lord Dufferin, has gone to Syria as British Commissioner, and
she is in great anxiety for fear he should catch the fever, which
prevails there at this season. He is very amiable, accomplished, and good-looking, and in every respect worthy to be
son to such a mother. You know, of course, that Lady

Dufferin is sister to Mrs. Norton. The other sister, the Duchess of Somerset, has been kind enough to invite us to a wedding which is to take place on the 25th of this month in church, with the breakfast afterwards at her house, thinking that we might like to see an English wedding. The couple to be married are a very pretty Miss Graham with a young officer named Baring.

I feel that I am writing a very stupid letter, but in truth I have got very much out of the way of writing anything but history. I feel rather anxious about my new volumes, and for this reason. When I handed in my MS. to Murray some two or three months ago, I called it, and supposed it, Volume I.; but to my horror, I found that it would make two large volumes. Now the time covered is so short, although it is a most important epoch, I thought it even rather too brief for one volume. Of course, therefore, the objection is double for two. However, if the matter seems only one-tenth part as interesting to the reader as it did to me when writing, he will not quarrel with the slow movement in point of time. I can hardly now understand how I managed to write so much, for I have just calculated that I was exactly ten months and a half writing the whole, which is rather rapid work for two octavo volumes. It is true that from November 1858, when I began to write, till May 1860, when the book was finished, are eighteen months; but I lost the whole period from May 1859 to November in travelling and loafing. You must not think, however, that I have written in a hurry, for I have not done so at all, and I am only surprised that what I thought one volume has turned out two.

The remainder of the work will be about as much more, namely, two volumes, but they will go over six times as much ground.

I hope that you have had better weather than ours. I never knew that such a summer could be as this has been. Literally and honestly, I do not think we have had three really fine days since the 1st of May, and not one hot, or even warm, day. We never think of sunshine any more than if such an article did not exist, as it rains regularly every day. The possibility

of such a season is certainly a great set-off to the certainty
that we can never have one of our horrible winters. A New
England winter and an Old England summer, such as this has
been, would bring the world to an end very soon.

I am always most affectionately yours,

J. L. M.

To his Mother.

Studley Royal, Ripon,
September 27th, 1860.

MY DEAREST MOTHER,—I am going to take advantage of
your permission to write you a little note instead of a long
letter, for which it seems to me that I never shall find time.
It is no joke to do what I am now doing, namely, making a
tour of country visits and correcting the sheets of two great
octavo volumes while on the road. I am pursued by printer's
devils at every turn and by every post, so that my holiday is
not a pure and absolute one as you may suppose, and when I
get back to London my hard labour will begin afresh, for there
are two more volumes unwritten, which must be finished as
soon as possible. It was a very great pleasure to us all to see
Tom, and to have such fresh and delightful news of you—for
he reports you as in better health than for some years.

We came to this place the day before yesterday.

Lord de Grey is a young man, one of the rising politicians
of England. He was in the House of Commons as Lord
Goderich when I first knew him two years ago, but since
then he has succeeded to the earldoms of Ripon and de
Grey by the deaths of his father and uncle, and he is now
of course in the House of Peers. He is Under-Secretary for
War, and he is a hard-working public man, and a most amiable
and agreeable companion. His wife is most charming and
fascinating, very pretty, very gentle, and very amiable, a
great favourite in London society. This place, Studley, is a
large house, the park of 400 acres is very magnificent, and the
deer swarm about it in every direction. They have become

so familiar, however, as hardly to seem like wild animals, and like the beasts roaming over the plain commemorated by Mr. Selkirk—

" Their tameness is shocking to me."

The crowning glory of the place, however, is Fountain's Abbey. I do not know whether you ever heard of it, and I doubt whether it is as famous as Melrose or Tintern ; but I suspect that it is the first ecclesiastical ruin in the world.

It stands in the most beautiful part of Lord de Grey's park, and is very extensive. The tall tower, looking at a little distance as if belonging to a cathedral, is still in good preservation, but as you come nearer you find that all the rest of the spacious church is a mass of most picturesque ruin, with large trees growing in the nave, and ivy and wild-flowers festooning the old Norman pillars and the beautiful lancet-shaped windows. The cloisters are very extensive, and still preserve their roofs, so that you walk through their whole range and look out through the windows at a beautiful stream which murmurs along among the ruins, and at twilight or moonlight it would not require a violent imagination to picture the forms of hooded monks stalking through the cloisters, or to hear a midnight mass pealing from the ruined choir of the beautiful chapel. Descriptions of buildings and scenery are a bore, so I shall say nothing further of this exquisite ruin, save to repeat that it is far the most impressive one that I have ever seen, and much more beautiful than Melrose Abbey. We have a small but pleasant party here. The father and mother of Lady de Grey, Mr. and Lady Mary Vyner, Mr. Sidney Herbert (the Minister of War), and his very pretty wife, Mrs. Hughes, wife of Tom Hughes, author of ' Tom Brown's Schooldays,' and a most excellent fellow, who I am sorry to say is only coming when we are going, and one or two others. Mr. Herbert is one of the most distinguished persons in London, being very handsome, with considerable talents, of famous lineage, as he is a descendant of the family which numbers Sir Philip Sidney among their illustrations. He is himself brother and heir to the present Earl of Pembroke.

We leave this I suppose on Saturday (day after to-morrow) for Keir, where we shall stop a day, and on Monday we go to Aberdeen, where Mary and Susie are passing the time of our absence in the house of our excellent friends, the Miss Forbes's, of whom you have often heard us speak, and they have been making several visits among the friends of that family, and passing their time very agreeably.

Our house in Hertford Street, which I have taken on for six months, is small, but very neat and clean, and sufficiently comfortable, and my books and papers are all ready in my library, which is a satisfactory room enough, commanding an uninterrupted view of the water-butt and the dead wall of an adjacent house, but perfectly quiet and retired. This is a wretched little letter, my dear mother, but it will serve to express my affection for you, and my delight to hear that your health is so much improved.

Your ever affectionate son,
J. L. M.

To his Mother.

Taymouth Castle,
October 28th, 1860.

MY DEAREST MOTHER,—I am ashamed to think how long it is since I have written to you. . . . You may imagine, however, that letter-writing—even to you—has been an absolute impossibility. And even now I am only sending you a little note—no more—only for the pleasure of talking to you for the moment, and sending you my warmest greetings of affection not in the shape of writing anything worth the trouble of reading. Most unluckily, too, I have taken up my headaches again, and have been and am still enduring one unceasing one of four days and nights long. After having, as I thought, entirely distanced them, I am much disappointed. I think Lily has written to you a pretty full account of our journeyings. At Keir we have been several times. We passed a week in the wildest part of the Highlands, at a place called Glen Quoich, the property of Mr. Ellice, an old gentleman much known in the world of London, once a Cabinet Minister and still in Parliament, and as vigorous and active almost as Lord Palmerston, at almost the same age, seventy-six. He went to America two years ago (where both in New York and Canada he is a large landowner), and returned extremely delighted with everything he saw and heard in our country. His place in the Highlands he has created out of the wilderness during the last twenty years. His estate runs thirty miles long, through mountain, ravine, torrent, waterfall, deer forest, and lonely rocks, and his house is the only habitation, except the cabins of some of his own people, for miles and miles around. The house stands on the very edge of the wild Loch Quoich, surrounded by purple mountains on all sides. Beyond that lake is a magnificent sea inlet called Loch Hourn, hemmed in by precipitous crags, some of the more distant ones 3000 or 4000 feet high, with the heights of the Isle of Skye in the background. At the time of our visit, the second week in October, the mountains were all covered nearly to their base with new fallen snow, so that the scenery had an almost Alpine expression, and as the outlines are always bold and picturesque, the views were certainly of a very noble character.

The company was not a very large one. Many members of his family, Mrs. Ellice, his son's wife, who is a most delightful person, full of talent and amiable qualities, singing like a nightingale, and painting portraits or caricatures or scenery like a professional artist. Lord Stratford de Redcliffe, the ancient Ambassador in Turkey, with his wife and daughters, the young Chief of Lochiel, and a few others. In spite of rain, sleet, and snow, walked, drove, and fished, and were very sorry when our visit came to an end.

We afterwards passed a few days very pleasantly at Inveraray Castle, the seat of the Duke of Argyll. This is a great turreted building, standing near Loch Fyne on the west coast, surrounded by very grand scenery of cliff, wood, and water. The present head of all the Campbells, the MacCallum More, is comparatively young, about thirty-seven, handsome, with very Scottish golden locks. He is a member of the present Cabinet, is very clever, cultivated, a good speaker, an excel-

lent man of affairs, and very agreeable. The Duchess, who is
daughter to the Duchess of Sutherland, is gentle, amiable, and
very cultivated and attractive. They have a quiver full of
children to the number of eleven. We passed a few days
rather quietly, but much to our satisfaction.

We have now been spending a week at this magnificent
place, one of the most princely establishments in the kingdom,
Taymouth Castle, the seat of the Marquis of Breadalbane.
The house stands on the Tay, a dark, transparent, rapidly
rolling river, which flows out from Loch Tay, about two miles
off. The position is very beautiful, but perhaps in some degree
melancholy, as the house and pleasure-grounds are a little too
much shut in by the mountains like the happy valley of
Rasselas. There is a walk along the Tay on both sides, under
magnificent beeches two or three miles long, with the most
velvety lawn under foot, which is one of the most beautiful
things I ever saw. Nothing can be imagined much more
agreeable than these scenes, where a beautiful Nature has been
assisted to decorate itself by the hands of Art and intelligent
wealth. Lord Breadalbane is the chief of another branch of
the great Campbell family. He is about sixty-eight years of
age, the most amiable, kind-hearted, and benevolent of men,
evidently taking the greatest delight in making other people
happy. The Marchioness is somewhat of an invalid, but is
very amiable, accomplished, and agreeable. There are several
very charming young girls in the house, especially two nieces
of Lord Breadalbane, and other young people, so that there are
always pleasant excursions all day long, and in the evening,
after the magnificent dinner (which is always like a royal entertainment in a splendid hall, a table blazing with silver and
gold, with bag-pipes blowing martial airs in alternation with
a band of music), comes dancing till after midnight, reels and
flings, and strathspeys and Roger de Coverleys. Last night
several of the young men were in Highland costume, dancing
as only Scotchmen can, or do. It has been a very pleasant
week for Lily and for Mary. As for myself, I should have
enjoyed myself better if I had not been tormented with this
horrible headache, which still continues, and which must be

my excuse for the fearful stupidity of this letter. A hundred
pages of uncorrected proofs lie glaring at me in my dressing-
room; but I am absolutely incapable of reading, and I am
afraid that there will be some delay in the book if my head
will not stop. Good-bye, my dearest mother. I promise
faithfully to write again very soon, for before a great while
the printer's devils will have ceased for a while to torment
me.   Ever your most affectionate son,

J. L. M.

To his Mother.

31, Hertford Street,
November 19th, 1860.

MY DEAREST MOTHER,—Your kind letter of 22nd October
reached me a few days ago, and gave me, as your letters
always do, very great pleasure. As to the governor, he seems
to grow younger every day, and I am sure that I should not
have been up to dancing all night till five o'clock, and then
getting to breakfast in the country by 8.30.

The Prince of Wales has returned, after a passage of twenty-
eight days, safe and sound. I met him at dinner at Oxford
just before he sailed, as I think I mentioned to you. I am told
that the Queen is much pleased with the enthusiasm created
in America by his visit. I am sure that she has reason to be,
and all good Englishmen rejoice in it. It was certainly a
magnificent demonstration of the genuine and hearty good
feeling that exists between the two great branches of the
Anglo-Saxon race, and I read the long accounts given in the
Times by the special correspondent of his reception in New
York and Boston with the greatest pleasure.

I am very sorry that I cannot exchange congratulations with
the governor on the subject of the Presidential election.[1] The
account has this instant reached us by telegraph, and although
I have felt little doubt as to the result for months past, and
Tom will tell you that I said so at Keir, yet as I was so
intensely anxious for the success of the Republican cause, I

---

[1] The first election of Lincoln.

was on tenterhooks till I actually knew the result. I rejoice in the triumph at last of freedom over slavery more than I can express. Thank God, it can no longer be said, after the great verdict just pronounced, that the common law of my country is slavery, and that the American flag carries slavery with it wherever it goes. . . . .

To change the subject, you will be pleased to hear that Mr. Murray had his annual trade sale dinner last Thursday (15th). This is given by him in the City to the principal London booksellers, and after a three-o'clock dinner, he offers them his new publications. You will be glad to know that my volumes[1] quite took the lead, and that he disposed at once of about 3000 copies. As he only intended to publish 2000, you may suppose that he was agreeably disappointed. He has now increased his edition to 4000, and expects to sell the whole. After that he will sell a smaller and cheaper edition. The work is, however, not yet published, nor will it be for several weeks. I am very glad to hear that you are pleased with the opening pages. The volumes have cost me quite as much labour as the other work; but, alas, I have no William of Orange for a hero. I hope the governor will be pleased with them.   Ever most affectionately your son,

J. L. M.

From M. Barthélemy St. Hilaire.

Paris, rue de l'Empereur, 54 (ancien Montmartre),
25 *décembre* 1860.

MONSIEUR ET TRÈS HONORABLE AMI,—J'ai reçu ces jours-ci les deux volumes que vous avez bien voulu m'envoyer, et je vous remercie de ce beau présent. C'est une digne suite à 'L'Histoire de la Fondation de la République des Provinces-Unies.' Je vous lirai avec le plus grand plaisir, et j'ai déjà vu avec un très vif intérêt votre chapitre sur l'invincible Armada. Je n'ai vu nulle part un récit plus attachant ni plus complet de cette abominable entreprise. Le portrait que vous avez tracé de Philippe II est aussi exact que le person-

---

[1] The first two volumes of the 'History of the Netherlands.'

nage est odieux. Je serai presque porté à croire que les souvenirs, qui datent de 270 ans, ne laissent pas que d'avoir aujourd'hui leur opportunité. Mais l'Angleterre ne se laissera pas surprendre par une nouvelle Armada, ni par un nouveau Philippe II. Le mouvement des volontaires atteste que la nation est plus vigilante encore que son gouvernement. Je crains que l'année prochaine ne démontre la haute nécessité de cette vigilance.

Il faut espérer que les dissensions qui agitent votre patrie se calmeront bientôt, et les dernières nouvelles sont plus favorables. Il me semble, autant que j'en puis juger, que le message de M. Buchanan offre un terrain d'assez facile conciliation, mais il faudrait, de part et d'autre, beaucoup de sagesse et de prudence.

Nos amis les Mohl sont très bien, ainsi que nos amis de l'Institut.   Votre bien dévoué,

B^Y. St. Hilaire.

From M. Guizot.

Paris, 52, Rue du Faubourg St. Honoré,
7 *janvier* 1861.

J'ai reçu, Monsieur, les deux nouveaux volumes de votre histoire des Provinces-Unies, et je vous remercie d'avance du plaisir que j'aurai à vous lire ; je suis sûr que j'y trouverai le même esprit de philosophie chrétienne et le même talent dramatique qui ont assuré à votre premier ouvrage un succès si légitime et si général. Désirez-vous que ces deux volumes soient traduits et publiés en France comme les précédents ? Je ne veux faire, à ce sujet, aucune démarche avant de savoir quelles sont vos intentions.

Je ne me promets pas de pouvoir vous lire tout de suite, au milieu du bruit de Paris en hiver. Mais je retournerai à la campagne dès que le printemps reparaîtra, et je reprendrai là les lectures qui charment mes loisirs.

Recevez, je vous prie, Monsieur, avec mes remercîments, l'assurance de toute ma considération et de mes sentiments les plus distingués.   Guizot.

CHAPTER XIII.

THE CRISIS IN AMERICA.

To his Mother.

31, Hertford Street,
February 9th, 1861.

MY DEAREST MOTHER, ... I wrote you a long letter of eight pages yesterday, and then tossed it into the fire, because I found I had been talking of nothing but American politics. Although this is a subject which, as you may suppose, occupies my mind almost exclusively for the time being, yet you have enough of it at home, as before this letter reaches you it will perhaps be decided whether there is to be civil war, peaceable dissolution, or a patch up; it is idle for me to express any opinions on the subject. I do little else but read American newspapers, and we wait with extreme anxiety to know whether the pro-slavery party will

be able to break up the whole compact at its own caprice, to
seize Washington, and prevent by force of arms the inauguration of Lincoln. That event must necessarily be followed by
civil war, I should think. Otherwise, I suppose it may be
avoided. But whatever be the result, it is now proved beyond
all possibility of dispute that we never have had a government,
and that the much eulogised constitution of the United States
never was a constitution at all, for the triumphant secession
of the Southern States shows that we have only had a league
or treaty among two or three dozen petty sovereignties, each
of them insignificant in itself, but each having the power to
break up the whole compact at its own caprice. Whether the
separation takes place now, or whether there is a patch up,
there is no escaping the conclusion that a government proved
to be incapable of protecting its own property and the honour
of its own flag is no government at all, and may fall to pieces
at any moment. The pretence of a people governing itself,
without the need of central force and a powerful army, is an
exploded fallacy which can never be revived. If there is a
compromise now, which seems possible enough, because the
Northern States are likely to give way, as they invariably
have done, to the bluster of the South, it will perhaps be the
North which will next try the secession dodge, when we find
ourselves engaged in a war with Spain for the possession of
Cuba, or with England on account of the reopened African
slave trade, either of which events are in the immediate future.

But I find myself getting constantly into this maelstrom of
American politics and must break off short.

I send you by this mail the London *Times* of the 7th of
February. You will find there (in the parliamentary reports)
a very interesting speech of Lord John Russell; but it will be
the more interesting to you because it contains a very handsome compliment to me, and one that is very gratifying. I
have not sent you the different papers in which my book has
been reviewed, excepting three consecutive *Times*, which contain a long article. I suppose that 'Littell's Living Age'
reprints most of these notices. And the *Edinburgh, Quarterly*
and *Westminster Reviews* (in each of whose January numbers the

work has been reviewed) are, I know, immediately reprinted. If you will let me know, however, what notices you have seen, I will send you the others in case you care for them.

We are going on rather quietly. We made pleasant country visits at Sidney Herbert's, Lord Palmerston's, Lady Stanhope's, Lord Ashburton's, but now the country season is pretty well over, parliament opened, and the London season begun. I am hard at work in the State Paper Office every day, but it will be a good while before I can get to writing again.

I am most affectionately your son,

J. L. M.

From Dr. O. W. Holmes.

Boston,
February 16th, 1861.

MY DEAR MOTLEY,—It is a pleasing coincidence for me that the same papers which are just announcing your great work are telling our little world that it can also purchase, if so disposed, my modest two volume story. You must be having a respite from labour. You will smile when I tell you that I have my first vacation since you were with us—when was it? in '57?—but so it is. It scares me to look on your labours, when I remember that I have thought it something to write an article once a month for the *Atlantic Monthly*; that is all I have to show, or nearly all, for three and a half years, and in the meantime you have erected your monument more perennial than bronze in these two volumes of alto relievo. I will not be envious, but I must wonder—wonder at the mighty toils undergone to quarry the ore before the mould could be shaped and the metal cast. I know you must meet your signal and unchallenged success with little excitement, for you know too well the price that has been paid for it. A man does not give away the best years of a manhood like yours without knowing that his planet has got to pay for his outlay. You have won the name and fame you must have fore-seen were to be the accidents of your career. I hope, as you partake the gale with your illustrious brethren, you are well ballasted with those other accidents of successful authorship.

I am thankful for your sake that you are out of this wretched country. There was never anything in our experience that gave any idea of it before. Not that we have had any material suffering as yet. Our factories have been at work, and our dividends have been paid. Society—in Boston, at least—has been nearly as gay as usual. I had a few thousand dollars to raise to pay for my house in Charles Street, and sold my stocks for more than they cost me. We have had predictions, to be sure, that New England was to be left out in the cold if a new confederacy was formed, and that the grass was to grow in the streets of Boston. But prophets are at a terrible discount in these times, and, in spite of their predictions, Merrimac sells at 1125. It is the terrible uncertainty of everything—most of all the uncertainty of opinion of men. I had almost said of principles. From the impracticable Abolitionist, as bent on total separation from the South as Carolina is on secession from the North, to the Hunker, or Submissionist, or whatever you choose to call the wretch who would sacrifice everything and beg the South's pardon for offending it, you find all shades of opinion in our streets. If Mr. Seward or Mr. Adams moves in favour of compromise, the whole Republican party sways like a field of grain before the breath of either of them. If Mr. Lincoln says he shall execute the laws and collect the revenue though the heavens cave in, the backs of the Republicans stiffen again, and they take down the old revolutionary king's arms, and begin to ask whether they can be altered to carry minie bullets.

In the meantime, as you know very well, a monstrous conspiracy has been hatching for nobody knows how long, barely defeated in its first great move by two occurrences— Major Anderson's retreat to Fort Sumter, and the exposure of the great defalcations. The expressions of popular opinion in Virginia and Tennessee have encouraged greatly those who hope for union on the basis of a compromise; but this evening's news seems to throw doubt on the possibility of the North and the Border States ever coming to terms; and I see in this same evening's paper the threat thrown out that if the Southern ports are blockaded, fifty regiments will be

set in motion for Washington! Nobody knows, everybody
guesses. Seward seems to be hopeful. I had a long talk with
Banks; he fears the formation of a powerful Southern military
empire, which will give us trouble. Mr. Adams predicts that
the Southern Confederacy will be an ignominious failure.

A Cincinnati pamphleteer, very sharp and knowing, shows
how pretty a quarrel they will soon get up among themselves.
There is no end to the shades of opinion. Nobody knows
where he stands but Wendell Phillips and his out-and-outers.
Before this political cataclysm we were all sailing on as
quietly and harmoniously as a crew of your good Dutchmen
in a treckschuyt. The Club has flourished greatly, and proved
to all of us a source of the greatest delight. I do not believe
there ever were such agreeable periodical meetings in Boston
as these we have had at Parker's. We have missed you, of
course, but your memory and your reputation were with us.
The magazine which you helped to give a start to has
prospered since its transfer to Ticknor and Fields. I suppose
they may make something directly by it, and as an adver-
tising medium it is a source of great indirect benefit to them.
No doubt you will like to hear in a few words about its small
affairs. I don't believe that all the Oxfords and Institutes can
get the local recollections out of you. I suppose I have made
more money and reputation out of it than anybody else, on the
whole. I have written more than anybody else, at any rate.
Miss Prescott's stories have made her quite a name. Wentworth
Higginson's articles have also been very popular. Lowell's
critical articles and political ones are always full of point, but
he has been too busy as editor to write a great deal. As for
the reputations that were *toutes faites*, I don't know that they
have gained or lost a great deal by what their owners have
done for the *Atlantic*. But oh! such a belabouring as I
have had from the so-called "Evangelical" press for the last
two or three years, almost without intermission! There must
be a great deal of weakness and rottenness when such extreme
bitterness is called out by such a good-natured person as I can
claim to be in print. It is a new experience to me, but is
made up by a great amount of sympathy from men and

women, old and young, and such confidences and such senti-
mental *épanchements*, that if my private correspondence is ever
aired, I shall pass for a more questionable personage than
my domestic record can show me to have been.

Come now, why should I talk to you of anything but yourself
and that wonderful career of well-deserved and hardly-won
success which you have been passing through since I waved my
handkerchief to you as you slid away from the wharf at East
Boston? When you write to me, as you will one of these days,
I want to know how you feel about your new possession, a
European name. I should like very much, too, to hear something of your everyday experiences of English life,—how
you like the different classes of English people you meet—the
scholars, the upper class, and the average folk that you may
have to deal with. You know that, to a Bostonian, there is
nothing like a Bostonian's impression of a new people or mode
of life. We all carry the Common in our heads as the unit of
space, the State House as the standard of architecture, and
measure off men in Edward Everetts as with a yard-stick. I
am ashamed to remember how many scrolls of half-an-hour's
scribblings we might have exchanged with pleasure on one side,
and very possibly with something of it on the other. I have
heard so much of Miss Lily's praises, that I should be almost
afraid of her if I did not feel sure that she would inherit a
kindly feeling to her father and mother's old friend. Do
remember me to your children; and as for your wife, who
used to be Mary once, and I have always found it terribly
hard work to make anything else of, tell her how we all
long to see her good, kind face again. Give me some stray
half-hour, and believe me always your friend,

O. W. HOLMES.

To his Mother.

31, Hertford Street,
March 15th, 1861.

MY DEAREST MOTHER,—. . . . . It is not for want of
affection and interest, not from indolence, but I can hardly tell
you how difficult it is to me to write letters. I pass as much

of my time daily as I can at the State Paper Office, reading hard in the old MSS. there for my future volumes; and as the hours are limited there to from ten till four, I am not really master of my own time.

I am delighted to find that the success of the 'United Netherlands' gives you and my father so much pleasure. It is by far the pleasantest reward for the hard work I have gone through to think that the result has given you both so much satisfaction. Not that I grudge the work, for, to say the truth, I could not exist without hard labour, and if I were compelled to be idle for the rest of my days, I should esteem it the severest affliction possible.

My deepest regret is that my work should be for the present on the wrong side of the Atlantic. Before leaving the subject of the new volumes, I should like to say that I regret that no one has sent me any of the numerous reviews and notices in the American papers and magazines to which you allude. I received a number of the *New York Times* from the governor, and also the *Courier*, containing notices. The latter, which was beautifully and sympathetically written, I ascribed to Hillard's pen, which I do not think I can mistake. If this be so, I hope you will convey my best thanks to him.

These are the only two which have been sent to me, and it is almost an impossibility for me to procure American newspapers here. Of course both Mary and Lily, as well as myself, would be pleased to see such notices, and it seems so easy to have a newspaper directed to 31, Hertford Street, with a three cent stamp. Fortunately I recently subscribed to the *Atlantic Monthly*, and so received the March number, in which there is a most admirably written notice, although more complimentary than I deserve. It is with great difficulty that I can pick up anything of the sort, and I fear now that as the time passes it will be difficult for me to receive them from America.

The Harpers have not written to me, but I received a line from Tom showing that the book was selling very well considering the times. As to politics, I shall not say a word, except that at this moment we are in profound ignorance as to what will be the policy of the new administration, how the inauguration business went off, and what was the nature of Mr. Lincoln's address, and how it was received, all which you at home at this moment have known for eleven days. I own that I can hardly see any medium between a distinct recognition of the Southern Confederacy as an independent foreign power, and a vigorous war to maintain the United States Government throughout the whole country. But a war without an army means merely a general civil war, for the great conspiracy to establish the Southern Republic, concocted for twenty years, and brought to maturity by Mr. Buchanan's Cabinet Ministers, has, by that wretched creature's connivance and vacillation, obtained such consistency in these fatal three months of interregnum as to make it formidable. The sympathy of foreign powers, and particularly of England, on which the seceders so confidently relied to help them on in their plot, has not been extended to them. I know on the very highest authority and from repeated conversations that the English Government looks with deepest regret on the dismemberment of the great American Republic. There has been no negotiation whatever up to this time of any kind, secret or open, with the secessionists. This I was assured of three or four days ago. . . . . At the same time I am obliged to say that there has been a change, a very great change, in English sympathy since the passing of the Morrill Tariff Bill. That measure has done more than any commissioner from the Southern Republic could do to alienate the feelings of the English public towards the United States, and they are much more likely to recognise the Southern Confederacy at an early day than they otherwise would have done. If the tariff people had been acting in league with the secessionists to produce a strong demonstration in Europe in favour of the dissolution of the Union, they could not have managed better.

I hear that Lewis Stackpole is one of the most rising young lawyers of the day, that he is very popular everywhere, thought to have great talents for his profession, great industry, and that he is sure to succeed. You may well suppose with how much delight we hear such accounts of him.

My days are always spent in hard work, and as I never work at night, going out to dinners and parties is an agreeable and useful relaxation, and as I have the privilege of meeting often many of the most eminent people of our times, I should be very stupid if I did not avail myself of it; and I am glad that Lily has so good an opportunity of seeing much of the most refined and agreeable society in the world.

The only very distinguished literary person that I have seen of late for the first time is Dickens. I met him last week at a dinner at John Forster's. I had never even seen him before, for he never goes now into fashionable company. He looks about the age of Longfellow. His hair is not much grizzled and is thick, although the crown of his head is getting bald. His features are good, the nose rather high, the eyes largish, greyish and very expressive. He wears a moustache and beard, and dresses at dinner in exactly the same uniform which every man in London or the civilised world is bound to wear, as much as the inmates of a penitentiary are restricted to theirs. I mention this because I had heard that he was odd and extravagant in his costume. I liked him exceedingly. We sat next each other at table, and I found him genial, sympathetic, agreeable, unaffected, with plenty of light easy talk and touch-and-go fun without any effort or humbug of any kind. He spoke with great interest of many of his Boston friends, particularly of Longfellow, Wendell Holmes, Felton, Sumner, and Tom Appleton.

I have got to the end of my paper, my dearest mother, and so with love to the governor and A——, and all the family great and small, I remain,

Most affectionately your son,
J. L. M.

P.S.—I forgot to say that another of Forster's guests was Wilkie Collins (the 'Woman in White's' author). He is a little man, with black hair, a large white forehead, large spectacles, and small features. He is very unaffected, vivacious, and agreeable.

From Rt. Hon. W. E. Forster.

Burnley, near Otley,
March 30th, 1861.

My DEAR MR. MOTLEY,—I am very much obliged to you for both your letters, and can assure you that they, especially the longer one, will be of the greatest service to me, if I take part in the debate on the 16th prox.

As I go up to London next Friday, and as I hope to see you and talk the matter over fully between then and the 16th, I will do little more now than thank you.

So far as I can judge from the newspapers, the chances of avoiding war increase. It seems to me Lincoln's policy is shaping itself into first attempting, by refraining from hostile measures, by keeping the door for return open on the one hand, and by making their exclusion on the other as uncomfortable as possible, to get the seceding States back ; and secondly, should this turn out to be impossible, to let them go peaceably, straining every nerve to keep the Border States. My great fear still is, lest the Republicans should, in order to keep the Border States, compromise principle ; but as yet they have stood as firm as one can reasonably expect.

You must excuse my saying that I do not agree with you that supposing the Union patched up again, or the Border Slave States left with the North, you will even then get rid of the negro question. So long as the Free States remain in union with Slave States, that question will every day press more and more urgently for solution. Such union will be impossible without a Fugitive Slave law, and any Fugitive Slave law will become every day more and more impossible to execute; and again, slave-holding in one State, with freedom of speech and pen in the next State, will become more and more untenable. I do not doubt, however, that the question will, in case of the Border States being left by themselves with the North, be solved by their freeing themselves before long from their slave population, partly by sale and partly by emancipation. Did I not think so, I would wish them to join the South.

As it is, however, unless the North degrades and enslaves itself by concession of principle, the cause of freedom must gain by present events, either in case of the cotton States returning, as they would have to do on Northern terms, or in case of their going on by themselves, when they will be far less powerful for harm than they were while backed by the whole strength of the North.   I am therefore most anxious that our Government should not, as yet, recognise the South, not only because I think a premature recognition would be an interference in your affairs, and an interference most unjust and unfriendly to the old Union—our ally, but because I think it would strengthen the South, and so either tend to harden her against concession to the North, or give her a fairer chance, and therefore more power for evil in a separate start.   Such recognition would also, I fear, do harm by making it less unlikely for the seceding States to join the South.   I thought I ought to write this much in order to show you why I feel so interested in this matter; but the best mode of meeting the debate in the House must be left for consideration nearer the time, when I hope to see you.

Yours most faithfully,
W. E. FORSTER.

To Dr. O. W. Holmes.

31, Hertford Street, Mayfair, W.
April 19th, 1861.

MY DEAR HOLMES,—. . . . . I did not wish to let this steamer go without thanking you for your delightful letter of 16th February. I wish I had deserved such a pleasure as it gave me, or that at this moment I had entitled myself to just such another at an early day. I can only promise that I will send another note on the heels of this one, and thus give myself a better chance. I only desire at this moment to tell you that I have read ' Elsie Venner.' I refrained on purpose from reading it until it was all finished, and then I gobbled it up at a single meal—so hungry was I

for the long deferred banquet. I assure you that I admire it
extremely. I was in some anxiety before I began, because I
knew that you had never written a novel before, and I felt
somehow as if you had announced yourself to come out as
Hamlet, or to walk over Niagara on a tight rope, or to do, in
short, some of those things by which men achieve fame, but to
which they are apt to have apprenticed themselves in their
tender epochs. One ceases to suspect a man

> " Cujus octavum trepidavit ætas
> Claudere lustrum "

of such romantic delinquencies as you have just committed—
with even (shall we say it?) an additional lustre or so to those
which Horace confesses. But fortunately your reputation·has
gained infinite lustre by your crimes. Then I knew how hard
it was to write a novel. *Haud inexpertus loquor.* Did I not
have two novels killed under me (as Balzac phrases it) before
I found that my place was among the sappers and miners and
not the lancers? And was it not natural, having thus come
to grief in the bygone ages, that I should feel solicitous when
I saw you setting off on the same career?

But you have been perfectly successful. I assure you that the
interest is undying throughout the book—that the characters
are sharply and vigorously drawn and coloured—that the
scenery is fresh, picturesque, and poetical, and the dialogue,
particularly when it is earnest and thoughtful, is suggestive,
imaginative, and stimulating in the highest degree. As to the
mother-thought of the book, it is to me original, poetical, and
striking. I knew that there was no resemblance to 'Christabel';
but I had not read 'Lamia' since college days. So after finishing 'Elsie' I took up Keats and read the poem, but found no
resemblance whatever. There is a snake, to be sure, and so
there is in 'Paradise Lost,' and plenty in 'Virginia,' but none
with a family likeness. I took the deepest interest in Elsie,
and was passionately in love with her myself, and could not
approve your excellent but somewhat calm-blooded Bernard
C. Langdon (I never will forgive you that " C.") for not taking
the snake out of her heart and her to his bosom at that last
most touching appeal, 'Love me.' I thought of Rachel's

'*M'aimes tu?*' as I saw her years ago as Thisbe in 'Angelo,' which nobody but a Connecticut schoolmaster could have resisted, any more than your Elsie's despairing cry. Do not be angry with me if I seem to underrate your hero. He has all the necessary heroic New England romance, but he is perhaps a little too poison proof and has too clear an eye to the main chance to be much more interesting than all his family of heroes.

In truth I suspect it is only when the hero has a tragic ending, like the Master of Ravenswood, that one cares very much about him. If the Master had married the Lord Keeper's daughter, and Sir William had come down with handsome settlements, and the Master had grown opulent and fat, and repaired his residence of Wolf's Crag, we should have found his slouched hat and black feathers less exciting. On the other hand, you have succeeded in inspiring a true and legitimate interest in the school-mistress and her energetic and gentle life. The pure, vaporous but still sufficiently definite shape comes and goes like the true indigenous American angel—flitting through all the book, and filling it with a health-giving atmosphere. I did not mean to write a criticism on the book. You have enough of that in the journals. But I feel that you will like to hear me say how cordially I appreciate and how thoroughly I have enjoyed it, as we do all. After all, the sympathy of so old and true a friend as I claim to be will not be indifferent to you, even though it blends with the general chorus of praise which salutes you from all sides. The 'Autocrat' has sold a great deal here. Dickens told me he had read it through twice —with great interest and admiration. He remembers you well, and speaks of you as all who know you are prone to speak. He promised to read 'Elsie Venner' at once, and when I next see him I will get him to tell me what he thinks of it. I hope you are not thinking hardly of me for not elaborately criticising the book. It is not from want of sympathy or admiration, but from a momentary feeling of incompetency. Besides, a letter should not be a newspaper notice. I read it through from beginning to end in a single day and evening with unflagging interest, and I read and re-read with increased delight the

choice passages, and I consider it a most undeniably successful
novel. . . . .

I am most sincerely yours,

J. L. M.

P.S.—I wrote a note to Longfellow, acknowledging from
my heart the cordial greeting sent me by the Saturday Club.
I send another response by you, and pray give my love to them
one and all.

To the Duchess of Argyll.

31, Hertford Street, Mayfair,
May 16th, 1861.

MY DEAR DUCHESS OF ARGYLL,—I hope that you will kindly
accept the accompanying volumes, in memory of the delightful
days, during which we had the privilege of enjoying your
hospitality at Inveraray.

You were my first reader, or rather my first and only *listener*,
for you may recollect that you allowed me to read a chapter
from the proof sheets.

I have just taken the liberty of writing a hurried note to
the Duke. I do hope that you will use your influence to persuade him and the English Government and all England, that
the cause of the United States Government is a righteous
cause; that we are disappointed and mortified at the idea
that there should be any party in England, least of all in the
Liberal Government, who should look coldly on the chance of
our dismemberment, while we are struggling with the most
gigantic rebellion with which a civilized commonwealth was
ever called on to grapple. We are but in the beginning of
the conflict. Of course, we do not expect anything but
neutrality; but why we are not as much entitled to moral
sympathy as Italy ever was, I cannot understand.

With the greatest regard,

Believe me, very faithfully yours,

J. L. MOTLEY.

From Lord Lyndhurst.

George Street,
June 12th, 1861.

DEAR MR. MOTLEY,—Will you do me the favour to dine
here on *Thursday* the 21st., and meet a countryman of *ours,*[1]
at a quarter to eight o'clock?

Very faithfully yours,
LYNDHURST.

To his Wife and Daughters.

Woodland Hill,
June 14th, 1861.

MY DEAREST MARY AND DEAREST DARLINGS,—My note from
Halifax, with the announcement which you must have seen in
the papers, will have told you enough of my voyage.[2] It was
a singularly favourable one, and we reached Boston Wednesday
morning at 8 o'clock. I found my dear mother looking not
worse than I had anticipated, but very feeble. She had had
an attack of neuralgic pain the day before, and was not able
to come out of her room. She was, however, pretty well the
next day, and is not very much changed in the face, although
she has evidently become more infirm.

My father seems a good deal older, but is very active and in
vigorous health. All the various members of the family are
very well. I walked out about eleven o'clock, and went first
to the State House to see Governor Andrew. He received me
with the greatest cordiality, I may say distinction, and thanked
me very warmly for my papers in the *Times.* I may as well
mention once for all, that *not a single person* of the numbers
with whom I have already spoken has omitted to say the same
thing. You know how enthusiastic our people are when

---

[1] Lord Lyndhurst was born in
America in 1772, an English subject.

[2] Mr. Motley's anxiety in this crisis
of American affairs led to a sudden
visit to Boston, his family then expect-

ing to follow him. His appointment
to the post of U.S. Minister to Austria,
which became vacant after his return,
changed the plan.

pleased, and you can therefore imagine the earnest and perhaps somewhat exaggerated commendations which I receive.[1]

The paper was at once copied bodily into the Boston and
New York papers, with expressions of approbation, and I make
a point of stating this to you, both because I was myself surprised at the deep impression which the article seems to have
made here, and in order that you may let any of our English
friends who are interested, know that the position taken in
the article is precisely that which is recognised by all men
throughout the Free States as the impregnable one in this
momentous conflict.

The reason why I am saying so much about it now, is simply
because it is the text, as it were, to all I have or probably shall
have to say on the subject of American politics in my letter to
you. Any one who supposes that this civil war is caused by
anything else than by an outrageous and unprovoked insurrection against a constituted government, because that government had manifested its unequivocal intention to circumscribe
slavery, and prevent for ever its further extension on this continent, is incapable of discussing the question at all, and is not
worth listening to. Therefore it is (and with deep regret I
say it), that there is so deep and intense a feeling of bitterness
and resentment towards England just now in Boston. Of
course I only speak of Boston, because having been here but
two days, I have as yet taken no wider views, and I intend,
when I write, to speak only of that " which I do know." The
most warm-hearted, England-loving men in this England-loving
part of the country are full of sorrow at the attitude taken
up by England. It would be difficult to exaggerate the
poisonous effects produced by the long-continued, stinging,
hostile articles in the *Times*. The declaration of Lord John
Russell, that the Southern privateers were to be considered
belligerents, was received, as I knew and said it would be, with
great indignation. Especially the precedent cited of Greece

---

[1] At the beginning of the Civil War,
Mr. Motley wrote an elaborate letter to
the London *Times*, explaining clearly
and comprehensively the nature of the
union and the actual causes of the
struggle. There was so much misun-
derstanding upon the subject that the
letter was of the greatest service. It
was republished in the United States,
and universally read and approved.

struggling against Turkey, to justify, as it were, before England and the world, the South struggling against the United States Government. This then is the value, men say to me every moment, of the anti-slavery sentiment of England, of which she has boasted so much to mankind. This is the end of all the taunts and reproaches which she has flung at the United States Government—for being perpetually controlled by the slavery power, and for allowing its policy to be constantly directed towards extending that institution.

Now that we have overthrown that party, and now that we are struggling to maintain our national existence, and with it, liberty, law, and civilization, against the insurrection which that overthrow has excited, we are treated to the cold shoulder of the mother country, quite as decidedly as if she had never had an opinion or a sentiment on the subject of slavery, and as if the greatest *war of principle* which has been waged in this generation at least was of no more interest to her, except as it bore on the cotton question, than the wretched squabbles of Mexico or South America. The ignorance, assumed or actual, of the nature of our constitution, and the coolness with which public speakers and writers have talked about the Southern States and the Northern States, as if all were equally wrong, or equally right, and as if there had never *been such a State in existence* as the one which the Queen on her throne not long ago designated as the "great Republic," has been the source of surprise, disappointment, and mortification to all. Men say to me, We did not wish England to lift a little finger to help us—we are not Austria calling in Russia to put down our insurrections for us —but we have looked in vain for any noble words of encouragement and sympathy. We thought that some voice, even of men in office, or of men in opposition, might have been heard to say, We are sorry for you, you are passing through a terrible ordeal, but we feel that you are risking your fortunes and your lives for a noble cause, that the conflict has been forced upon you, that you could not recede without becoming a by-word of scorn among the nations; our hands are tied— we must be neutral in action—you must fight the fight yourself, and you would be ashamed to accept assistance; but our hearts are with you, and God defend the right. But of all this there is not a word.

. . . . Now it is superfluous for *me* to say to *you* that I am not expressing my own opinions in what I am writing. In my character of your own correspondent, I am chronicling accurately my first impressions on arriving here. You see that the language I hear does not vary so much in character as in intensity from that which I have used myself on all occasions in England to our friends there. But the intensity makes a great difference, and I am doing my best, making use of whatever influence and whatever eloquence I possess, to combat this irritation towards England, and to bring about, if I can, a restoration of the old kindliness.

You cannot suppose that I am yet in condition to give you much information as to facts. One thing, however, is certain, there is no difference of opinion here. There is no such thing as party. Nobody asks or cares whether his neighbour was a republican, or democrat, or abolitionist. There is no very great excitement now—simply because it is considered a settled thing which it has entered into no man's head to doubt, that this great rebellion is to be put down, whatever may be the cost of life and treasure it may entail. We do not know what General Scott's plan is, but every one has implicit confidence in his capacity, and it is known that he has matured a scheme on a most extensive scale. There are now in Washington and Maryland, or within twelve hours' march of them, about 80,000 Union troops. There are, including these, 240,000 enrolled and drilling and soon to be ready. The idea seems to be, that a firm grasp will be kept upon Maryland, Washington, Western Virginia—and that Harper's Ferry, Richmond, and Norfolk, will be captured this summer—that after the frosts of October, vast columns of men will be sent down the Mississippi, and along it, co-operating with others to be sent by sea; that New Orleans will be occupied, and that thus with all the ports blockaded, and a "cordon" of men hemming them in along the border of the middle States, the rebellion will be suffocated with the least possible effusion of blood. Of course there will be terrible fighting in Virginia this summer, and I am by no means confident that we shall not sustain reverses at first, for the rebels have had longer time to prepare than we, and they are desperate. General Scott promises to finish the war triumphantly before the *second* frost, unless *England interferes.* This was his language to the man who told me.

You see that it was no nightmare of mine, this possibility of a war with England. General Scott loves and admires England, but there is a feeling in Washington that she intends to recognise the Southern Confederacy. This would be considered by our Government, under the present circumstances, as a declaration of war—and war we should have, even if it brought disaster and destruction upon us. But I have little fear of such a result. I tell every one what is my profound conviction, that England will never recognise the " Confederacy " until the *de facto* question is placed beyond all doubt, and until her recognition is a matter of absolute necessity. I have much reliance on Forster. I know that his speech will do infinite good, and I doubt not that Buxton will be warm and zealous. I hope that Milnes and Stirling will keep their promise; but what nonsense it is for me to tell of what you know already, and what I shall know in a few days.

Yesterday afternoon I came out here to stop for a couple of nights. My first object was to visit Camp Andrew. This is the old Brook farm, the scene of Hawthorne's 'Blithedale Romance,' and his original and subtle genius might, I should think, devise a new romance out of the wonderful transformation effected now in that locality.

Five regiments, in capital condition, have already gone from Massachusetts to the seat of war—being, as you know, the very first to respond to the President's summons. We have more enlisted for the war, which are nearly ready to move, and will have their marching orders within a fortnight. Of these, the crack one is Gordon's regiment—the Massachusetts Second. Lawrence Motley is one of the first lieutenants in this corps, and you would be as pleased as I was, to see what a handsome, soldierly fellow he is. And there is no boy's play before his regiment, for it is the favourite one.

All the officers are of the *jeunesse dorée* of Boston—Wilder
Dwight, young Quincy, Harry Russell, Bob Shaw, Harry
Higginson, of Dresden memory, and others whose names would
be familiar to you, are there, and their souls are in their work.
No one doubts that the cause is a noble and a holy one; and
it is certainly my deliberate opinion that there was never a
war more justifiable and more inevitable in history.

We went to the camp to see the parade.   To my unsophisticated eye there was little difference between these young
volunteers and regular soldiers. But of course, my opinion is
of little worth in such matters.   I had a good deal of talk
with Colonel Gordon.   He is about thirty, I should think.
He graduated first in his class at West Point—served through
the Mexican War, and is, I should think, an excellent soldier.
He is very handsome, very calm and gentle in manner, with a
determined eye.   You will watch, after this, with especial
interest the career of the Massachusetts Second.

. . . . Gordon's regiment will, it is hoped, be taken into the
permanent service, after the war, as the regular army must
always be on a much larger scale than before.   In that case,
these officers will have a profession, which has been one of
the great wants for young men of rich families in our part of
the country.

I am now going into town, when I shall post this letter, and
order your Boston newspaper.   *No event* has taken place of
any very great moment, since I left you.   General Scott, I
am very glad to say, is in no hurry.   He is too old a campaigner
and strategist to wish to go unprepared into petty conflicts to
furnish food for telegrams.   The thing is to be done on a
great scale.   There is no thought of peace, and there is a
settled conviction in the minds of the most pacific by nature,
that, even had the United States Government been base enough
to *acknowledge* the Southern Confederacy, it would necessarily
have been involved in war with it.   There are at least half a
dozen *casus belli*, which, as between two belligerent nations,
could only be settled by the sword, unless the North chose to
go on its knees, and accept the dictation of the South.   There
is no need of saying more.   The Mississippi alone speaks war

out of its many mouths. The Union hardly intended, when it bought Louisiana and the Mississippi valley, in order to take it from the control of one enemy, to make a present of it to another and more bitter foe.

The girls here are all pretty and nice. N—— sings very well, with a fine, fresh, ringing voice, and gave me 'The Star-spangled Banner' last night, with great spirit.

God bless you all, dearest ones. I will write from Washington.   Ever most affectionately,

J. L. M.

I shall go to see Mrs. Greene[1] to-day, who is in town and in good health. It was impossible for me to do so yesterday, as I was detained by many visitors. Amory came almost the first. He is delightful as ever, and sends his love to you.

To his Wife.

Washington,
June 17th, 1861.

MY DEAR MARY,— .... After being at home three days, I left by the afternoon boat of Saturday, 15th, for New York, where I was obliged to remain all Sunday till 6 P.M. I did not find Mr. Grinnell, unluckily, who is out of town for the summer. In the night I came on to Washington, reaching here at six this morning. I went up to the State Department in the forenoon, and had the merest moment of a conversation with Mr. Seward, who begged me to come and dine with him to-day at seven, and requested, as it was his despatch day, to defer all further colloquy until then. I had afterwards a very brief interview with the Secretary of War, Cameron, to whom Governor Andrew begged me to give some information concerning Cobb's battery of flying artillery, which is of more interest to the War Department than to you, so I will not enlarge on that subject. I also introduced Tom, who had something to communicate concerning Gordon's regiment;

[1] Sister to Lord Lyndhurst.

and the Secretary took occasion to say that Massachusetts—
and, indeed, all New England—did everything so well that
improvement seemed impossible, and that the country was
more indebted to it than could ever be repaid for its conduct
in the present crisis.

Afterwards I saw a small crowd waiting on the pavement,
and Lee, who was with us (and who, as you know, has a place
in the War Department), told me that they were waiting to
see General Scott come out of his office. It reminded me
of the group I so often saw in Piccadilly waiting to see Lord
Palmerston come out. We stood looking on, too, and very
soon he appeared. He has a fine soldierly, and yet benignant
countenance, very much resembling Dr. Reynolds in face as
well as stature, and not seeming much older than he. Presently Lee, who knows him very well, went up and mentioned
my name. He turned round with much vivacity, with his
hand stretched out very cordially, and expressed himself very
happy to make my acquaintance, being pleased to add that
my writings " were an honour to the age." Of course, I say
these little things to you because it will please you and the
children. He asked us to come and see him of an evening,
and I certainly shall do so as soon as possible.

No one here knows what the plans of the campaign are—
all is conjecture. You will see by the papers that go with
this that Harper's Ferry has just been evacuated by the rebels.
Those with whom I converse seem to imagine that the plan
is to strengthen and improve day by day the great national
army gradually surrounding the rebellion by an impenetrable
" cordon," and thus compelling them, by sheer exhaustion, to
lay down their arms before the close of a year. The blockade,
bankruptcy, and famine, it is thought, will be potent enough
without many very severe pitched battles. The show of force
is already so imposing and so utterly beyond any previous
calculation of the rebels that they are thought to be rapidly
demoralizing, while, on the other hand, every day strengthens
the Government. There are at least 100,000 well-furnished
Government troops here and in the immediate neighbourhood,
or within twelve hours' march, and they are coming daily.

The Government has plenty of money, plenty of men, and is constantly improving its commissariat, and arranging all the details of a great war. It has entered into no man's head that the rebellion is not to be put down. I doubt not that the English Government have been fully informed upon this point now, for when I expressed this sentiment just now to Lord Lyons, he responded, " Certainly not; it is only a question of time."

I went to see him after leaving Mr. Seward. In fact Seward was kind enough to send me there in his carriage. I found him little changed from the Dresden days, except that he has grown stouter. He was very cordial, frank and friendly, and we had a long and full conversation on American affairs. He was himself sure that every thinking person in England would deplore a rupture between the two countries as a calamity too painful to contemplate, and that all his efforts would be to avert it.

There is a review of 8,000 Government troops on the sacred soil of Virginia going on just now. General MacDowell invited us to go. My dinner engagement prevents me, but Tom has gone. The town is full of troops. A Massachusetts regiment left Boston the day we did, and a Michigan regiment arrived the same day. All are enlisted for the war just now. There is no lack of good officers. McClellan, who commands the Western Division, and is next to Scott, is very competent to command the whole if anything should happen to the veteran. But of that there seems no fear. He looks vigorous, healthful, and young. There seems nothing senile about him.

To-morrow we are going across the Potomac to see the encampments, the fortifications, etc. Pay no heed to anything you may see from time to time of intentions of the rebels to attack Washington. They are as likely to attack Boston. The thing I believe to be utterly out of the question. Although Scott would like nothing better than that they should try it on.

I dine with Lord Lyons to-morrow, and I dare say I shall spend the rest of the week here. I have not quite decided whether to go to Fortress Monroe or not, but probably shall

do so.   Secretary Cameron has given us a pass recommending
us especially to the commander of troops, etc., etc.   I may as
well repeat what I said in my last; that here as in Boston
every one to whom I speak thanks me for the article in the
Times.   Lord Lyons said it was considered the principal document in the whole affair, and the French Minister said the
same thing.   Everybody says it has done much good, and it
most sincerely rejoices me to hear it.

June 18th, *Tuesday morning,* 7 A.M.—I continue my letter for
a moment before breakfast.   We are going across the Potomac
at nine—Tom and I and the two Lees.   I dined with Seward
entirely *en famille*, no one being present but his son and son's
wife. . . .

We had, among the first acts of the new anti-slavery administration, agreed to do, what we have been so freely
reproached for not doing, when our Government was controlled
by an administration of which Jefferson Davis was a member,
and we are met on the threshold by the declaration that his
invitation to pirates of all nations is sufficient to convert them
into good, honest belligerents.[1]

Had the English declaration been delayed a few weeks or
even days, I do not think it would ever have been made, and
I cannot help thinking that it was a most unfortunate mistake.   Nevertheless I am much less anxious about the relations between our two countries than I was.   Nobody really
wishes a rupture on either side, and I think that the natural

[1] Early in the administration of Mr.
Lincoln, the Government of the United
States proposed to accede to the four
articles in regard to maritime warfare
adopted at the Congress of Paris in
1856.   The British Government, however, wished to state that by the
proposed convention for such accession Great Britain did not mean to
undertake any engagement bearing
upon the Civil War in America.   The
President deciding that such a declaration was inadmissible, as the United
States could accede to the Articles
only upon a perfectly equal footing
with all the other parties.   The American Government was aggrieved by
the obstruction offered by Great Britain
to its accession to the four articles,
especially as Great Britain was at the
time secretly proposing to the Con-
federate Government to accept but
three of them.   The exequatur of the
British Consul at Charleston, who had
been the intermediary of the negotia-
tions of his Government with the Con-
federate authorities, was revoked by
the President.

love of justice and fair play which characterises England will cause regret at the mistake which has been committed. Moreover, there can hardly be much doubt, despite the misrepresentations of an influential portion of the English press and of some public men, that the English nation will understand the true position of the American Government in this great crisis.

We have circumscribed slavery, and prevented for ever its extension by one square inch on this continent, and at the same time we mean to preserve our great republic one and indivisible. It is impossible that so simple and noble a position as this should fail to awaken the earnest sympathy of nine-tenths of the English nation. To the question whether the task is beyond our strength, I can only repeat that General Scott—than whom a better strategist or a more loftyminded and honourable man does not exist—believes that he can do it in a year; and so far as I can make out his design, it is by accumulating so much force and by making such imposing demonstrations everywhere, as to convince the rebels that their schemes—already proved to have been false in all their calculations founded on co-operations in the Free States— have become ridiculous. Thus without any very great effusion of blood perhaps, the rebellion may be starved out and broken to pieces. Mr. Seward says that the great cause of the revolt is the utter misapprehension in the Slave States of the Northern character. It has hitherto been impossible to make the sections thoroughly acquainted with each other. Now they will be brought together by the electric shock of war. And they will learn to know each other thus, which is better than not knowing each other at all—and so on. I give you a brief idea of his schemes and hopes.

He read me a long despatch which he is sending to-day to the French and English Governments. He did this of course confidentially, and because, as he was pleased to say, I had been fighting our battles so manfully in England, for he, like every one else, praised warmly my *Times'* letter. I suppose ultimately this despatch will be published; but I have only room now to say that I think it unobjectionable in every way—dignified, reasonable, and not menacing, although very decided. I said little in reply, and soon afterwards we went to the White House, in order to fall upon Abraham's bosom. I found the President better- and younger-looking than his pictures. He is very dark and swarthy, and gives me the idea of a very honest, confiding, unsophisticated man, whose sincerity of purpose cannot be doubted. I will say more of him in my next, for I am obliged to close suddenly. By the way, let me correct one statement in another part of my letter. Both the President and Seward tell me that, in Scott's opinion, an attack by the rebels on the lines before Washington is not impossible. It would be a desperate and hopeless venture. Maryland has just gone for the Union by a very large majority, electing all members of Congress.

Good-bye. God bless you and my darlings!

Ever your affectionate

J. L. M.

To his Wife.

Washington,
June 20th, 1861.

MY DEAREST MARY,—I told you that I went with Seward in the evening of Monday to see the President. He looks younger than I expected—less haggard than the pictures— and on the whole, except for his height, which is two or three inches above six feet, would not be remarked in any way as ill- or well-looking. His conversation was commonplace enough, and I can hardly remember a single word that he said, except when we were talking—all three—about the military plans in progress, he observed, not meaning anything like an epigram, " Scott will not let us outsiders know anything of his plans." He seemed sincere and honest, however, and steady, but of course it is quite out of the question for me to hazard an opinion on so short an acquaintance as to his moral or intellectual qualities.

Seward impresses me as being decidedly a man of intellect, but seems an egotist. . . . There is no doubt whatever that the early impressions of the Foreign Ministers here were favourable to the success of the rebellion, and that these impressions were conveyed to their Governments. Mercier, the French Minister, was most decided in his views and his sympathies, while Lord Lyons, calm and quiet as you know him to be, as well as sagacious and right-minded, had also little doubt, I suspect, six or seven weeks ago that the secession or revolution was an accomplished fact. Hence the anxiety of their Governments to be on good terms with the rebels, particularly after the astounding misrepresentations of the Southern commissioners. It amuses Americans very much when I tell them that the recognition of Mr. Adams was remonstrated against by those individuals.

I dined with Lord Lyons yesterday, and M. Mercier was there. Of course we spoke of little else but American affairs. There is no need of quoting the conversation, but it is sufficient to say that little doubt seems now to exist in the minds of either that the United States Government is sure to put down this rebellion and remain a great power—greater than ever before.

The encouragement which the rebels have derived from their premature recognition which they have received as belligerents, and still more by the exclusion of *our ships of war* as well as their pirates from the English ports *all over the world* for the purpose of bringing in prizes, while on the contrary France does not exclude our ships of war, but only privateers, has already given the rebellion a new lease of life. Still more pernicious is the hope which is now entertained by the rebels, that so soon as the new cotton crop is ready to come forward—say in October—England will break up our blockade, and of course become instantly involved in war with us. I refuse to contemplate such a possibility. It would be madness on the part of England, for at the very moment when it would ally itself with the South against the United States, for the sake of supplying the English manufacturers with their cotton, *there would be a cry of twenty millions as from one mouth for the instant emancipation of all the slaves.*

Nothing could resist that cry. The sentiment of the Free

States would be more overwhelming even than its manifestation so lately, which has surprised the world by the rising as it were out of the earth in the brief space of six weeks, of a well equipped and disciplined army of 250,000 men.   The alliance of England with the South for the sake of re-opening the cotton ports would have for its instant result the total destruction of the cotton interest.   An invading army at half a dozen different ports would proclaim the instant abolition of slavery.

There is not the slightest exaggeration in this.   No logic can be more inexorable, and the opinion is avowed on all sides.

To break our blockade for the sake of getting cotton for Manchester, would lead to the total extermination of the cotton crop for many a long year.   No English statesman can be blind to this, and therefore I do not fear any interference on the part of England.   The South, however, does expect such interference, and will in consequence prolong its struggle a little.

I passed the whole of the day before yesterday on the other side of the Potomac—the "sacred soil of Virginia." We hired a carriage and took it on board a small steamer plying to Alexandria.   The sail for about half a dozen miles along the broad, magnificent Potomac, under a cloudless sky, but protected by an awning, was very pleasant. The heat is not excessive yet, and there is usually a good air stirring. The expanse of hill and dale and the wooded heights which surround the margin of the beautiful river make a delightful passage of scenery.   Alexandria, but lately a bustling tobacco port, is now like a city of the dead so far as anything like traffic is concerned.   It is the head-quarters of General McDowell, an experienced army officer, who commands all the Union troops (some 25,000) in this part of Virginia.

We went to the Marshall House, the principal hotel of the place, where, as I suppose you read in the papers, Colonel Ellsworth of the New York Zouaves was killed. He had gone in person to the top of the house to cut down a Secession flag, and was coming down the stairs with it, when he was shot by the master of the house, one Jackson, who in his turn was instantly despatched by a private in the regiment. Ellsworth is much regretted as a young officer of great courage and irreproachable character.

By the way, you should read in the *Atlantic* for June and July a very spirited account of the march of the New York 7th to Washington. It was written by Major Winthrop of New York, who was killed the other day in that unlucky and blundering affair of General Pierce at Great Bethel. These outpost skirmishes are of little consequence to their ultimate results, but they serve to encourage the enemy a little. On the other hand, they read a useful lesson to Government upon the folly of appointing militia officers to high command when there is no lack of able and experienced army officers. Of these there are plenty, and no idea is more ridiculous than that the South has got all the officers and all the military material. The bone and sinew of the Free States are probably the best raw material for troops in the world. General Scott told me last night that the Massachusetts volunteers in a few months would be equal to the best regulars. To an unsophisticated eye they are nearly so already.

A regiment marched into Washington yesterday morning— the Massachusetts 1st—and with their steady march, stout frames, good equipments, and long train of baggage waggons, drawn by admirable teams of horses, following them, they looked very business-like, I assure you. And this regiment is but a tenth part of the men whom Massachusetts has already contributed. As for New York, I am afraid to say how many are already here, and they are wonderfully well-drilled—at least 20,000—and they can send on as many more as can possibly be required. The contention now among the States is to get the largest proportion of their regiments accepted. The manner in which these great armies have been so suddenly improvised is astounding to foreigners. " *C'est le pays des improvisations*," said Mr. Mercier to me yesterday. From Alexandria we went on to Shuter's Hill, one of the heights commanding Washington, where, under guidance of Colonel Wright, the engineer who built the works, we examined the very considerable fortifications which have been erected here.

It is very interesting to see the volunteers working with pick and spade under the broiling sun of Virginia, without complaint or inconvenience. They are men who have never doubted that labour was honourable.

We afterwards went to Arlington House, formerly the seat of Washington Custis, and now the property of General Lee. He is an excellent officer, and was, before his defection, a favourite of General Scott. The place has great natural beauties of hill and dale, lawn and forest, and commands a magnificent view of Washington and the whole valley of the Potomac; but the house is mean. It is now the head-quarters of General McDowell (I was wrong in saying further back that these were at Alexandria). Colonel Heintzelmann commands there, and there are some New York regiments encamped in the grounds. I observed one alley through the tents had been christened Fifth Avenue. The property is thoroughly respected, and the soldiers have even amused their leisure in planting little gardens about their tents instead of destroying or defacing anything.

Thus we passed the day in going about the lines from one point to another, receiving explanations of everything from most intelligent officers—generally of the regular army. The works at the Tête du Pont, to defend the mile-long bridge which crosses the Potomac from the Virginia side to Washington, are very thorough, and the attempt upon Washington, if made, must, I think, result in a total defeat. I passed an hour with General Scott last night at his house in Washington. He tells me still that he expects an attack daily along the whole line, says that the rebels are perhaps in greater number than those which he has in the immediate neighbourhood, but that his are much better troops. I could not make out that he had any reasons to expect an attack, except upon the logical ground that they must do it, or come to grief by remaining inactive. They are poorly provisioned, impatient, and in danger of disbanding. Meantime, Scott has secured Harper's Ferry, a most important strategical position, without striking a blow. They were forced to evacuate the place to escape being surrounded. " *Reste à savoir* " how it will be at Manassas Junction. The

General pleases me exceedingly. He is in manner quiet, but hale, vigorous, and full of energy, and has no doubt whatever of bringing the whole matter to a happy issue within a reasonable time. But the things which annoy him most are the lying telegrams of the newspapers and the general impatience of outsiders. I spent an hour and a half with Seward last evening, and afterwards called at the White House on Mrs. Lincoln. She is rather nice-looking, youngish, with very round white arms, well dressed, chatty enough, and if she would not, like all the South and West, say "Sir" to you every instant, as if you were a royal personage, she would be quite agreeable.

Woodland Hill,
June 23rd, 1861.

I continue my letter interrupted at Washington. Thursday evening I passed with Mr. Chase, the Secretary of the Treasury, the hardest worked man, except Mr. Cameron, just now in Washington. He is a tall, well-made, robust man, with handsome features, fine blue eye, and a ready and agreeable smile —altogether "*simpatico*." The conversation, of course, turned very much upon our English relations, and I told him I would stake my reputation on the assertion that the English Government would never ally itself with the Southern Confederacy, or go any further in the course already taken towards its recognition. I said that I had been over and over again assured, by those in whom I had entire confidence, that the sympathy of the English nation was with the American cause, but that it was exceedingly difficult to make the English understand that which to us was so self-evident a proposition, that we meant two things—first, to put an end for ever to slavery extension and the nationalisation of slavery; secondly, to maintain the constitution and laws of the Great Republic one and indivisible; that war was not contemplated as possible between the two countries, except by a small and mischievous faction in England.

Mr. Chase is a frank, sincere, warm-hearted man, who has always cordially detested slavery and loved the American constitution as the great charter of American liberty and nationality. Like every man, public or private, throughout the Free States, he is convinced of the simple truth that the constitutional union of the whole people is all which guarantees to each individual the possession of his life and property, because it is the basis of all our laws. Destroy this, and anarchy and civil war are the inevitable results. He expressed a most undoubting conviction that the rebellion would be put down and the Union restored. It was not of much consequence who was in power—who occupied this or that office. The people was resolved that it would not be disinherited of its constitution and its national life, nor of the right possessed by every individual in the country to set his foot at will on any part of the whole broad country of the United States. It was as idle to attempt resistance to the great elemental forces of nature as to oppose this movement. The people would put down the rebellion without a government, were it necessary. In six weeks an army of 250,000 men had been put into the field, armed and equipped for service. In six months there would be half a million, and as many more as might be necessary. There is nothing of the braggart about Mr. Chase, nor about the President, nor about Cameron, and, after all, the Minister of Finance and the Secretary of War are the men who are of necessity most alive to the stern realities of the crisis. They know that money, men, beef, bread and gunpowder in enormous amounts are necessary for suppressing this insurrection, but they have not the slightest doubt as to the issue.

" Already a great result is secured," said Chase. The *idea* even of extending slavery has for ever vanished from men's minds. It can never go an inch further on this continent, and, in addition, slavery as a governing power (as it has been for forty years) is for ever dethroned. It can never be nationalised, but must, so long as it remains, be local, exceptional, municipal and subordinate, restricted to the States where it at present exists, while the policy of the Government will be the policy of freedom. The South will be forced to come back into the Union, such as it has ever existed under the Constitution. This, he thinks, will be brought about by the pressure caused by the blockade, by the sufferings of the people thus imprisoned, as it were, and thrown out of employment, by the steady pressing down upon them of immense disciplined armies, backed by the boundless resources of a fertile country and a well-organised commissariat and vast wealth; while, on the other hand, the South cannot be inspired by the enthusiasm which has often enabled a feebler nation to resist triumphantly a *foreign* invasion. The United States Government is no foreigner. It is at home everywhere upon its own soil, from the Canada line to the Gulf of Mexico, but conspirators have excluded it for a time from its own rights, its own property, and the exercise of its benignant functions over the whole people of which it is the minister and guardian, appointed by the people itself. The inhabitants of the Slave States must ere long awake from the madman's dream which has deprived them of their reason. For the leaders, of course, there is no returning.

There is already a beginning, and a good beginning, on the border. Maryland, which seemed but a few weeks ago so rabid in the Secession cause, has just voted largely for the Union. The progress of the counter revolution in Virginia is steady. The inhabitants of Western Virginia have repudiated the action of the State Convention, and are about establishing a government of their own—not as a separate state, but as claiming *to be Virginia*, with the intention of sending members and senators to Congress, and electing governor and legislature. This course is supported by United States troops, and will be recognised by Congress, which has had to deal with similar cases before, and *is the sole judge* according to the Constitution as to the claims of its members to their seats. According to Chase and other Cabinet Ministers with whom I have conversed, this movement will be triumphant. Thus in the rebel States, fire is fighting fire, as in a prairie conflagration. The same phenomenon will be manifested in Eastern Tennessee, where there are 30,000 or 40,000 fighting men, who will fiercely dispute the power of a Convention to deprive them of their rights as citizens of the United States, and who will maintain the Union with arms in their hands to the death. The same will be sooner or later the case in North Carolina, in North Alabama, in Louisiana.

In short, the whole white population of the Seceding States is five and a half millions, against twenty-two or twenty-three millions. Not another State can secede by any possibility, and within the five and a half million seceders there are large numbers who are fierce against the rebels, and still larger numbers among the ignorant masses, who will be soon inquiring, What is all this about? Why is all this bloodshed and misery? And they will be made to understand, despite the lies of the ringleaders of the rebellion, that the United States Government is their best friend; that not one of their rights has been menaced—that it wishes only to maintain the constitution and laws under which we have all prospered for three-quarters of a century, and which have now been assaulted, because the people at the ballot-box, last November, chose to elect Mr. Lincoln president, instead of Mr. Breckenridge. This plunging into " pronunciamiento " and civil war, by a party defeated at the polls, may be very good Mexican practice, but it will not go down in the United States; and ere long the people, even at the South, will make this discovery. So thinks Mr. Chase, and I think he is right. I am much pleased with the directness and frankness of his language. "And if all these calculations fail," said he, " if the insurrection is unreasonably protracted, and we find it much more difficult and expensive in blood and treasure to put it down than we anticipated, we shall then draw that sword which we prefer at present to leave in the sheath, and *we shall proclaim the total abolition of slavery on the American continent.* We do not wish this, we deplore it, because of the vast confiscation of property, and of the servile insurrections, too horrible to contemplate, which would follow. We wish the Constitution and Union as it is, with slavery, as a municipal institution, existing till such time as each State in its wisdom thinks fit to mitigate or abolish it, but with freedom the law of the territories and of the land; but if the issue be distinctly presented— death to the American Republic or death to slavery, slavery *must die.* Therefore," said he, " the great Republic cannot be destroyed. The people will destroy slavery, if by no other means they can maintain their national existence." In this connection we came to talk again of England and its policy. But it is hardly worth while to repeat anything more to you on this subject. Every man with whom I have conversed holds the same language.

I battle stoutly for England and the English, for no man knows better than I all the noble qualities of that great nation; and how necessary it is to our moral greatness and true prosperity to cultivate the closest and warmest relations with our ancient mother. I maintain, and I think have partly convinced many minds, that England has only acted under a great delusion as to the permanence of our institutions, for which error we are ourselves somewhat to blame; that the great heart of the nation is in sympathy with us; that the idea of going to war with us, has never entered the minds of any but a few mischief-makers; that the *Times* is no representative of English opinion, nor of the English Government. I would pledge myself for a marked difference before long in the whole attitude of England, and that the last thing she contemplated was allying herself with the South in a war against the United States Government. Already my words have been partly justified. Recent news from England to the 8th of June has produced a good effect. Notwithstanding the violence of language which I have described to you (in order that you and such of our dear English friends who care to read my first impressions may hear and see exactly as I have seen and heard), I believe that the hearts of this, the most excitable and the most warmhearted people on the earth, will soon turn to England, if they catch any warm manifestations of sympathy with our cause.

While I was at Mr. Chase's, General McDowell, with one of his aides, came in. He is a firm, square, browned, powerful-looking soldier, some forty years of age, educated at West Point, and thoroughly experienced in all the active warfare which we have had in his time. He commands, as I mentioned, all the forces on the Virginia side of the Potomac, for the defence of Washington. He told us of an alarm the night before; that the rebels were about attacking his lines, and that they were in force to the number of 3000 in the immediate vicinity of Alexandria. He went there, but the 3000 melted to three, who were taken prisoners. Nevertheless, there is no doubt that there are ready 100,000 rebels under arms in Virginia, and that they are bound by every rule of war to carry out their boasts and make the attack.

On the other hand it is the object of the Government daily to strengthen itself. This, as I told you, was the language of General Scott to me the evening before. By the way, I did not tell you that on that occasion we rather took the General by surprise (as I think Jefferson Davis will never do). The servant ushered us at once into his little drawing-room. He inhabits a small, modest house in—I forget what street—and we found him, the evening being very sultry, taking a nap in his shirt sleeves, with an aide-de-camp at each knee, and a servant brushing flies, at his back. He started up, somewhat confused, and beat a hasty retreat to an adjoining room, whence he emerged, a quarter of an hour later, arrayed in all the splendour of an old black bombazine frock coat. But he is a magnificent old fellow. He told us, with a smile, that a price had been set upon his head by his native State of Virginia, but he doubted whether it would ever be earned. Nevertheless his house was only guarded by a sergeant and ten men. The rest of his conversation I have already reported to you.

As I told you before, there is no lack of good officers. The great cause of future trouble may be in neglecting to make proper use of them, through this detestable system of appointing politicians and militia men to be brigadiers and major-generals. General Mansfield, who commands in Washington, seems to me a first-class man in every respect, and so do McDowell and Colonel Heinzelmann. McClellan, who commands in the West, is said to be equal to Scott in talent, and thirty years his junior; while General Lyon, a Connecticut man and a West Pointer, seems to be carrying all before him in Missouri, and is rather the favourite of the hour. I do not go quite into military details, because you get them,

true or false, in the papers. I have already ordered you the
Daily Advertiser, and to-morrow I shall see that you get the
New York Times regularly. Up to this time nothing of importance has happened, and I think that you will derive from
my letters as much information to be relied upon as you could
get anywhere. With regard to Missouri, there is not the
slightest possibility of her getting out of the Union. The
Governor is a Secessionist and a fugitive, and his following is
comparatively small. I had a long conversation last evening
with the Attorney-General of the United States, Mr. Bates, who
is himself of Missouri, and he tells me that secession there is
simply an impossibility. General Lyon with his United States
forces has already nearly put down secession there; but should
the insurrection be protracted much longer, the State would be
entered on three sides at once (for it is surrounded by Free
States) and 150,000 slaves liberated. There is no child's play
intended any longer, and the word compromise, which has
been the country's curse for so long, has been expunged from
the dictionary. Bates has been the champion of freedom for
many years, and he has lived to sit in a cabinet with men of
his own faith. He is a plain man, shrewd, intelligent.

Sumner, who arrived Wednesday night, told me that Montgomery Blair, the Postmaster-General, was desirous of making
my acquaintance. Friday morning I was engaged to breakfast
with Mr. Chase. The conversation was very pleasant and
instructive to me, turning on the topics already mentioned,
and as I walked down with him to the Treasury Department,
he insisted on my going with him into his office to finish the
subject, the purport of which, he said, I have already given
you. Afterwards I went with Sumner to Mr. Blair's. He is a
Virginian by birth and education, and it is therefore the more
to his credit that, like General Scott, he is of the warmest
among Unionists, and perhaps the most go-ahead, uncompromising enemy to the rebels in the cabinet, not even excepting
Mr. Chase. While we were talking, he asked me what I
thought of the President's views. I told him that I had only
passed half-an-hour with him a few evenings before, when I
had been introduced to him by Mr. Seward, and that since

then it had been advertised conspicuously in all the papers that the President would receive no visitors, being engaged in preparing his message to Congress. "But you must see him; it is indispensable that you should see him, and tell him about English affairs," said Blair. I told him that I was leaving Washington that afternoon. He asked if I could not defer my departure. I said no, for my arrangements were already made.

The truth is, I had resolved not to force myself upon the President. If he did not care to converse with me, it was indifferent to me whether I saw him or not. But Mr. Blair begged me to stop a moment in his library, and incontinently rushed forth into the street to the White House, which was near, and presently came back, saying that the President would be much obliged if I would pay him a visit.

I went and had an hour's talk with Mr. Lincoln. I am very glad of it, for had I not done so, I should have left Washington with a very inaccurate impression of the President. I am now satisfied that he is a man of very considerable native sagacity; and that he has an ingenuous, unsophisticated, frank, and noble character. I believe him to be as true as steel, and as courageous as true. At the same time there is doubtless an ignorance about State matters, and particularly about foreign affairs, which he does not affect to conceal, but which we must of necessity regret in a man placed in such a position at such a crisis. Nevertheless his very modesty in this respect disarms criticism.

Our conversation was, of course, on English matters, and I poured into his not unwilling ear everything which my experience, my knowledge, and my heart, could suggest to me, in order to produce a favourable impression in his mind as to England, the English Government, and the English people. There is no need of my repeating what I said, for it is sufficiently manifest throughout this letter. And I believe that I was not entirely unsuccessful, for he told me that he thought that I was right, that he was much inclined to agree with me, but, he added, it does not so much signify what I think, you must persuade Seward to think as you do. I told him that I found the secretary much mitigated in his feelings compared with what I had expected. He expressed his satisfaction. I do not quote any of his conversation because he was entirely a listener in this part of the interview. Afterwards he took up his message, which was lying in loose sheets upon the writing-table, and read me nearly the whole of it, so far as it was written. On the whole, the document impressed me very favourably. With the exception of a few expressions, it was not only highly commendable in spirit, but written with considerable untaught grace and power. These were my first impressions, which I hope will not be changed when the document comes before the world. It consists mainly of a narrative of events from the 4th of March up to the present hour. Nothing had yet been written as to foreign relations, but I understand from Seward that they are all to be dismissed in a brief paragraph, such as will create neither criticism nor attention anywhere.

We parted very affectionately, and perhaps I shall never set eyes on him again, but I feel that so far as perfect integrity and directness of purpose go, the country will be safe in his hands. With regard to the great issue, we have good generals, good soldiers, good financiers, twenty-three millions of good people "whose bosoms are one," a good cause, and endless tin.

The weather has been beautiful ever since I landed, magnificent sunshine and delicious heat. Just now there is a heavy shower. When it is over I am going to drive over to Camp Andrew, to see the Massachusetts 2nd.

Ten more regiments have been ordered from Massachusetts, and seven, including Gordon's, will soon be ready to take the field at once. This will make 15,000 men from Massachusetts alone. New York has already sent 20,000, and has a reserve of 20,000 ready. Pennsylvania about the same, and so on. The only struggle is who shall get the greatest number accepted.

Give my love to all my English friends. Kiss my three darlings 3000 times, and believe me,

Most lovingly,
J. L. M.